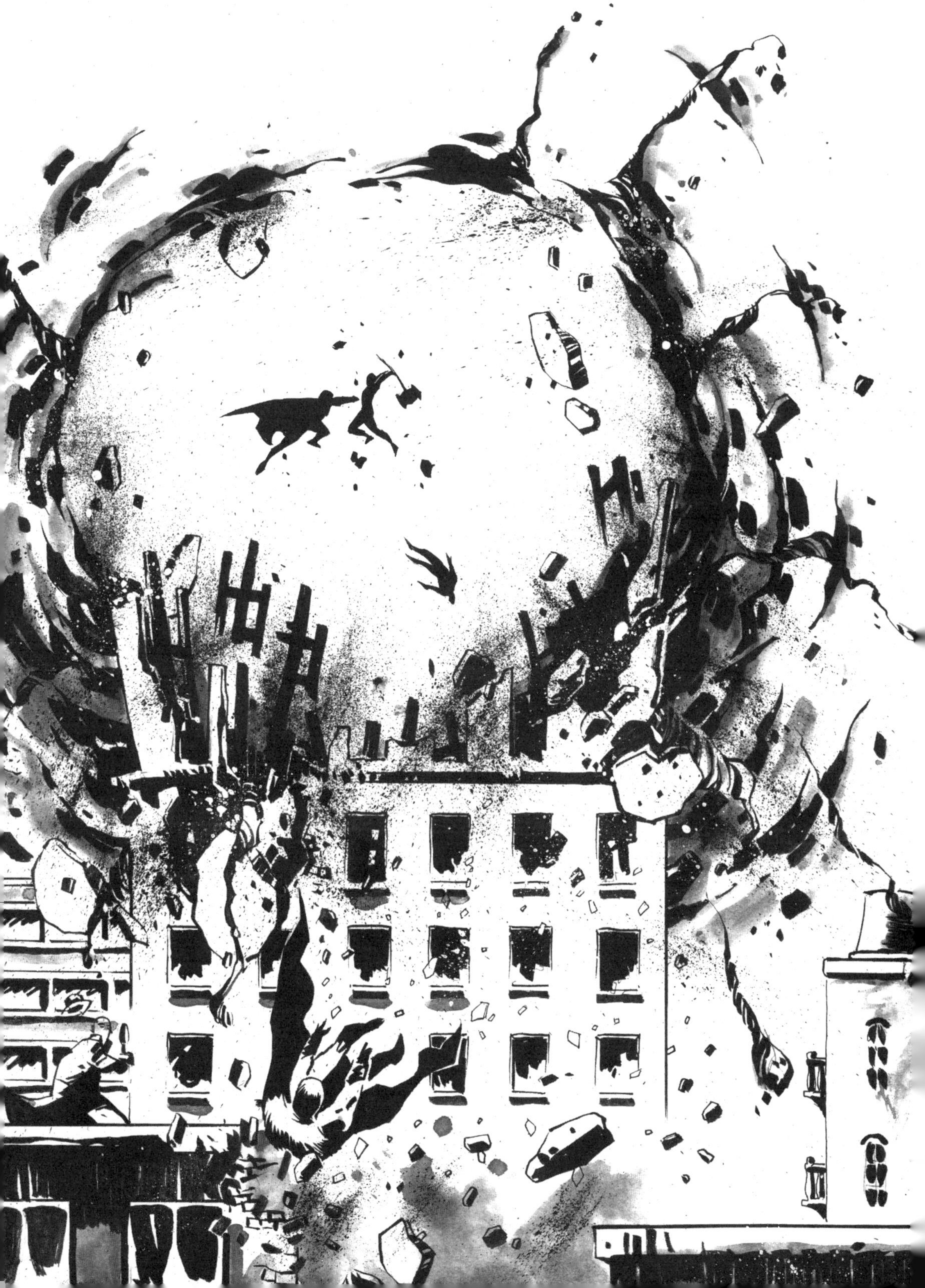

ISBN: 978-1-60706-765-8

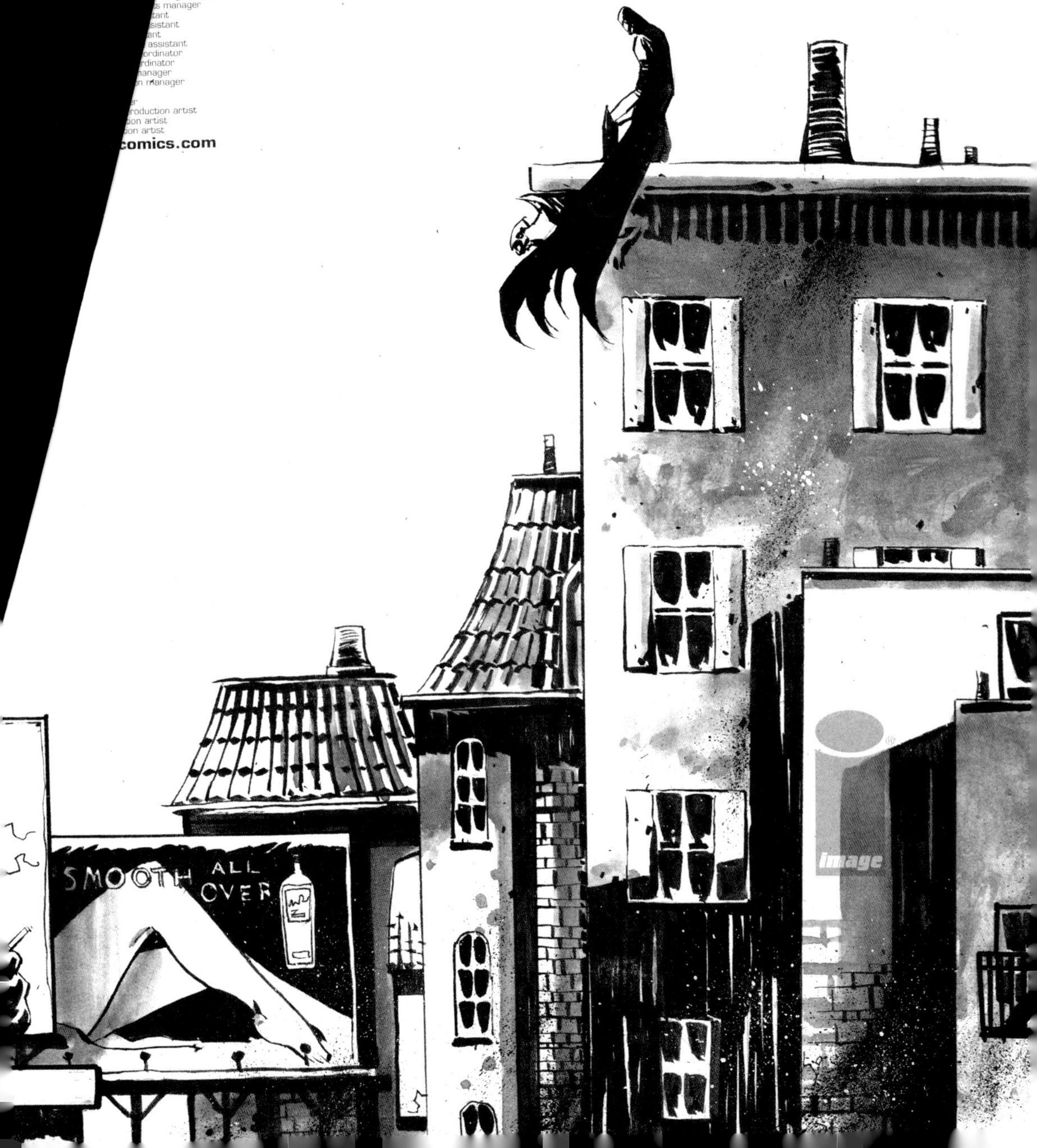
SMOOTH ALL OVER
image

MAS &
MOBSTE

VOLUME ONE

MASKS AND MOBSTERS, VOLUME ONE
FIRST PRINTING: July, 2013
Published by Image Comics, Inc.

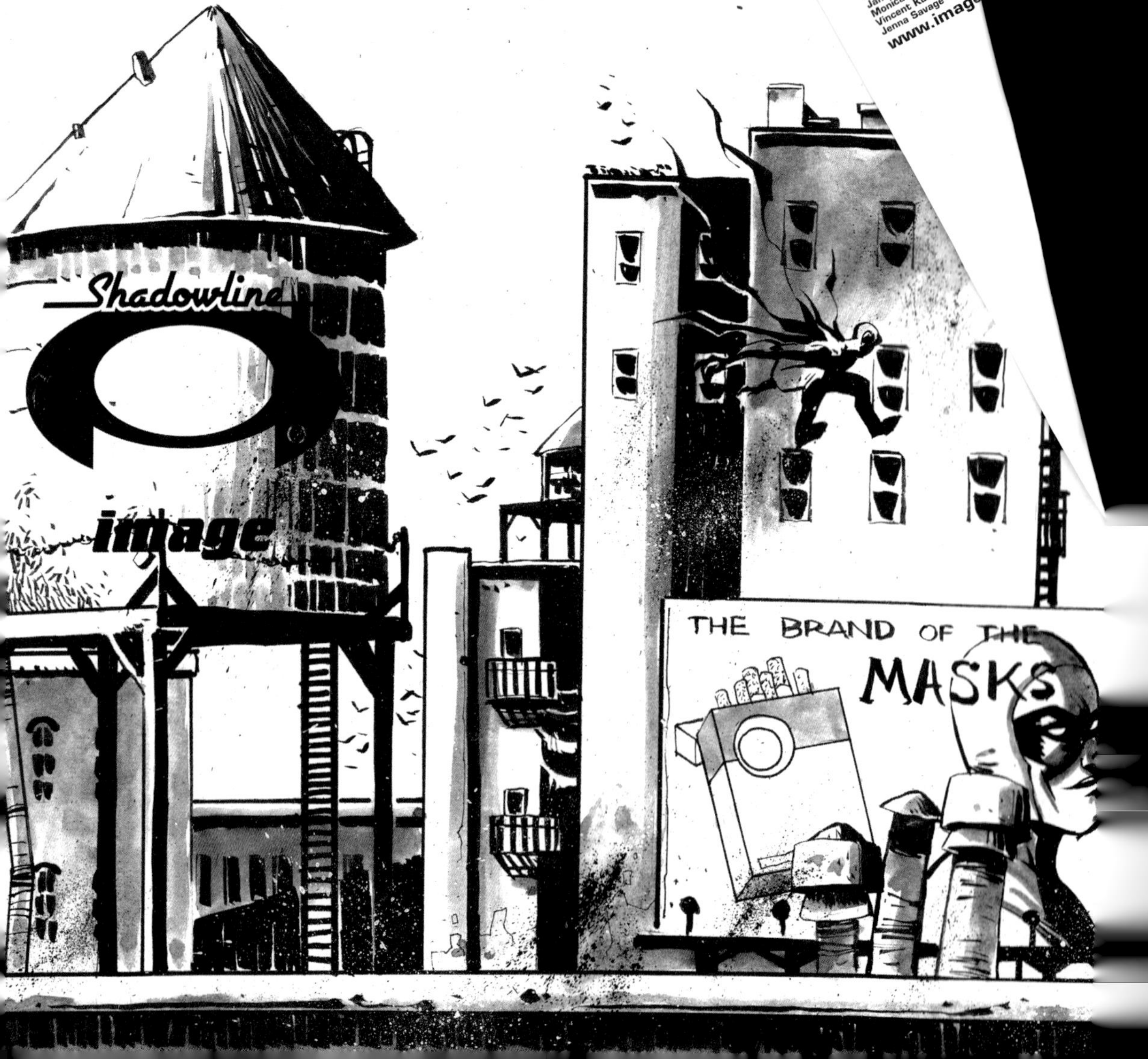
THE BRAND OF THE
MASKS

Joshua Williamson - WRITER
Mike S. Henderson- ARTIST
(CHAPTERS 1, 2, 3, 5, 7, 10)

Jason Copland- CHAPTER 4
Justin Greenwood-CHAPTER 6
Ryan Cody-CHAPTER 8
Seth Damoose- CHAPTER 9

Zen- LETTERING
Williamson & Henderson- BOOK DESIGN
Tim Daniel- LOGO DESIGN
Mike S. Henderson- COVER

Laura Tavishati- BOOK EDITOR
Chris Roberson & Allison Baker- ORIGINAL EDITORS

Jim Valentino- PUBLISHER
www.ShadowlineOnline.com
follow us on FACEBOOK and TWITTER at
ShadowlineComics

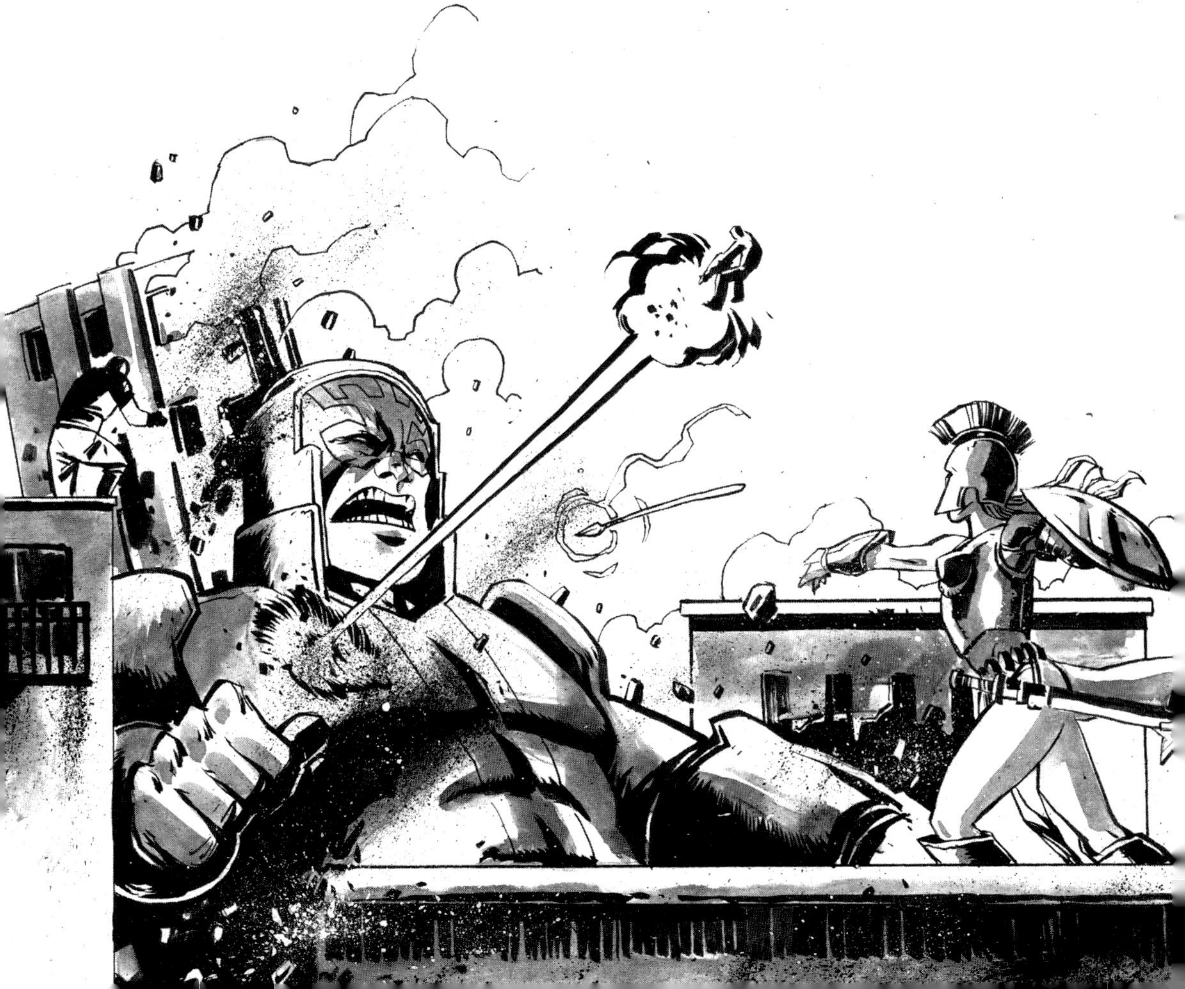

Thanks to all of the fans who helped spread the word.
To Chris and Allison for giving us a chance and a venue to do what we wanted, how we wanted. It saved my sanity.
And, of course, to Mike for being every writer's dream come true. A great artist and an even better friend.
Special thanks to Jim Valentino for putting up with me all these years and for publishing this book.

                                            Joshua Williamson

For everyone who read this and kept us going. And for everyone yet to read this, we'll keep going.
Special thanks to Josh, for making me an offer, then making me a friend.

                                            Mike S. Henderson

For our teachers:
Will Eisner and Scott McCloud

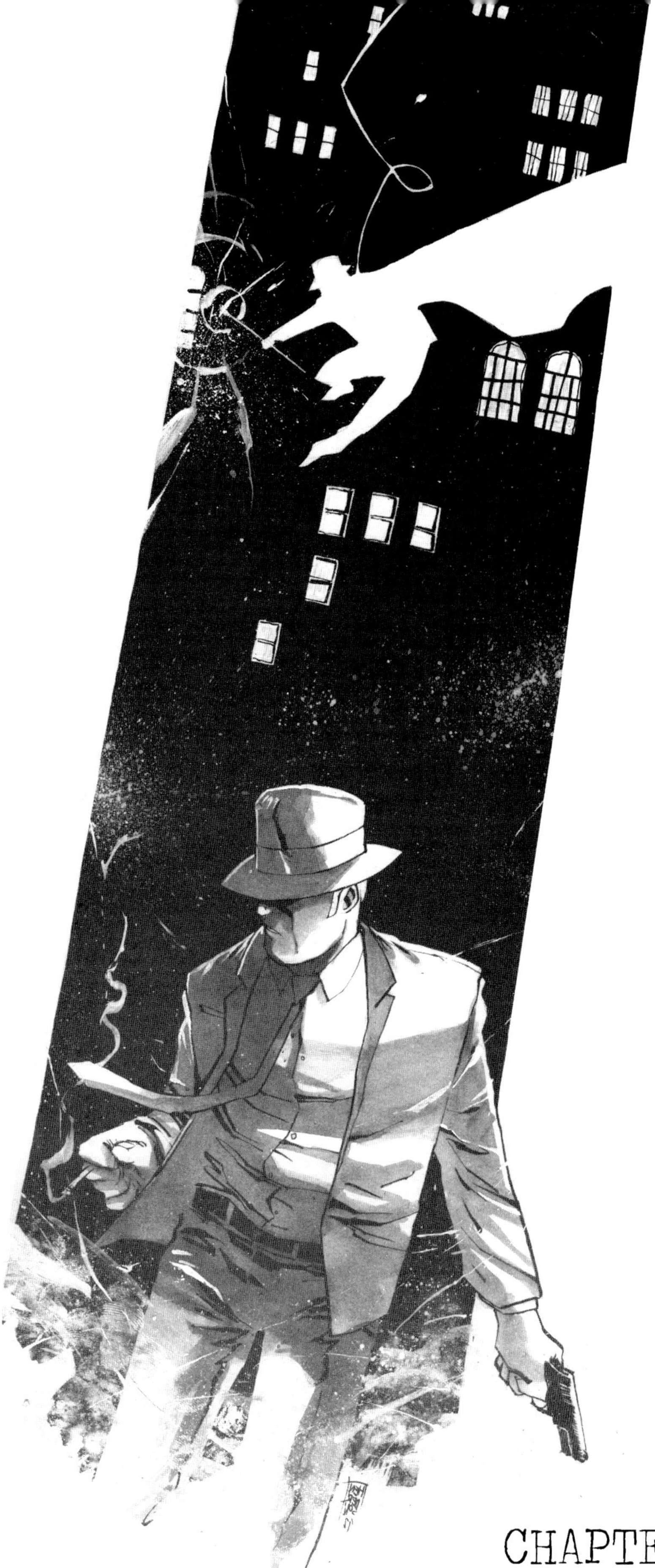

CHAPTER ONE

Roughs and the process that lead to the first cover.

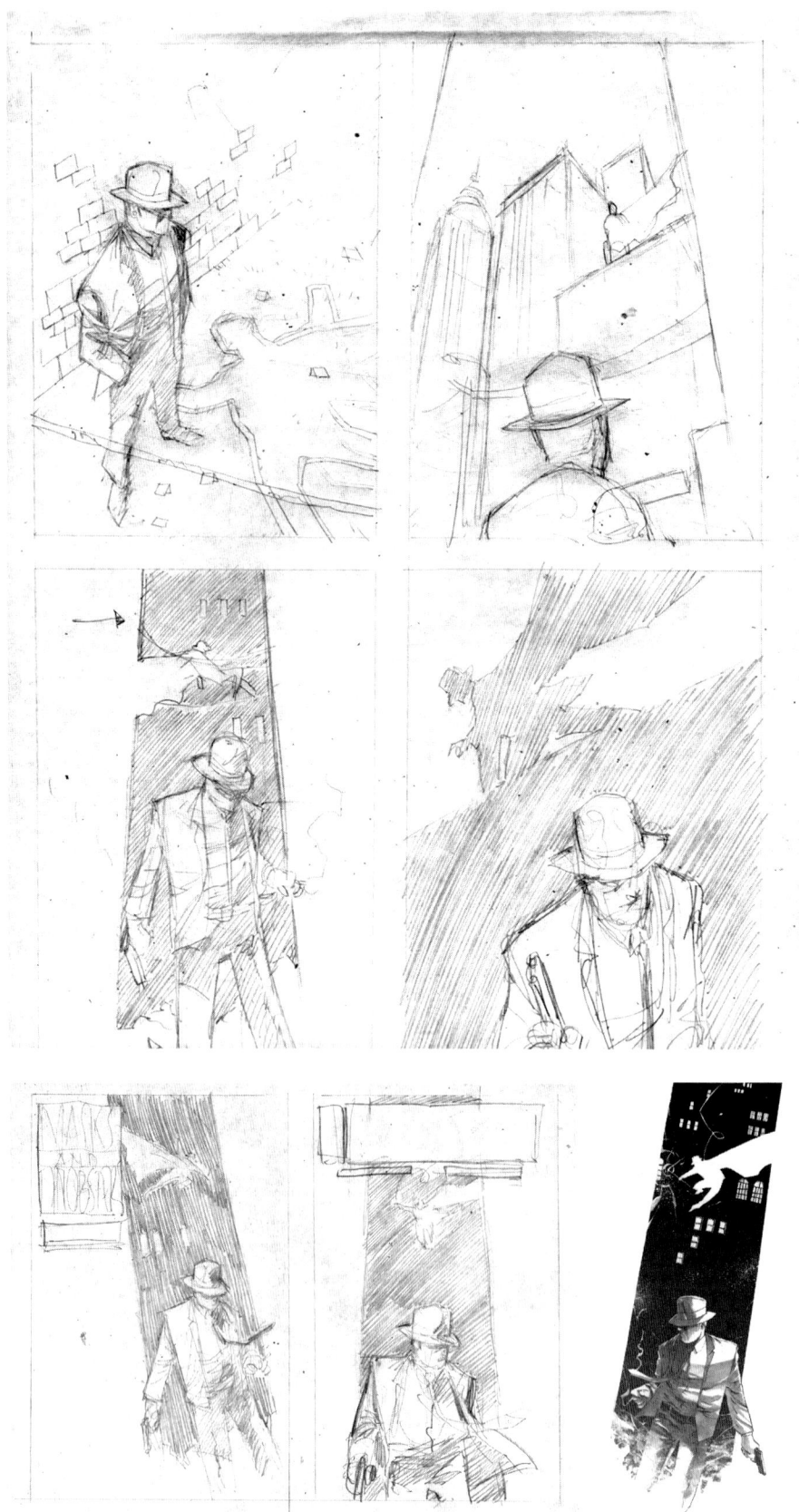

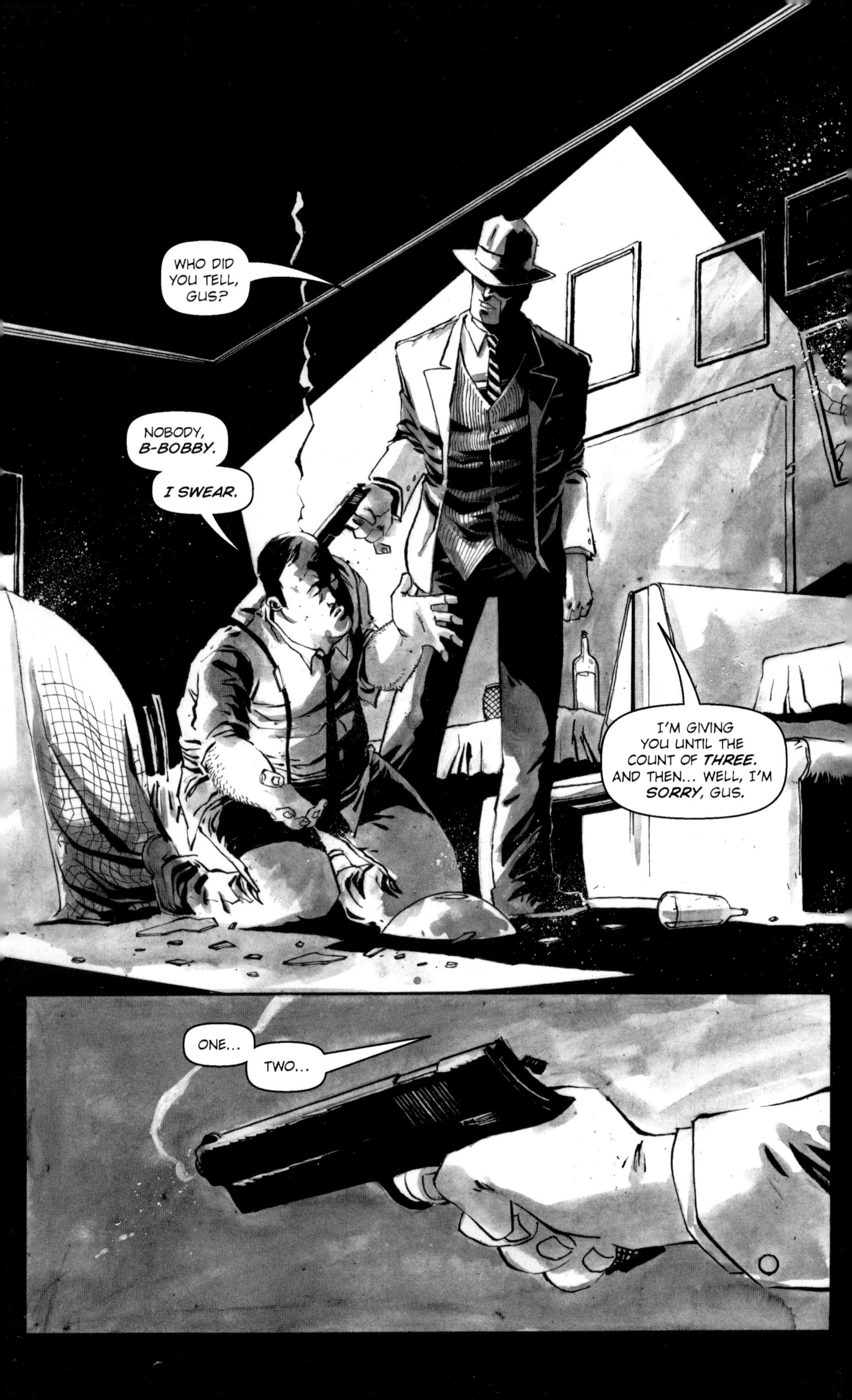
WHO DID YOU TELL, GUS?
NOBODY, *B-BOBBY.*
I SWEAR.
I'M GIVING YOU UNTIL THE COUNT OF *THREE.* AND THEN... WELL, I'M *SORRY,* GUS.
ONE...
TWO...

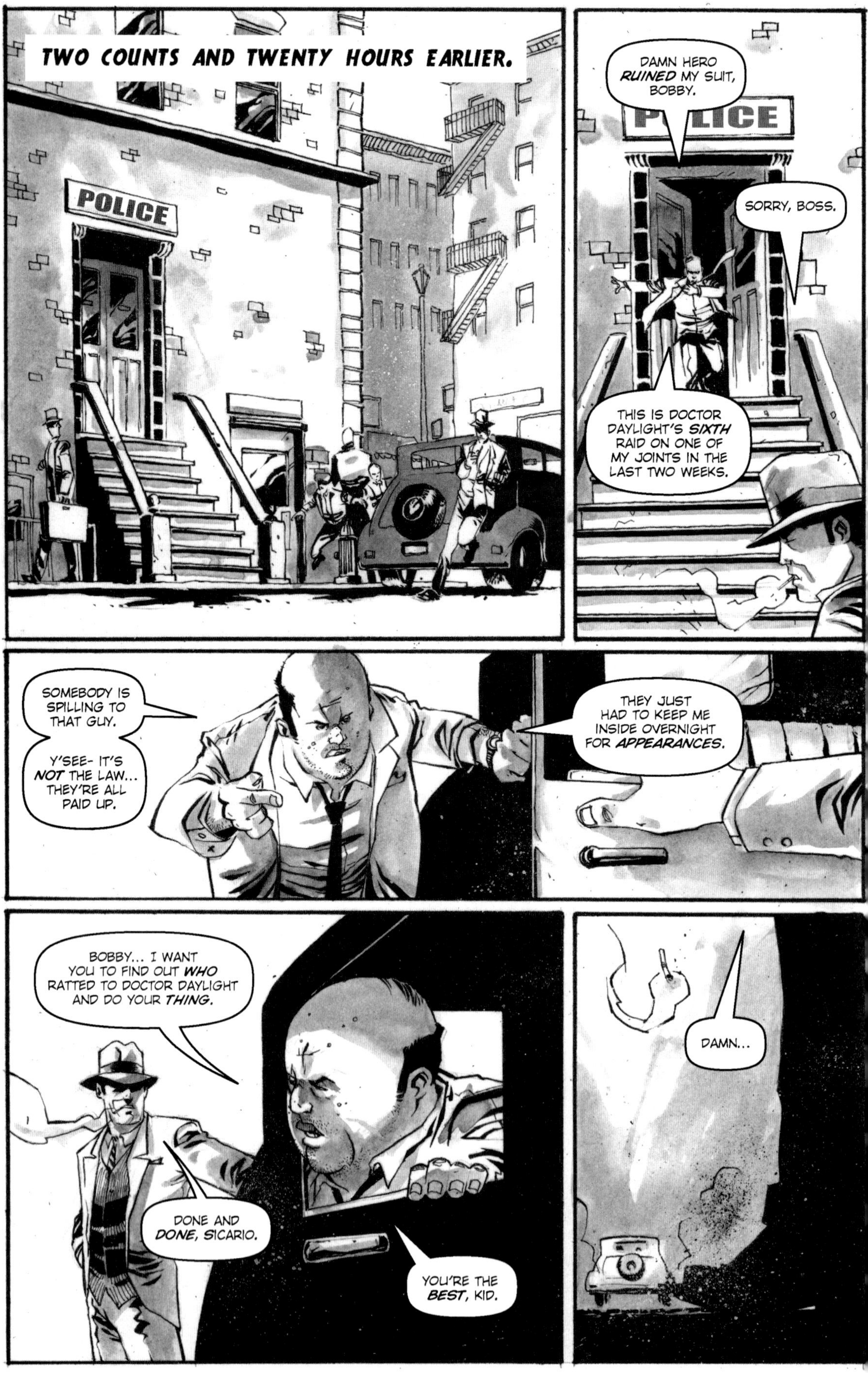
TWO COUNTS AND TWENTY HOURS EARLIER.
POLICE
DAMN HERO RUINED MY SUIT, BOBBY.
POLICE
SORRY, BOSS.
THIS IS DOCTOR DAYLIGHT'S SIXTH RAID ON ONE OF MY JOINTS IN THE LAST TWO WEEKS.
SOMEBODY IS SPILLING TO THAT GUY.
Y'SEE- IT'S NOT THE LAW... THEY'RE ALL PAID UP.
THEY JUST HAD TO KEEP ME INSIDE OVERNIGHT FOR APPEARANCES.
BOBBY... I WANT YOU TO FIND OUT WHO RATTED TO DOCTOR DAYLIGHT AND DO YOUR THING.
DONE AND DONE, SICARIO.
YOU'RE THE BEST, KID.
DAMN...

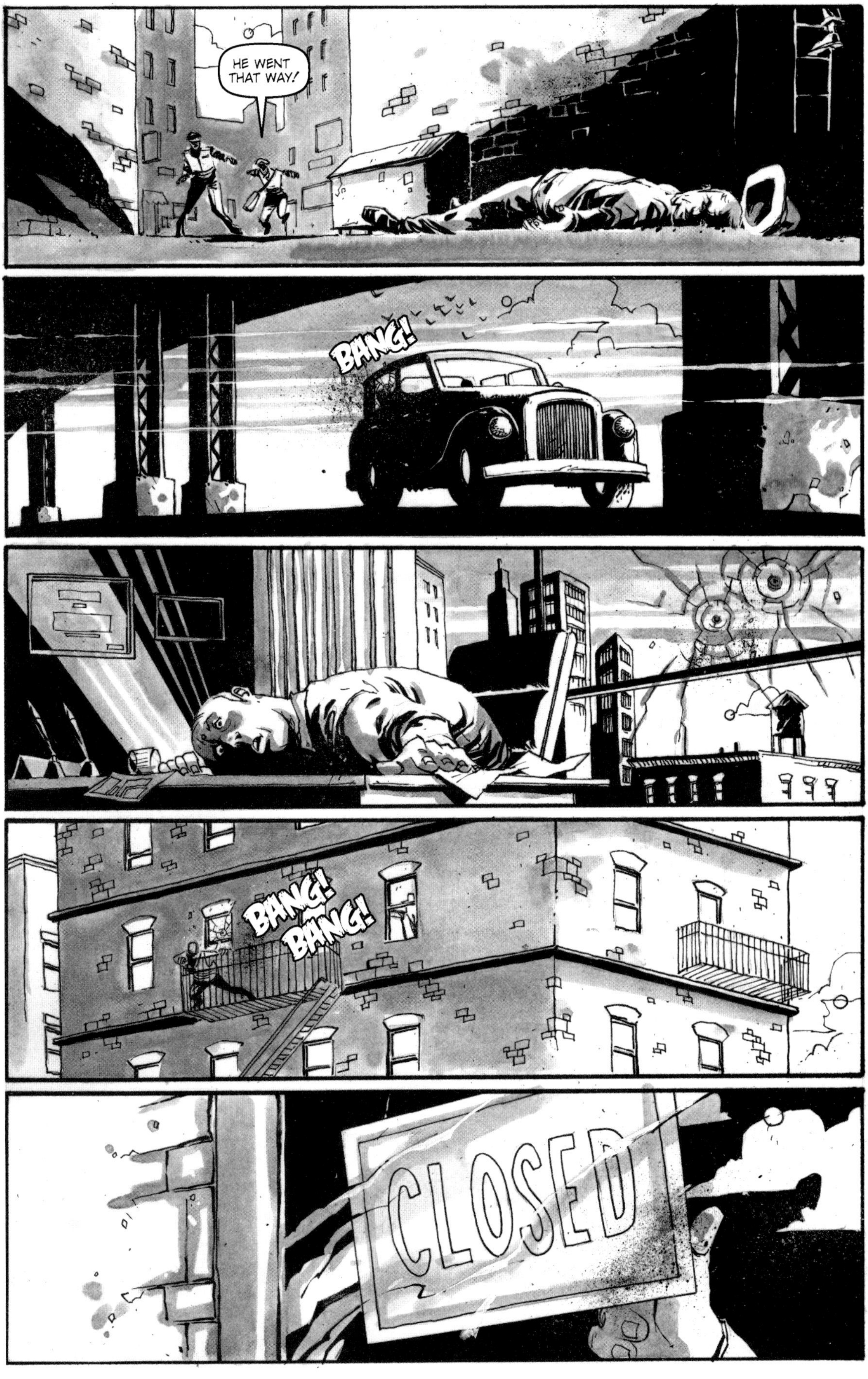
HE WENT THAT WAY!
BANG!
BANG!
BANG!
CLOSED

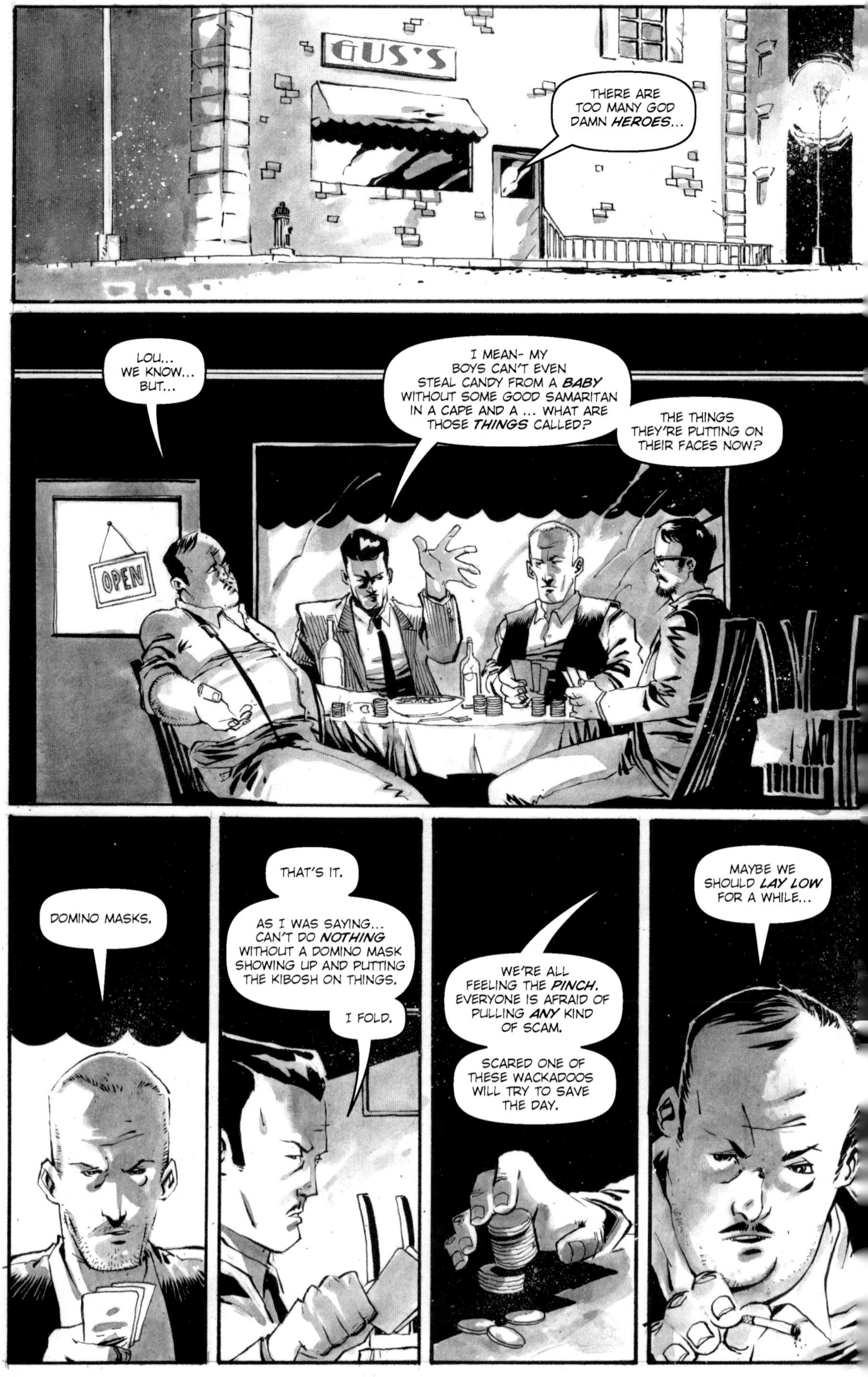
GUS'S
THERE ARE TOO MANY GOD DAMN HEROES...
LOU... WE KNOW... BUT...
I MEAN- MY BOYS CAN'T EVEN STEAL CANDY FROM A BABY WITHOUT SOME GOOD SAMARITAN IN A CAPE AND A ... WHAT ARE THOSE THINGS CALLED?
THE THINGS THEY'RE PUTTING ON THEIR FACES NOW?
OPEN
DOMINO MASKS.
THAT'S IT.
AS I WAS SAYING... CAN'T DO NOTHING WITHOUT A DOMINO MASK SHOWING UP AND PUTTING THE KIBOSH ON THINGS.
I FOLD.
WE'RE ALL FEELING THE PINCH. EVERYONE IS AFRAID OF PULLING ANY KIND OF SCAM.
SCARED ONE OF THESE WACKADOOS WILL TRY TO SAVE THE DAY.
MAYBE WE SHOULD LAY LOW FOR A WHILE...

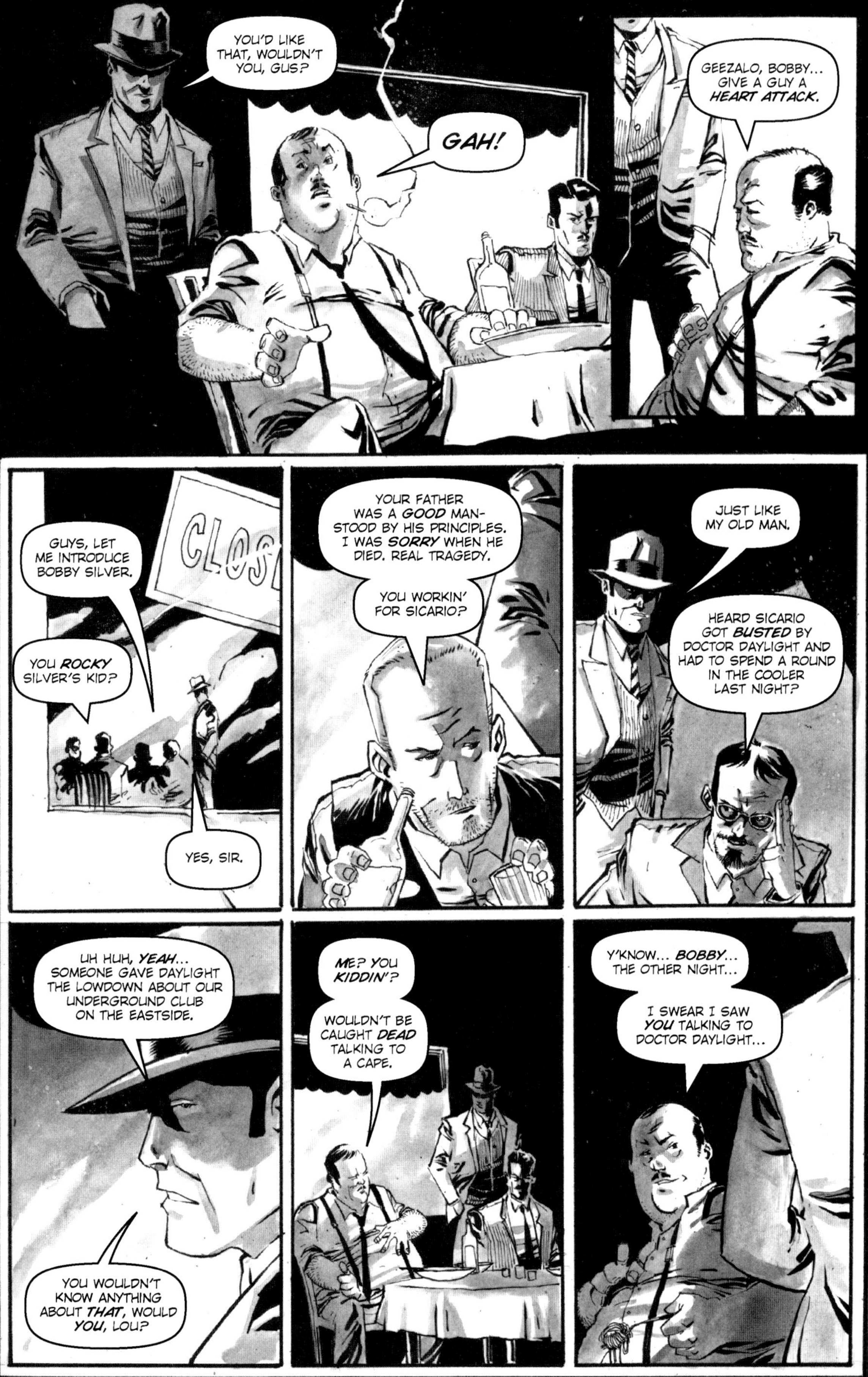

YOU'D LIKE THAT, WOULDN'T YOU, GUS?
GAH!
GEEZALO, BOBBY... GIVE A GUY A HEART ATTACK.
GUYS, LET ME INTRODUCE BOBBY SILVER.
CLOS
YOU ROCKY SILVER'S KID?
YES, SIR.
YOUR FATHER WAS A GOOD MAN- STOOD BY HIS PRINCIPLES. I WAS SORRY WHEN HE DIED. REAL TRAGEDY.
YOU WORKIN' FOR SICARIO?
JUST LIKE MY OLD MAN.
HEARD SICARIO GOT BUSTED BY DOCTOR DAYLIGHT AND HAD TO SPEND A ROUND IN THE COOLER LAST NIGHT?
UH HUH, YEAH... SOMEONE GAVE DAYLIGHT THE LOWDOWN ABOUT OUR UNDERGROUND CLUB ON THE EASTSIDE.
YOU WOULDN'T KNOW ANYTHING ABOUT THAT, WOULD YOU, LOU?
ME? YOU KIDDIN'?
WOULDN'T BE CAUGHT DEAD TALKING TO A CAPE.
Y'KNOW... BOBBY... THE OTHER NIGHT...
I SWEAR I SAW YOU TALKING TO DOCTOR DAYLIGHT...

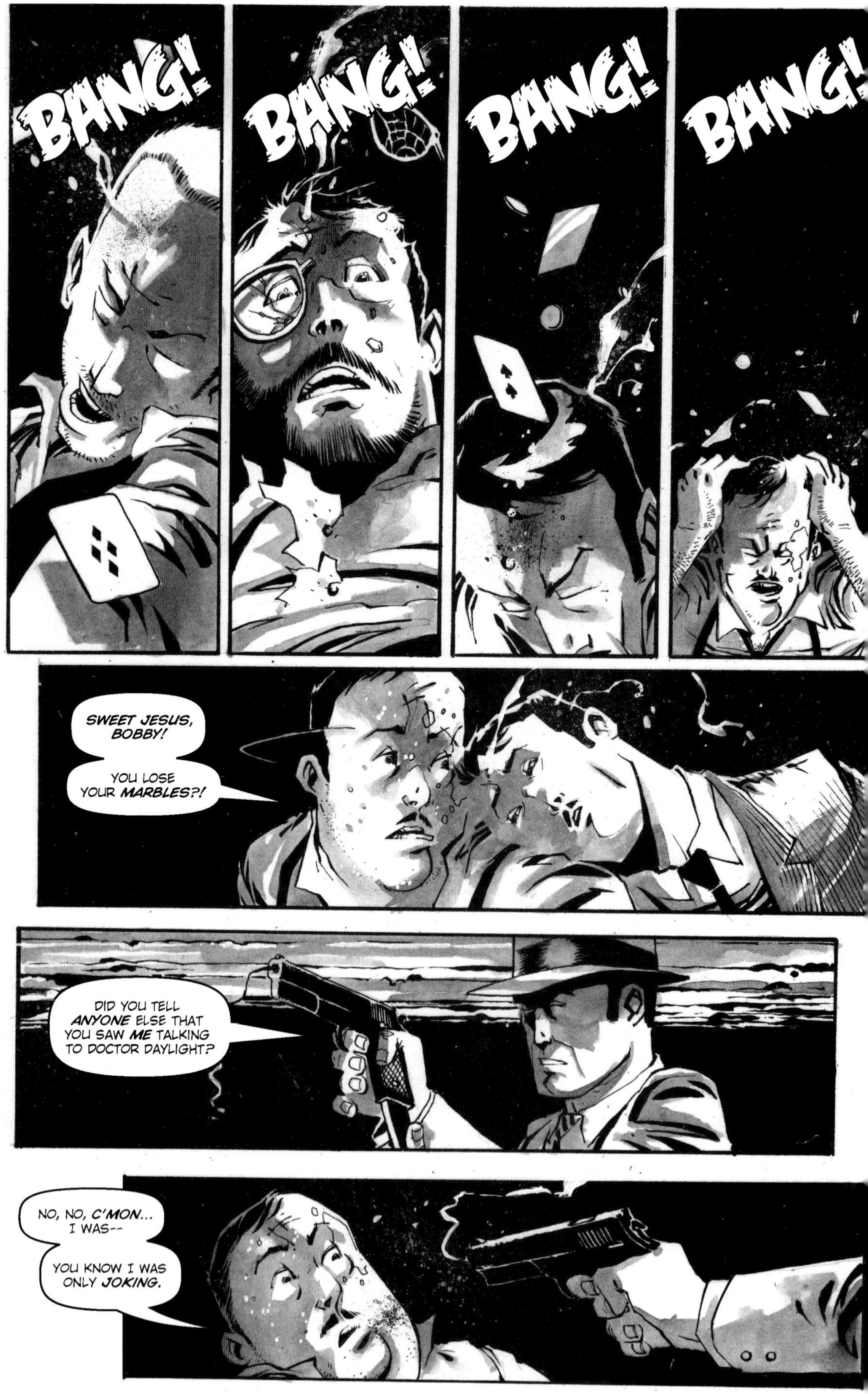
BANG!
BANG!
BANG!
BANG!
SWEET JESUS, BOBBY!
YOU LOSE YOUR MARBLES?!
DID YOU TELL ANYONE ELSE THAT YOU SAW ME TALKING TO DOCTOR DAYLIGHT?
NO, NO, C'MON... I WAS--
YOU KNOW I WAS ONLY JOKING.

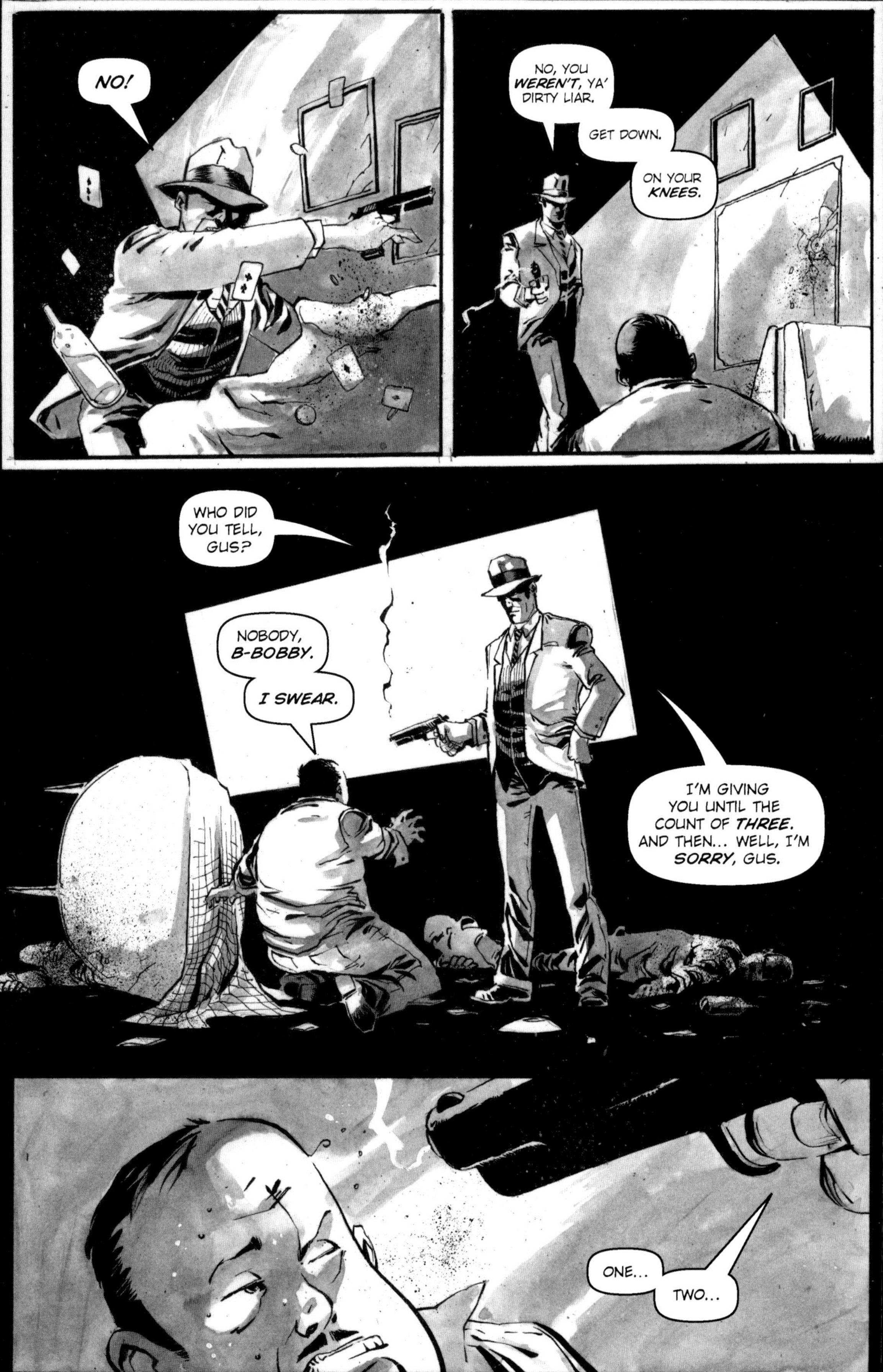
NO!
NO, YOU WEREN'T, YA' DIRTY LIAR.
GET DOWN.
ON YOUR KNEES.
WHO DID YOU TELL, GUS?
NOBODY, B-BOBBY.
I SWEAR.
I'M GIVING YOU UNTIL THE COUNT OF THREE. AND THEN... WELL, I'M SORRY, GUS.
ONE...
TWO...

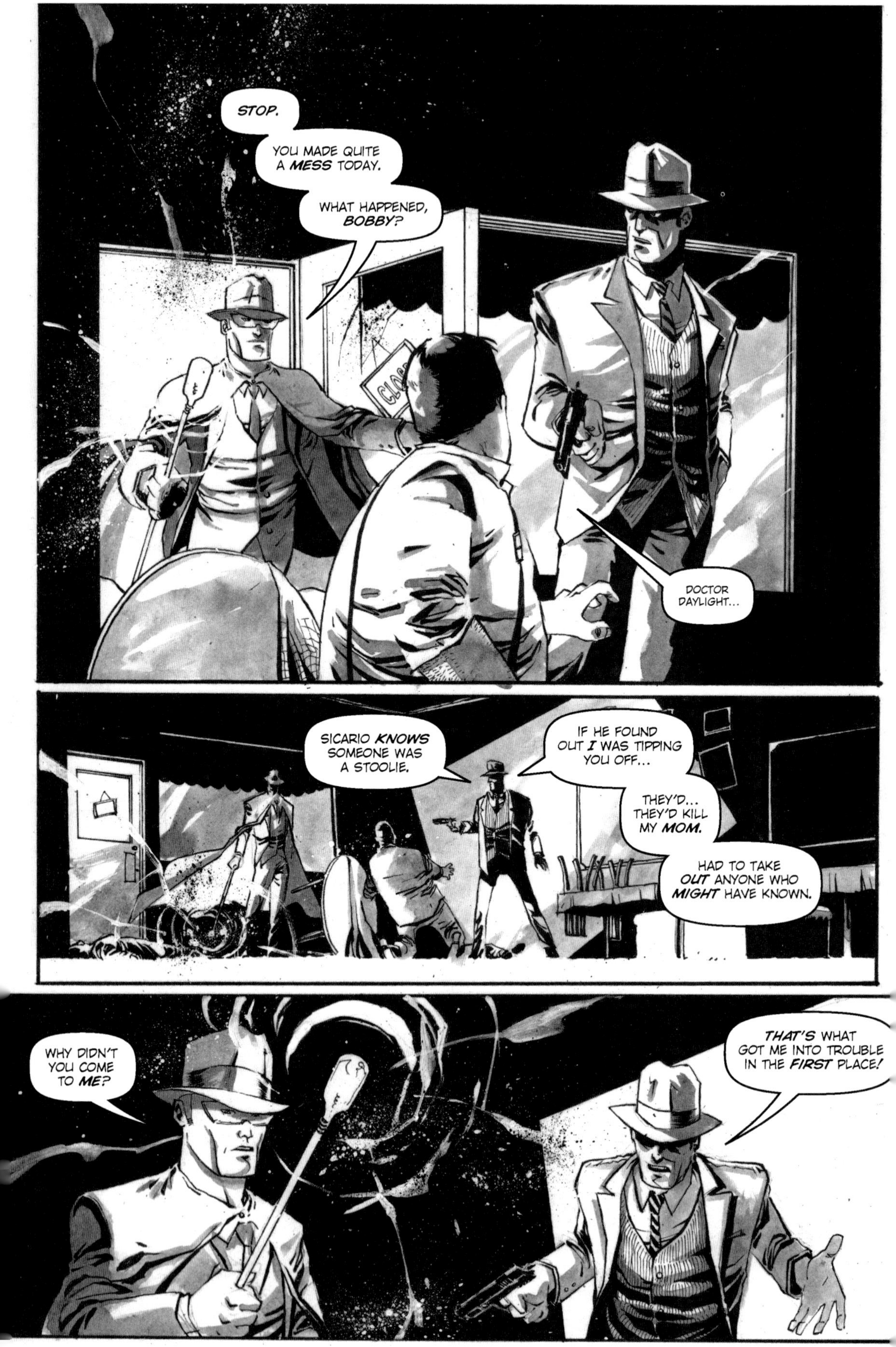
STOP.
YOU MADE QUITE A MESS TODAY.
WHAT HAPPENED, BOBBY?
DOCTOR DAYLIGHT...
SICARIO KNOWS SOMEONE WAS A STOOLIE.
IF HE FOUND OUT I WAS TIPPING YOU OFF...
THEY'D... THEY'D KILL MY MOM.
HAD TO TAKE OUT ANYONE WHO MIGHT HAVE KNOWN.
WHY DIDN'T YOU COME TO ME?
THAT'S WHAT GOT ME INTO TROUBLE IN THE FIRST PLACE!

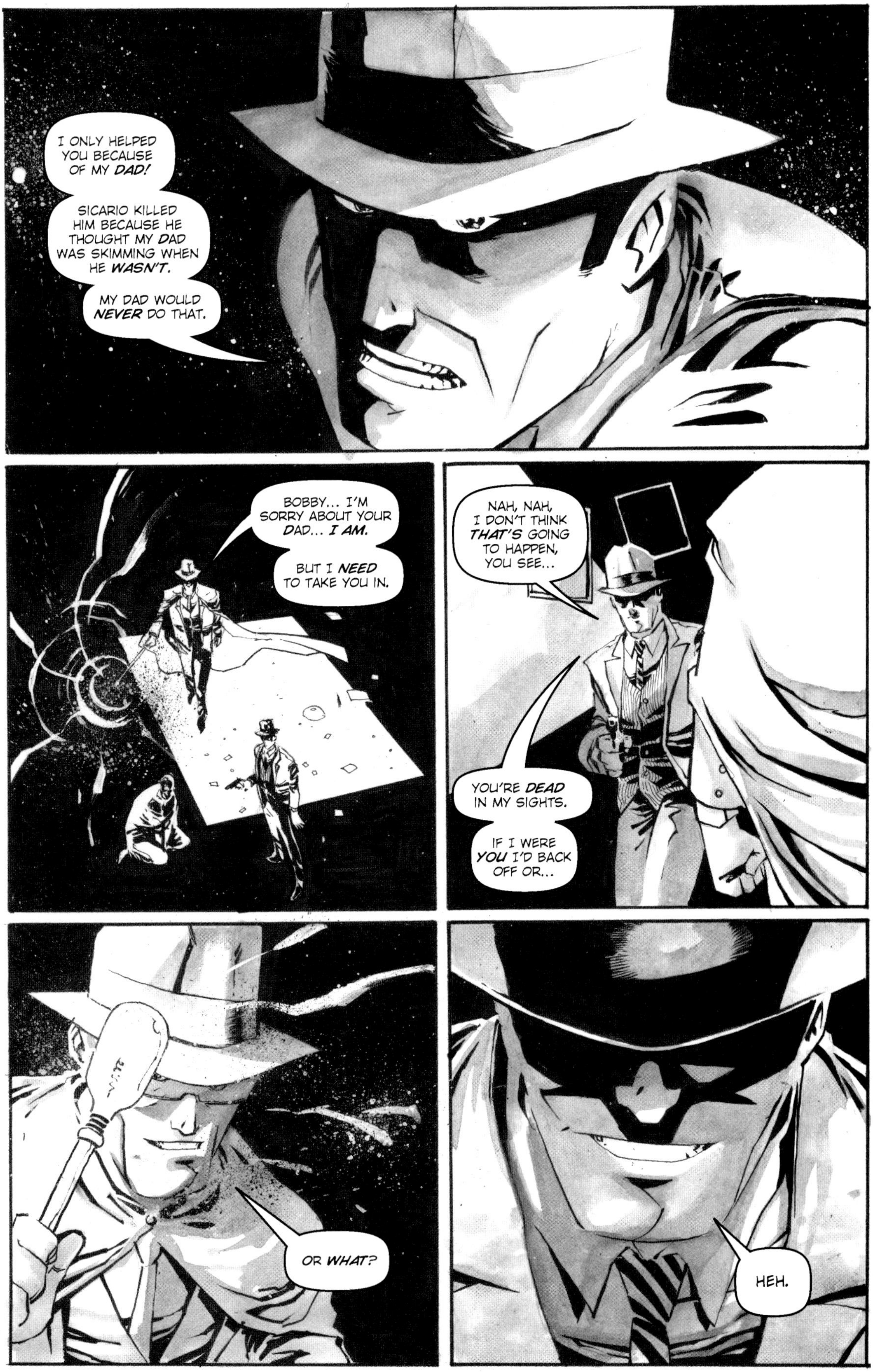
I ONLY HELPED YOU BECAUSE OF MY DAD!
SICARIO KILLED HIM BECAUSE HE THOUGHT MY DAD WAS SKIMMING WHEN HE WASN'T.
MY DAD WOULD NEVER DO THAT.
BOBBY... I'M SORRY ABOUT YOUR DAD... I AM.
BUT I NEED TO TAKE YOU IN.
NAH, NAH, I DON'T THINK THAT'S GOING TO HAPPEN, YOU SEE...
YOU'RE DEAD IN MY SIGHTS.
IF I WERE YOU I'D BACK OFF OR...
OR WHAT?
HEH.

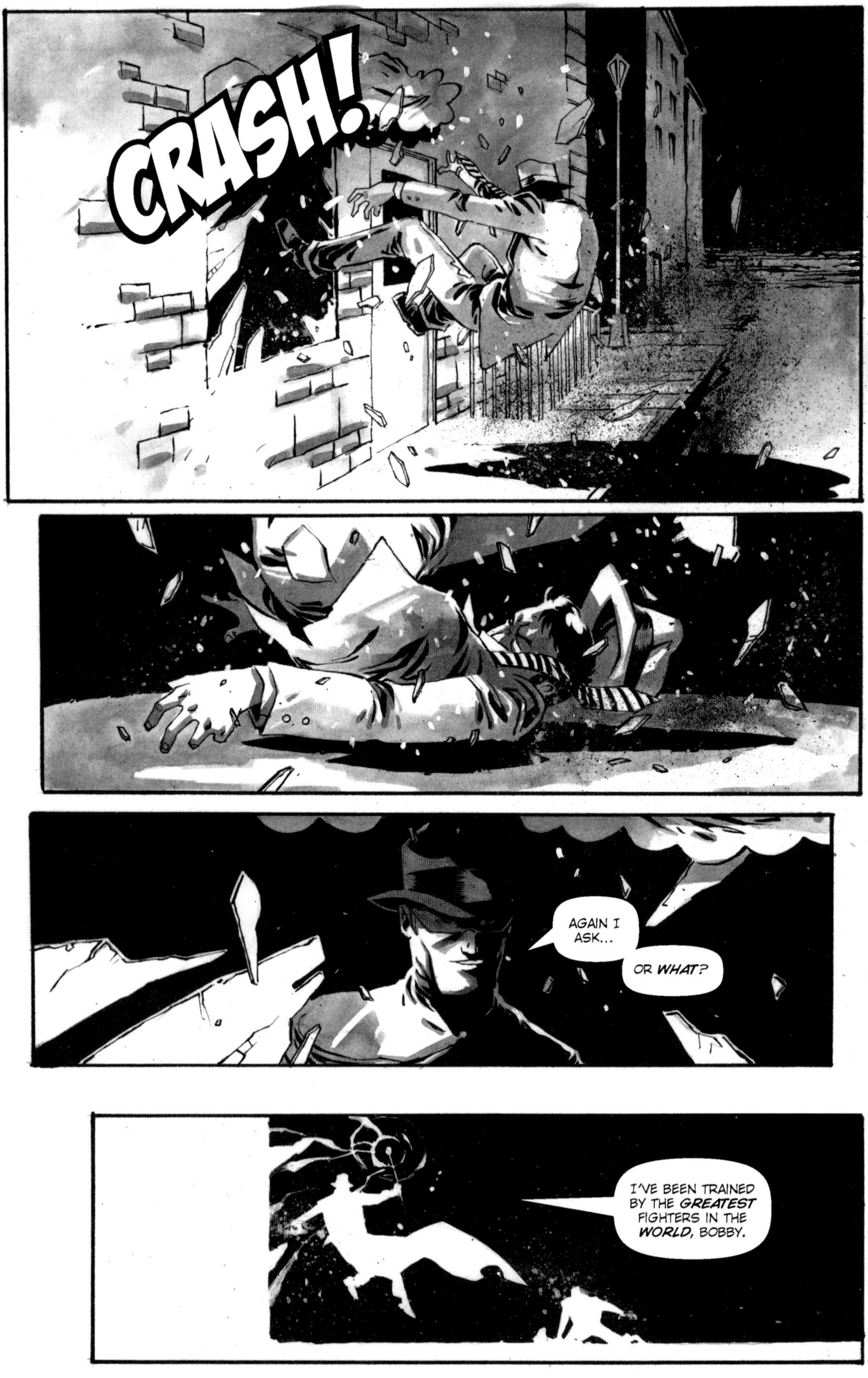
CRASH!
AGAIN I ASK...
OR WHAT?
I'VE BEEN TRAINED BY THE GREATEST FIGHTERS IN THE WORLD, BOBBY.

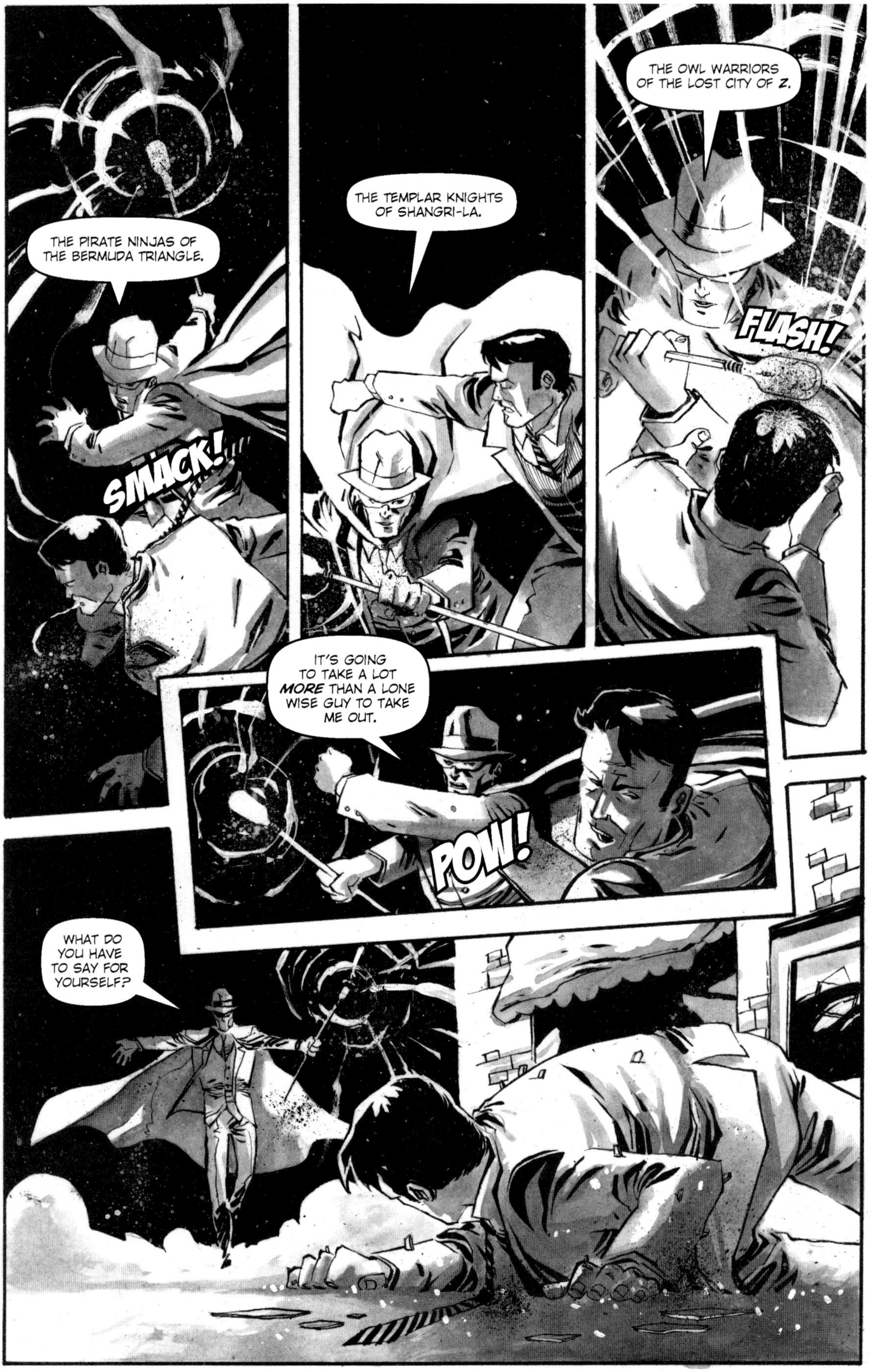

THE PIRATE NINJAS OF THE BERMUDA TRIANGLE.
SMACK!
THE TEMPLAR KNIGHTS OF SHANGRI-LA.
THE OWL WARRIORS OF THE LOST CITY OF Z.
FLASH!
IT'S GOING TO TAKE A LOT MORE THAN A LONE WISE GUY TO TAKE ME OUT.
POW!
WHAT DO YOU HAVE TO SAY FOR YOURSELF?

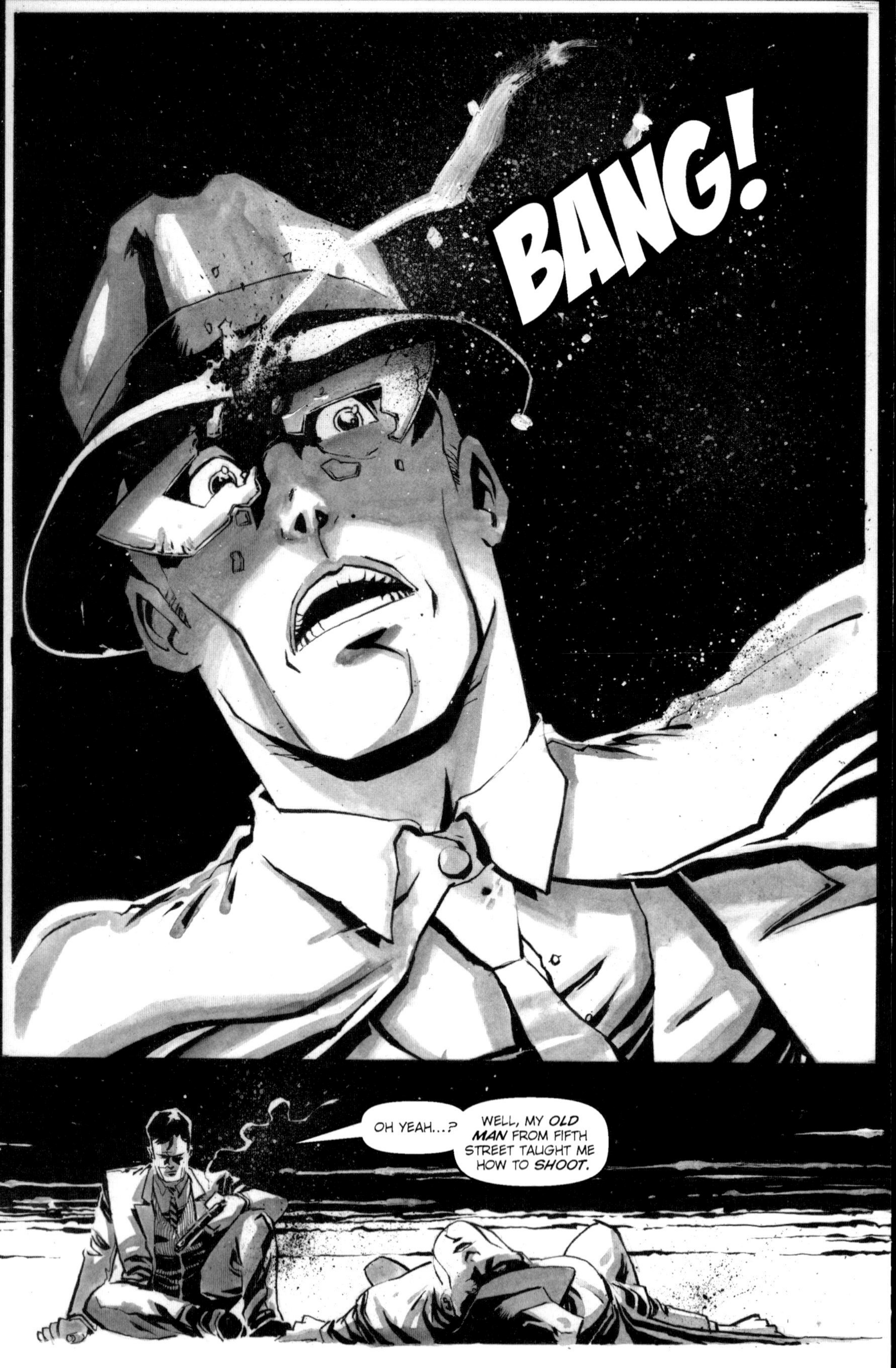
BANG!
OH YEAH...?
WELL, MY OLD MAN FROM FIFTH STREET TAUGHT ME HOW TO SHOOT.

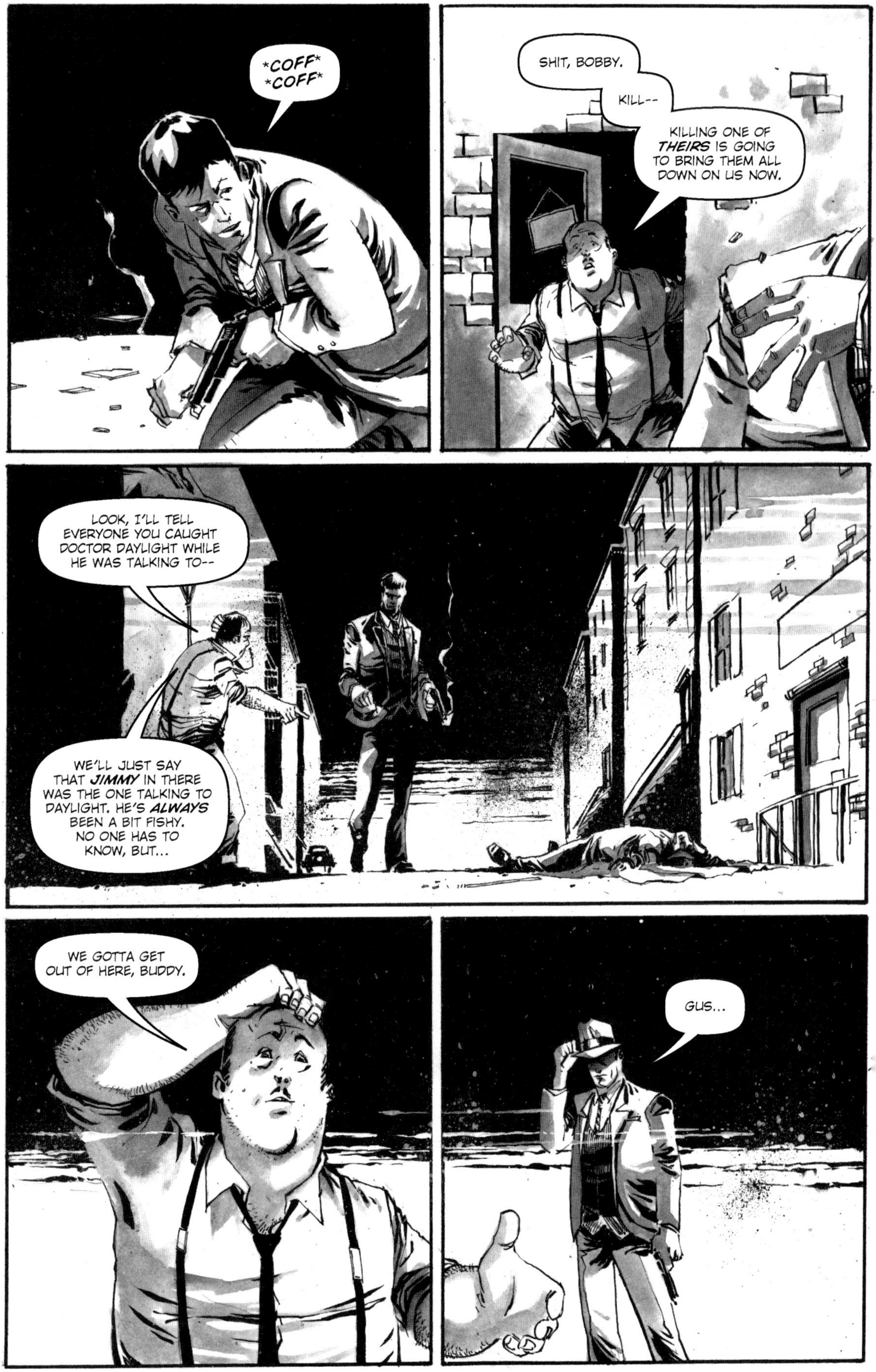
COFF
COFF
SHIT, BOBBY.
KILL--
KILLING ONE OF THEIRS IS GOING TO BRING THEM ALL DOWN ON US NOW.
LOOK, I'LL TELL EVERYONE YOU CAUGHT DOCTOR DAYLIGHT WHILE HE WAS TALKING TO--
WE'LL JUST SAY THAT JIMMY IN THERE WAS THE ONE TALKING TO DAYLIGHT. HE'S ALWAYS BEEN A BIT FISHY. NO ONE HAS TO KNOW, BUT...
WE GOTTA GET OUT OF HERE, BUDDY.
GUS...

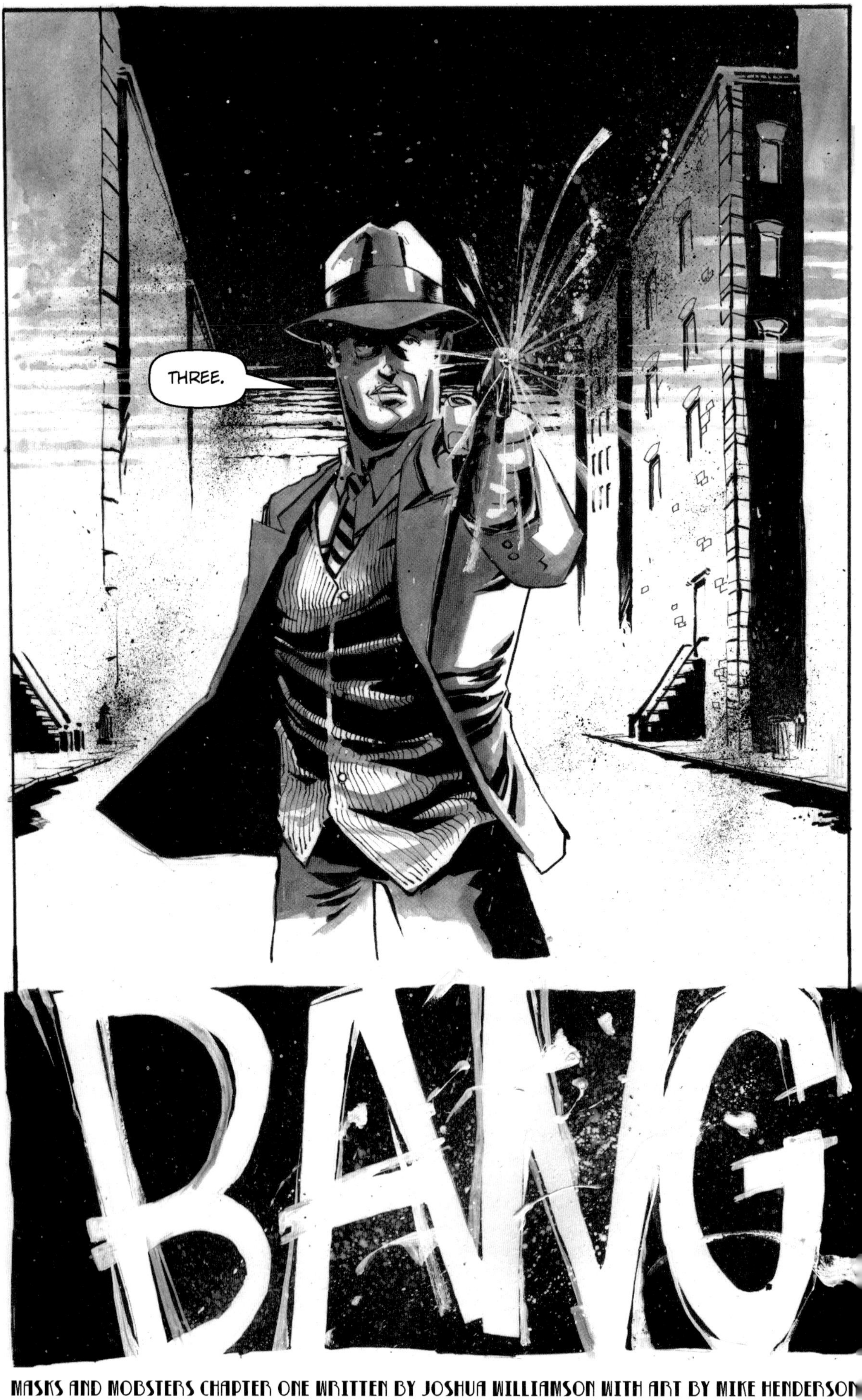
THREE.
BANG

MASKS AND MOBSTERS CHAPTER ONE WRITTEN BY JOSHUA WILLIAMSON WITH ART BY MIKE HENDERSON

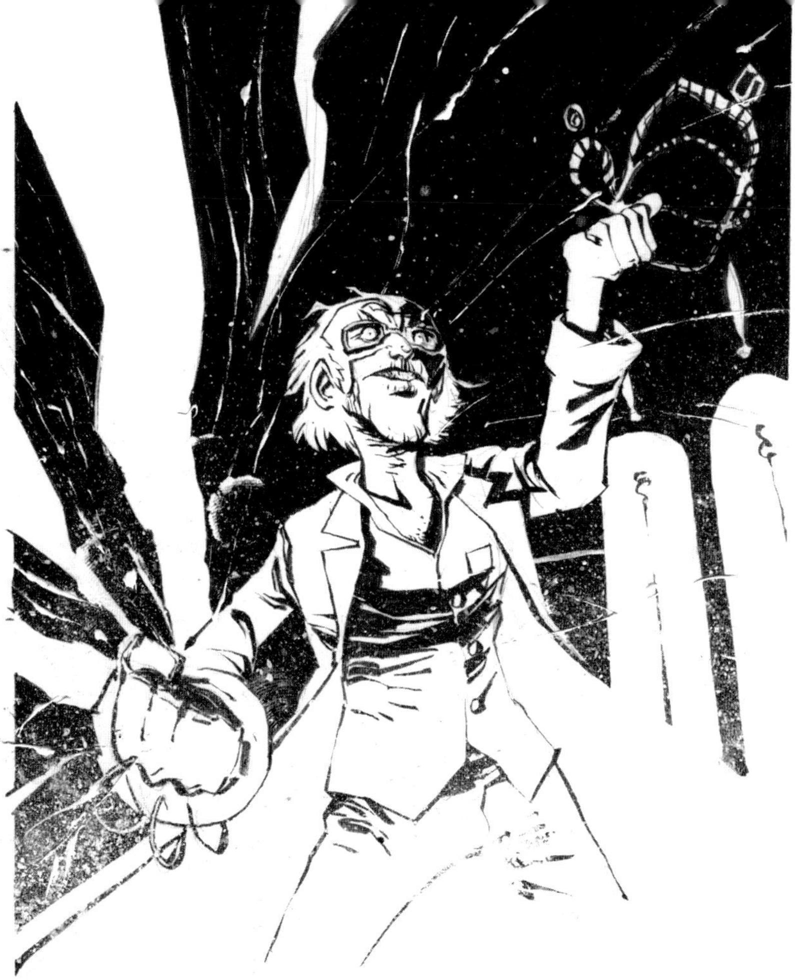

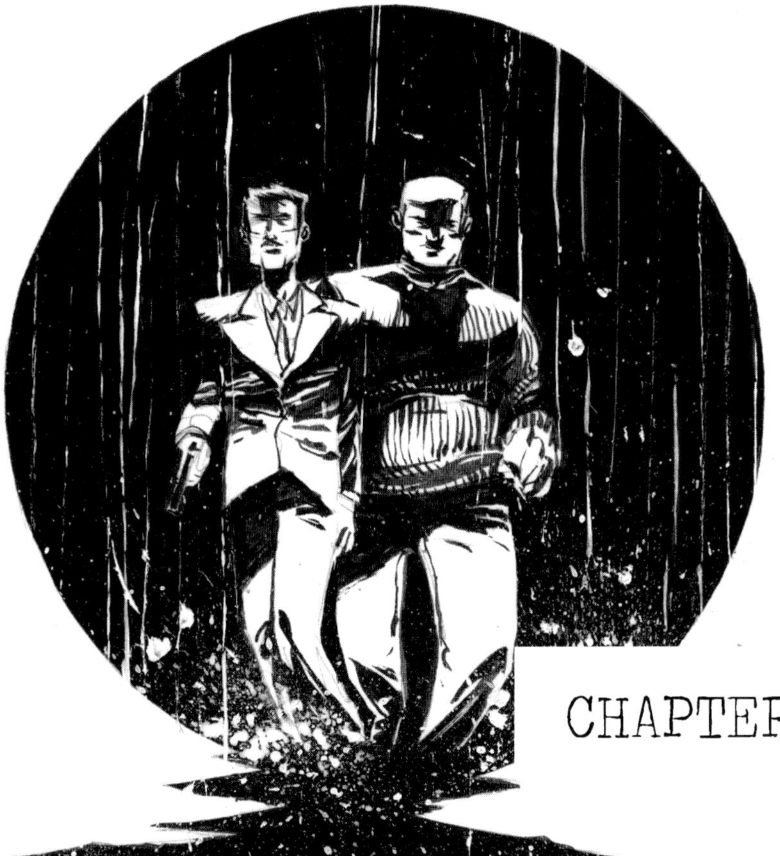

CHAPTER TWO

Mike's designs for the second chapter. Mike nailed the scientists but needed a few tries to get the robot.

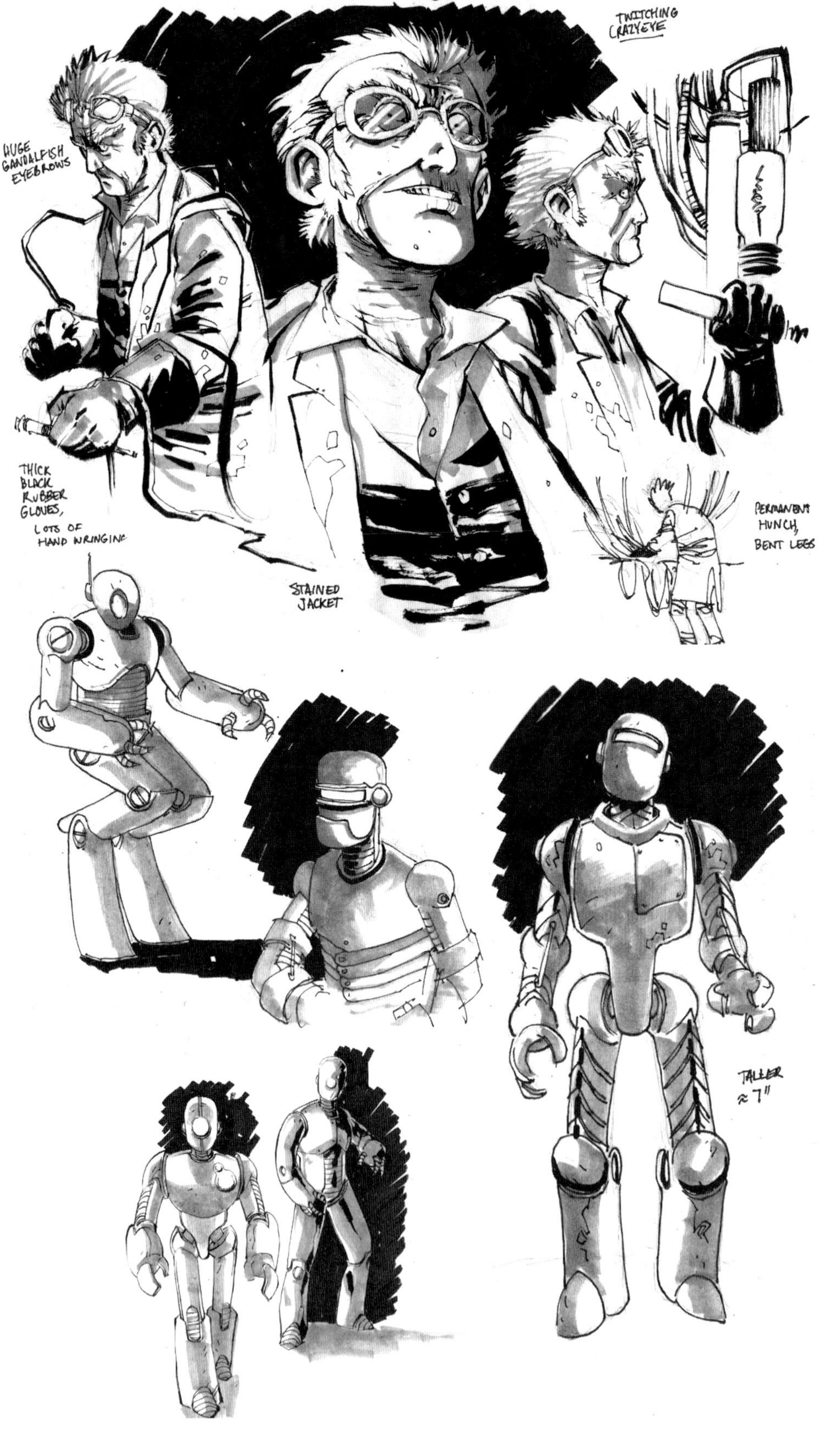
TWITCHING CRAZYEYE
HUGE GANDALFISH EYEBROWS
THICK BLACK RUBBER GLOVES, LOTS OF HAND WRINGING
STAINED JACKET
PERMANENT HUNCH, BENT LEGS
TALLER ≈ 7"

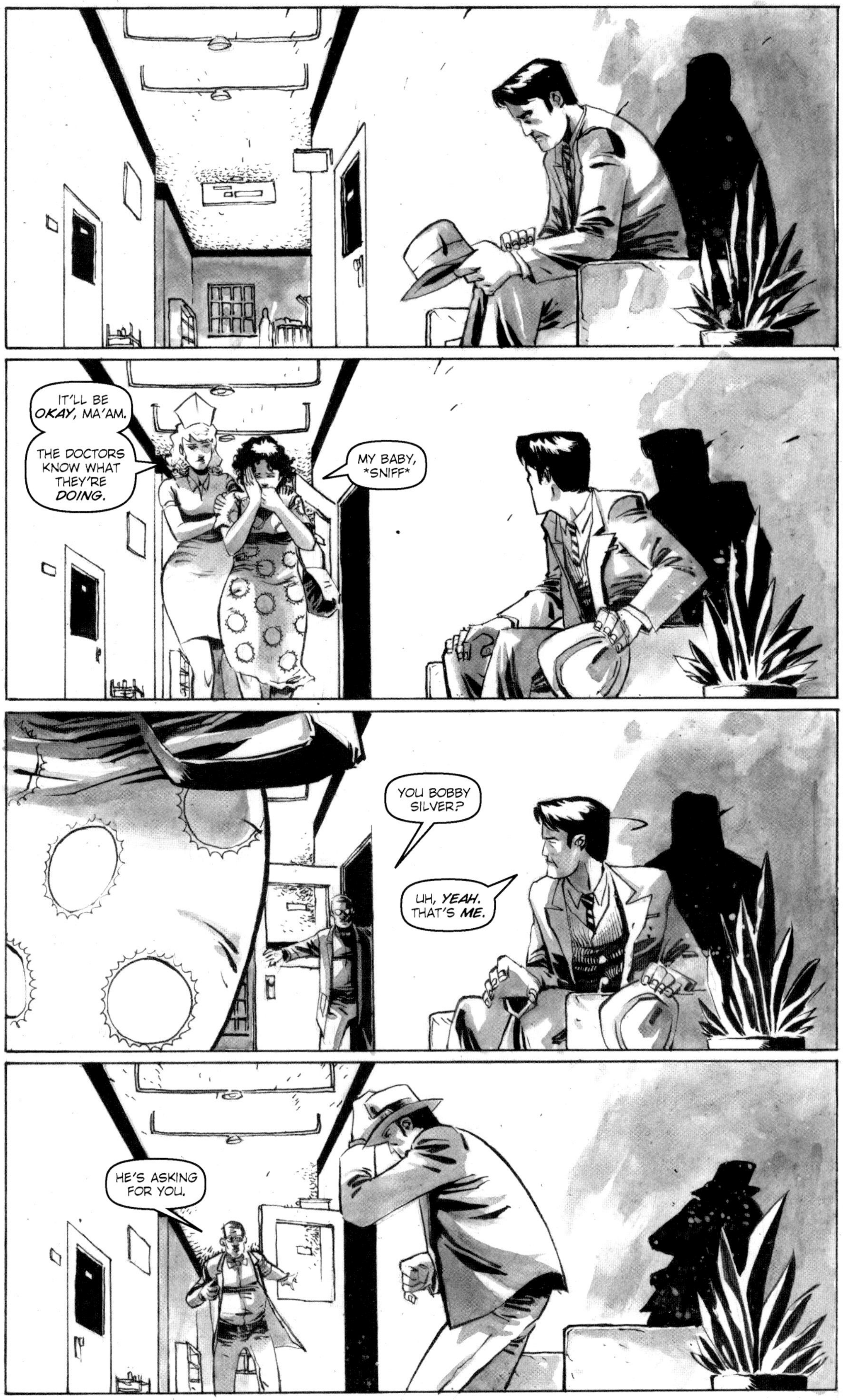
IT'LL BE OKAY, MA'AM.
THE DOCTORS KNOW WHAT THEY'RE DOING.
MY BABY, *SNIFF*
YOU BOBBY SILVER?
UH, YEAH. THAT'S ME.
HE'S ASKING FOR YOU.

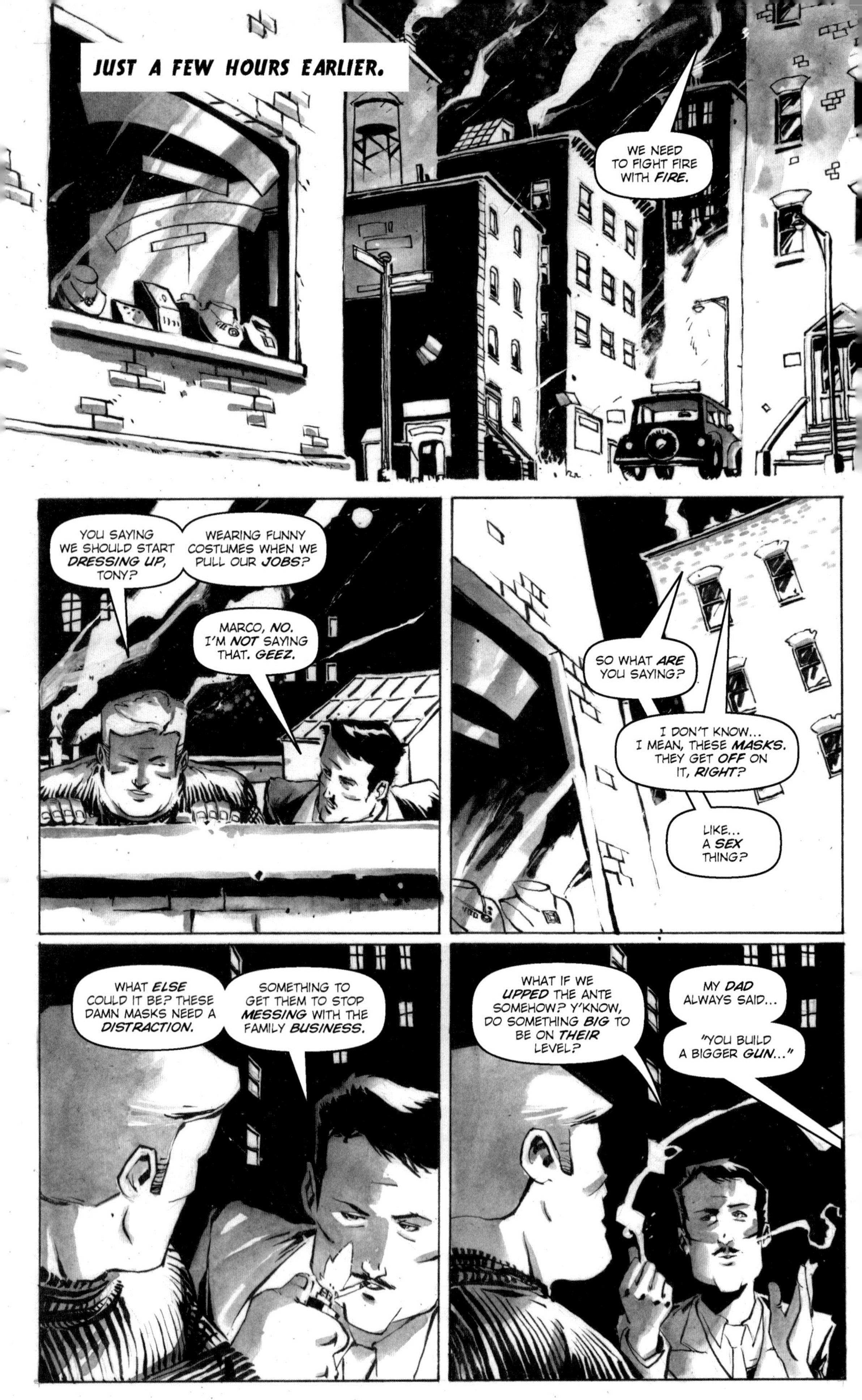
JUST A FEW HOURS EARLIER.
WE NEED TO FIGHT FIRE WITH FIRE.
YOU SAYING WE SHOULD START DRESSING UP, TONY?
WEARING FUNNY COSTUMES WHEN WE PULL OUR JOBS?
MARCO, NO. I'M NOT SAYING THAT. GEEZ.
SO WHAT ARE YOU SAYING?
I DON'T KNOW... I MEAN, THESE MASKS. THEY GET OFF ON IT, RIGHT?
LIKE... A SEX THING?
WHAT ELSE COULD IT BE? THESE DAMN MASKS NEED A DISTRACTION.
SOMETHING TO GET THEM TO STOP MESSING WITH THE FAMILY BUSINESS.
WHAT IF WE UPPED THE ANTE SOMEHOW? Y'KNOW, DO SOMETHING BIG TO BE ON THEIR LEVEL?
MY DAD ALWAYS SAID...
"YOU BUILD A BIGGER GUN..."

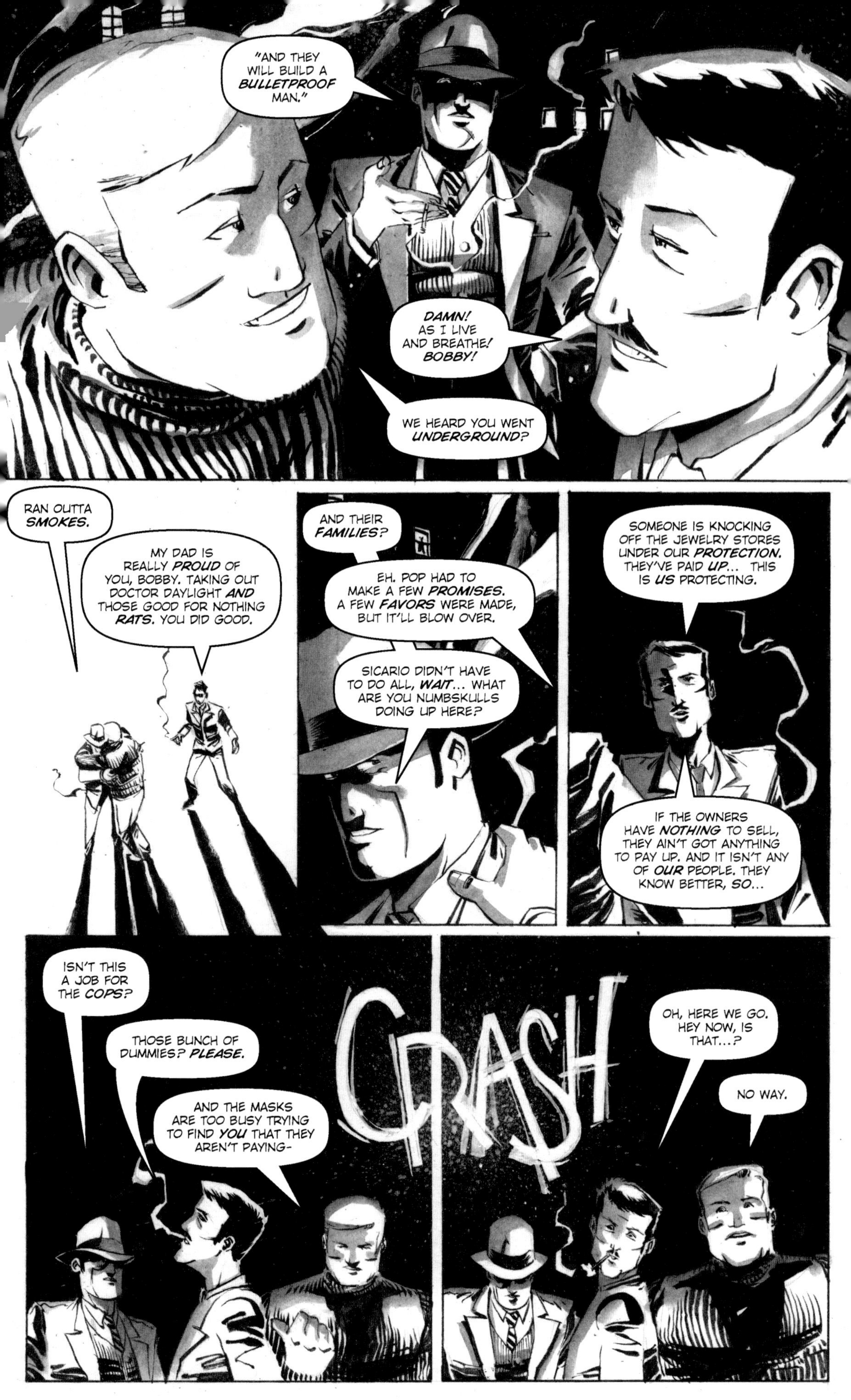
"AND THEY WILL BUILD A BULLETPROOF MAN."
DAMN! AS I LIVE AND BREATHE! BOBBY!
WE HEARD YOU WENT UNDERGROUND?
RAN OUTTA SMOKES.
MY DAD IS REALLY PROUD OF YOU, BOBBY. TAKING OUT DOCTOR DAYLIGHT AND THOSE GOOD FOR NOTHING RATS. YOU DID GOOD.
AND THEIR FAMILIES?
EH. POP HAD TO MAKE A FEW PROMISES. A FEW FAVORS WERE MADE, BUT IT'LL BLOW OVER.
SICARIO DIDN'T HAVE TO DO ALL, WAIT... WHAT ARE YOU NUMBSKULLS DOING UP HERE?
SOMEONE IS KNOCKING OFF THE JEWELRY STORES UNDER OUR PROTECTION. THEY'VE PAID UP... THIS IS US PROTECTING.
IF THE OWNERS HAVE NOTHING TO SELL, THEY AIN'T GOT ANYTHING TO PAY UP. AND IT ISN'T ANY OF OUR PEOPLE. THEY KNOW BETTER, SO...
ISN'T THIS A JOB FOR THE COPS?
THOSE BUNCH OF DUMMIES? PLEASE.
AND THE MASKS ARE TOO BUSY TRYING TO FIND YOU THAT THEY AREN'T PAYING-
CRASH
OH, HERE WE GO. HEY NOW, IS THAT...?
NO WAY.

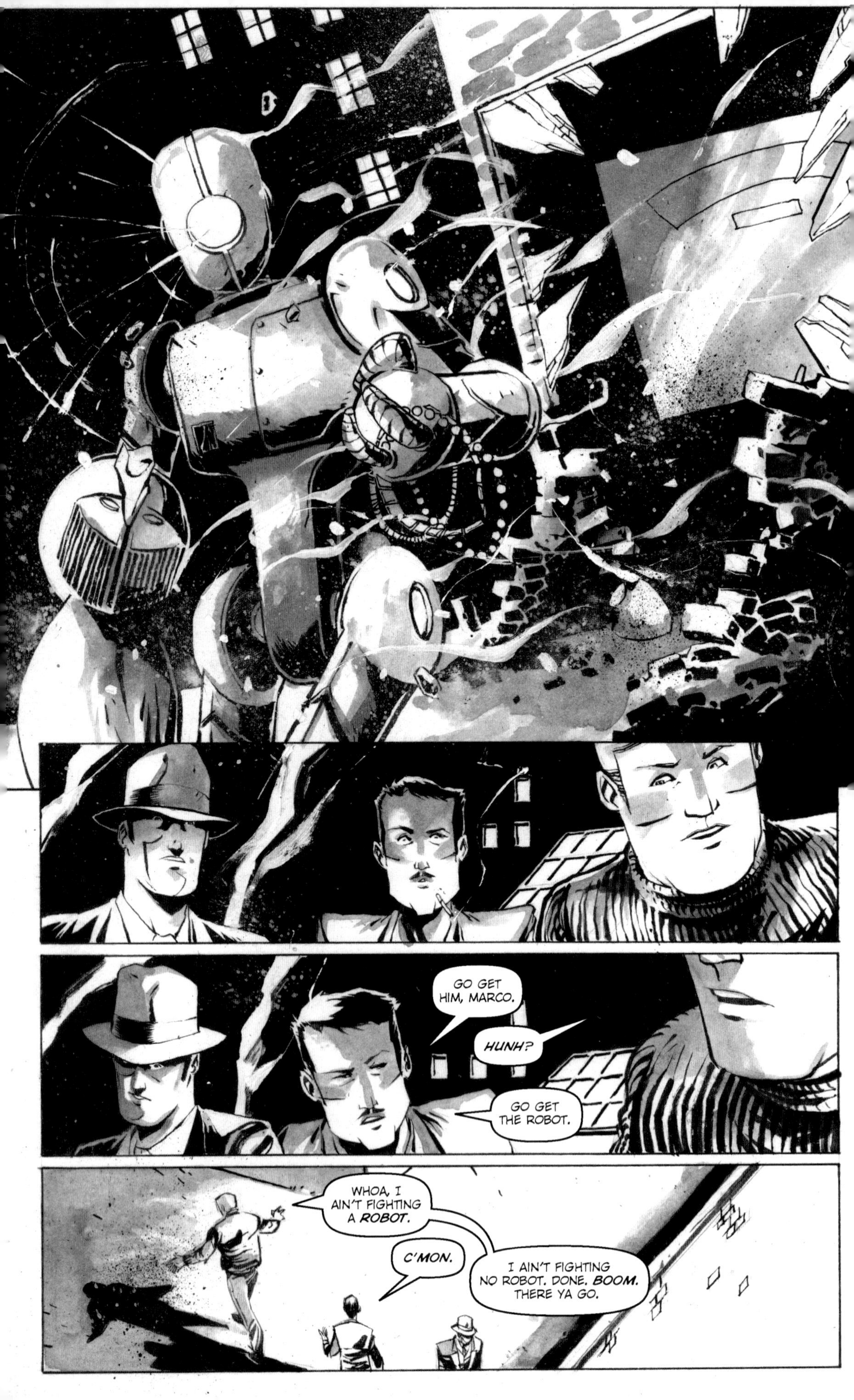
GO GET HIM, MARCO.
HUNH?
GO GET THE ROBOT.
WHOA, I AIN'T FIGHTING A ROBOT.
C'MON.
I AIN'T FIGHTING NO ROBOT. DONE. BOOM. THERE YA GO.

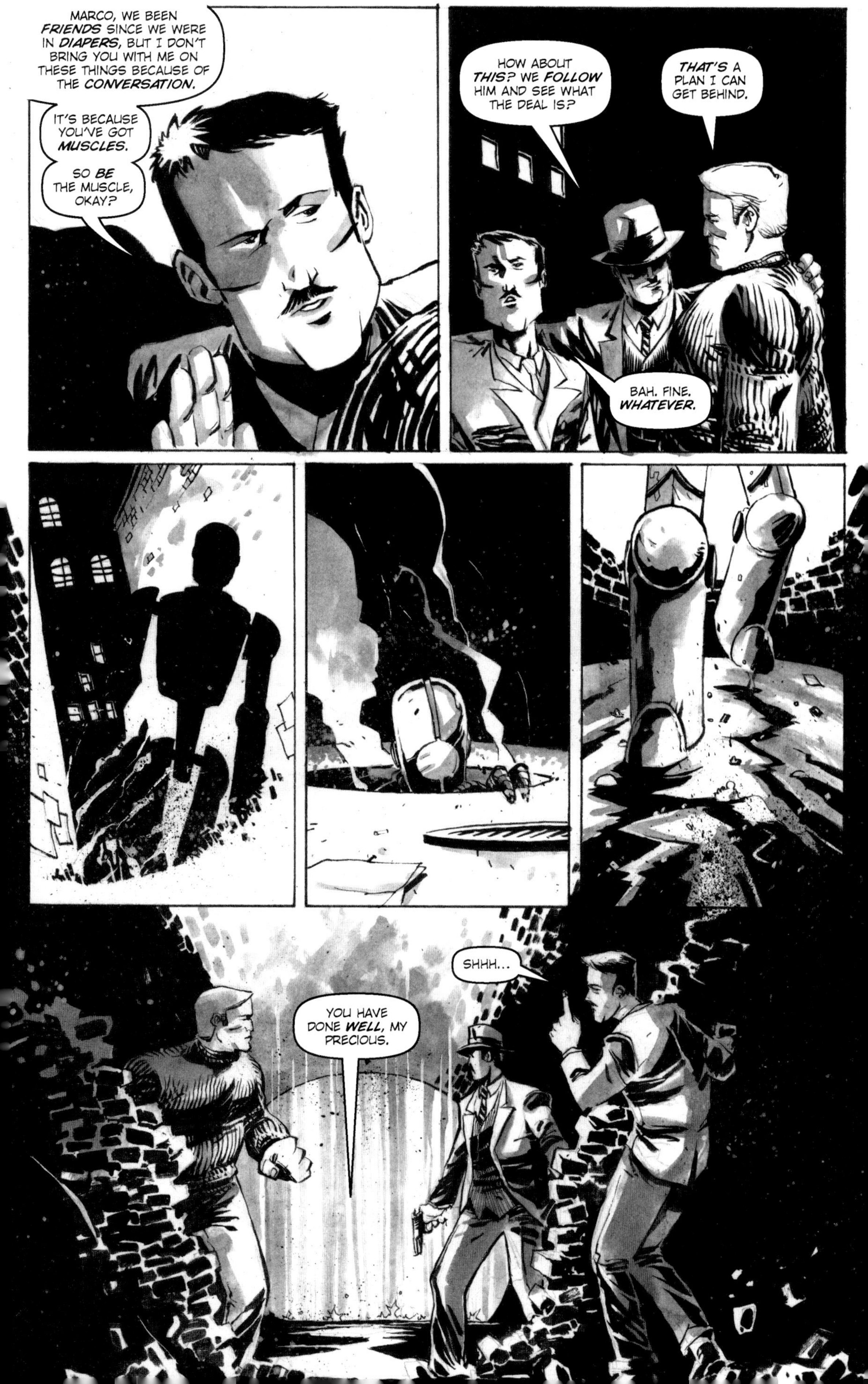
MARCO, WE BEEN FRIENDS SINCE WE WERE IN DIAPERS, BUT I DON'T BRING YOU WITH ME ON THESE THINGS BECAUSE OF THE CONVERSATION.
IT'S BECAUSE YOU'VE GOT MUSCLES.
SO BE THE MUSCLE, OKAY?
HOW ABOUT THIS? WE FOLLOW HIM AND SEE WHAT THE DEAL IS?
THAT'S A PLAN I CAN GET BEHIND.
BAH. FINE. WHATEVER.
SHHH...
YOU HAVE DONE WELL, MY PRECIOUS.

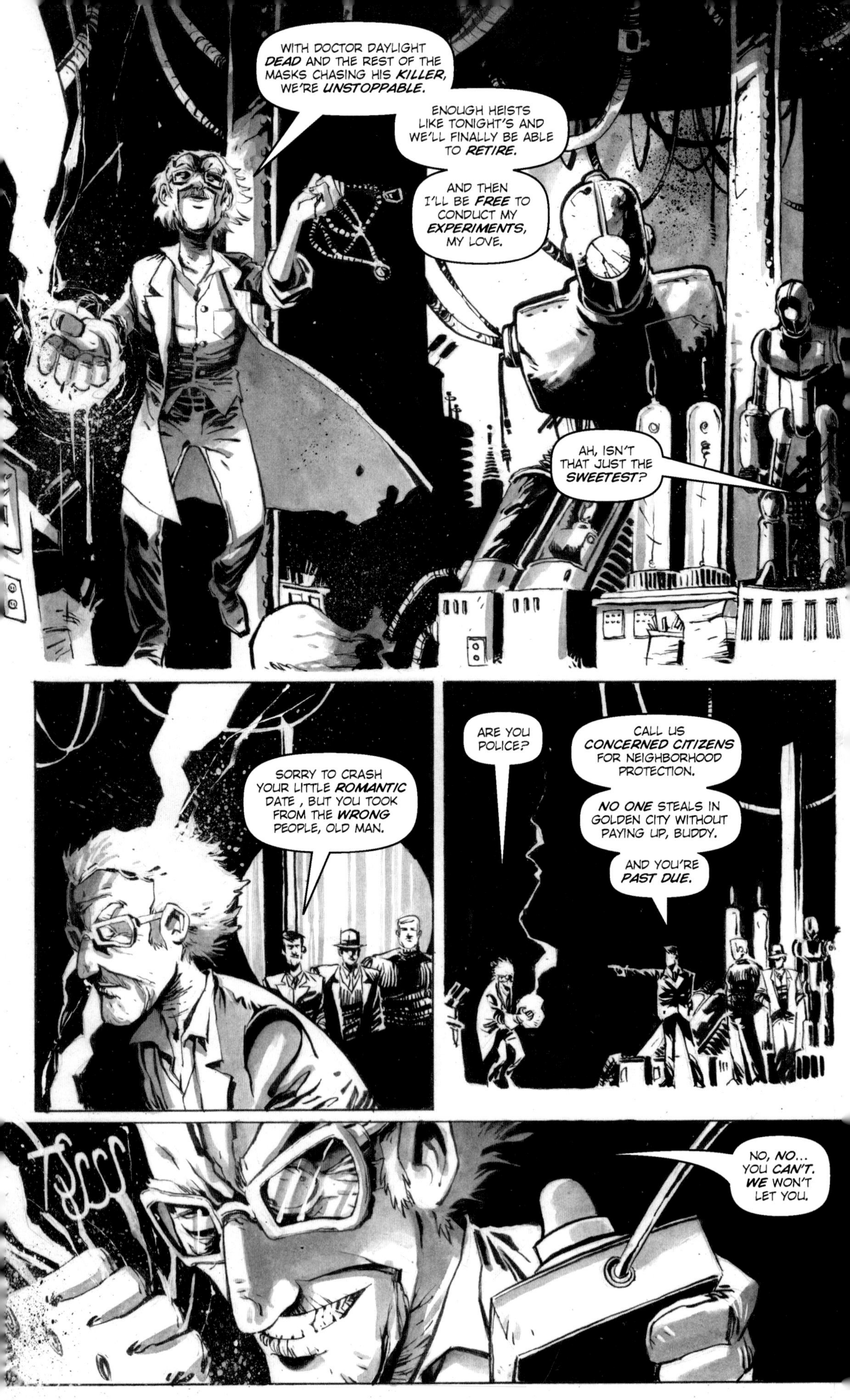
WITH DOCTOR DAYLIGHT DEAD AND THE REST OF THE MASKS CHASING HIS KILLER, WE'RE UNSTOPPABLE.
ENOUGH HEISTS LIKE TONIGHT'S AND WE'LL FINALLY BE ABLE TO RETIRE.
AND THEN I'LL BE FREE TO CONDUCT MY EXPERIMENTS, MY LOVE.
AH, ISN'T THAT JUST THE SWEETEST?
SORRY TO CRASH YOUR LITTLE ROMANTIC DATE , BUT YOU TOOK FROM THE WRONG PEOPLE, OLD MAN.
ARE YOU POLICE?
CALL US CONCERNED CITIZENS FOR NEIGHBORHOOD PROTECTION.
NO ONE STEALS IN GOLDEN CITY WITHOUT PAYING UP, BUDDY.
AND YOU'RE PAST DUE.
NO, NO... YOU CAN'T. WE WON'T LET YOU.

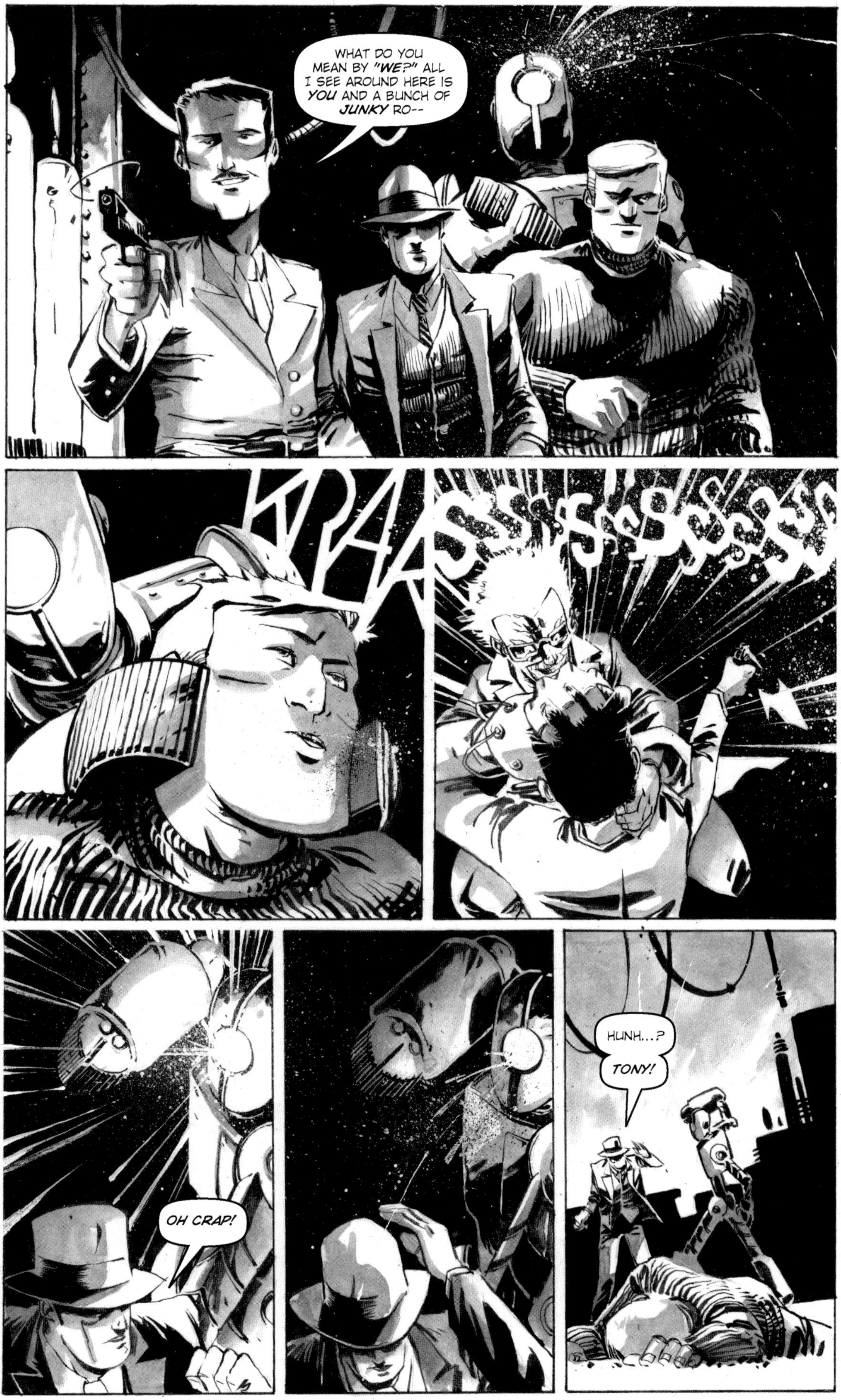
WHAT DO YOU MEAN BY "WE?" ALL I SEE AROUND HERE IS YOU AND A BUNCH OF JUNKY RO--
OH CRAP!
HUNH...?
TONY!

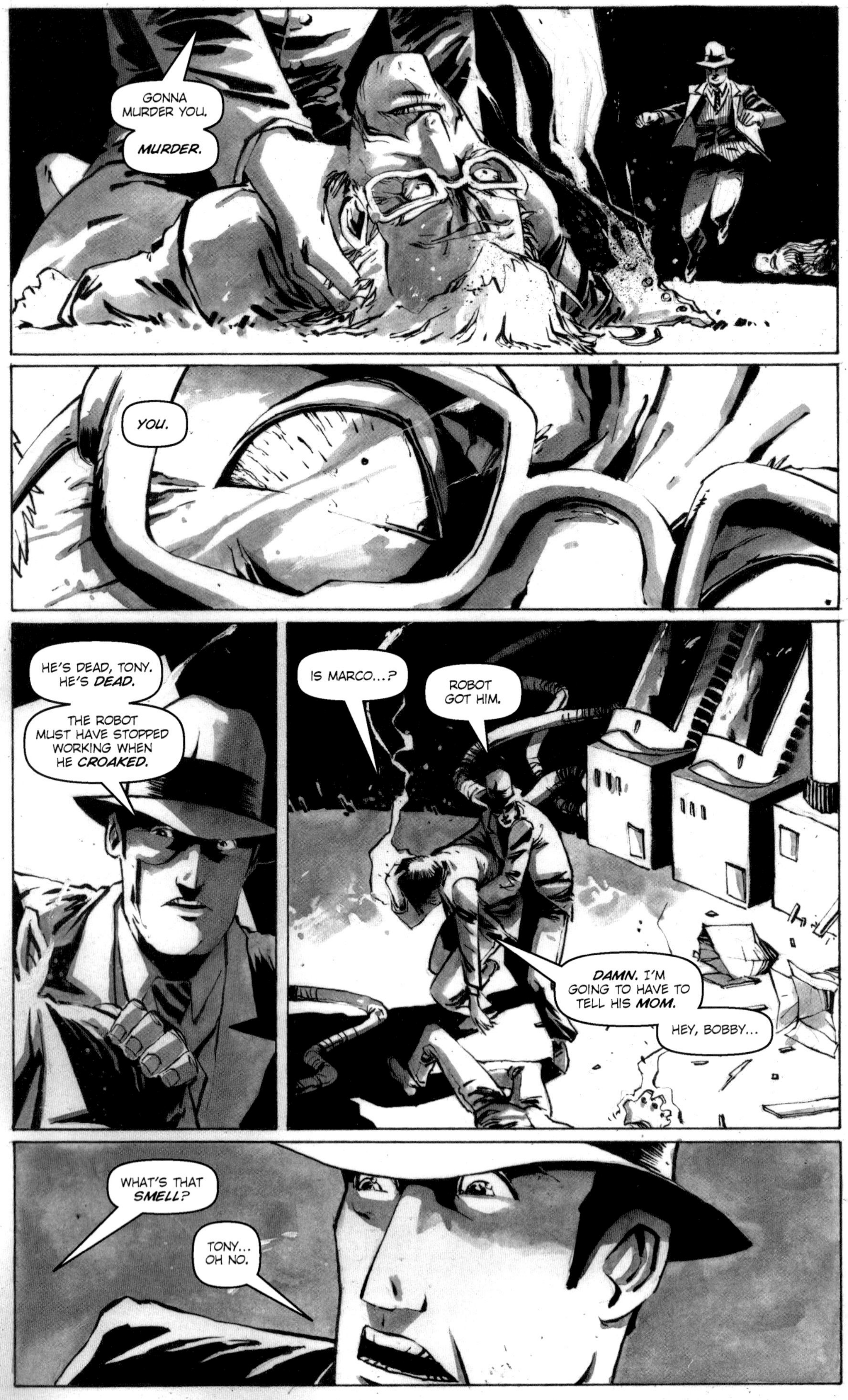
GONNA MURDER YOU.
MURDER.
YOU.
HE'S DEAD, TONY. HE'S DEAD.
THE ROBOT MUST HAVE STOPPED WORKING WHEN HE CROAKED.
IS MARCO...?
ROBOT GOT HIM.
DAMN. I'M GOING TO HAVE TO TELL HIS MOM.
HEY, BOBBY...
WHAT'S THAT SMELL?
TONY... OH NO.

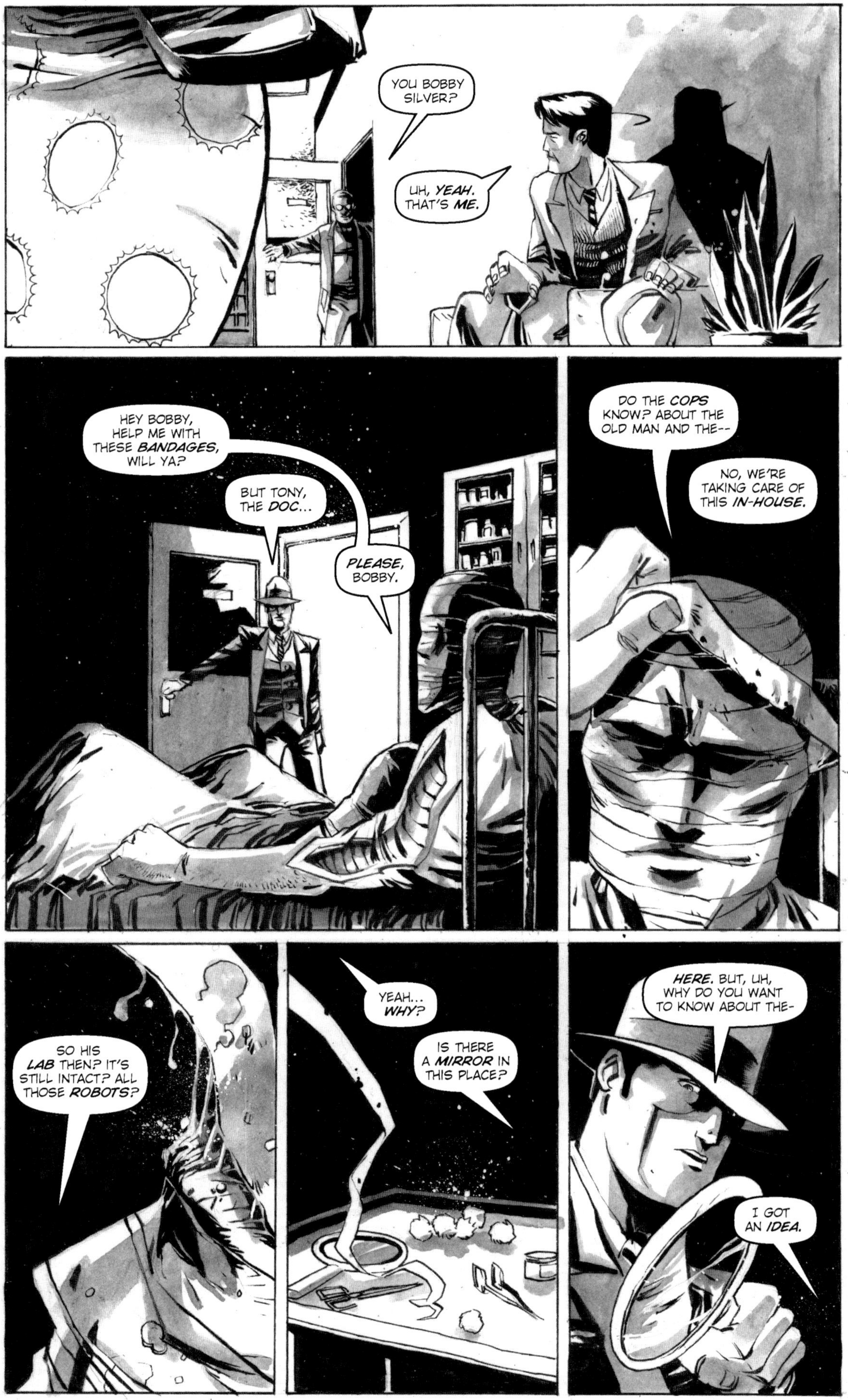
YOU BOBBY SILVER?
UH, YEAH. THAT'S ME.
HEY BOBBY, HELP ME WITH THESE BANDAGES, WILL YA?
BUT TONY, THE DOC...
PLEASE, BOBBY.
DO THE COPS KNOW? ABOUT THE OLD MAN AND THE--
NO, WE'RE TAKING CARE OF THIS IN-HOUSE.
SO HIS LAB THEN? IT'S STILL INTACT? ALL THOSE ROBOTS?
YEAH... WHY?
IS THERE A MIRROR IN THIS PLACE?
HERE. BUT, UH, WHY DO YOU WANT TO KNOW ABOUT THE-
I GOT AN IDEA.

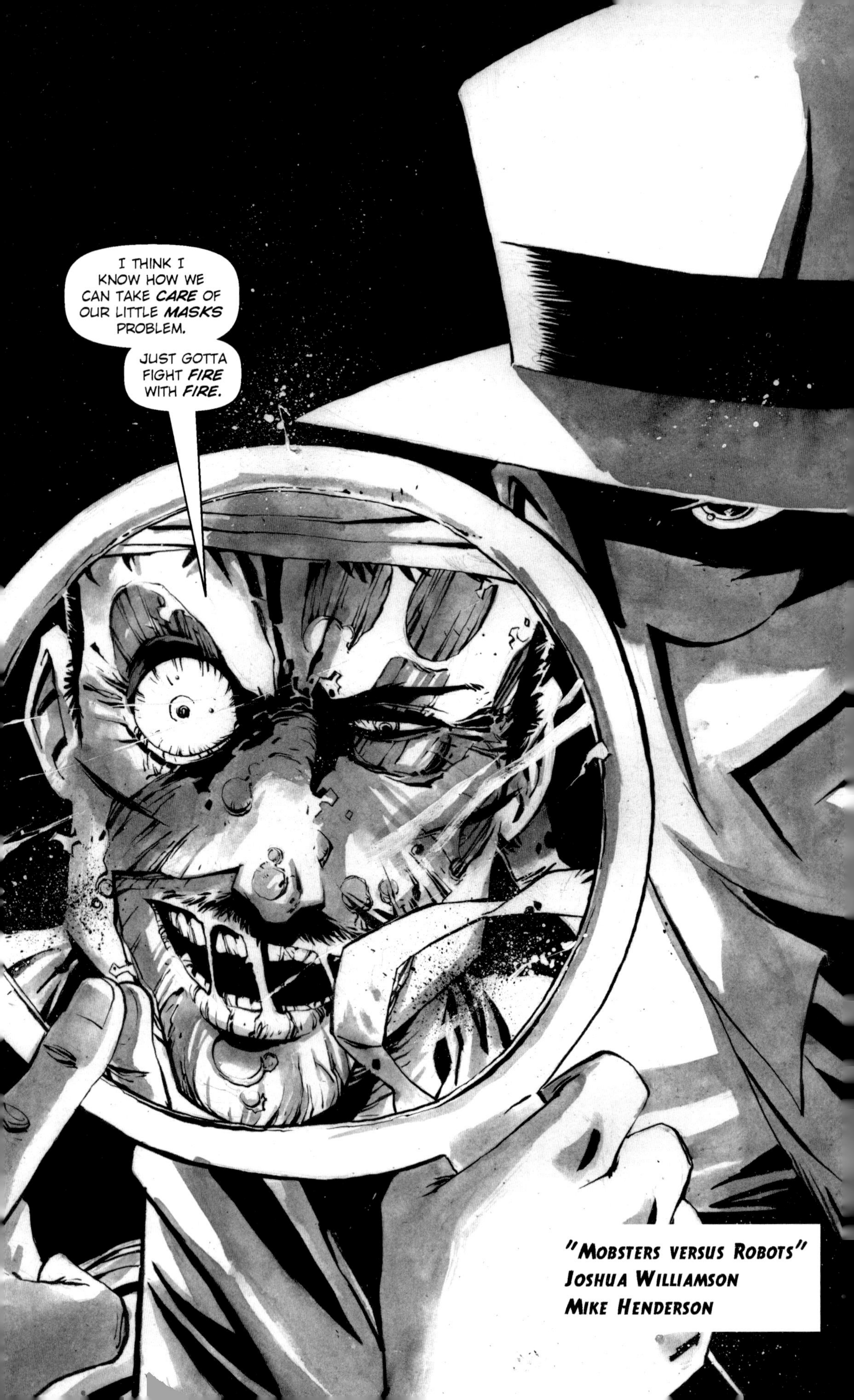

I THINK I KNOW HOW WE CAN TAKE CARE OF OUR LITTLE MASKS PROBLEM.
JUST GOTTA FIGHT FIRE WITH FIRE.
"Mobsters versus Robots"
Joshua Williamson
Mike Henderson

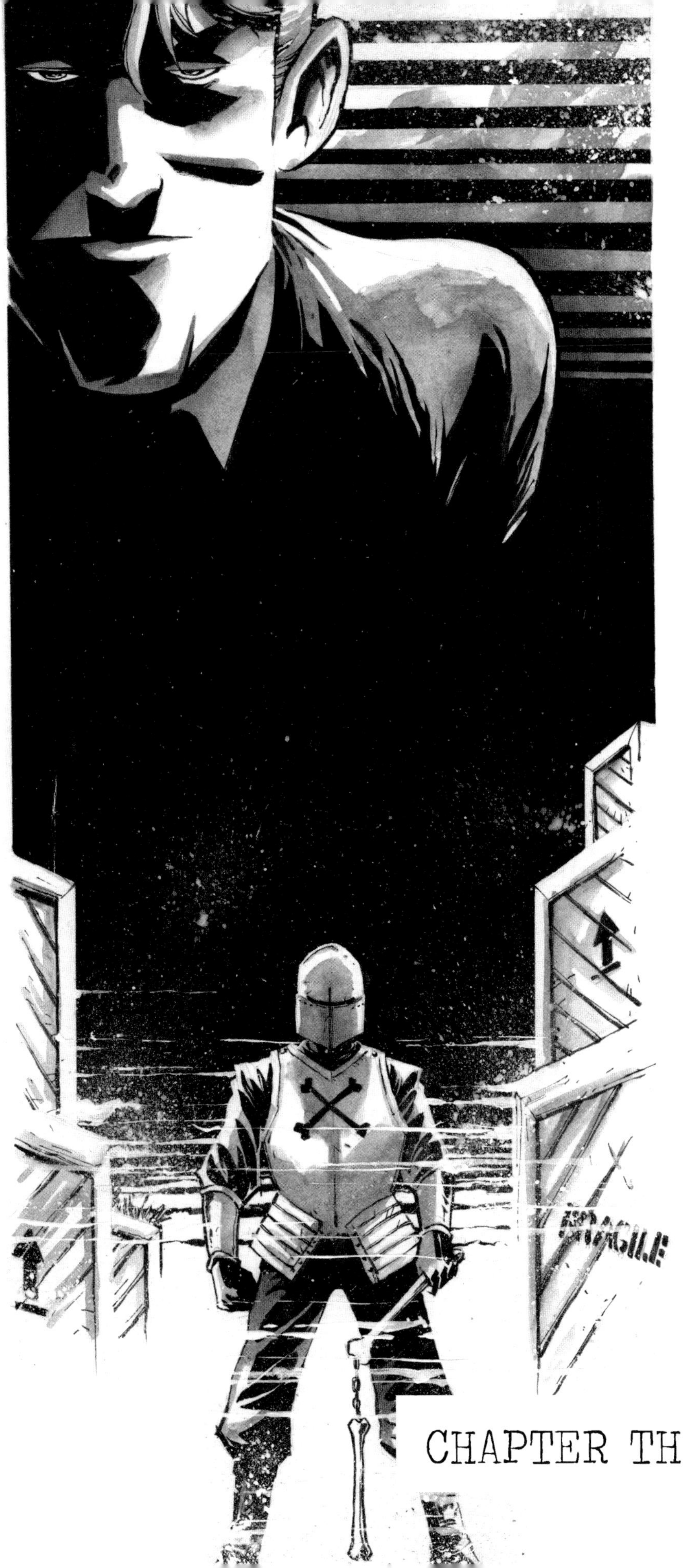
FRAGILE

CHAPTER THREE

The original designs for The Deadly Bones (left) and The Tower (below) were done by Scott Godlewski. Easily two of the best designs in the book.

Originally The Deadly Bones was going to be a handsome man as seen in the bottom left.

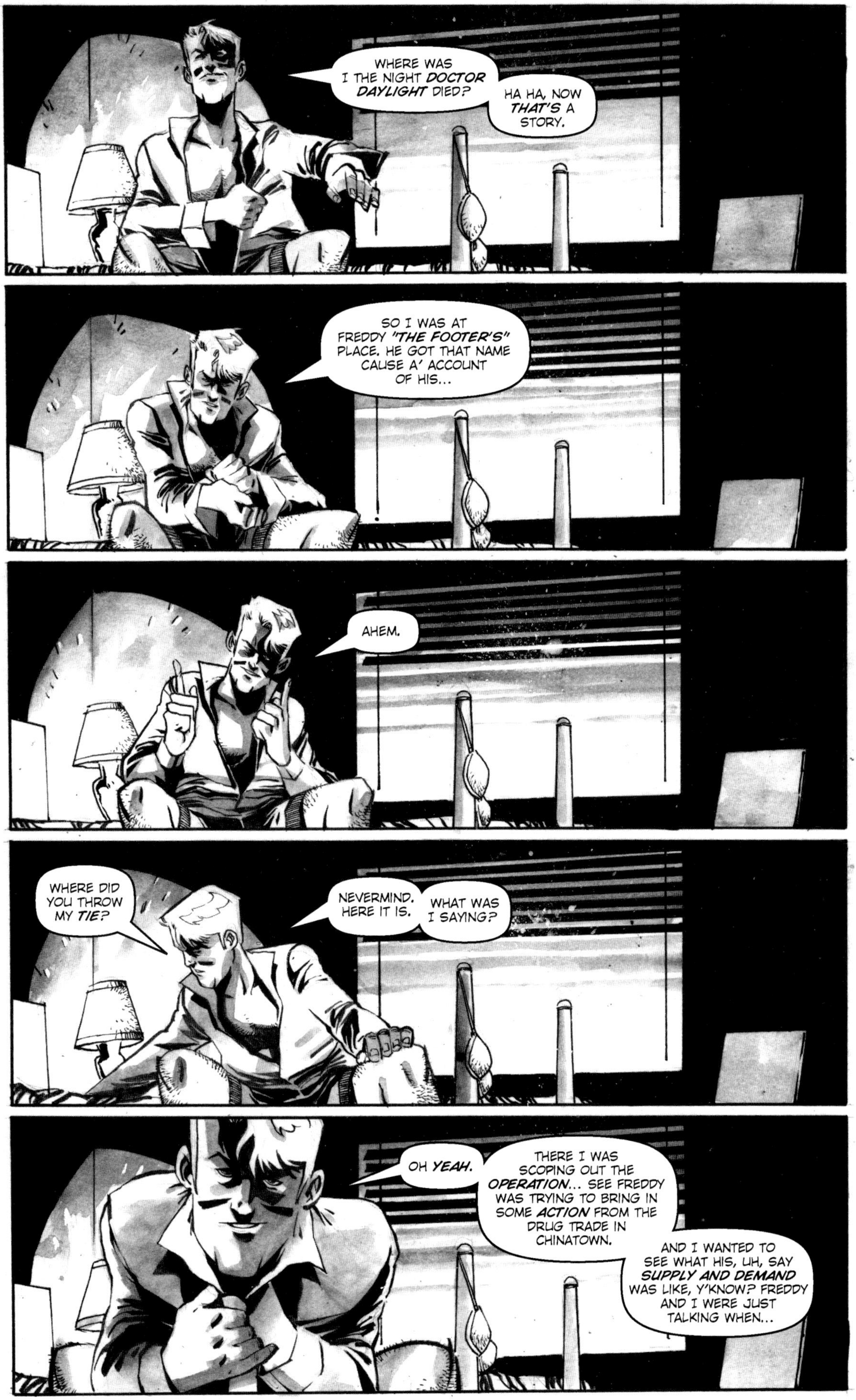

WHERE WAS I THE NIGHT DOCTOR DAYLIGHT DIED?
HA HA, NOW THAT'S A STORY.
SO I WAS AT FREDDY "THE FOOTER'S" PLACE. HE GOT THAT NAME CAUSE A' ACCOUNT OF HIS...
AHEM.
WHERE DID YOU THROW MY TIE?
NEVERMIND. HERE IT IS.
WHAT WAS I SAYING?
OH YEAH.
THERE I WAS SCOPING OUT THE OPERATION... SEE FREDDY WAS TRYING TO BRING IN SOME ACTION FROM THE DRUG TRADE IN CHINATOWN.
AND I WANTED TO SEE WHAT HIS, UH, SAY SUPPLY AND DEMAND WAS LIKE, Y'KNOW? FREDDY AND I WERE JUST TALKING WHEN...

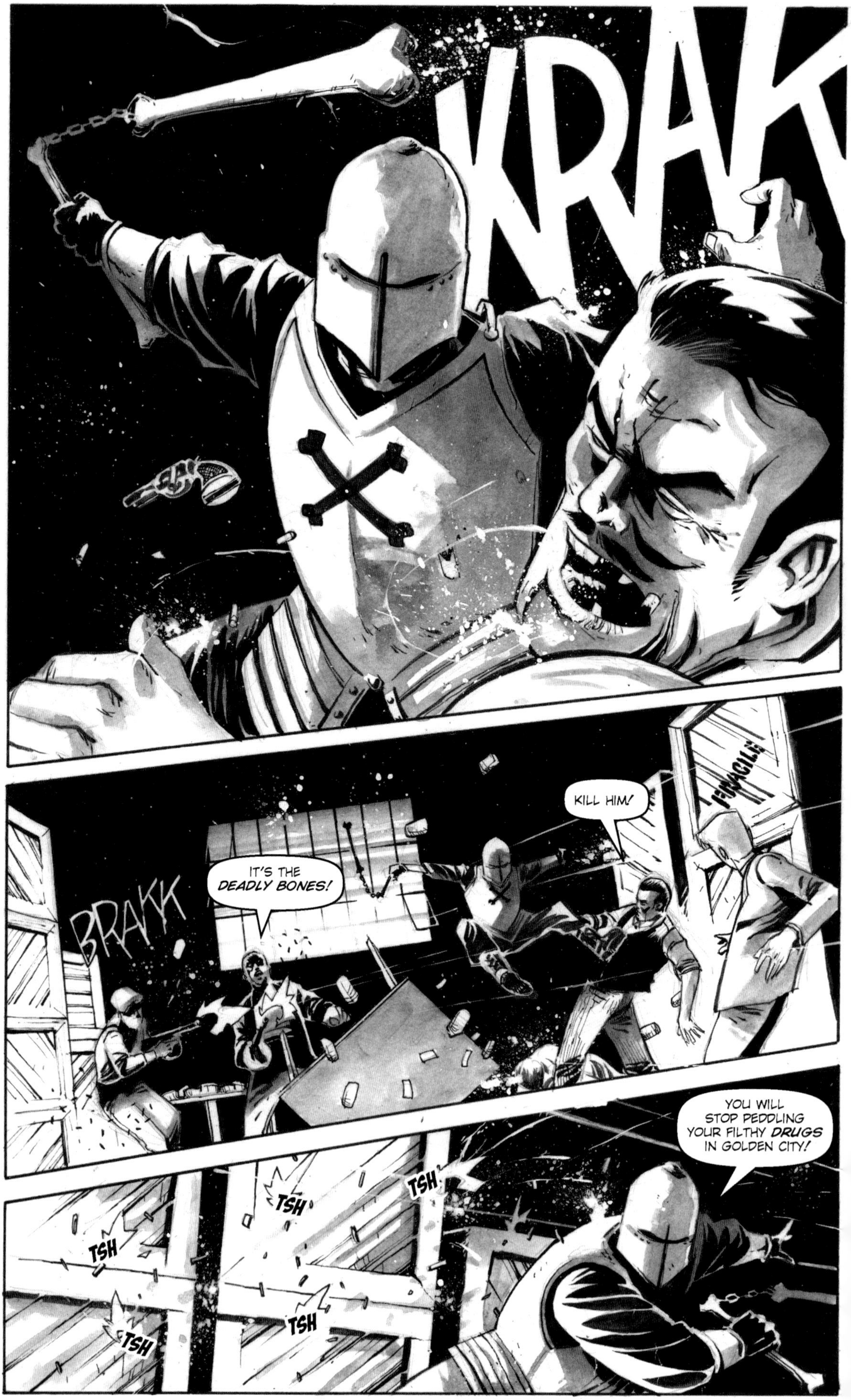
KRAK
BRAKK
IT'S THE DEADLY BONES!
KILL HIM!
FRAGILE
YOU WILL STOP PEDDLING YOUR FILTHY DRUGS IN GOLDEN CITY!
TSH
TSH
TSH
TSH
TSH

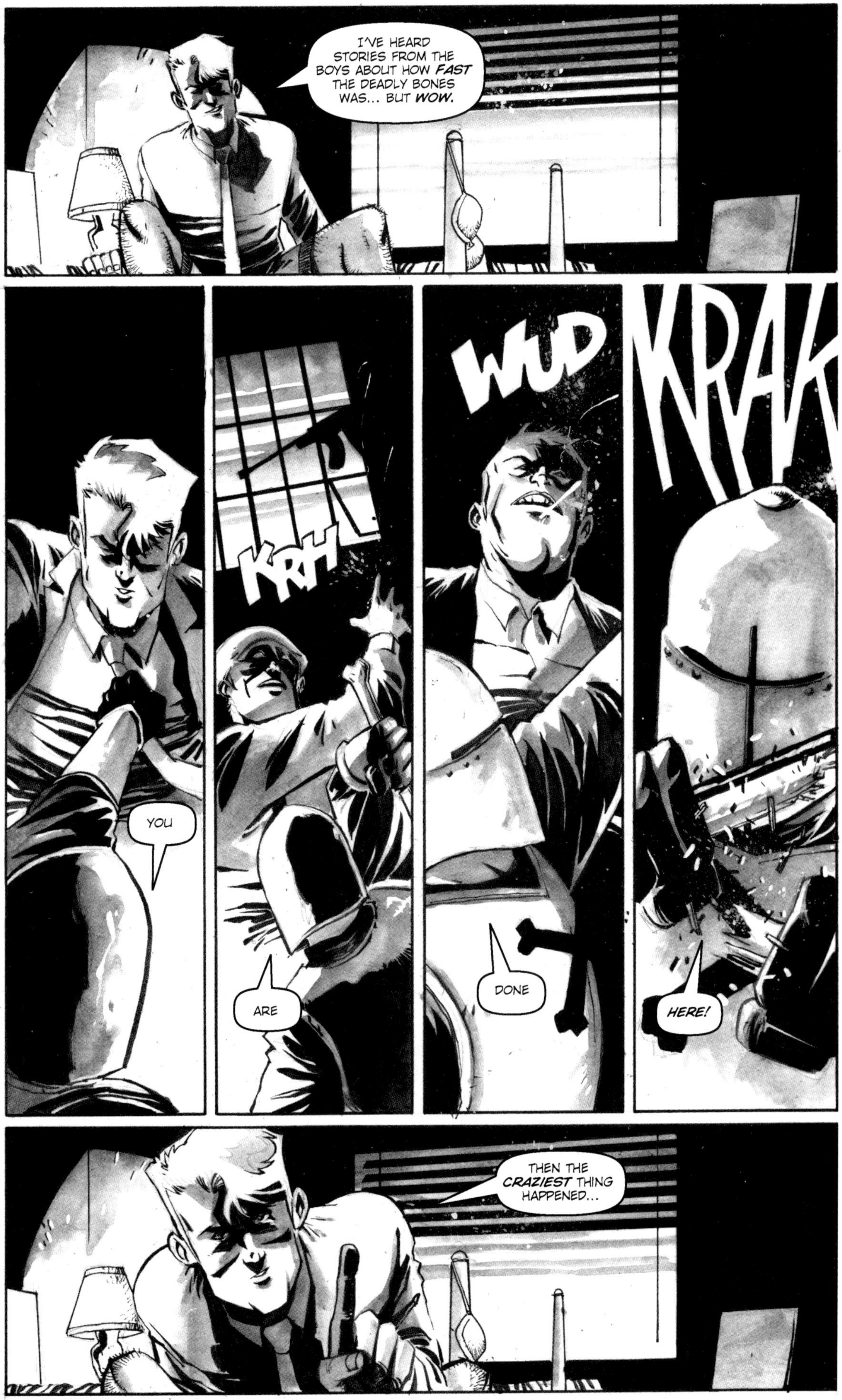
I'VE HEARD STORIES FROM THE BOYS ABOUT HOW *FAST* THE DEADLY BONES WAS... BUT *WOW.*
YOU
KRH
ARE
WUD
DONE
KRAK
HERE!
THEN THE *CRAZIEST* THING HAPPENED...

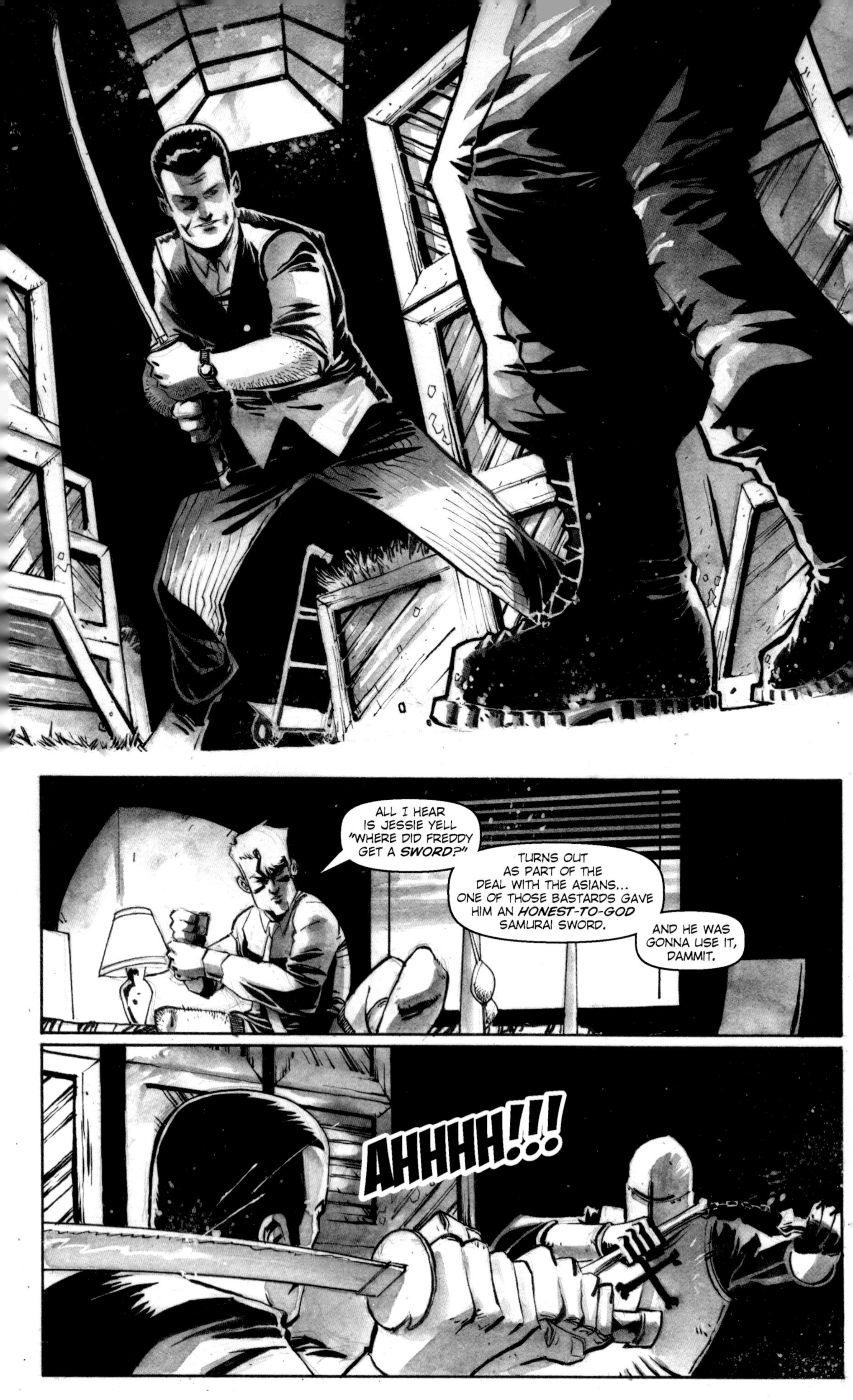

ALL I HEAR IS JESSIE YELL "WHERE DID FREDDY GET A SWORD?"
TURNS OUT AS PART OF THE DEAL WITH THE ASIANS... ONE OF THOSE BASTARDS GAVE HIM AN HONEST-TO-GOD SAMURAI SWORD.
AND HE WAS GONNA USE IT, DAMMIT.
AHHHH!!!

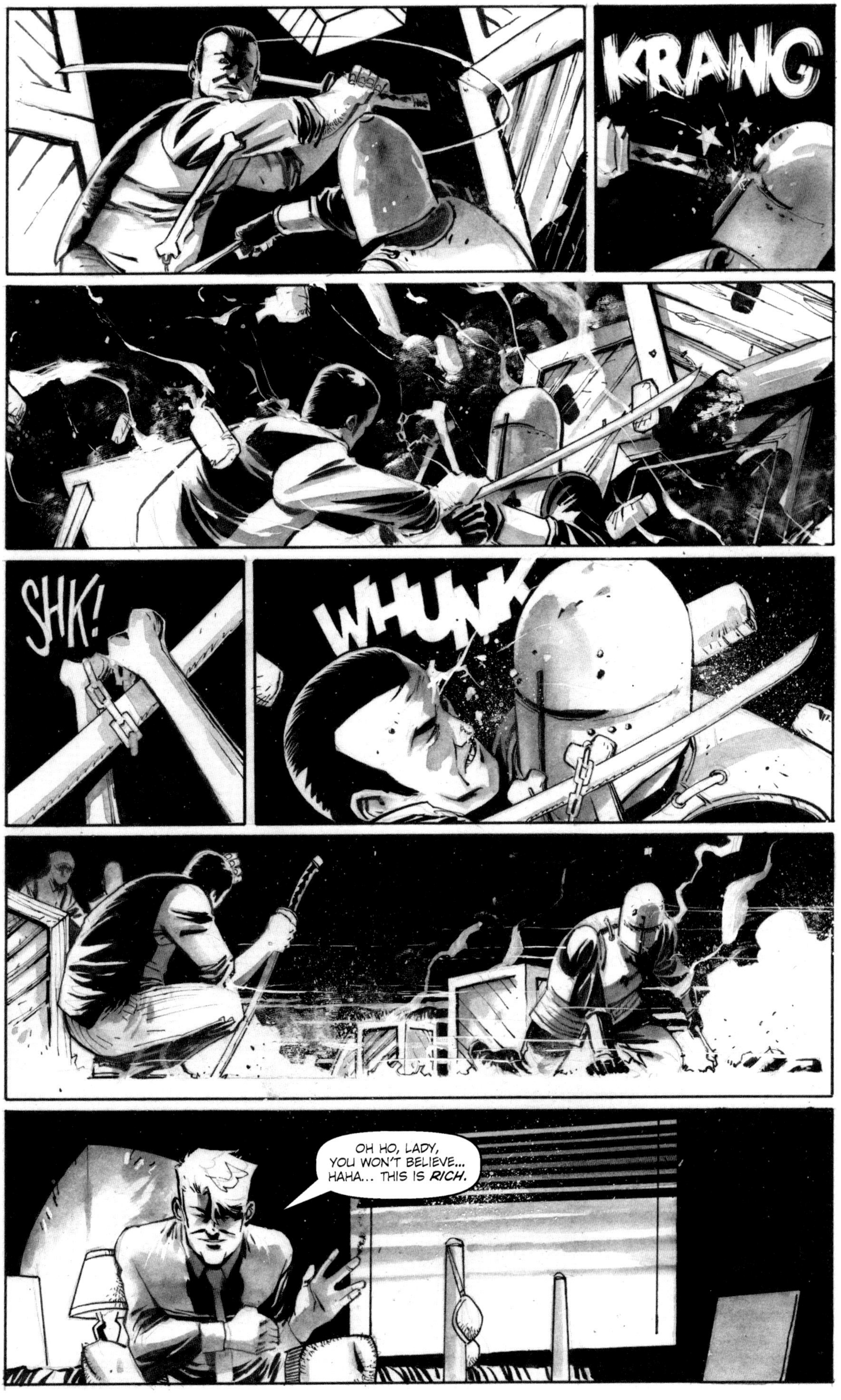
KRANG
SHK!
WHUNK
OH HO, LADY, YOU WON'T BELIEVE... HAHA... THIS IS *RICH*.

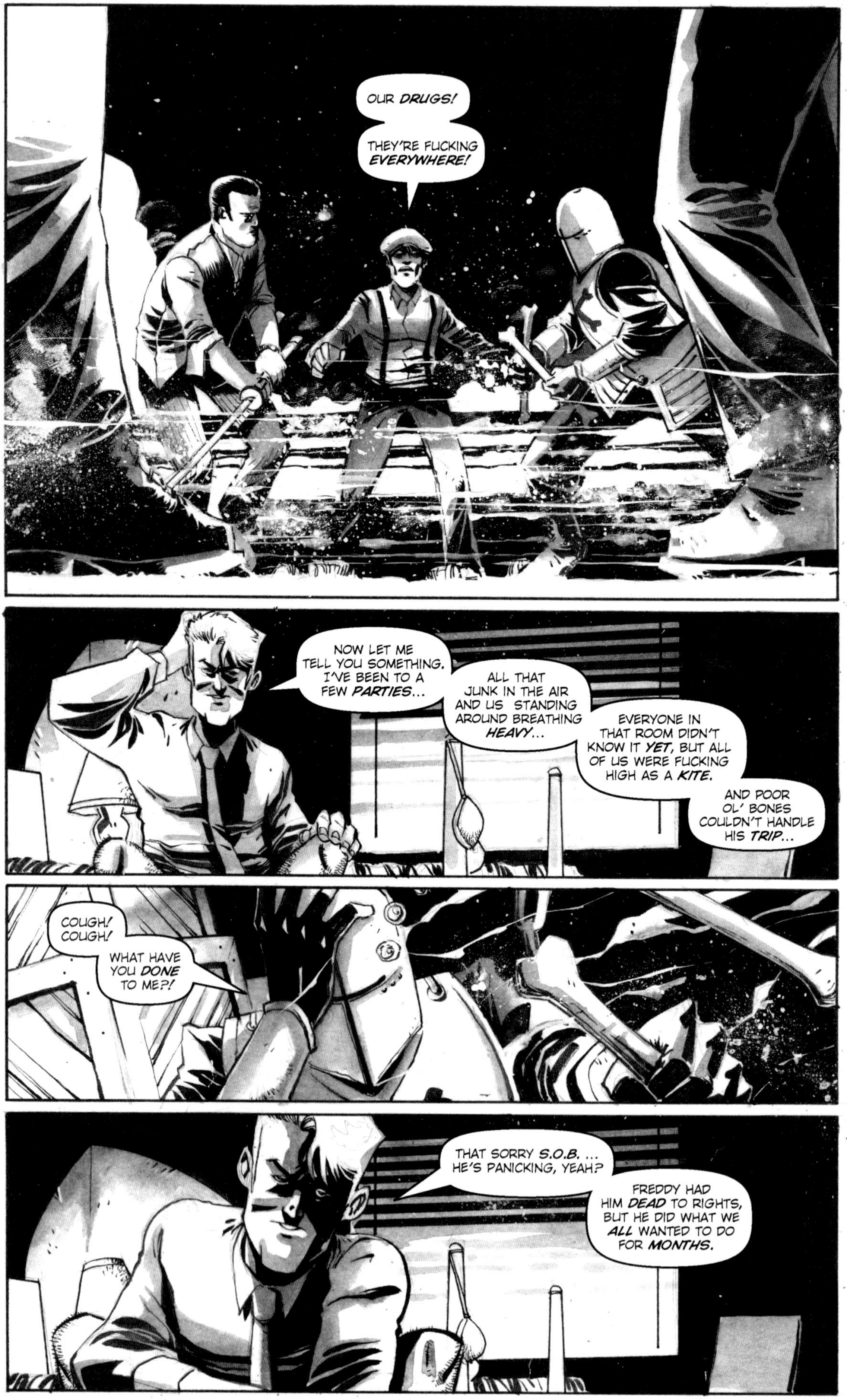
OUR DRUGS!
THEY'RE FUCKING EVERYWHERE!
NOW LET ME TELL YOU SOMETHING. I'VE BEEN TO A FEW PARTIES...
ALL THAT JUNK IN THE AIR AND US STANDING AROUND BREATHING HEAVY...
EVERYONE IN THAT ROOM DIDN'T KNOW IT YET, BUT ALL OF US WERE FUCKING HIGH AS A KITE.
AND POOR OL' BONES COULDN'T HANDLE HIS TRIP...
COUGH! COUGH!
WHAT HAVE YOU DONE TO ME?!
THAT SORRY S.O.B. ... HE'S PANICKING, YEAH?
FREDDY HAD HIM DEAD TO RIGHTS, BUT HE DID WHAT WE ALL WANTED TO DO FOR MONTHS.

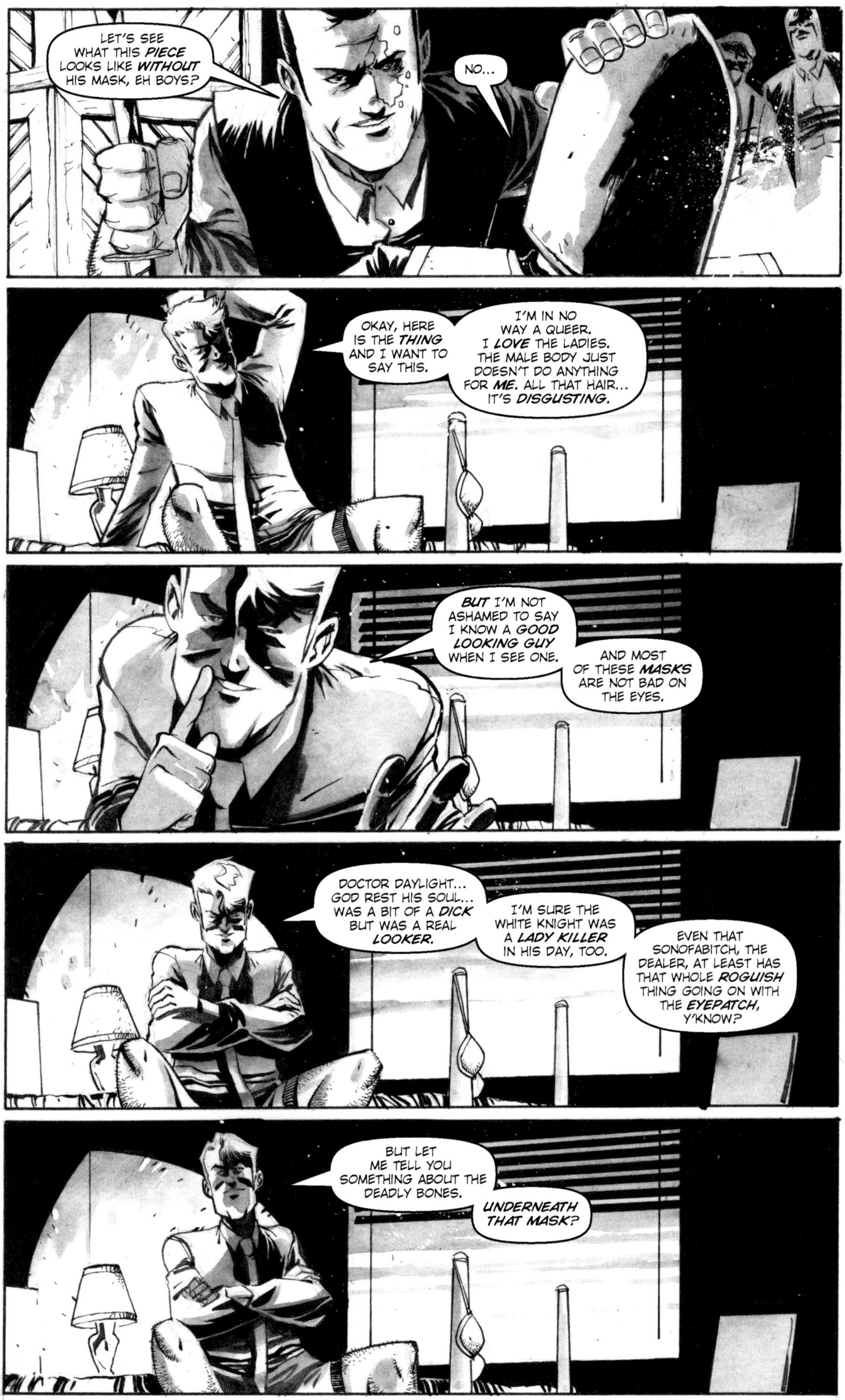
LET'S SEE WHAT THIS *PIECE* LOOKS LIKE *WITHOUT* HIS MASK, EH BOYS?
NO...
OKAY, HERE IS THE *THING* AND I WANT TO SAY THIS.
I'M IN NO WAY A QUEER. I *LOVE* THE LADIES. THE MALE BODY JUST DOESN'T DO ANYTHING FOR *ME.* ALL THAT HAIR... IT'S *DISGUSTING.*
BUT I'M NOT ASHAMED TO SAY I KNOW A *GOOD LOOKING GUY* WHEN I SEE ONE.
AND MOST OF THESE *MASKS* ARE NOT BAD ON THE EYES.
DOCTOR DAYLIGHT... GOD REST HIS SOUL... WAS A BIT OF A *DICK* BUT WAS A REAL *LOOKER.*
I'M SURE THE WHITE KNIGHT WAS A *LADY KILLER* IN HIS DAY, TOO.
EVEN THAT SONOFABITCH, THE DEALER, AT LEAST HAS THAT WHOLE *ROGUISH* THING GOING ON WITH THE *EYEPATCH,* Y'KNOW?
BUT LET ME TELL YOU SOMETHING ABOUT THE DEADLY BONES.
UNDERNEATH THAT MASK?

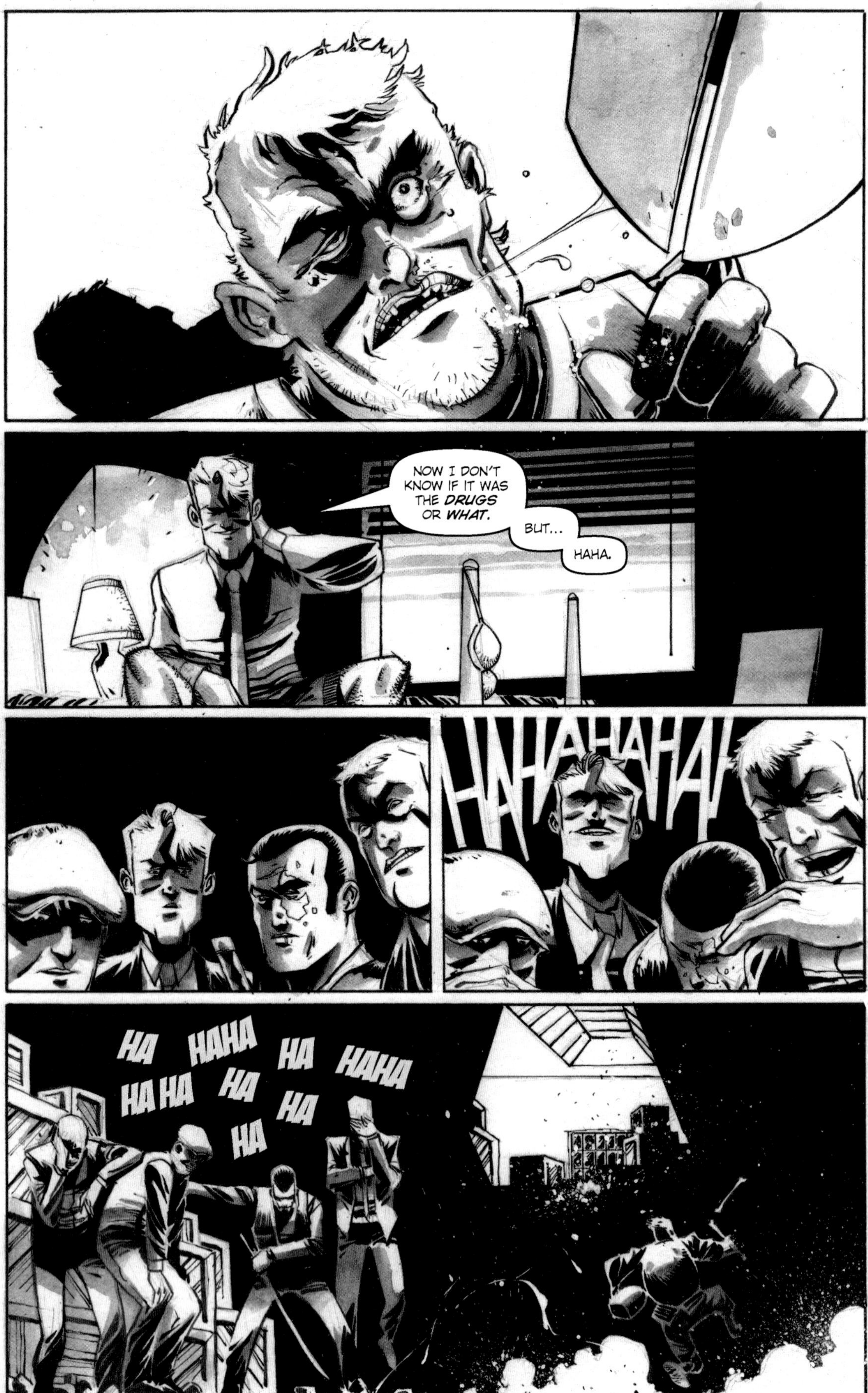
NOW I DON'T KNOW IF IT WAS THE DRUGS OR WHAT.
BUT...
HAHA.
HAHAHAHAH
HA HAHA HA HAHA
HA HA HA HA
HA

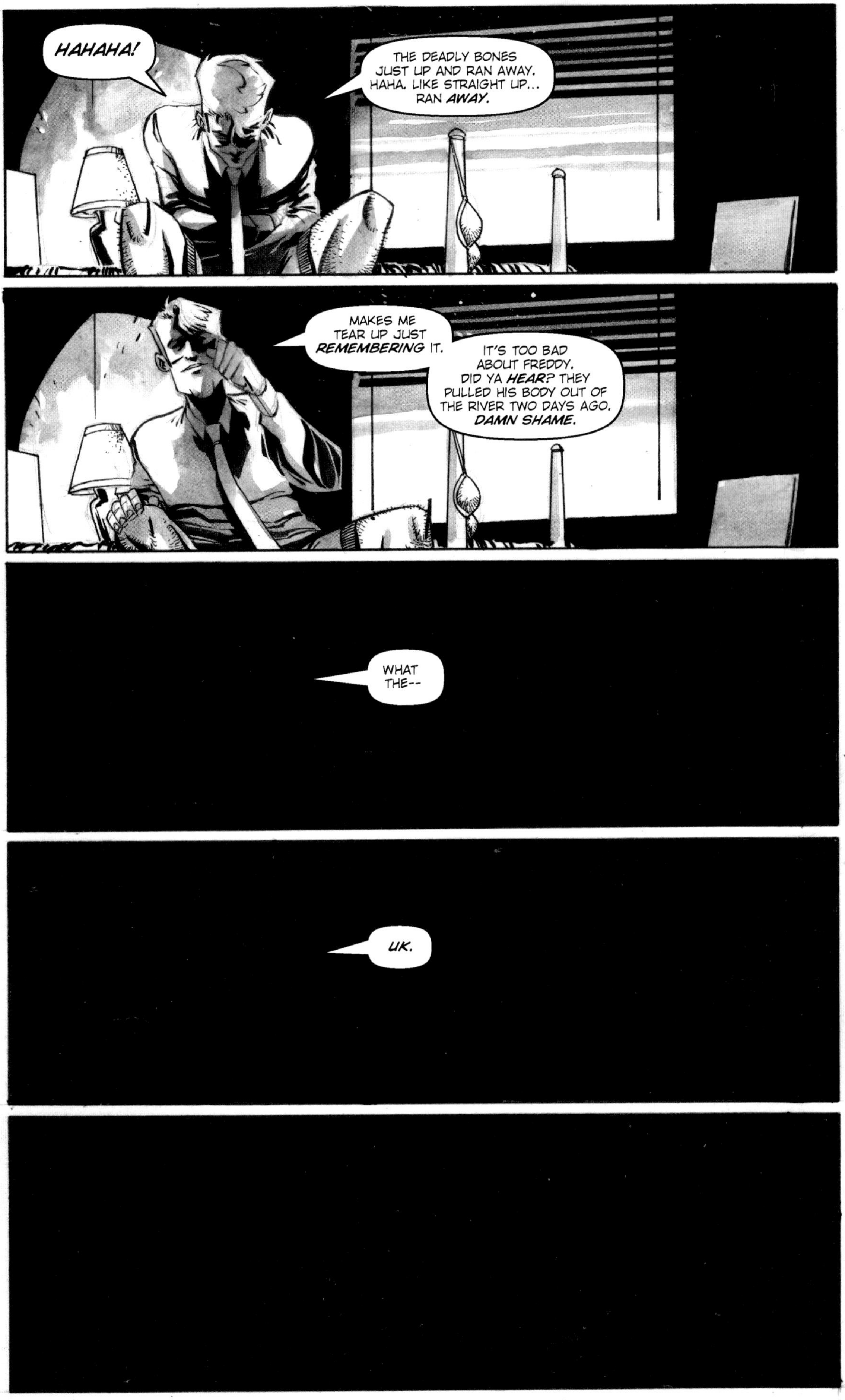
HAHAHA!
THE DEADLY BONES JUST UP AND RAN AWAY. HAHA. LIKE STRAIGHT UP... RAN AWAY.
MAKES ME TEAR UP JUST REMEMBERING IT.
IT'S TOO BAD ABOUT FREDDY. DID YA HEAR? THEY PULLED HIS BODY OUT OF THE RIVER TWO DAYS AGO. DAMN SHAME.
WHAT THE--
UK.

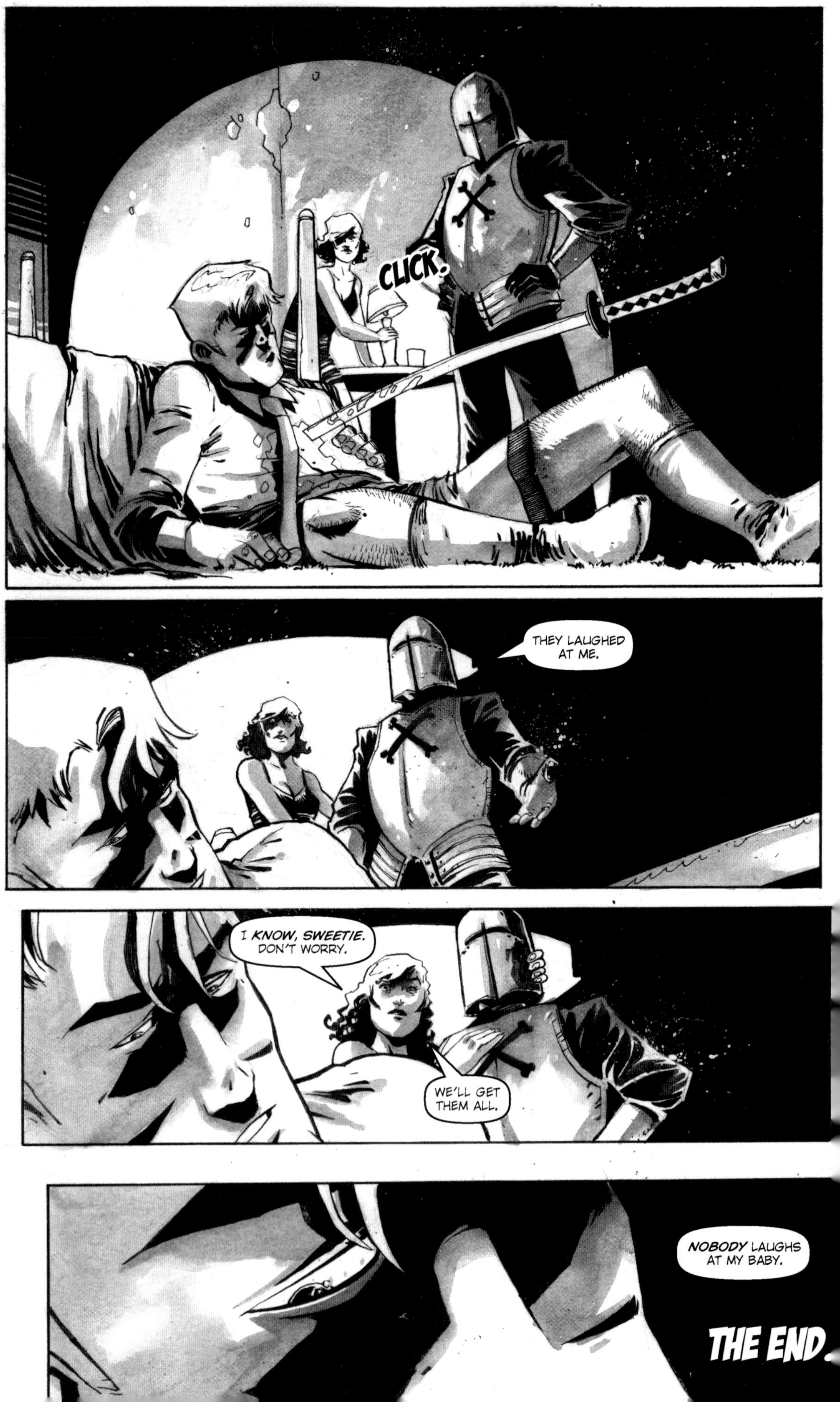
CLICK.
THEY LAUGHED AT ME.
I KNOW, SWEETIE. DON'T WORRY.
WE'LL GET THEM ALL.
NOBODY LAUGHS AT MY BABY.
THE END.

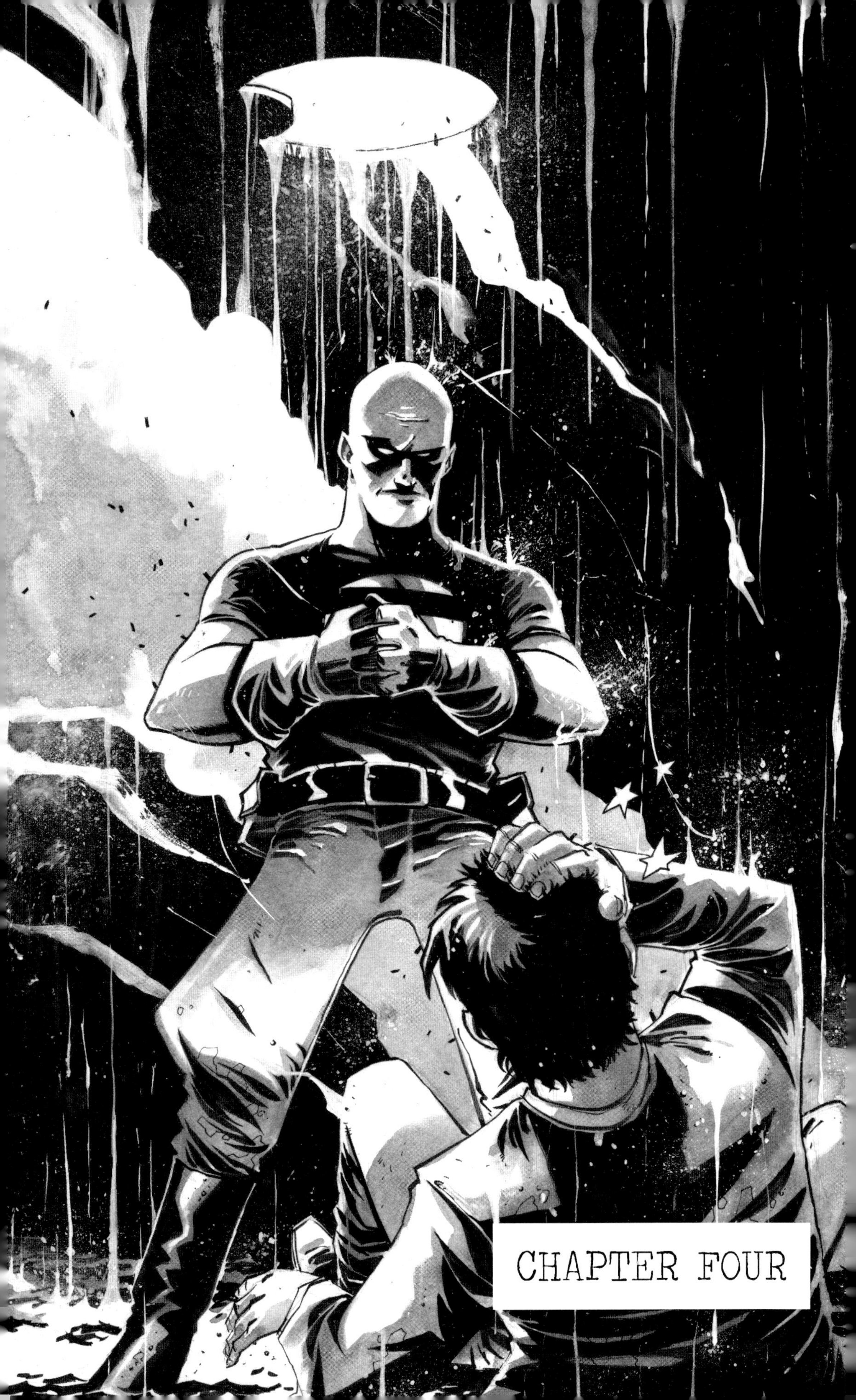
CHAPTER FOUR

Chapter Four cover roughs.

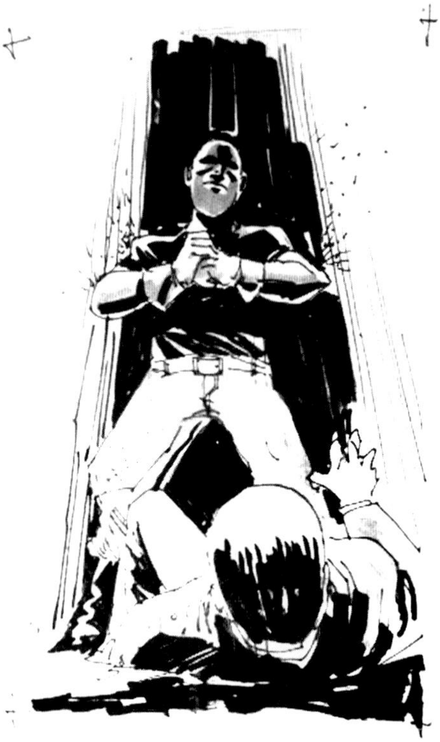

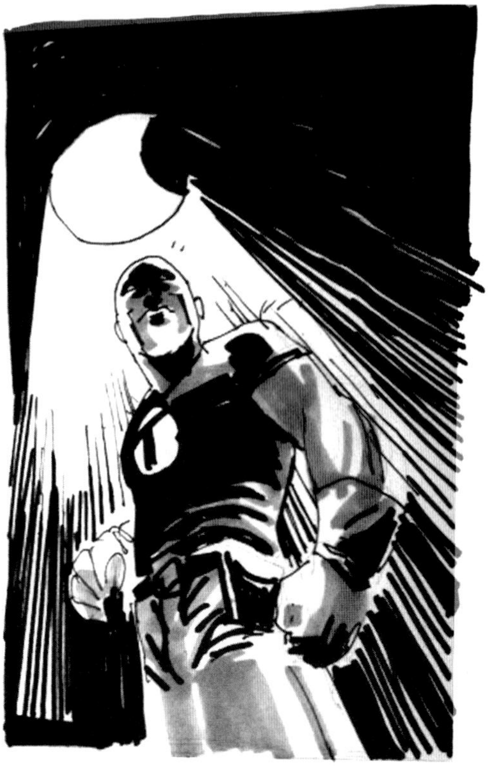

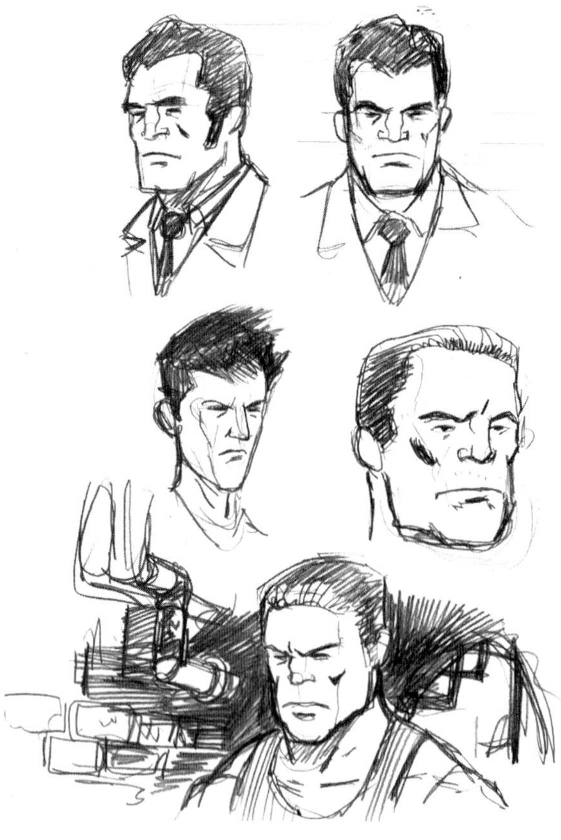

Jason Copland's designs for Ignacio. (left)

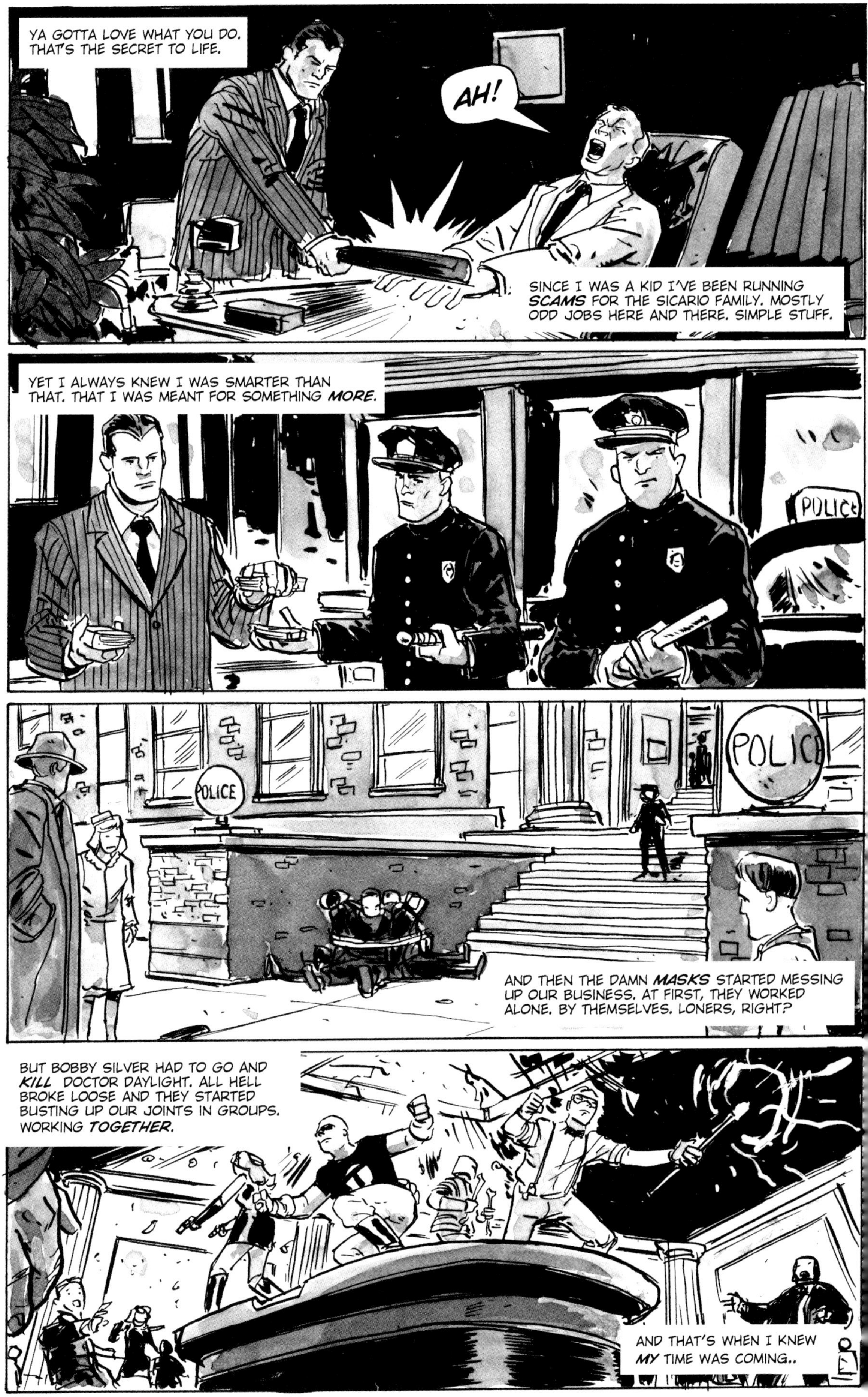
YA GOTTA LOVE WHAT YOU DO. THAT'S THE SECRET TO LIFE.
AH!
SINCE I WAS A KID I'VE BEEN RUNNING SCAMS FOR THE SICARIO FAMILY. MOSTLY ODD JOBS HERE AND THERE. SIMPLE STUFF.
YET I ALWAYS KNEW I WAS SMARTER THAN THAT. THAT I WAS MEANT FOR SOMETHING MORE.
POLICE
POLICE
POLICE
AND THEN THE DAMN MASKS STARTED MESSING UP OUR BUSINESS. AT FIRST, THEY WORKED ALONE. BY THEMSELVES. LONERS, RIGHT?
BUT BOBBY SILVER HAD TO GO AND KILL DOCTOR DAYLIGHT. ALL HELL BROKE LOOSE AND THEY STARTED BUSTING UP OUR JOINTS IN GROUPS. WORKING TOGETHER.
AND THAT'S WHEN I KNEW MY TIME WAS COMING..

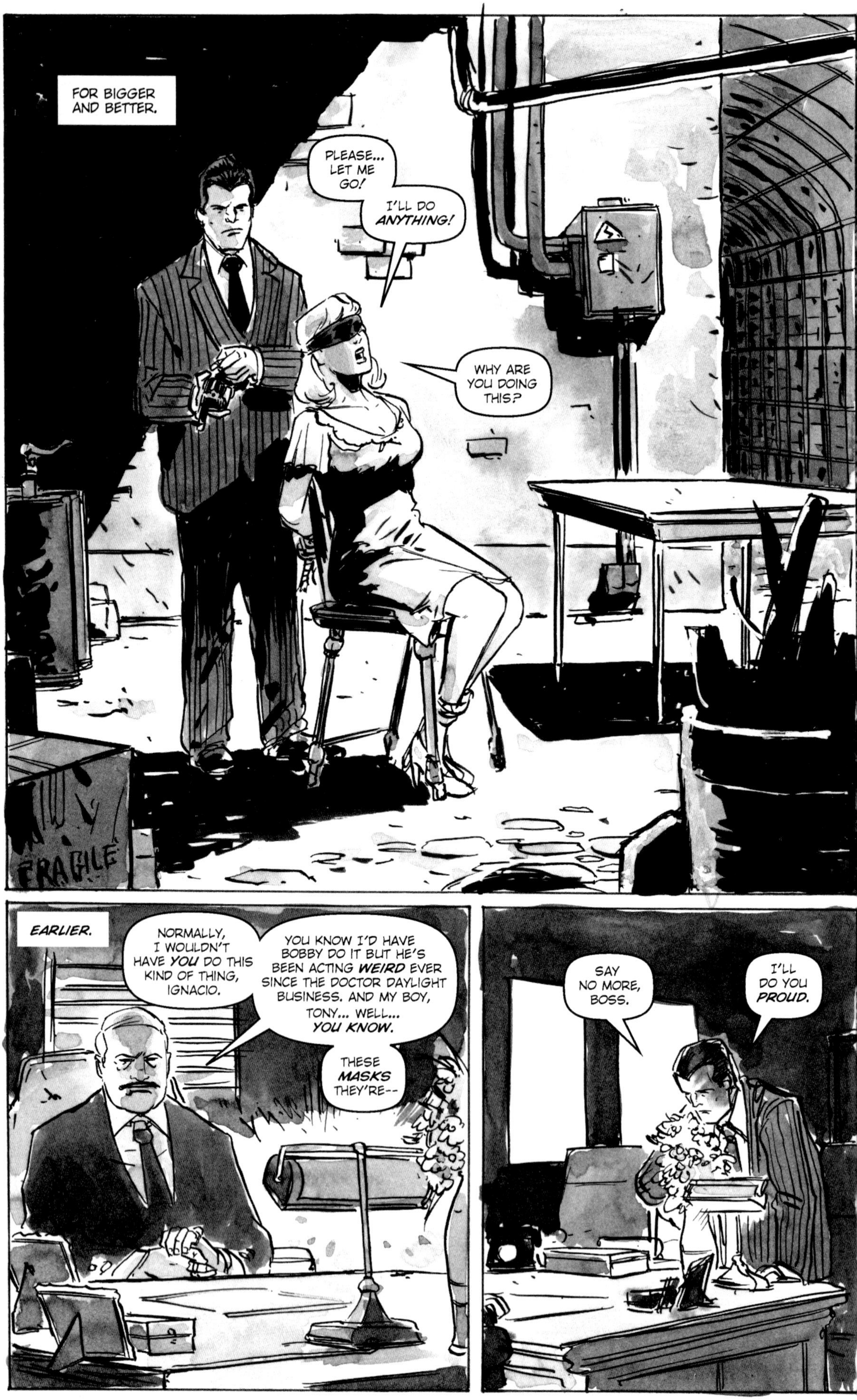
FOR BIGGER AND BETTER.
PLEASE... LET ME GO!
I'LL DO ANYTHING!
WHY ARE YOU DOING THIS?
FRAGILE
EARLIER.
NORMALLY, I WOULDN'T HAVE YOU DO THIS KIND OF THING, IGNACIO.
YOU KNOW I'D HAVE BOBBY DO IT BUT HE'S BEEN ACTING WEIRD EVER SINCE THE DOCTOR DAYLIGHT BUSINESS. AND MY BOY, TONY... WELL... YOU KNOW.
THESE MASKS THEY'RE--
SAY NO MORE, BOSS.
I'LL DO YOU PROUD.

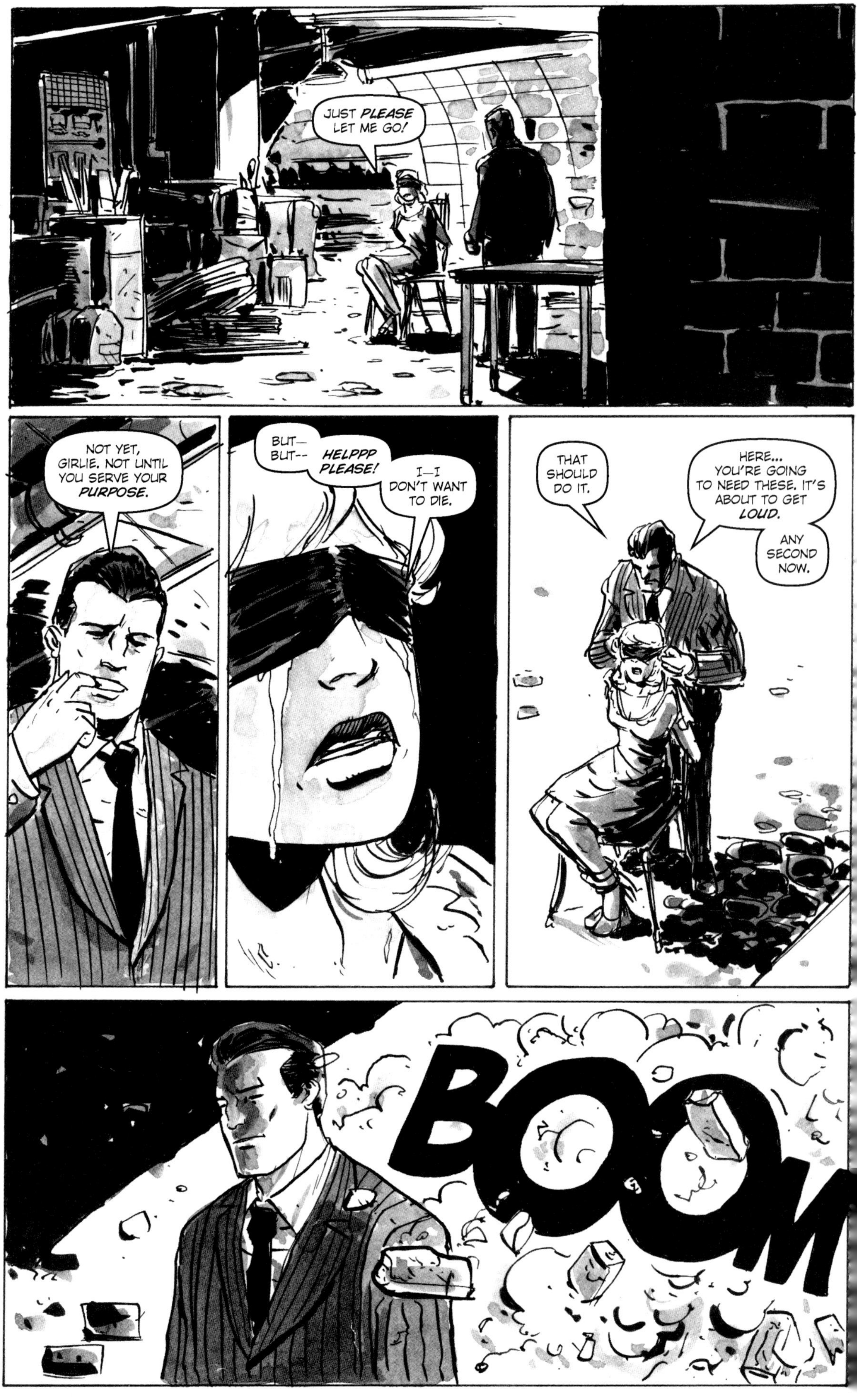
JUST *PLEASE* LET ME GO!
NOT YET, GIRLIE. NOT UNTIL YOU SERVE YOUR *PURPOSE*.
BUT— BUT--
HELPPP PLEASE!
I—I DON'T WANT TO DIE.
THAT SHOULD DO IT.
HERE... YOU'RE GOING TO NEED THESE. IT'S ABOUT TO GET *LOUD*.
ANY SECOND NOW.
BOOOM

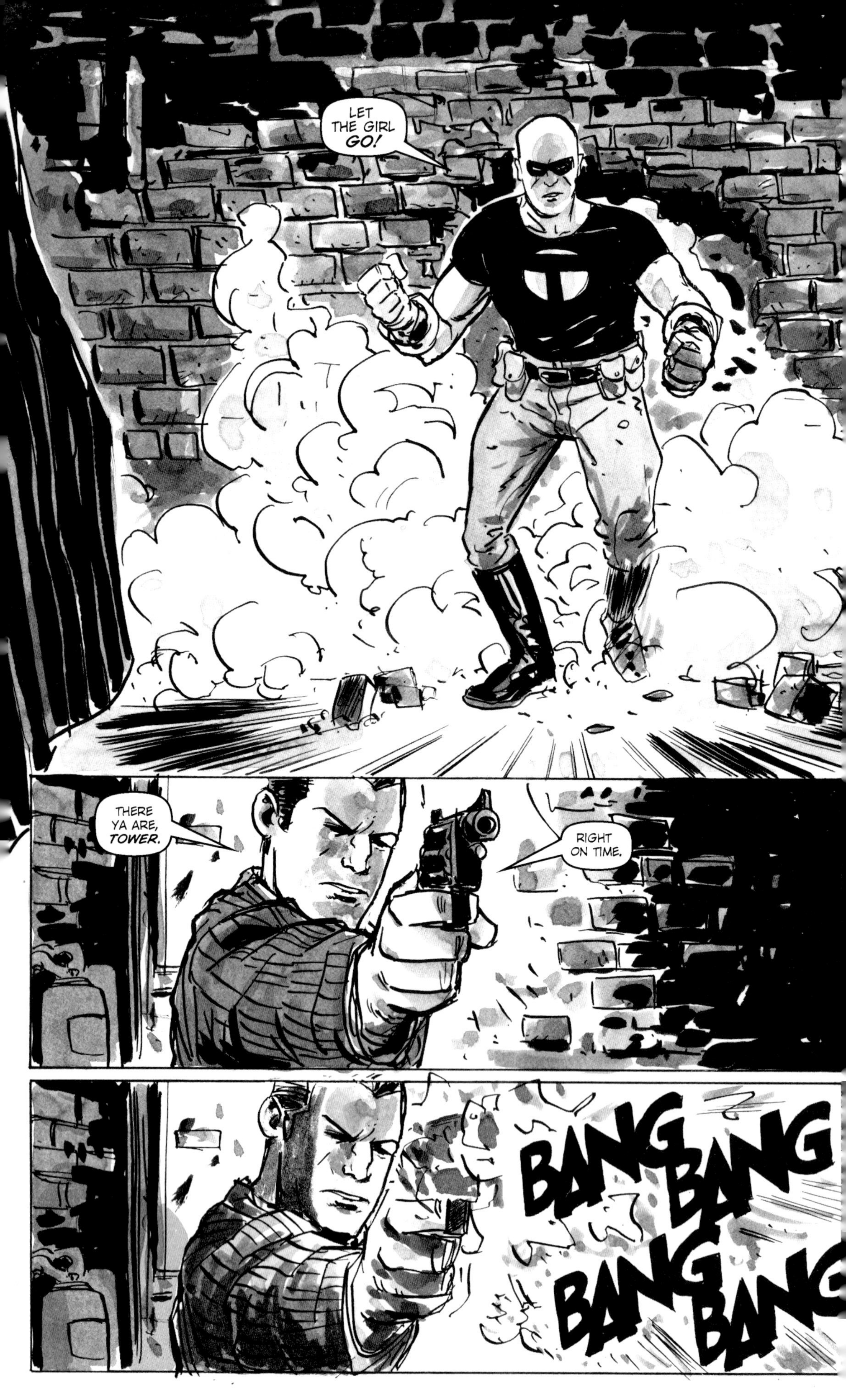
LET THE GIRL GO!
THERE YA ARE, TOWER.
RIGHT ON TIME.
BANG BANG
BANG BANG

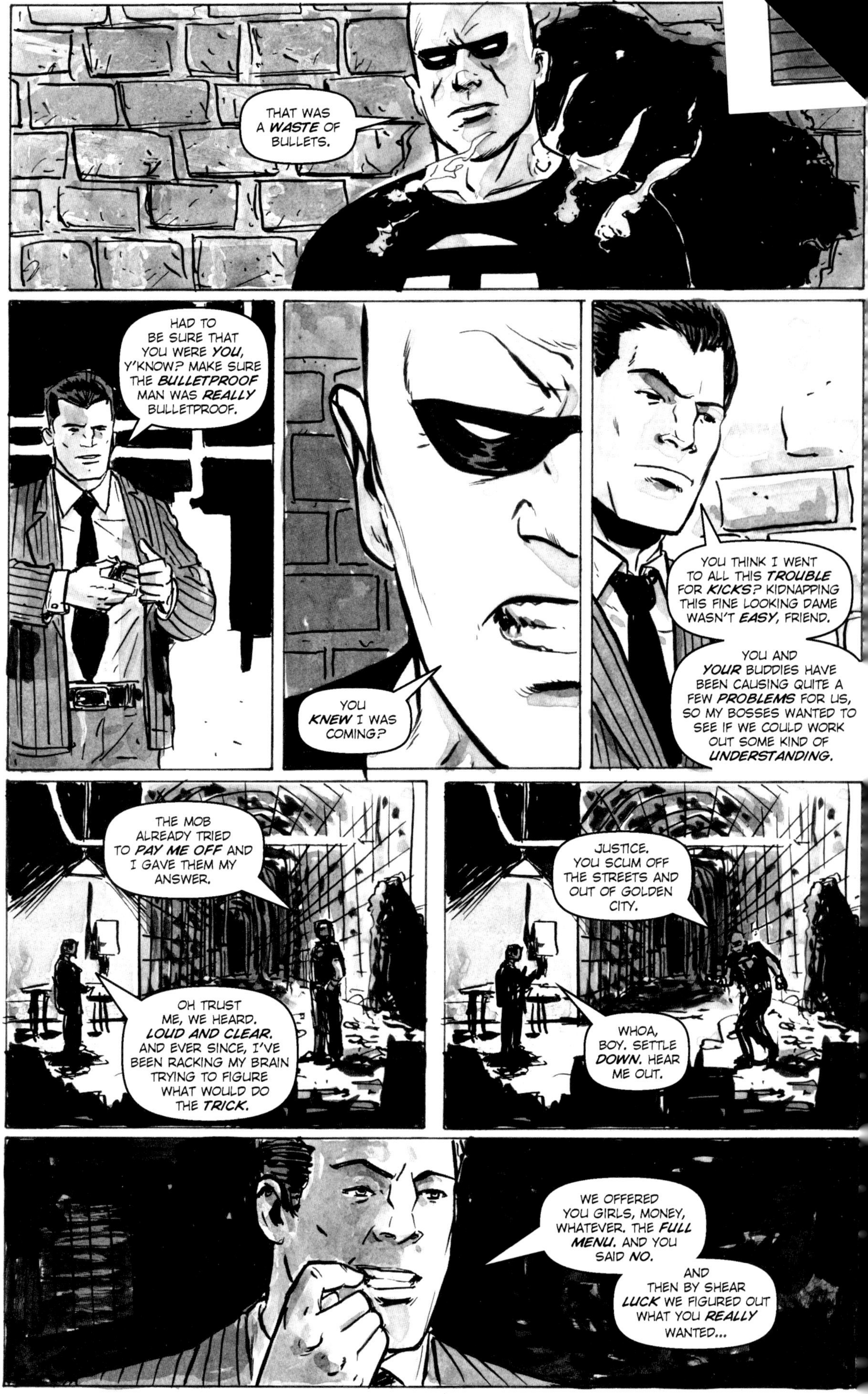
THAT WAS A WASTE OF BULLETS.
HAD TO BE SURE THAT YOU WERE YOU, Y'KNOW? MAKE SURE THE BULLETPROOF MAN WAS REALLY BULLETPROOF.
YOU KNEW I WAS COMING?
YOU THINK I WENT TO ALL THIS TROUBLE FOR KICKS? KIDNAPPING THIS FINE LOOKING DAME WASN'T EASY, FRIEND.
YOU AND YOUR BUDDIES HAVE BEEN CAUSING QUITE A FEW PROBLEMS FOR US, SO MY BOSSES WANTED TO SEE IF WE COULD WORK OUT SOME KIND OF UNDERSTANDING.
THE MOB ALREADY TRIED TO PAY ME OFF AND I GAVE THEM MY ANSWER.
OH TRUST ME, WE HEARD. LOUD AND CLEAR. AND EVER SINCE, I'VE BEEN RACKING MY BRAIN TRYING TO FIGURE WHAT WOULD DO THE TRICK.
JUSTICE. YOU SCUM OFF THE STREETS AND OUT OF GOLDEN CITY.
WHOA, BOY. SETTLE DOWN. HEAR ME OUT.
WE OFFERED YOU GIRLS, MONEY, WHATEVER. THE FULL MENU. AND YOU SAID NO.
AND THEN BY SHEAR LUCK WE FIGURED OUT WHAT YOU REALLY WANTED...

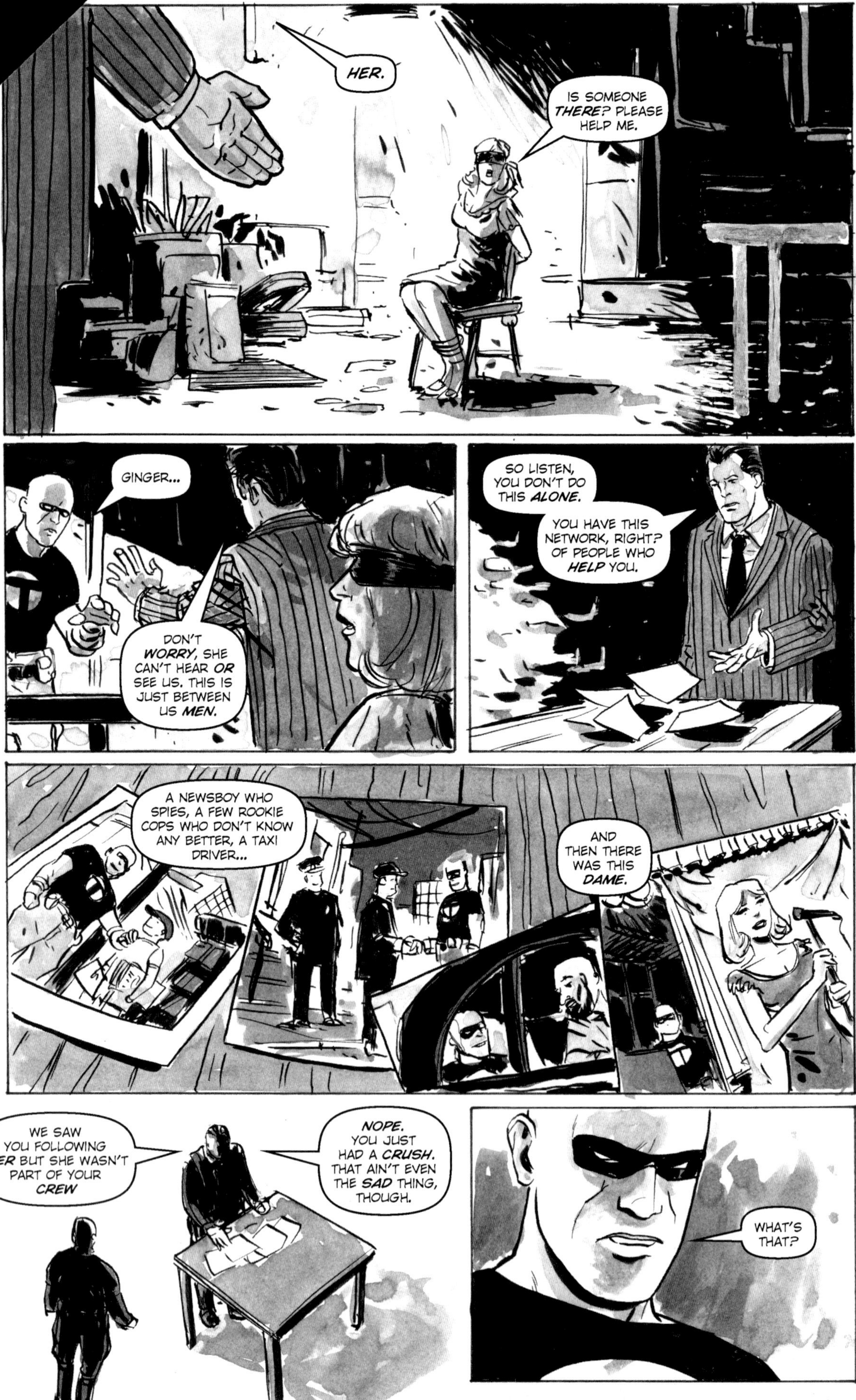
HER.
IS SOMEONE THERE? PLEASE HELP ME.
GINGER...
DON'T WORRY, SHE CAN'T HEAR OR SEE US. THIS IS JUST BETWEEN US MEN.
SO LISTEN, YOU DON'T DO THIS ALONE.
YOU HAVE THIS NETWORK, RIGHT? OF PEOPLE WHO HELP YOU.
A NEWSBOY WHO SPIES, A FEW ROOKIE COPS WHO DON'T KNOW ANY BETTER, A TAXI DRIVER...
AND THEN THERE WAS THIS DAME.
WE SAW YOU FOLLOWING HER BUT SHE WASN'T PART OF YOUR CREW
NOPE. YOU JUST HAD A CRUSH. THAT AIN'T EVEN THE SAD THING, THOUGH.
WHAT'S THAT?

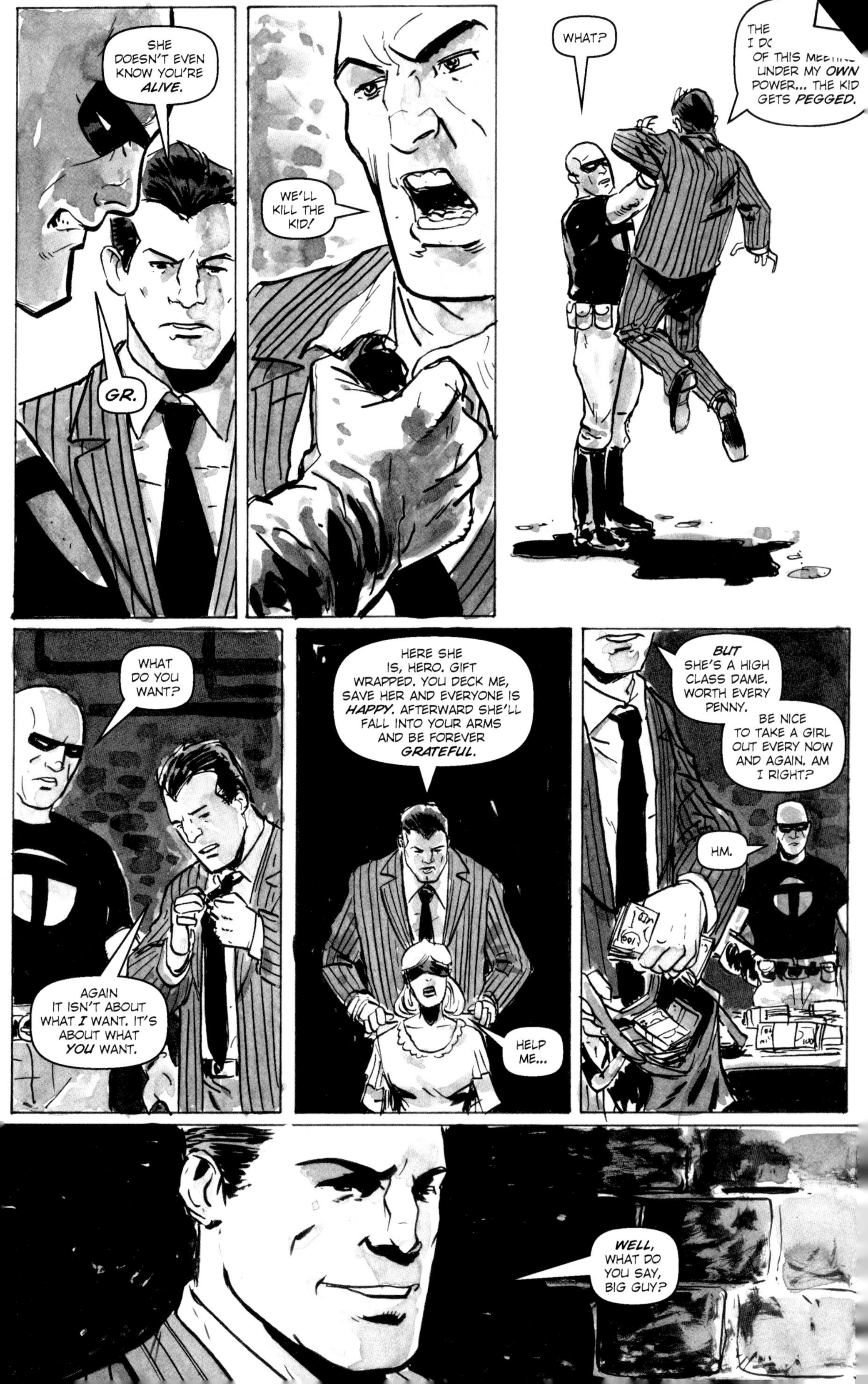

SHE DOESN'T EVEN KNOW YOU'RE ***ALIVE.***
GR.
WE'LL KILL THE KID!
WHAT?
THE
OF THIS
UNDER MY ***OWN*** POWER... THE KID GETS ***PEGGED.***
WHAT DO YOU WANT?
AGAIN IT ISN'T ABOUT WHAT ***I*** WANT. IT'S ABOUT WHAT ***YOU*** WANT.
HERE SHE IS, HERO. GIFT WRAPPED. YOU DECK ME, SAVE HER AND EVERYONE IS ***HAPPY.*** AFTERWARD SHE'LL FALL INTO YOUR ARMS AND BE FOREVER ***GRATEFUL.***
HELP ME...
BUT SHE'S A HIGH CLASS DAME. WORTH EVERY PENNY.
BE NICE TO TAKE A GIRL OUT EVERY NOW AND AGAIN. AM I RIGHT?
HM.
WELL, WHAT DO YOU SAY, BIG GUY?

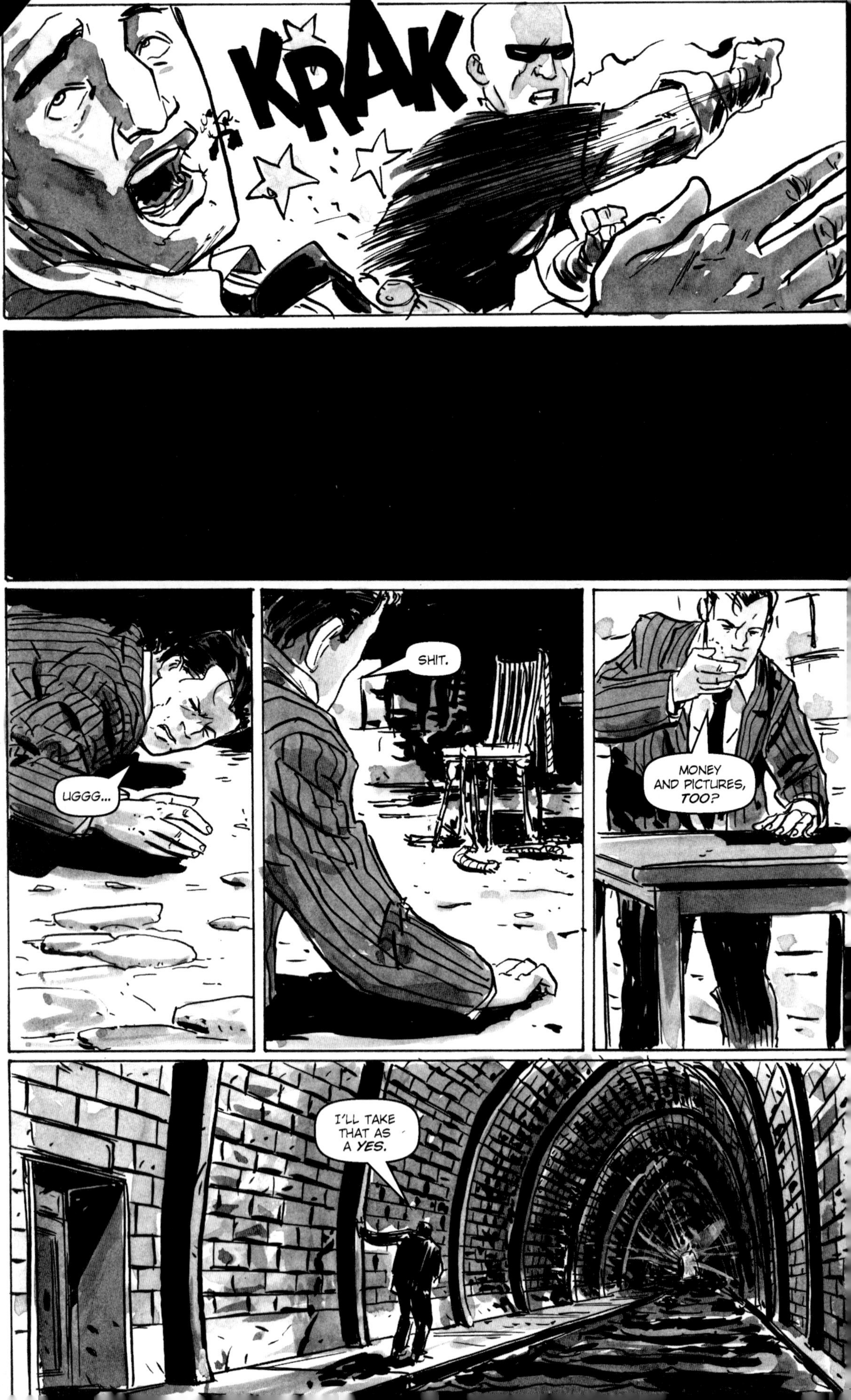
KRAK
UGGG...
SHIT.
MONEY AND PICTURES, *TOO?*
I'LL TAKE THAT AS A *YES*.

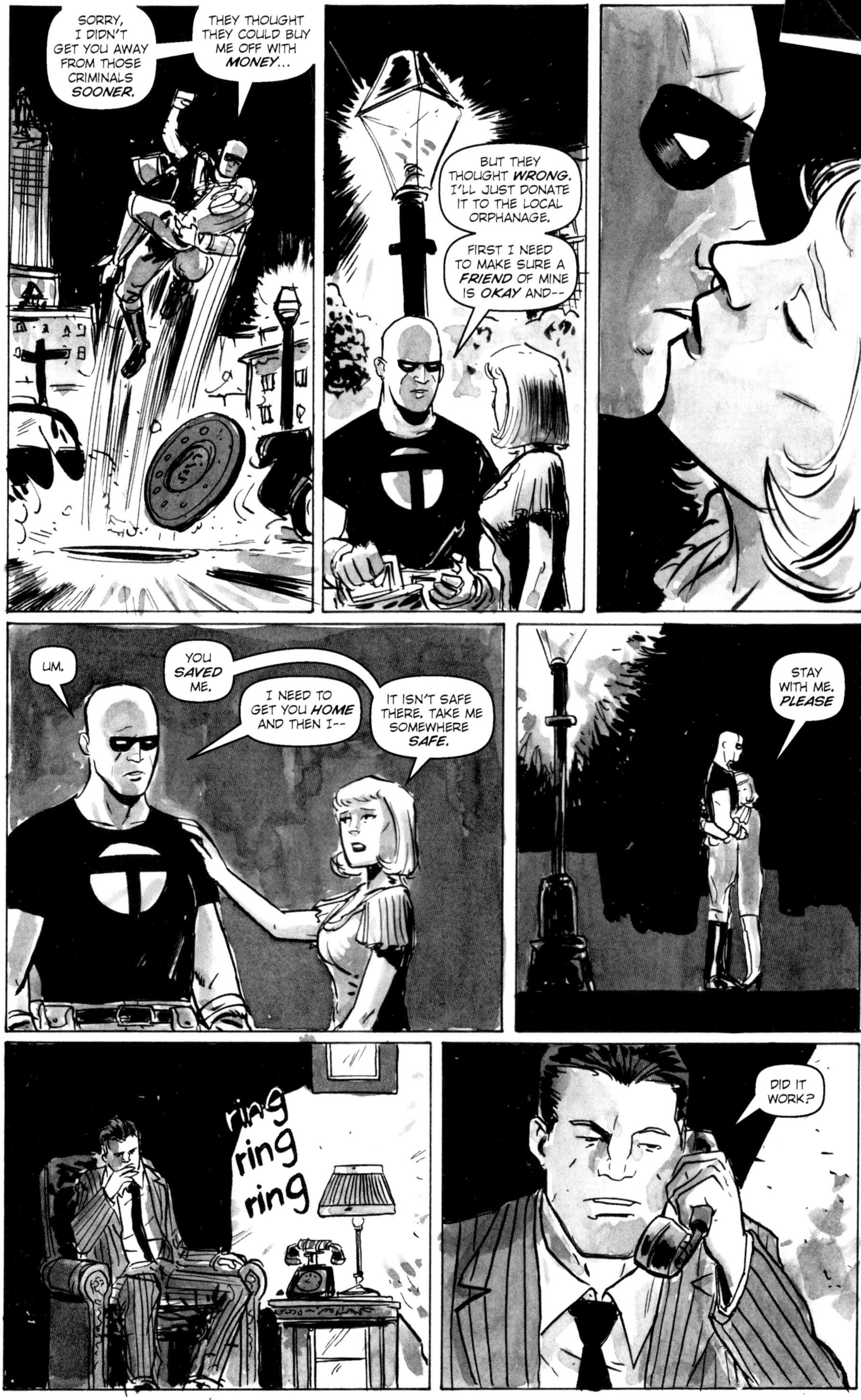
SORRY, I DIDN'T GET YOU AWAY FROM THOSE CRIMINALS SOONER.
THEY THOUGHT THEY COULD BUY ME OFF WITH MONEY...
BUT THEY THOUGHT WRONG. I'LL JUST DONATE IT TO THE LOCAL ORPHANAGE.
FIRST I NEED TO MAKE SURE A FRIEND OF MINE IS OKAY AND--
UM.
YOU SAVED ME.
I NEED TO GET YOU HOME AND THEN I--
IT ISN'T SAFE THERE. TAKE ME SOMEWHERE SAFE.
STAY WITH ME. PLEASE
ring ring ring
DID IT WORK?

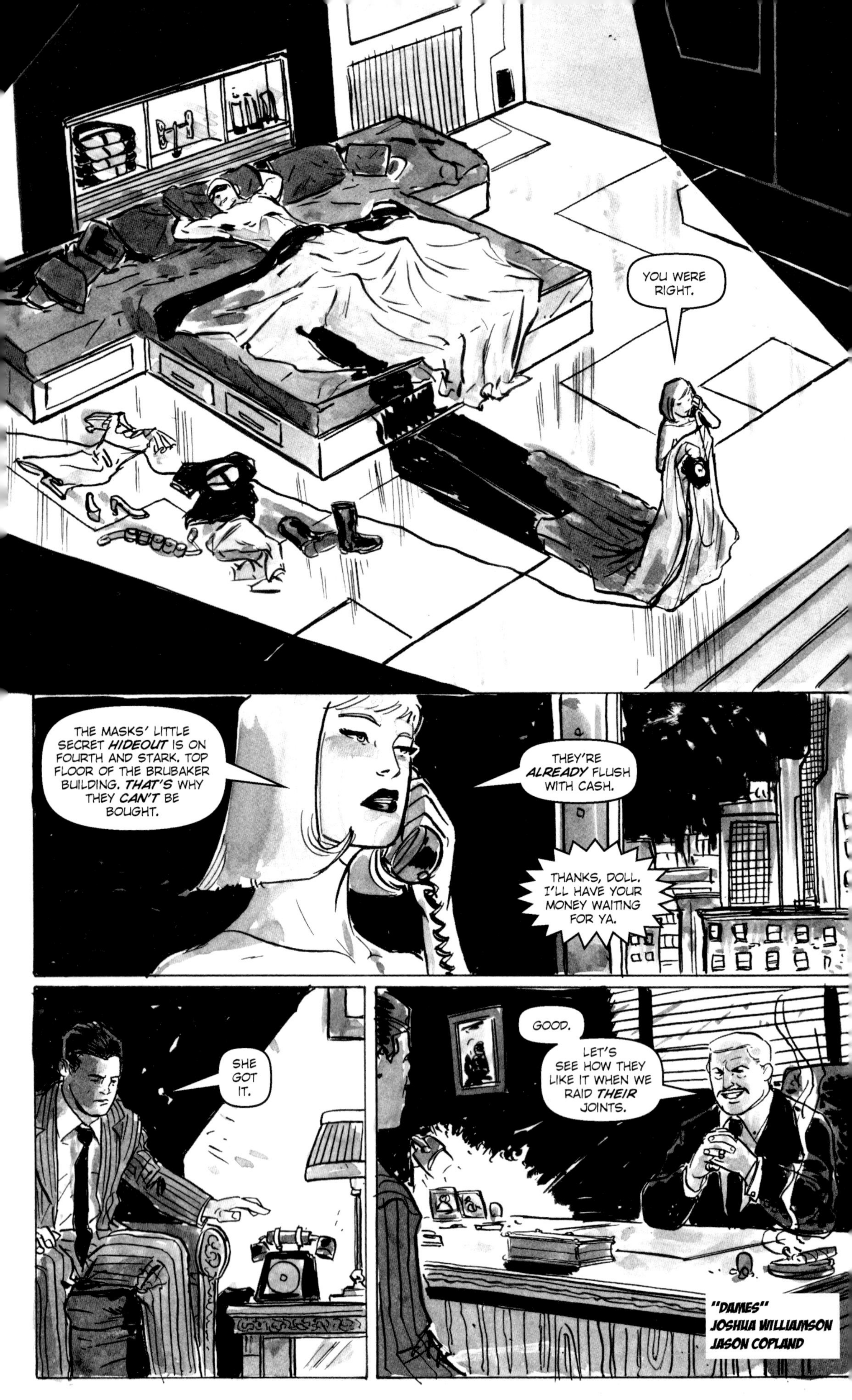
YOU WERE RIGHT.
THE MASKS' LITTLE SECRET HIDEOUT IS ON FOURTH AND STARK. TOP FLOOR OF THE BRUBAKER BUILDING. THAT'S WHY THEY CAN'T BE BOUGHT.
THEY'RE ALREADY FLUSH WITH CASH.
THANKS, DOLL. I'LL HAVE YOUR MONEY WAITING FOR YA.
SHE GOT IT.
GOOD.
LET'S SEE HOW THEY LIKE IT WHEN WE RAID THEIR JOINTS.
"DAMES"
JOSHUA WILLIAMSON
JASON COPLAND

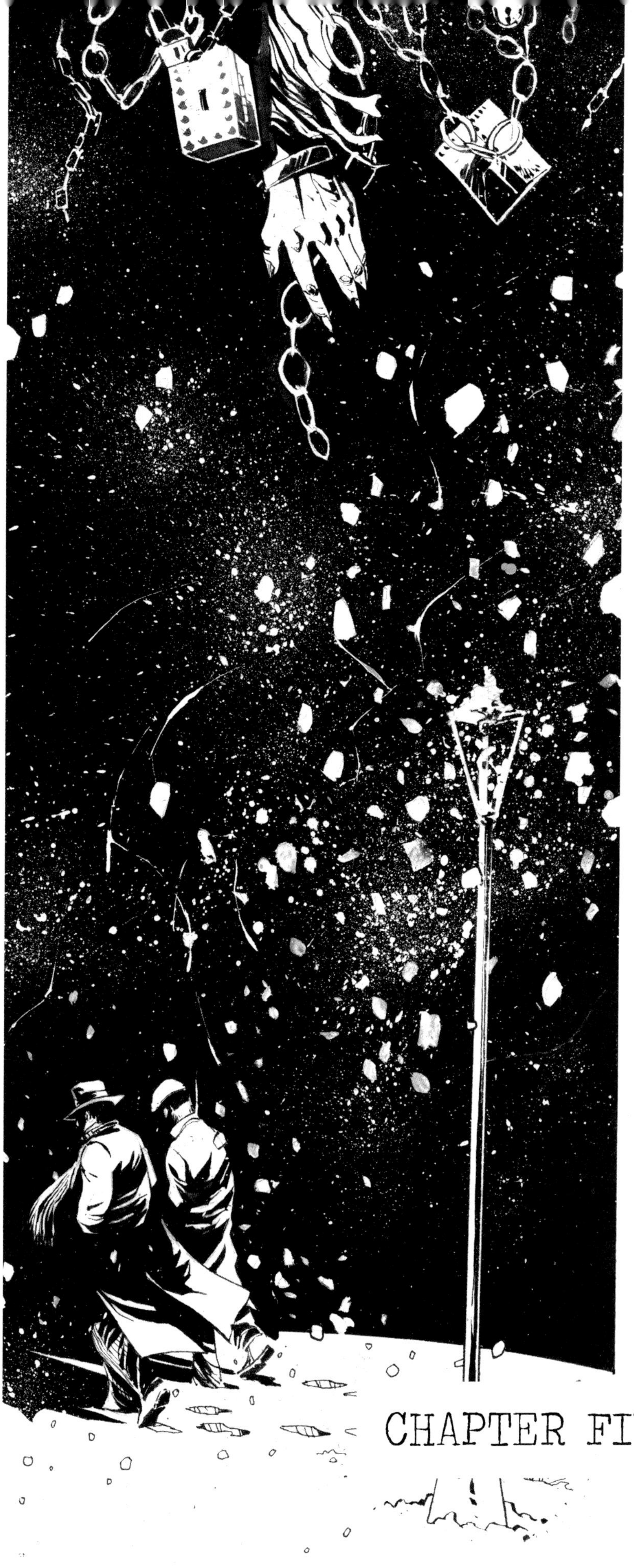

CHAPTER FIVE

The Christmas Chapter is one that we are especially proud of. Here are some of Mike's rough layouts and cover roughs.

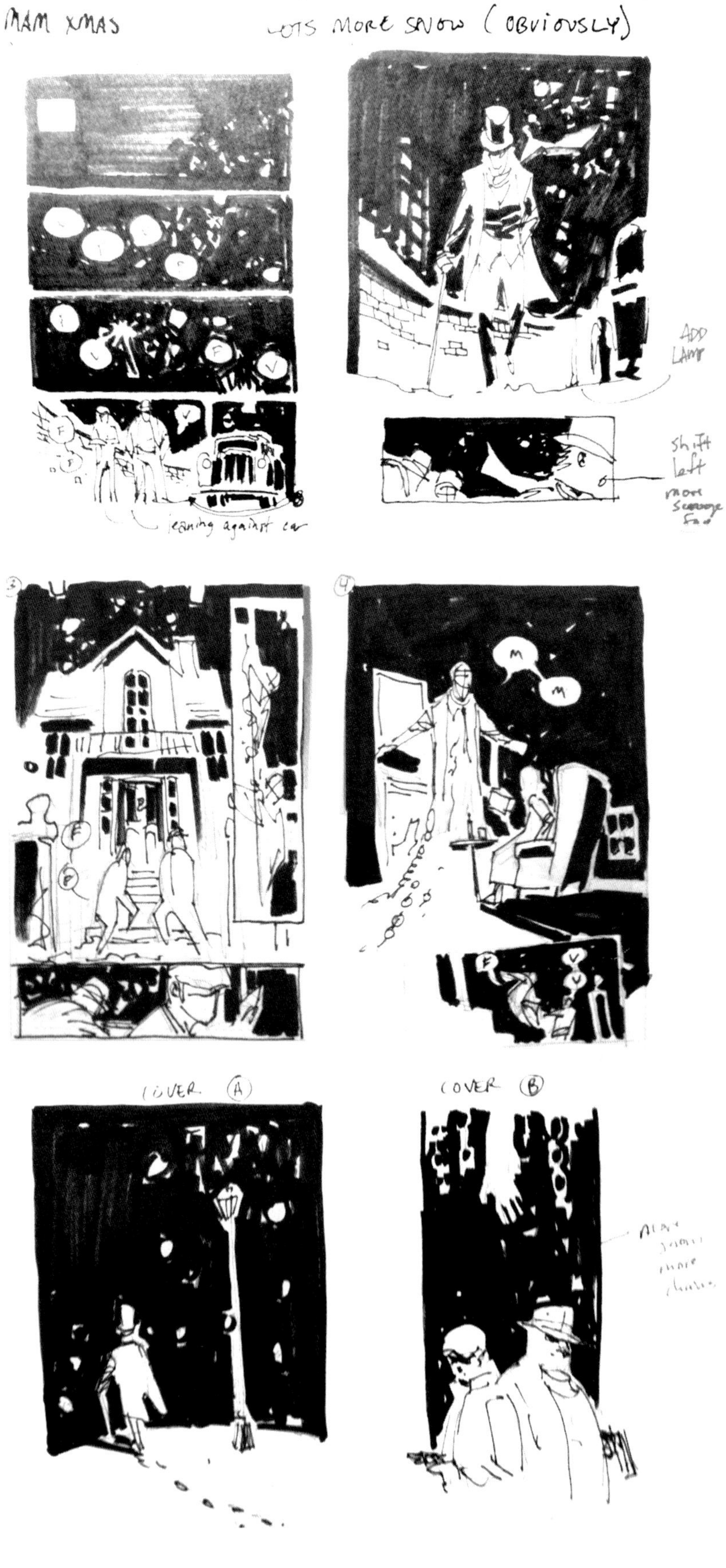
MAM XMAS
LOTS MORE SNOW (OBVIOUSLY)
ADD LAMP
leaning against car
Shift left
COVER (A)
COVER (B)

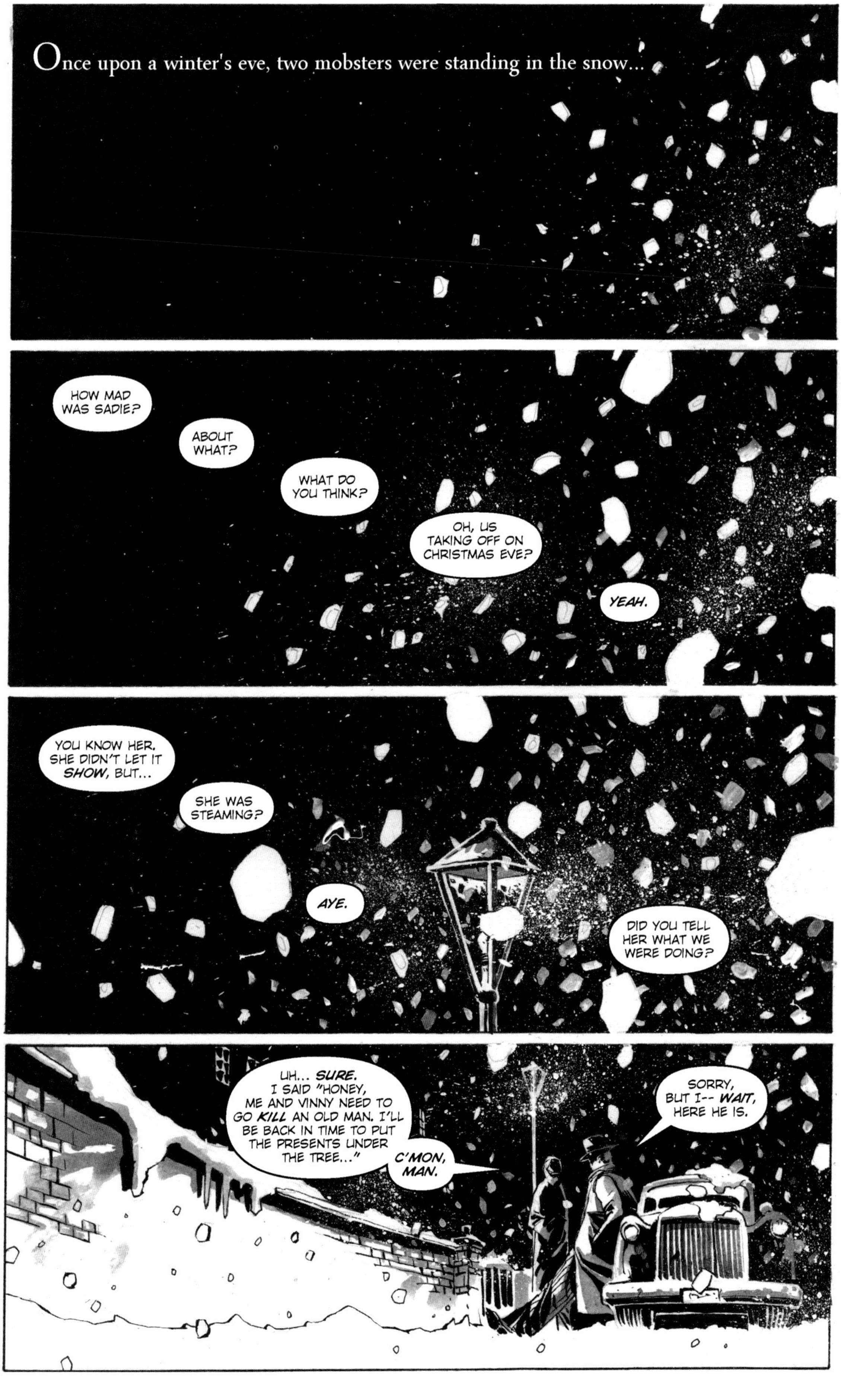
Once upon a winter's eve, two mobsters were standing in the snow...
HOW MAD WAS SADIE?
ABOUT WHAT?
WHAT DO YOU THINK?
OH, US TAKING OFF ON CHRISTMAS EVE?
YEAH.
YOU KNOW HER. SHE DIDN'T LET IT SHOW, BUT...
SHE WAS STEAMING?
AYE.
DID YOU TELL HER WHAT WE WERE DOING?
UH... SURE. I SAID "HONEY, ME AND VINNY NEED TO GO KILL AN OLD MAN. I'LL BE BACK IN TIME TO PUT THE PRESENTS UNDER THE TREE..."
C'MON, MAN.
SORRY, BUT I-- WAIT, HERE HE IS.

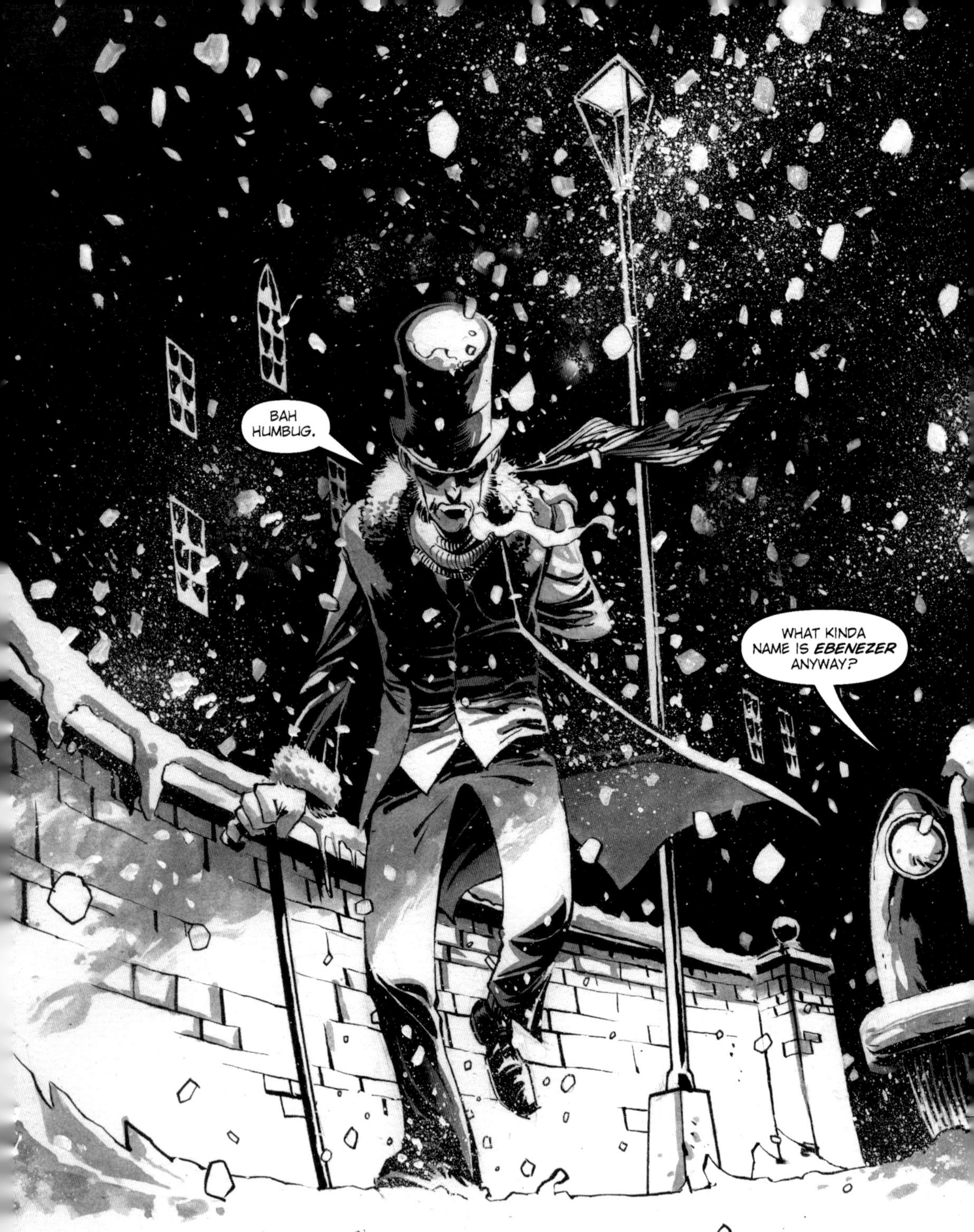
BAH HUMBUG.
WHAT KINDA NAME IS *EBENEZER* ANYWAY?

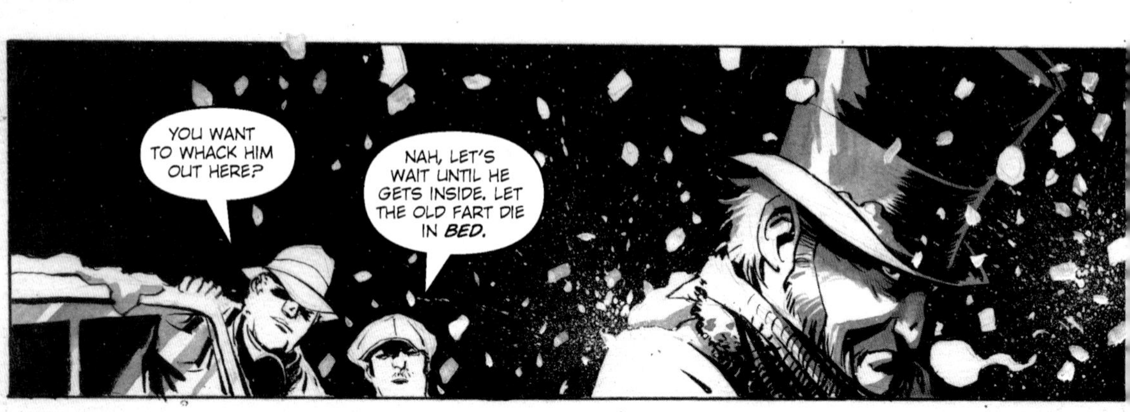
YOU WANT TO WHACK HIM OUT HERE?
NAH, LET'S WAIT UNTIL HE GETS INSIDE. LET THE OLD FART DIE IN *BED*.

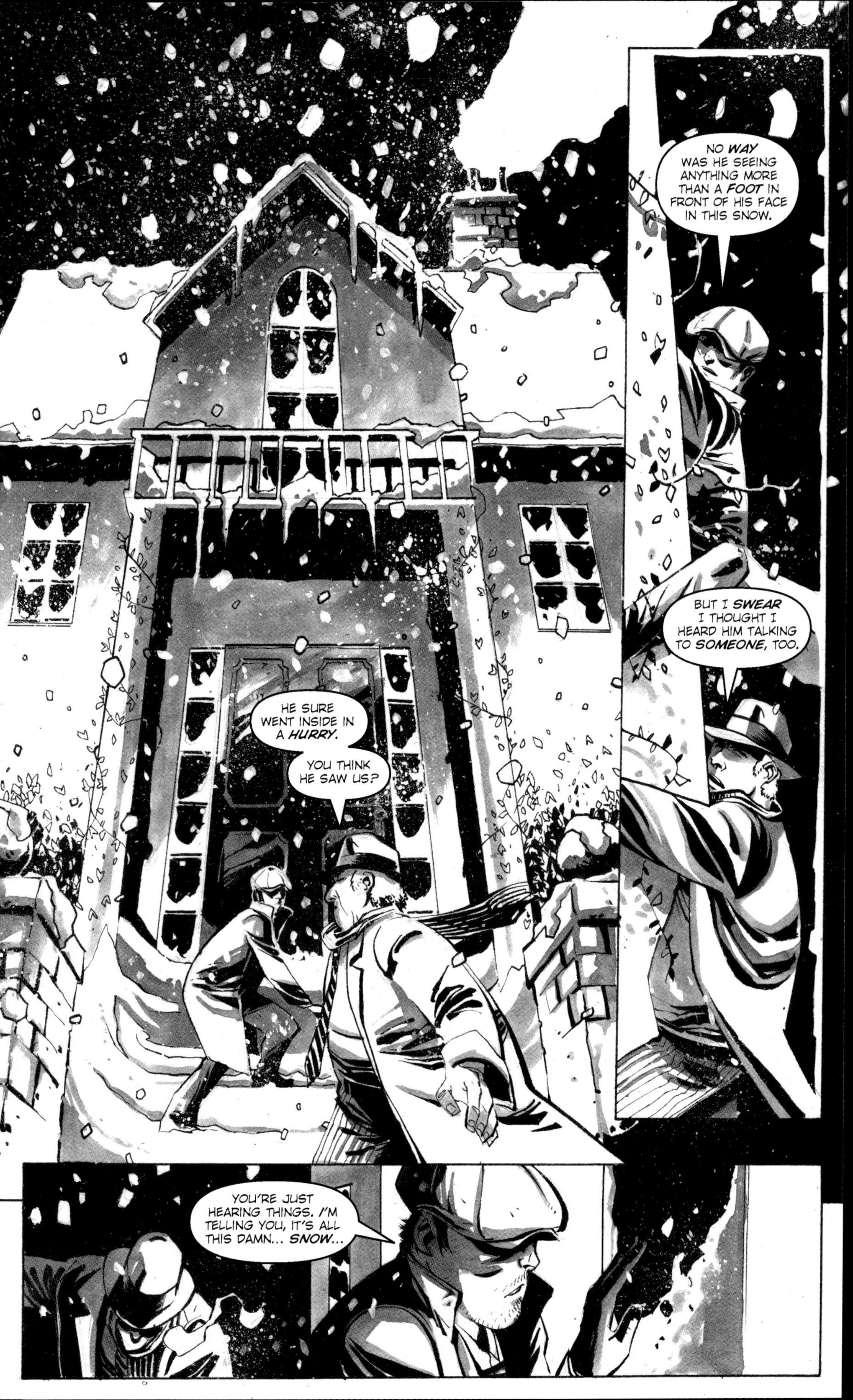
NO WAY WAS HE SEEING ANYTHING MORE THAN A FOOT IN FRONT OF HIS FACE IN THIS SNOW.
BUT I SWEAR I THOUGHT I HEARD HIM TALKING TO SOMEONE, TOO.
HE SURE WENT INSIDE IN A HURRY.
YOU THINK HE SAW US?
YOU'RE JUST HEARING THINGS. I'M TELLING YOU, IT'S ALL THIS DAMN... SNOW...

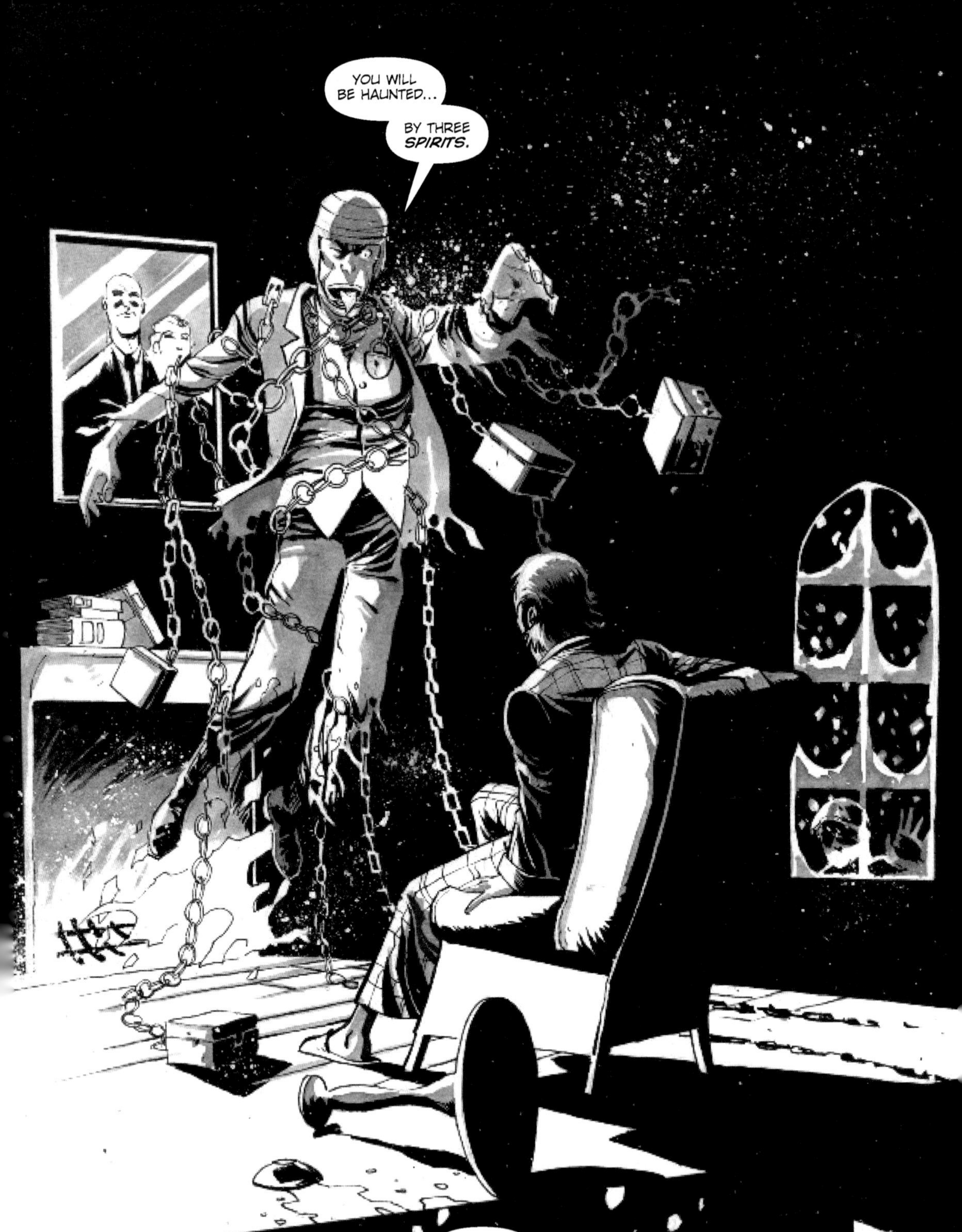
YOU WILL BE HAUNTED...
BY THREE *SPIRITS*.

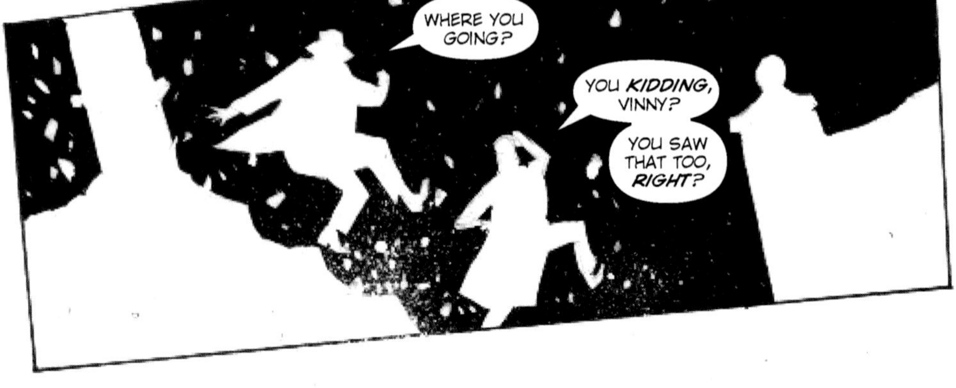
WHERE YOU GOING?
YOU *KIDDING*, VINNY?
YOU SAW THAT TOO, *RIGHT*?

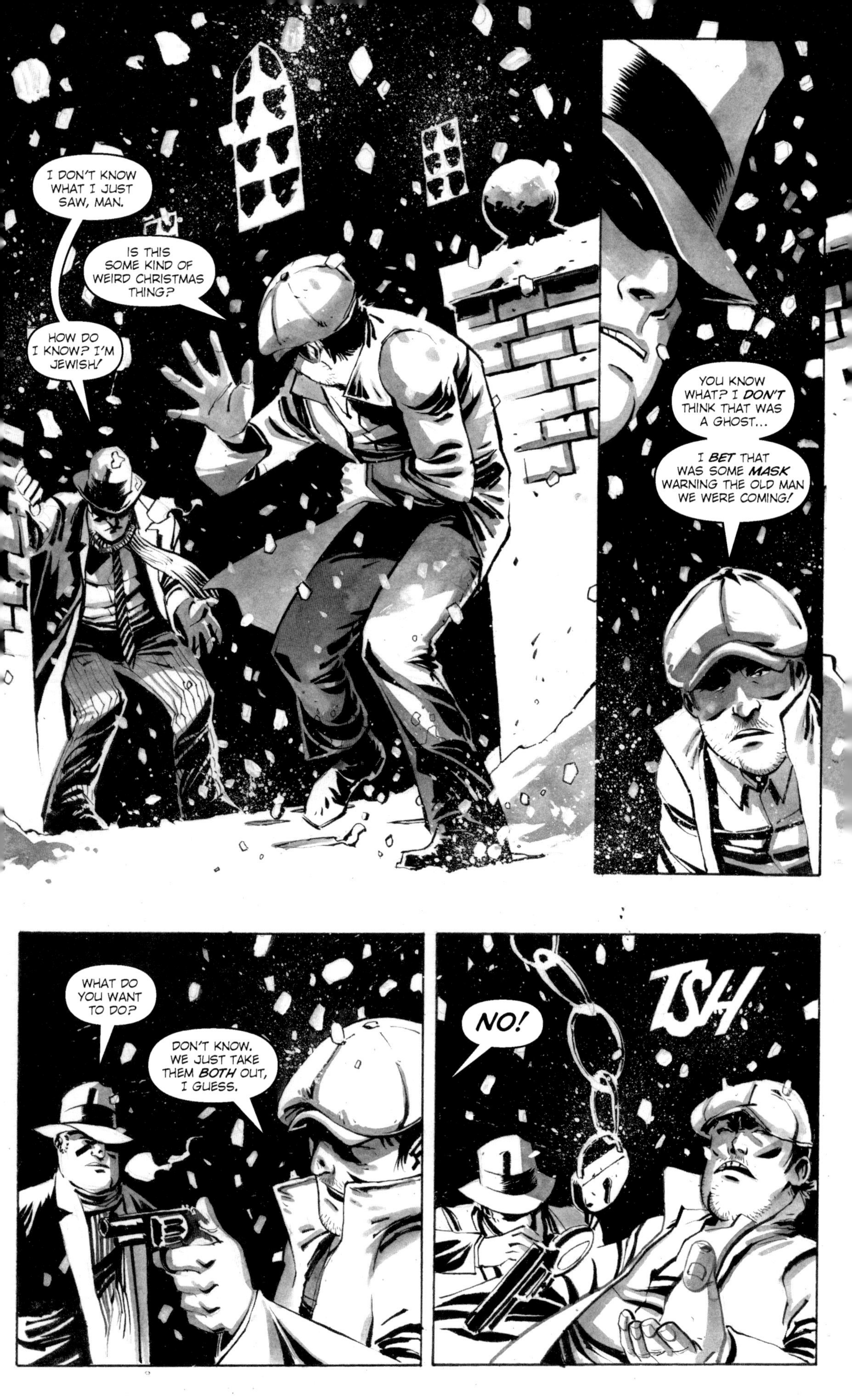
I DON'T KNOW WHAT I JUST SAW, MAN.
IS THIS SOME KIND OF WEIRD CHRISTMAS THING?
HOW DO I KNOW? I'M JEWISH!
YOU KNOW WHAT? I DON'T THINK THAT WAS A GHOST...
I BET THAT WAS SOME MASK WARNING THE OLD MAN WE WERE COMING!
WHAT DO YOU WANT TO DO?
DON'T KNOW. WE JUST TAKE THEM BOTH OUT, I GUESS.
NO!
TSH

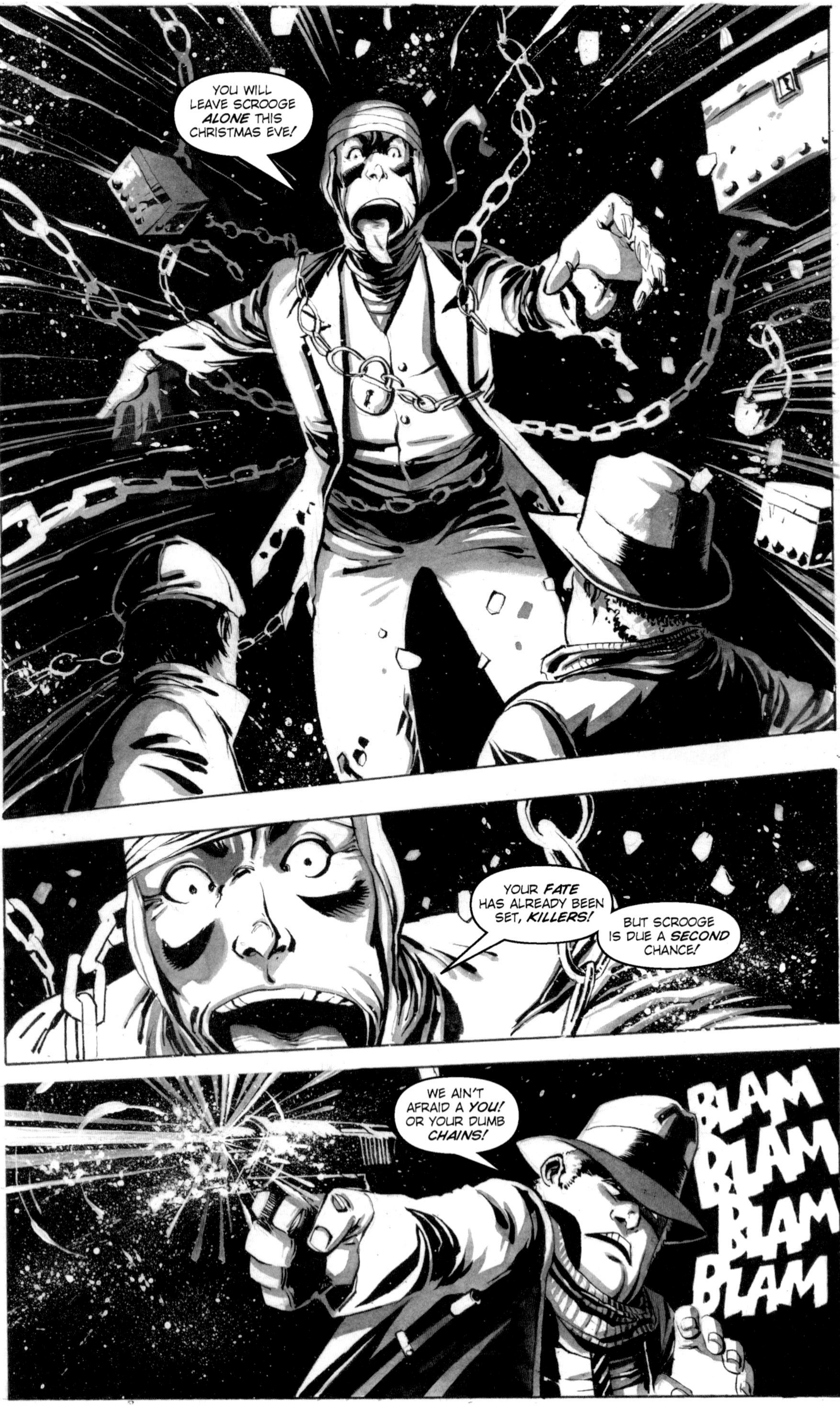
YOU WILL LEAVE SCROOGE ALONE THIS CHRISTMAS EVE!
YOUR FATE HAS ALREADY BEEN SET, KILLERS!
BUT SCROOGE IS DUE A SECOND CHANCE!
WE AIN'T AFRAID A YOU! OR YOUR DUMB CHAINS!
BLAM BLAM BLAM BLAM

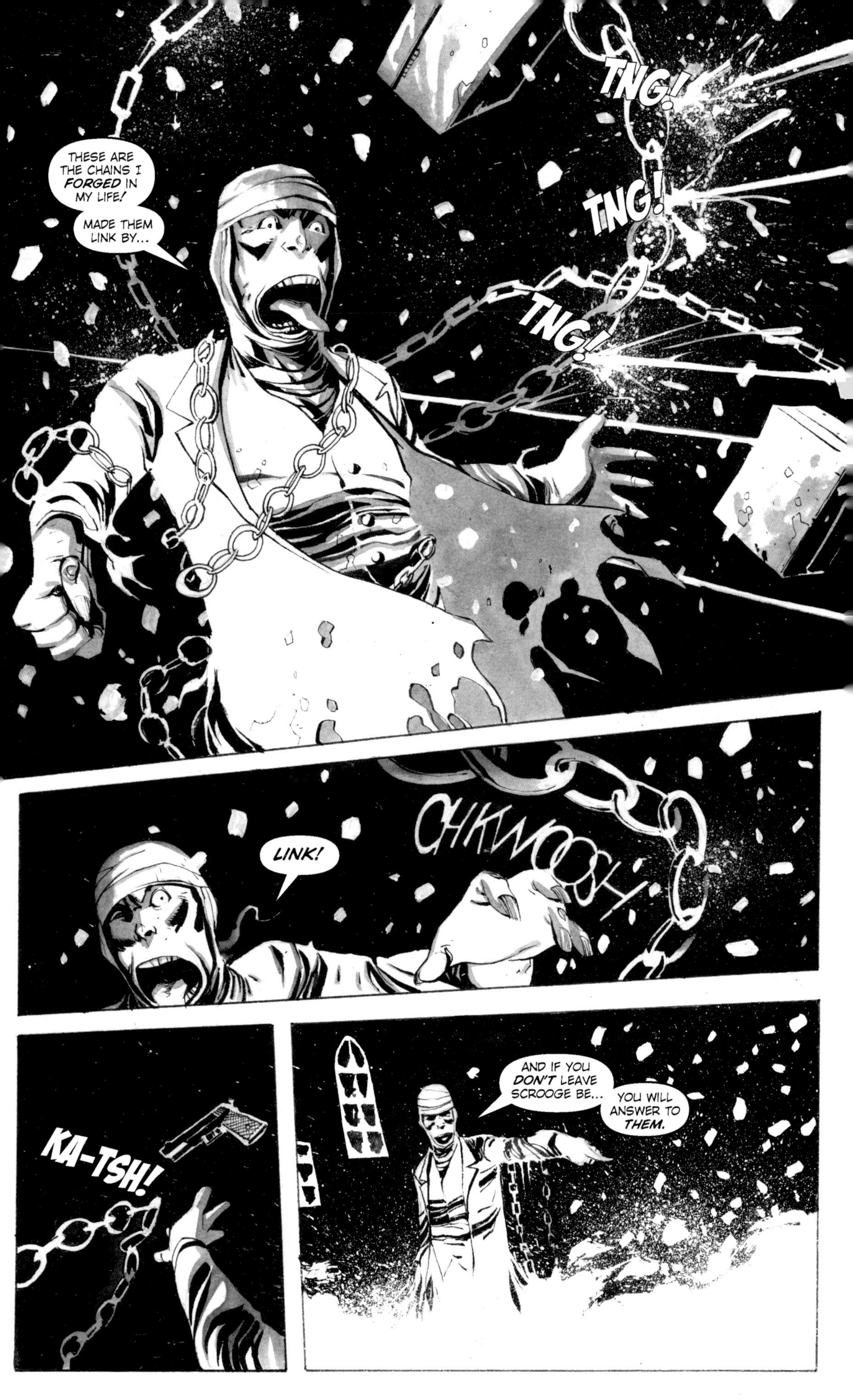
TNG!
TNG!
THESE ARE THE CHAINS I FORGED IN MY LIFE!
MADE THEM LINK BY...
TNG!
CHKWOOSH
LINK!
KA-TSH!
AND IF YOU DON'T LEAVE SCROOGE BE...
YOU WILL ANSWER TO THEM.

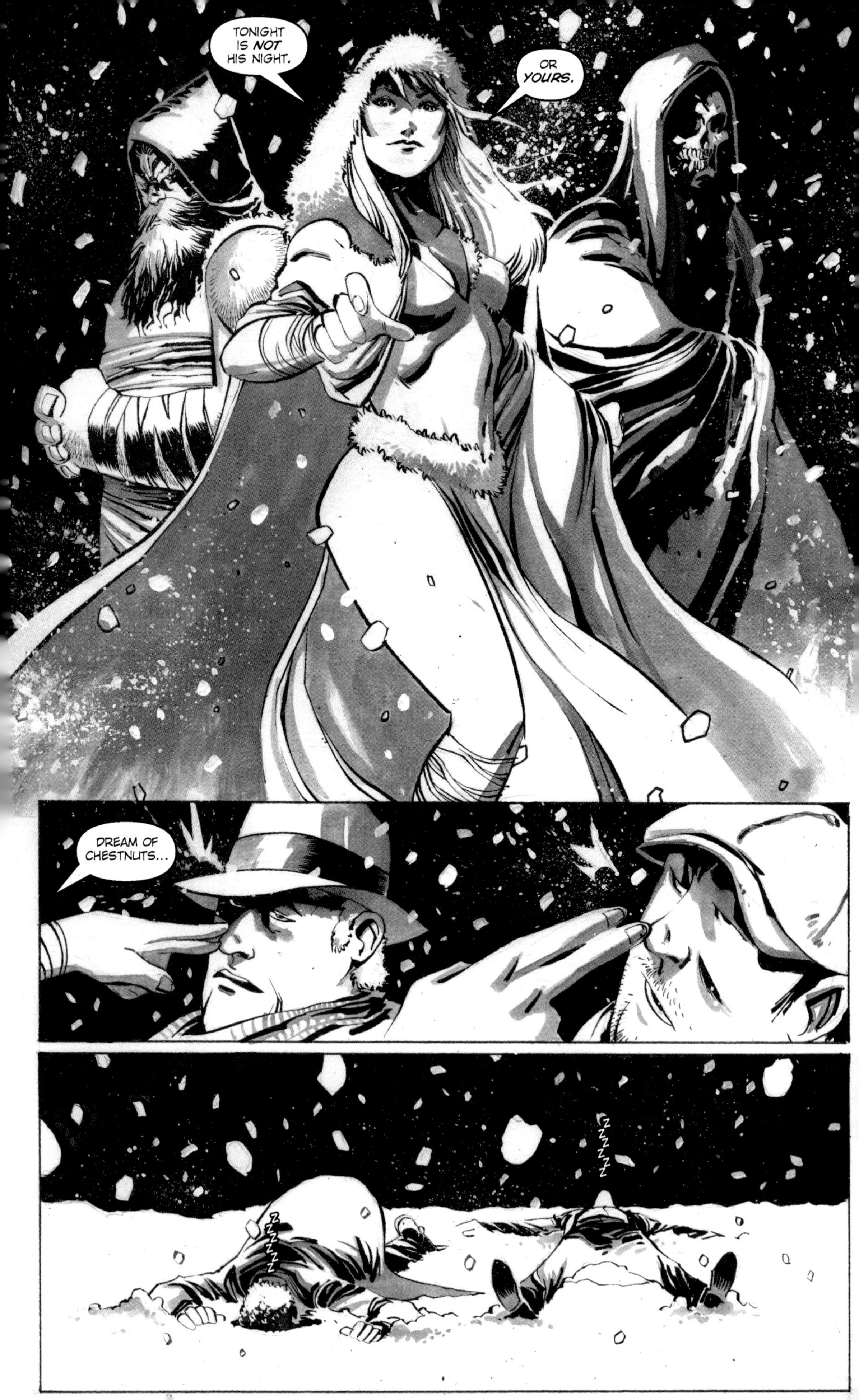
TONIGHT IS NOT HIS NIGHT.
OR YOURS.
DREAM OF CHESTNUTS...
ZZZZZ
ZZZZZ

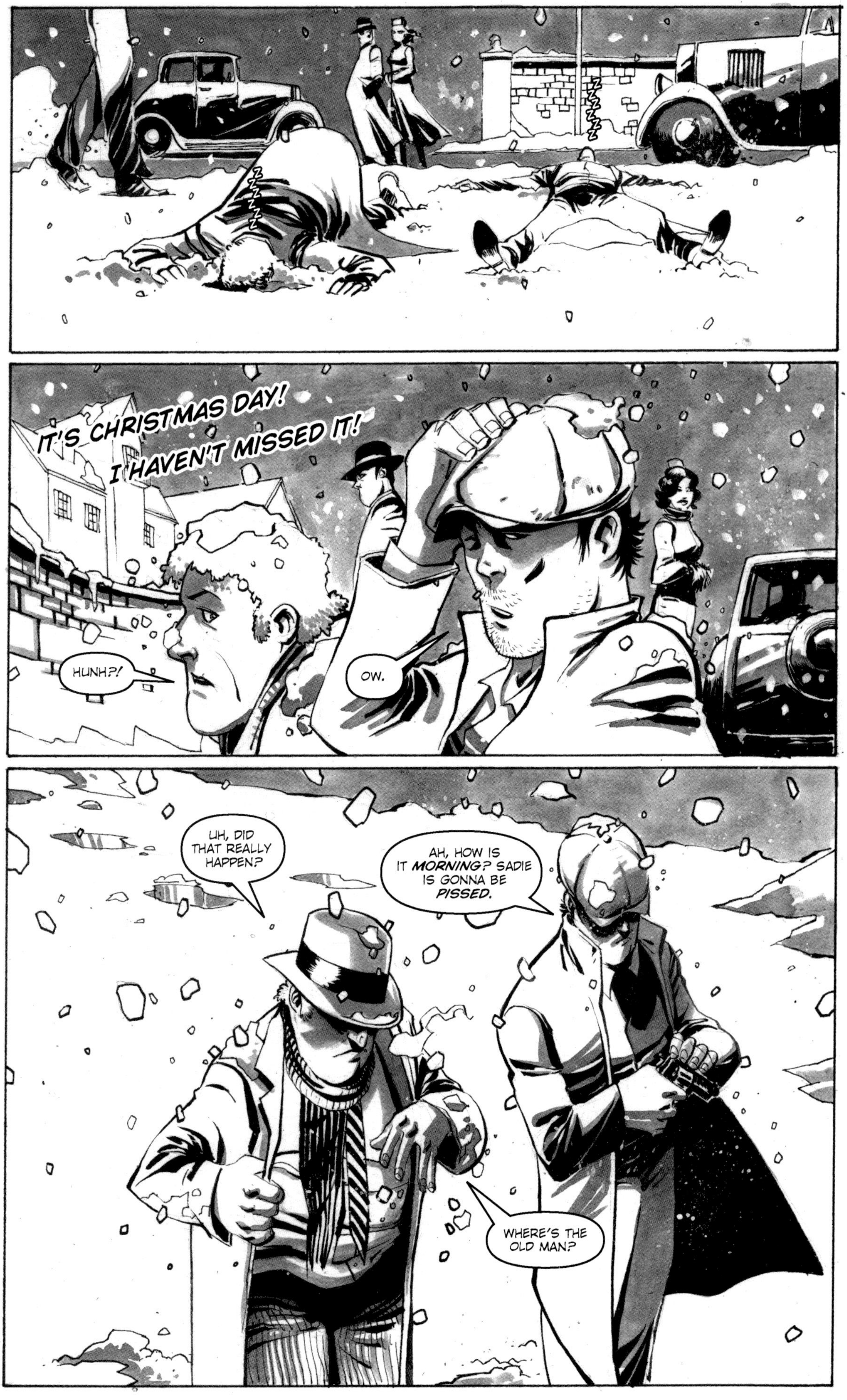
ZZZZZ
ZZZZZ
IT'S CHRISTMAS DAY!
I HAVEN'T MISSED IT!
HUNH?!
OW.
UH, DID THAT REALLY HAPPEN?
AH, HOW IS IT *MORNING?* SADIE IS GONNA BE *PISSED.*
WHERE'S THE OLD MAN?

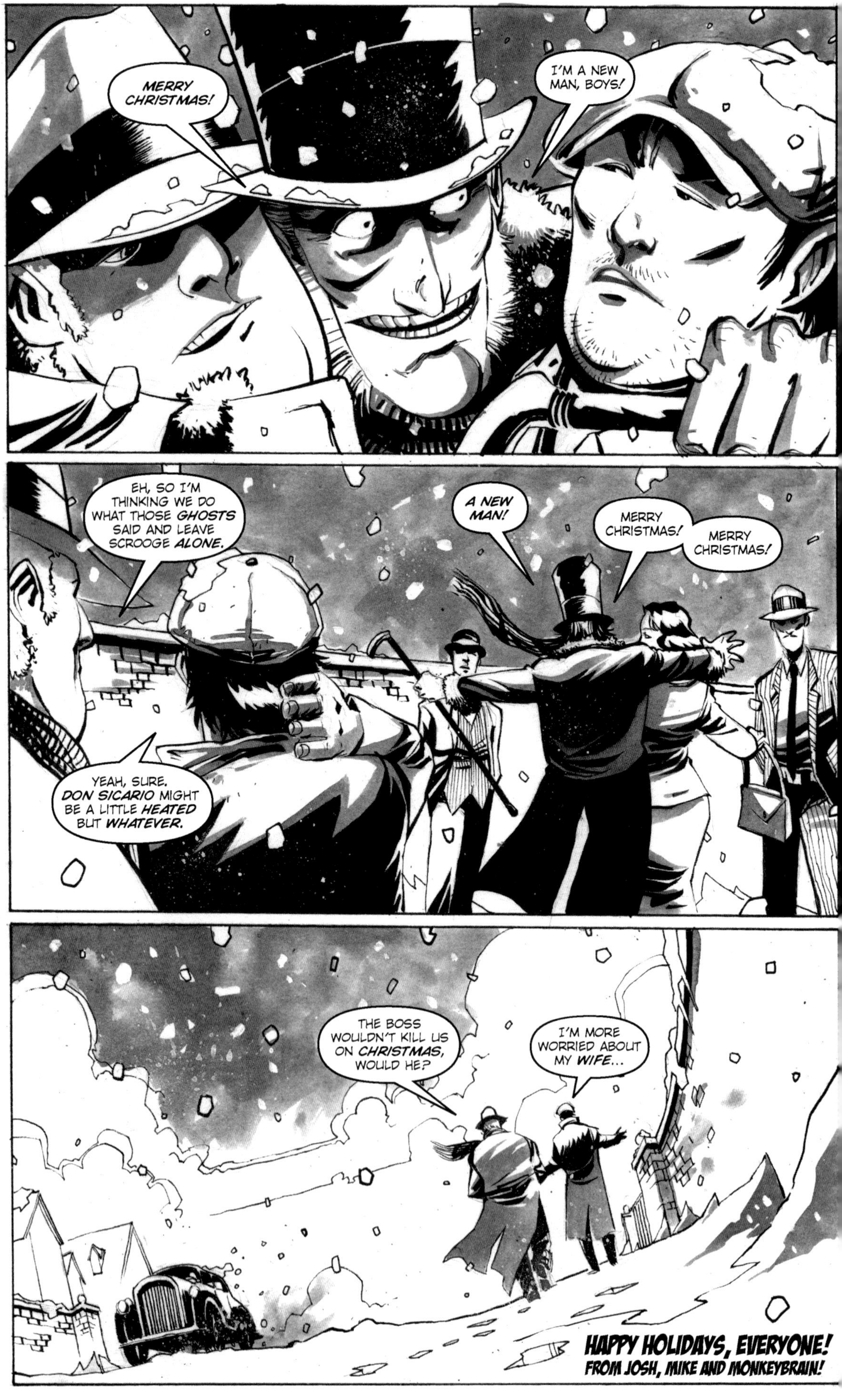
MERRY CHRISTMAS!
I'M A NEW MAN, BOYS!
EH, SO I'M THINKING WE DO WHAT THOSE GHOSTS SAID AND LEAVE SCROOGE ALONE.
A NEW MAN!
MERRY CHRISTMAS!
MERRY CHRISTMAS!
YEAH, SURE. DON SICARIO MIGHT BE A LITTLE HEATED BUT WHATEVER.
THE BOSS WOULDN'T KILL US ON CHRISTMAS, WOULD HE?
I'M MORE WORRIED ABOUT MY WIFE...
HAPPY HOLIDAYS, EVERYONE!
FROM JOSH, MIKE AND MONKEYBRAIN!

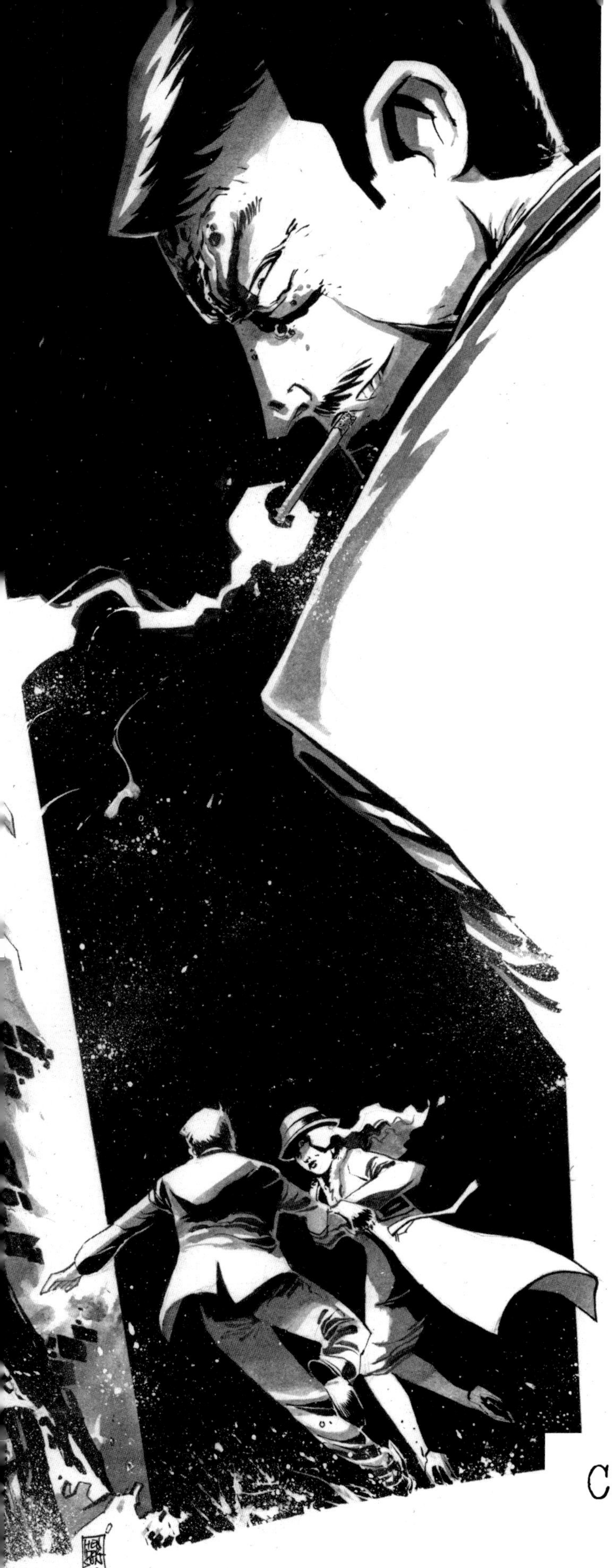

CHAPTER SIX

JK Greenwood did a TON of designs and character studies.

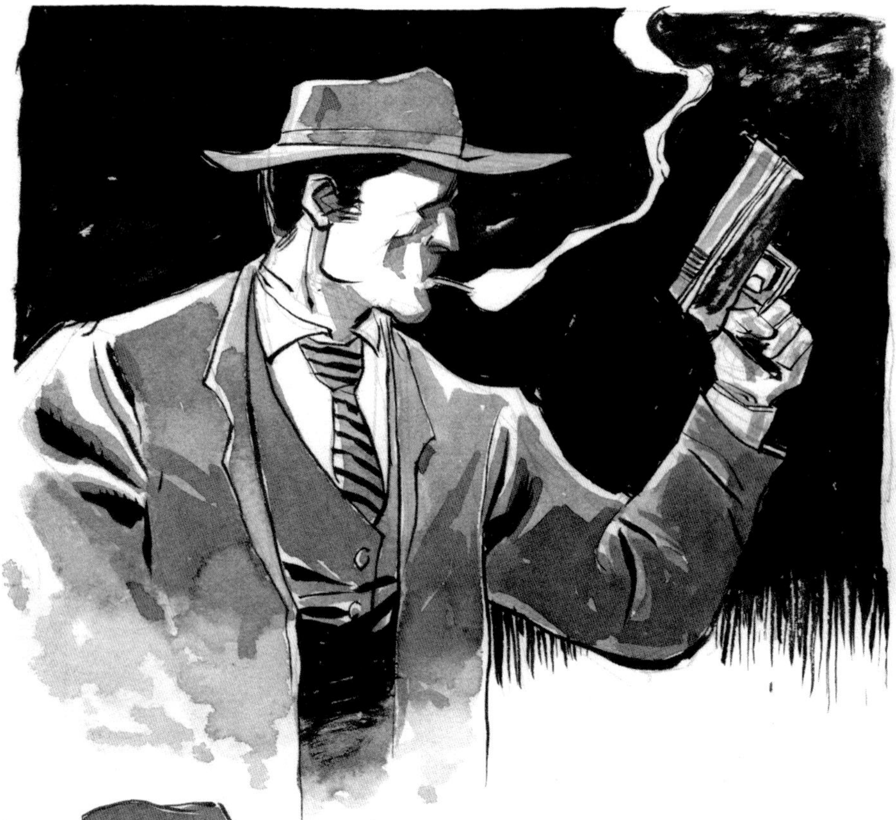

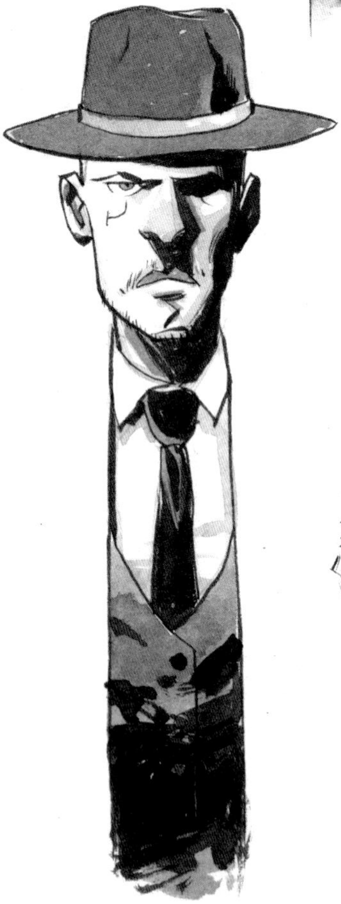

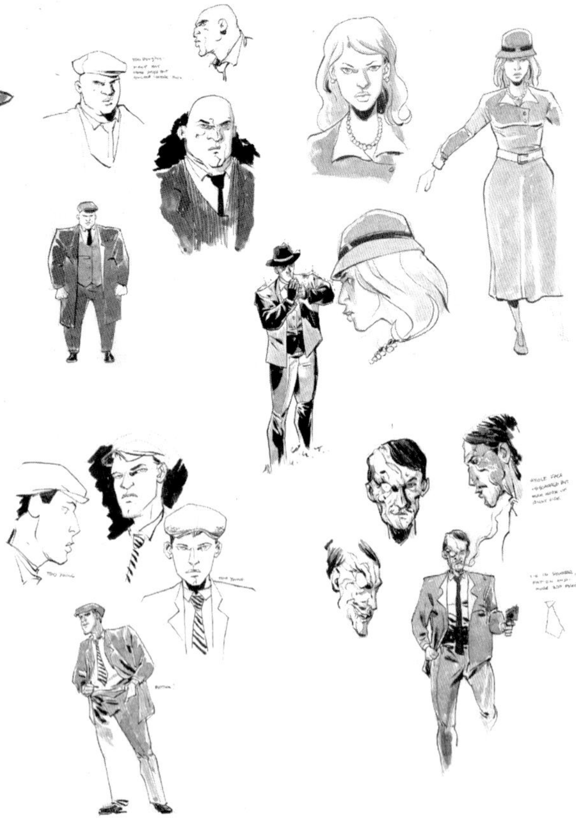

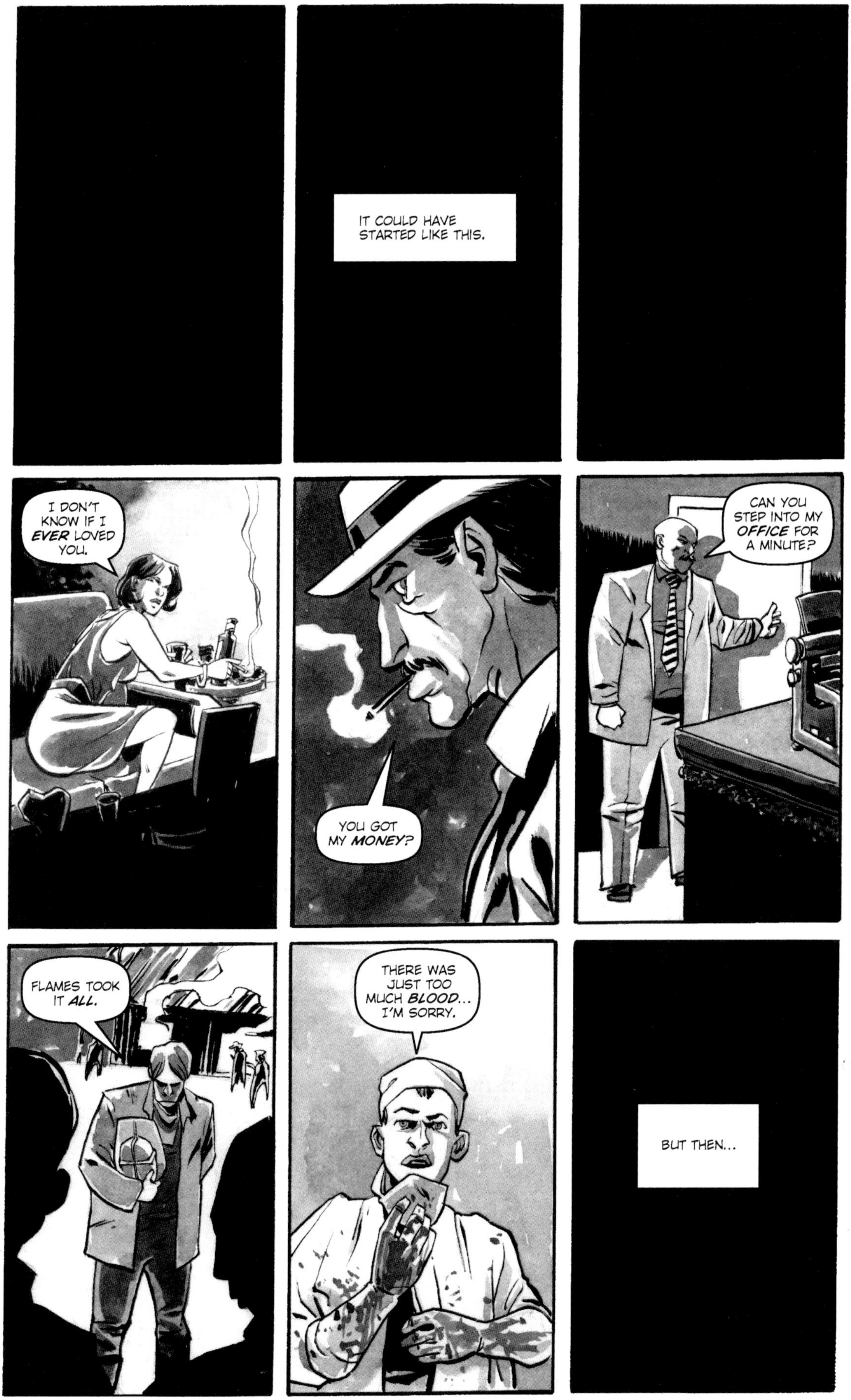

IT COULD HAVE STARTED LIKE THIS.
I DON'T KNOW IF I ***EVER*** LOVED YOU.
YOU GOT MY ***MONEY?***
CAN YOU STEP INTO MY ***OFFICE*** FOR A MINUTE?
FLAMES TOOK IT ***ALL.***
THERE WAS JUST TOO MUCH ***BLOOD***... I'M SORRY.
BUT THEN...

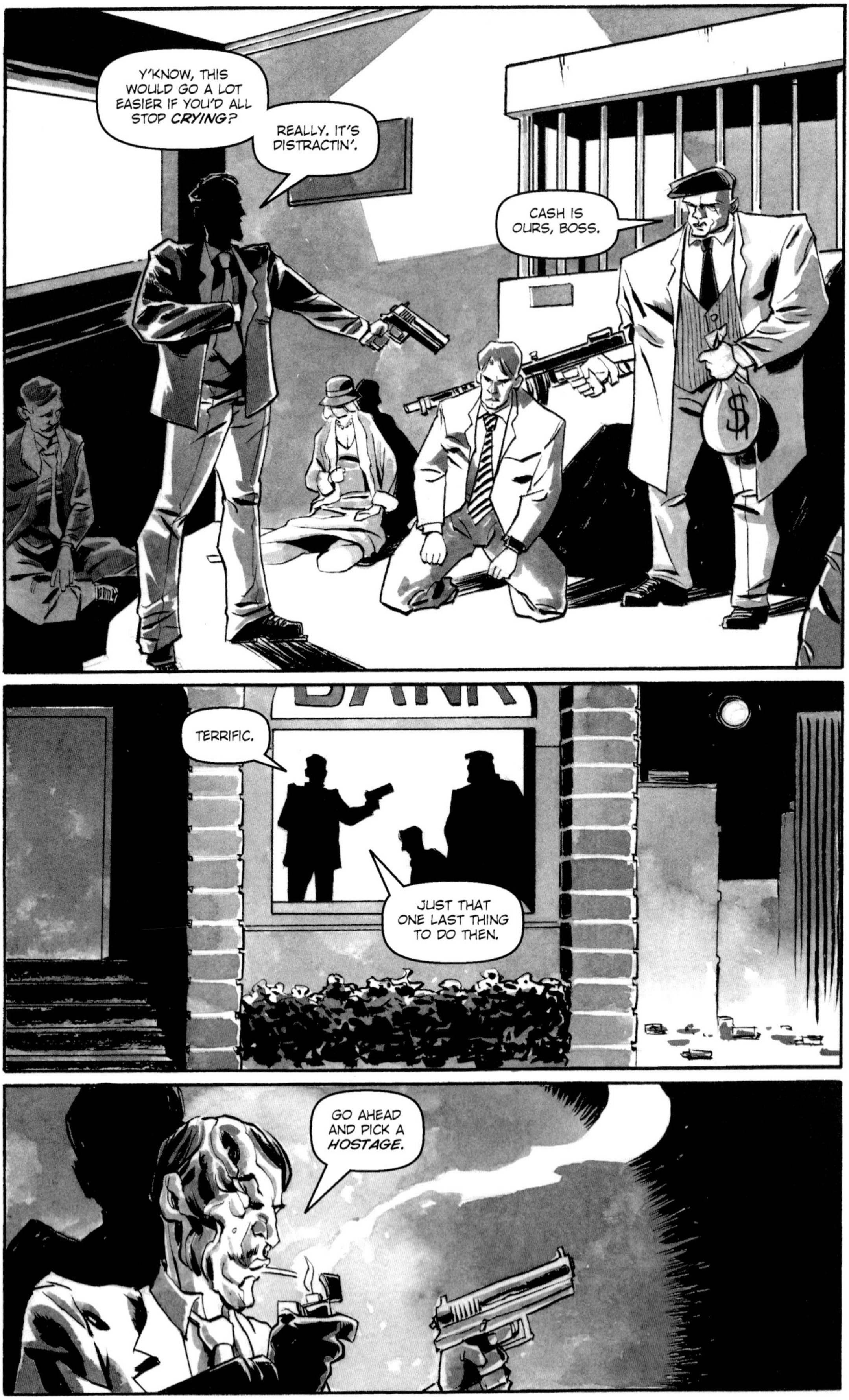
Y'KNOW, THIS WOULD GO A LOT EASIER IF YOU'D ALL STOP *CRYING*?
REALLY. IT'S DISTRACTIN'.
CASH IS OURS, BOSS.
TERRIFIC.
JUST THAT ONE LAST THING TO DO THEN.
GO AHEAD AND PICK A *HOSTAGE*.

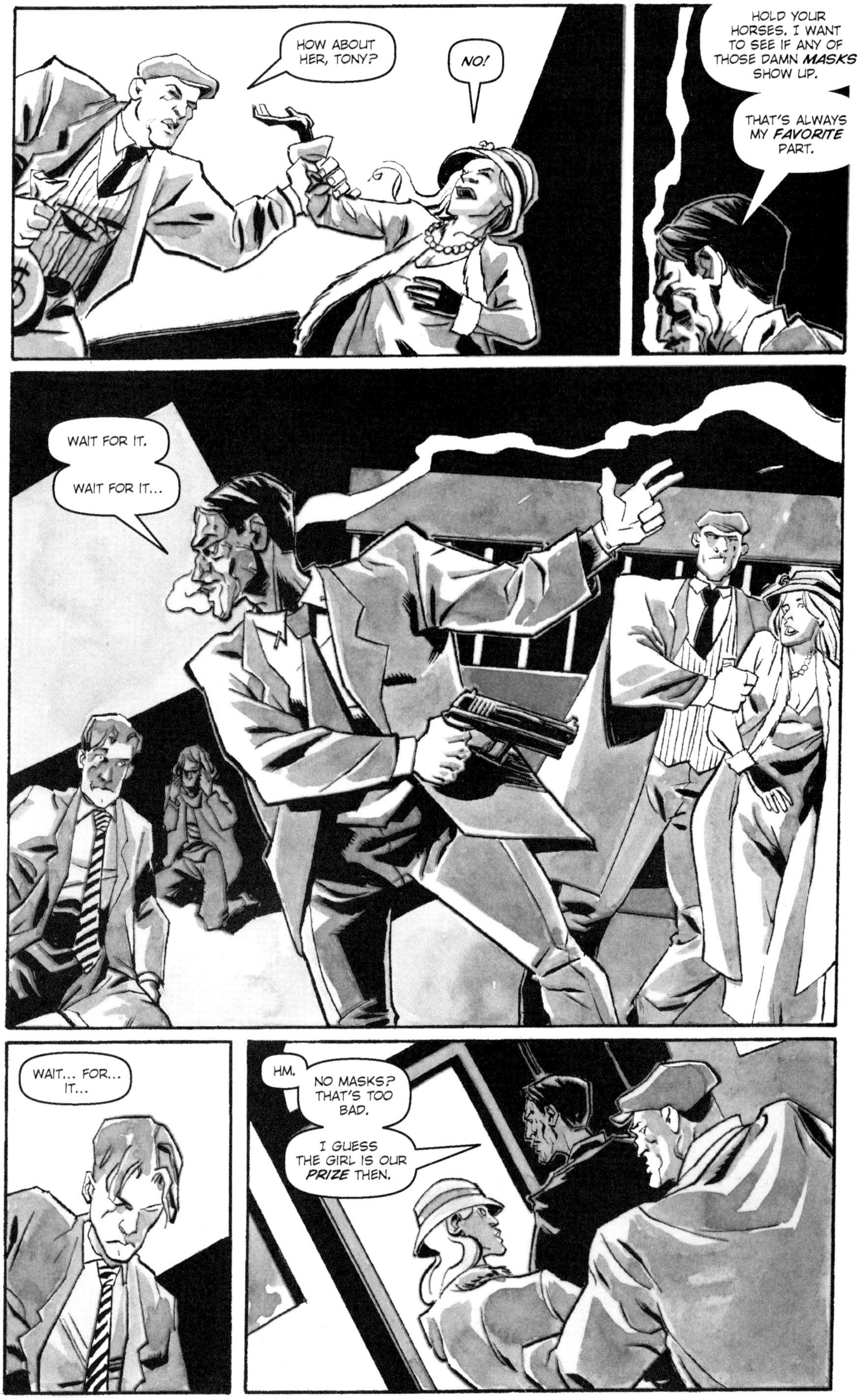
HOW ABOUT HER, TONY?
NO!
HOLD YOUR HORSES. I WANT TO SEE IF ANY OF THOSE DAMN MASKS SHOW UP.
THAT'S ALWAYS MY FAVORITE PART.
WAIT FOR IT.
WAIT FOR IT...
WAIT... FOR... IT...
HM.
NO MASKS? THAT'S TOO BAD.
I GUESS THE GIRL IS OUR PRIZE THEN.

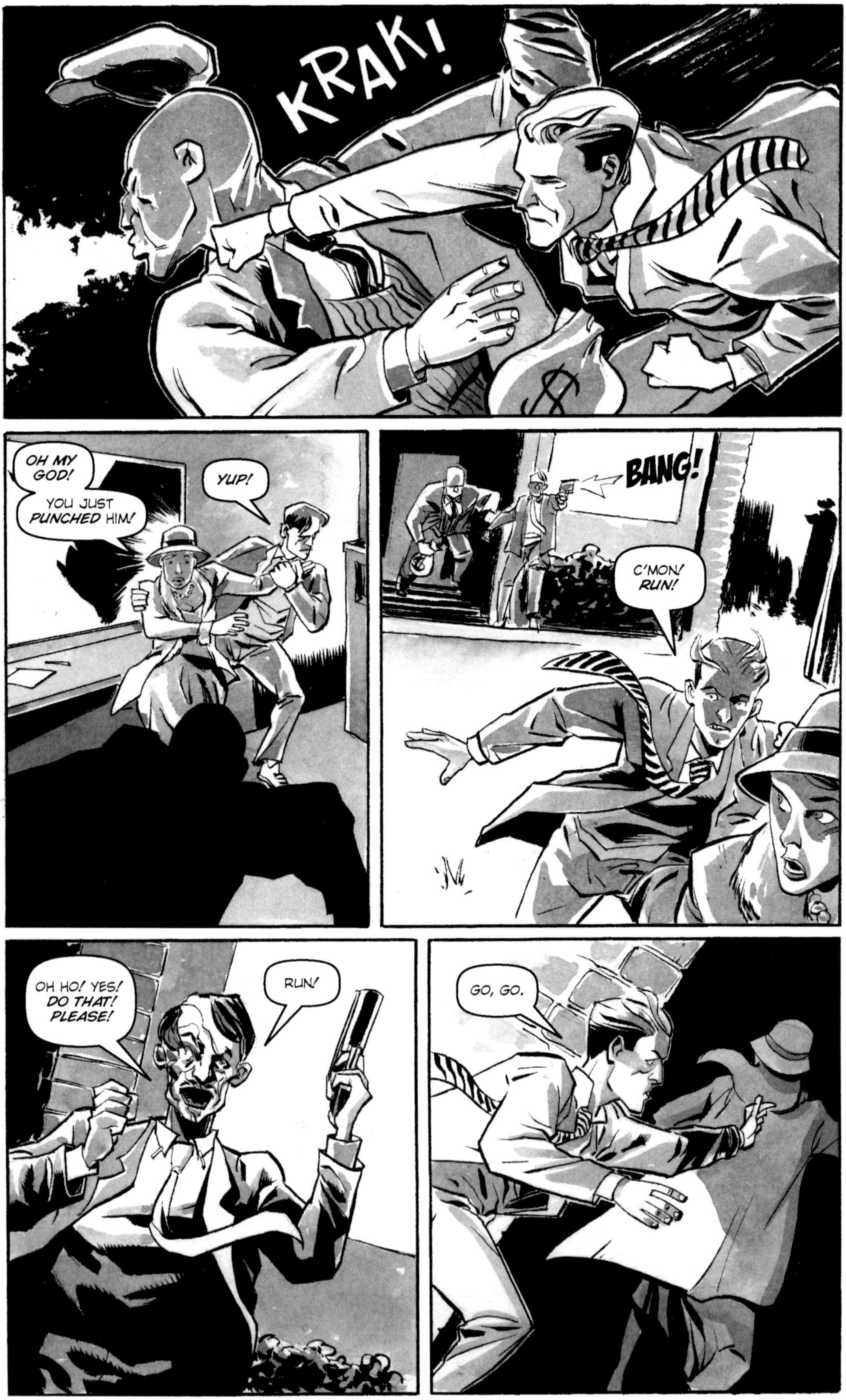
KRAK!
OH MY GOD!
YOU JUST PUNCHED HIM!
YUP!
BANG!
C'MON! RUN!
OH HO! YES! DO THAT! PLEASE!
RUN!
GO, GO.

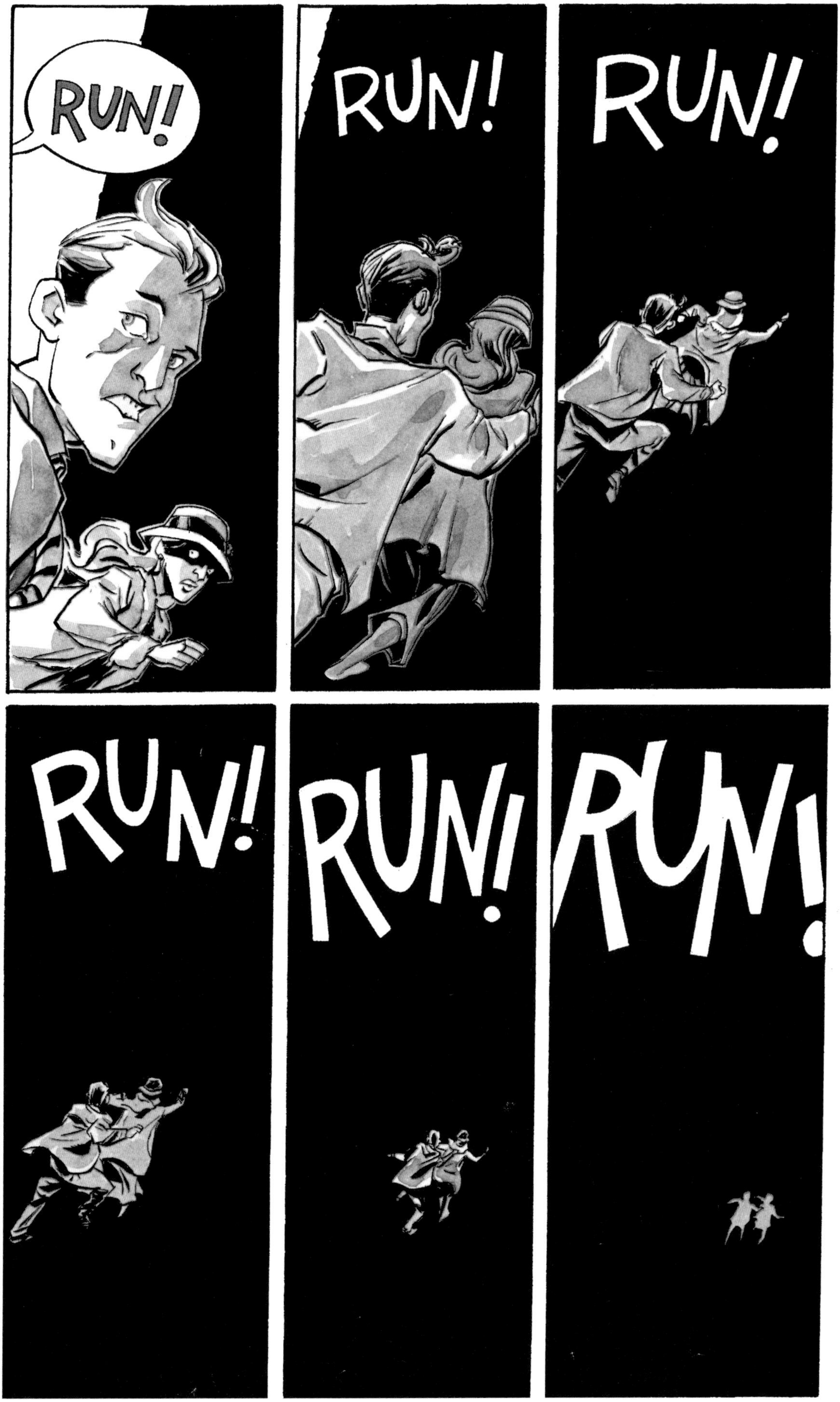
RUN!
RUN!
RUN!
RUN!
RUN!
RUN!

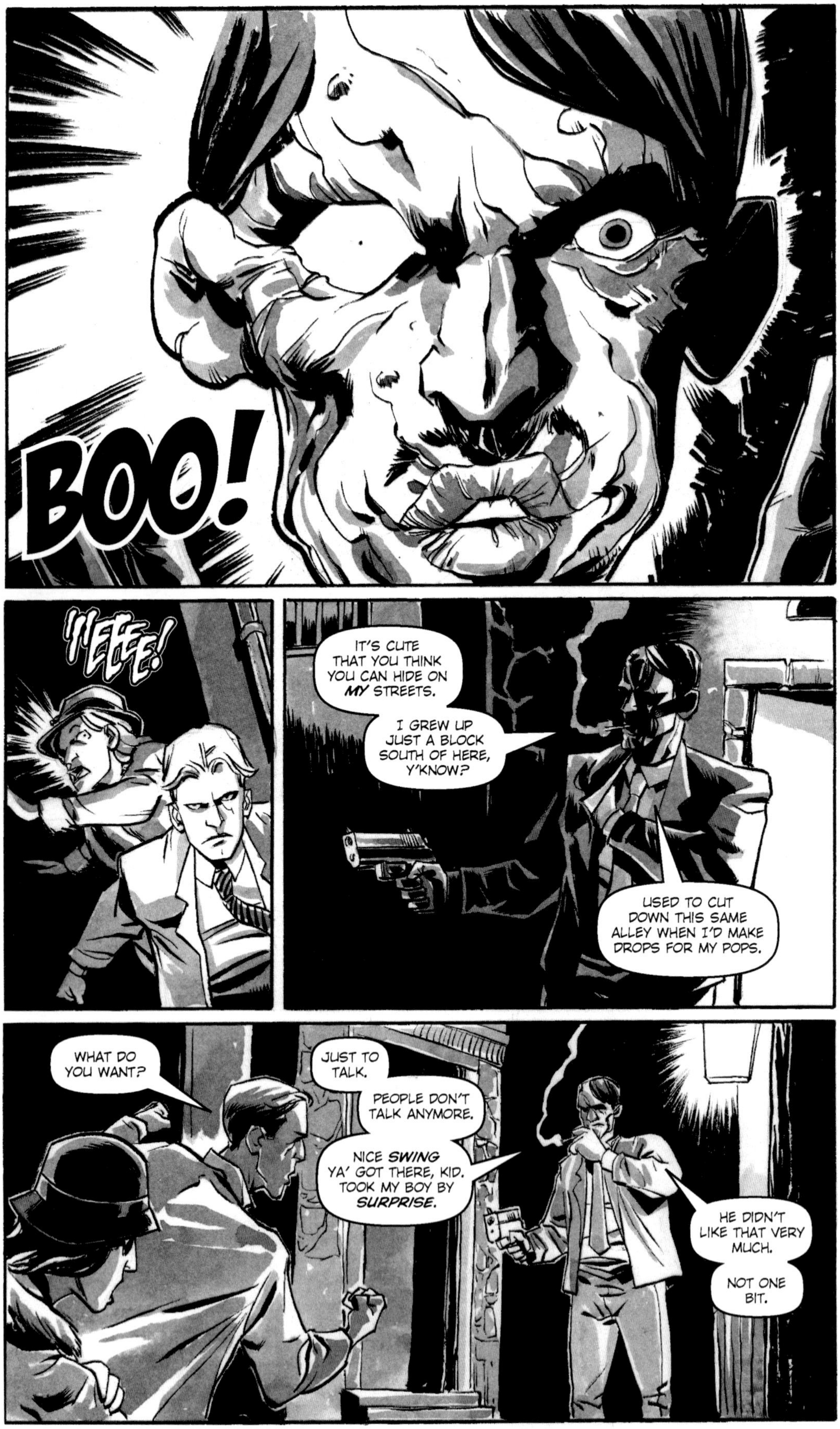
BOO!
YEEEE!
IT'S CUTE THAT YOU THINK YOU CAN HIDE ON MY STREETS.
I GREW UP JUST A BLOCK SOUTH OF HERE, Y'KNOW?
USED TO CUT DOWN THIS SAME ALLEY WHEN I'D MAKE DROPS FOR MY POPS.
WHAT DO YOU WANT?
JUST TO TALK.
PEOPLE DON'T TALK ANYMORE.
NICE SWING YA' GOT THERE, KID. TOOK MY BOY BY SURPRISE.
HE DIDN'T LIKE THAT VERY MUCH.
NOT ONE BIT.

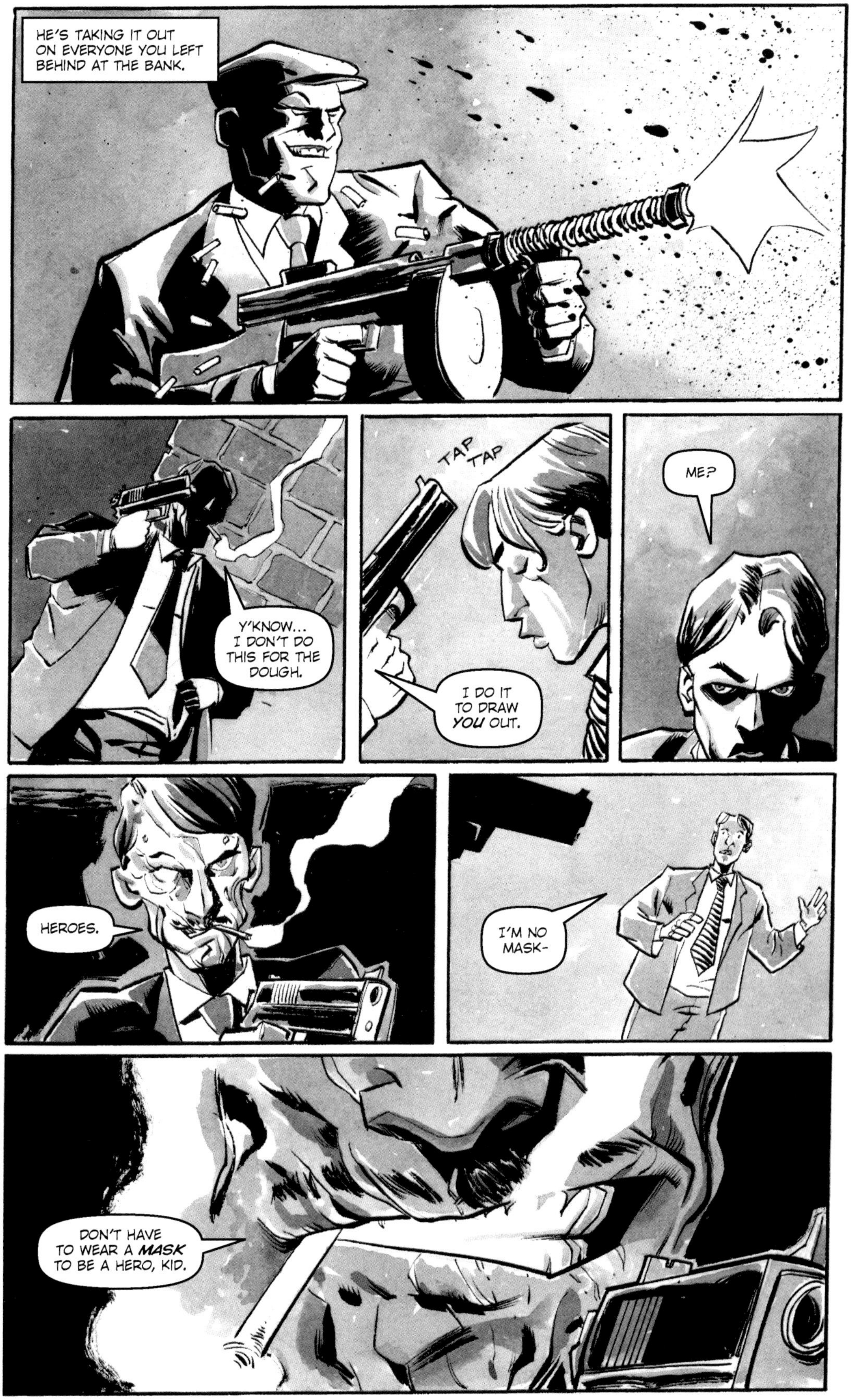
HE'S TAKING IT OUT ON EVERYONE YOU LEFT BEHIND AT THE BANK.
Y'KNOW... I DON'T DO THIS FOR THE DOUGH.
TAP TAP
I DO IT TO DRAW *YOU* OUT.
ME?
HEROES.
I'M NO MASK-
DON'T HAVE TO WEAR A *MASK* TO BE A HERO, KID.

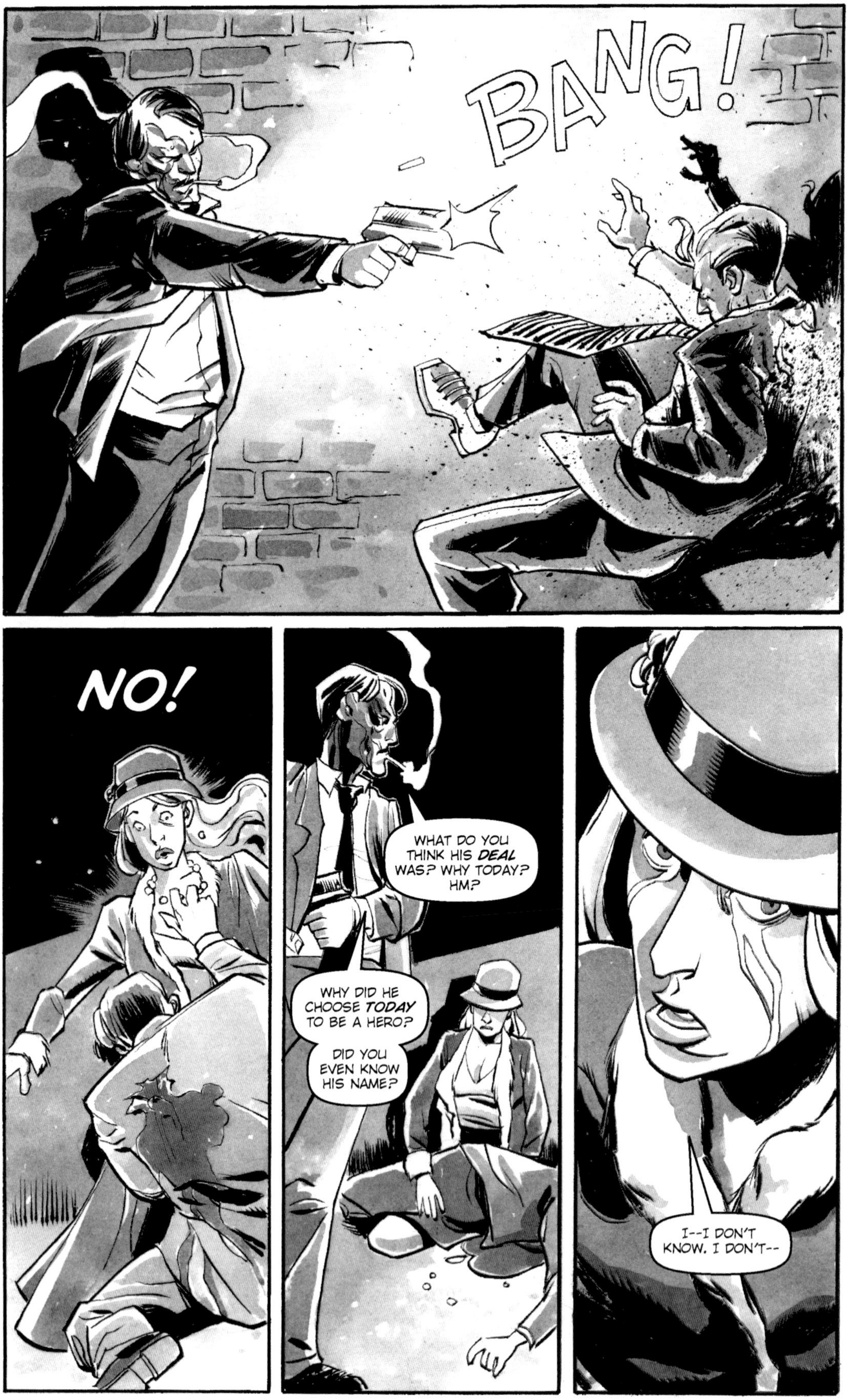
BANG!
NO!
WHAT DO YOU THINK HIS DEAL WAS? WHY TODAY? HM?
WHY DID HE CHOOSE TODAY TO BE A HERO?
DID YOU EVEN KNOW HIS NAME?
I--I DON'T KNOW. I DON'T--

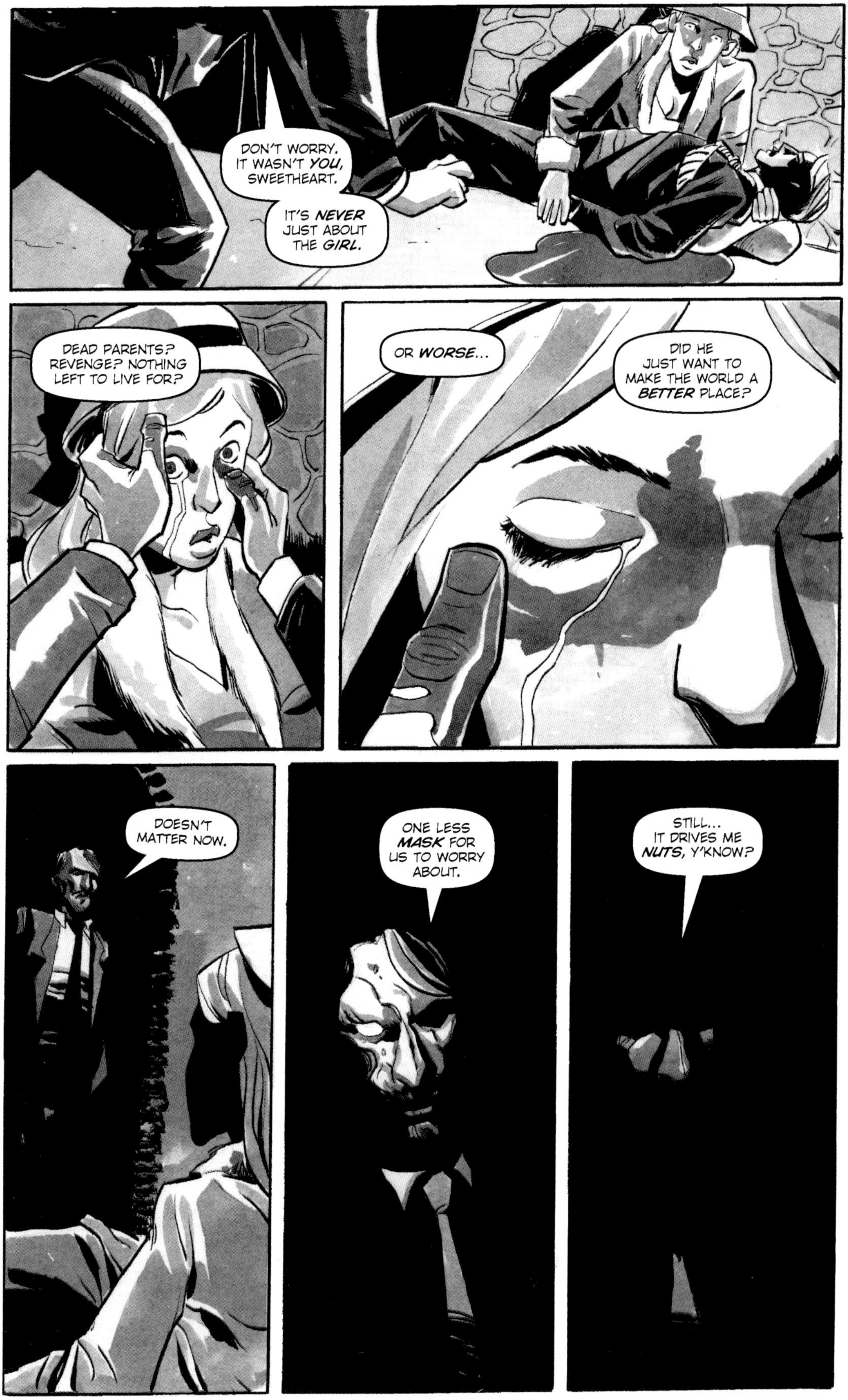
DON'T WORRY. IT WASN'T YOU, SWEETHEART.
IT'S NEVER JUST ABOUT THE GIRL.
DEAD PARENTS? REVENGE? NOTHING LEFT TO LIVE FOR?
OR WORSE...
DID HE JUST WANT TO MAKE THE WORLD A BETTER PLACE?
DOESN'T MATTER NOW.
ONE LESS MASK FOR US TO WORRY ABOUT.
STILL... IT DRIVES ME NUTS, Y'KNOW?

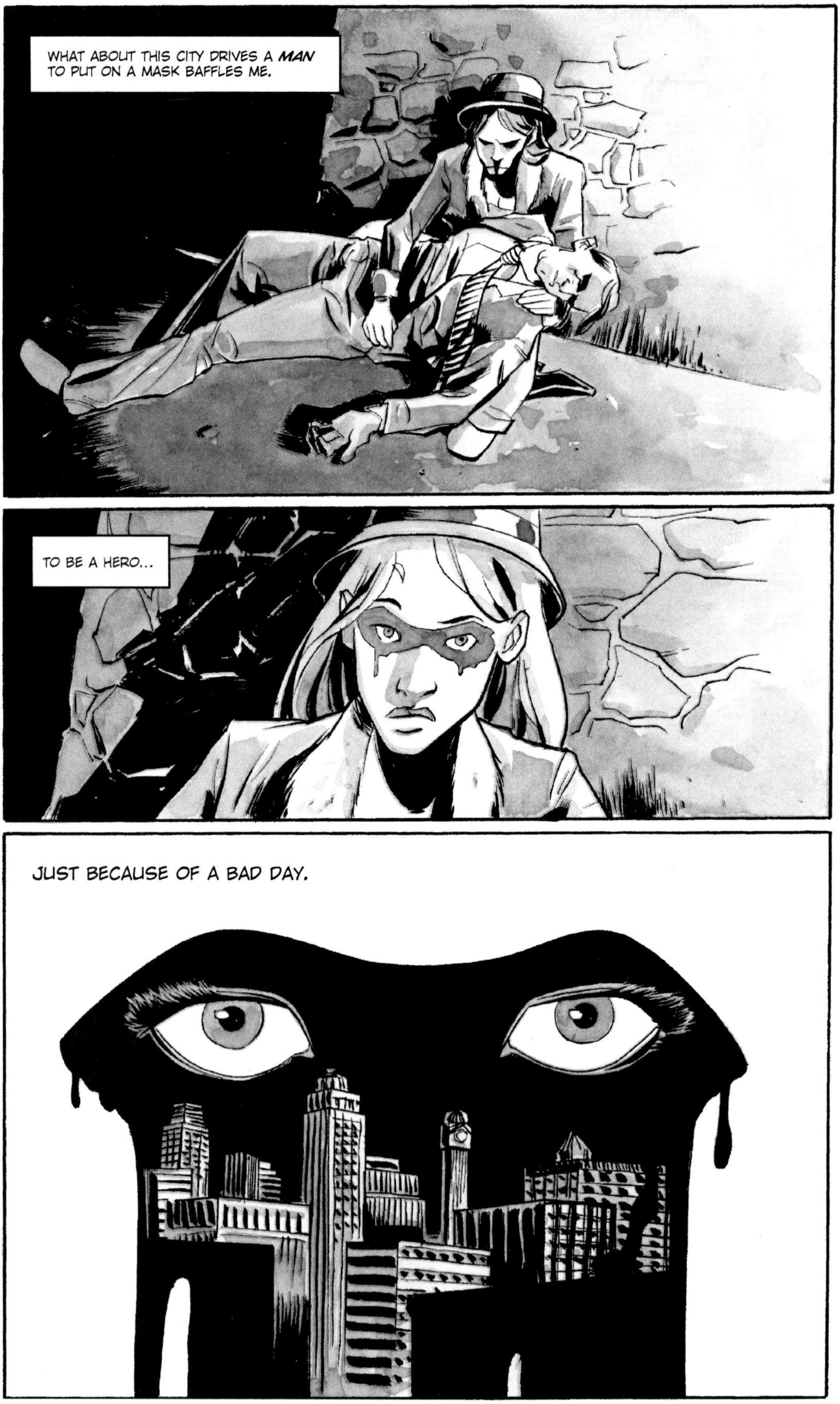
WHAT ABOUT THIS CITY DRIVES A ***MAN*** TO PUT ON A MASK BAFFLES ME.
TO BE A HERO...
JUST BECAUSE OF A BAD DAY.

ORIGINS JOSHUA WILLIAMSON- JUSTIN GREENWOOD

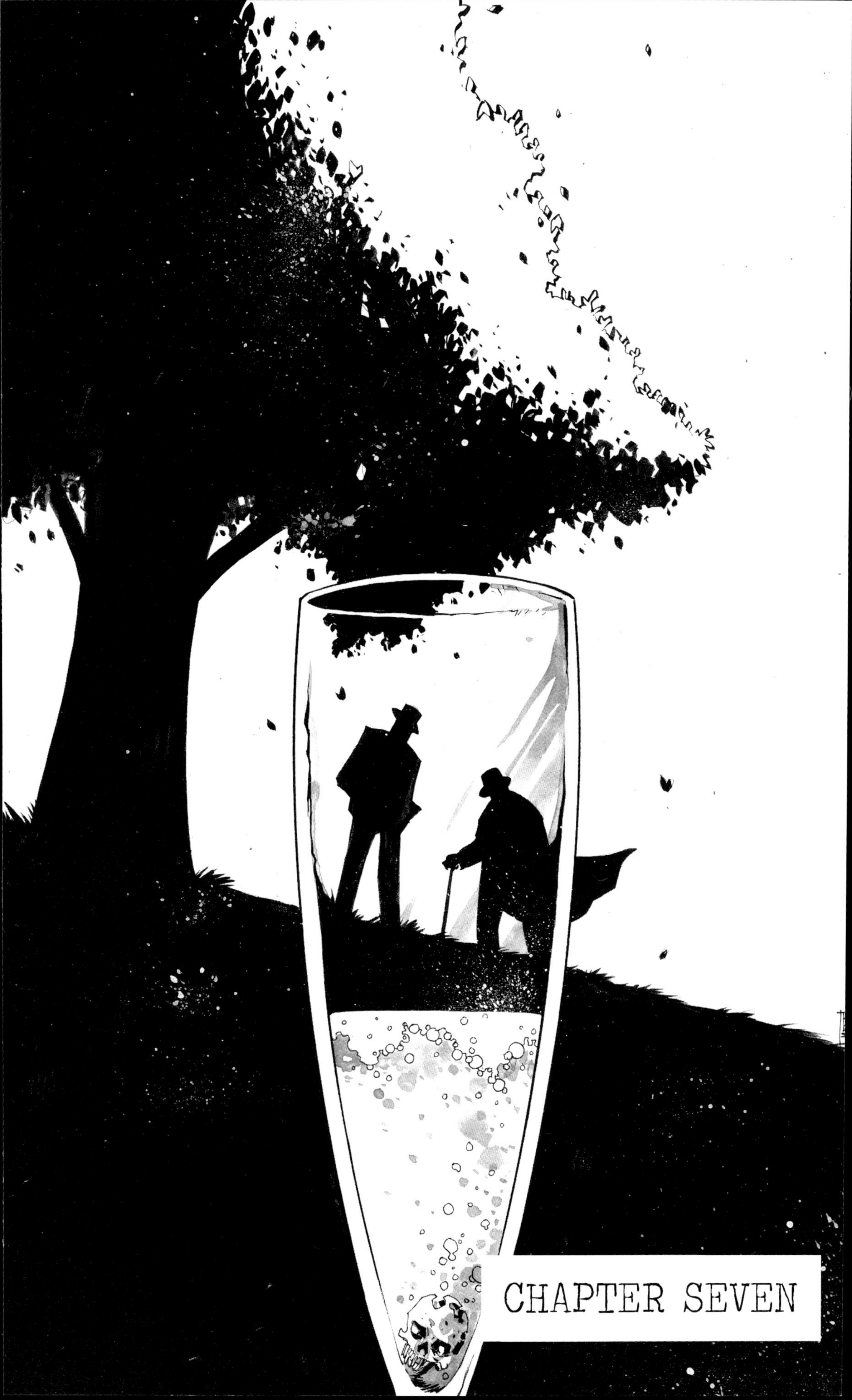

CHAPTER SEVEN

Chapter seven was one of the more unique and ambitious chapters of MASKS & MOBSTERS. Nailing down how it was going to be accomplished was complicated, but Mike got the look down quickly.

We were worried that readers wouldn't like the look of this story, but it was easily one of the book's most acclaimed.

Because of the nature of the story, Mike only did one set of thumbnails (left).

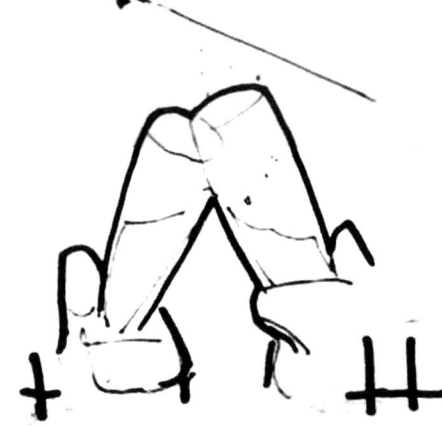

(Above and left) Mike's cover roughs for Chapter Seven.

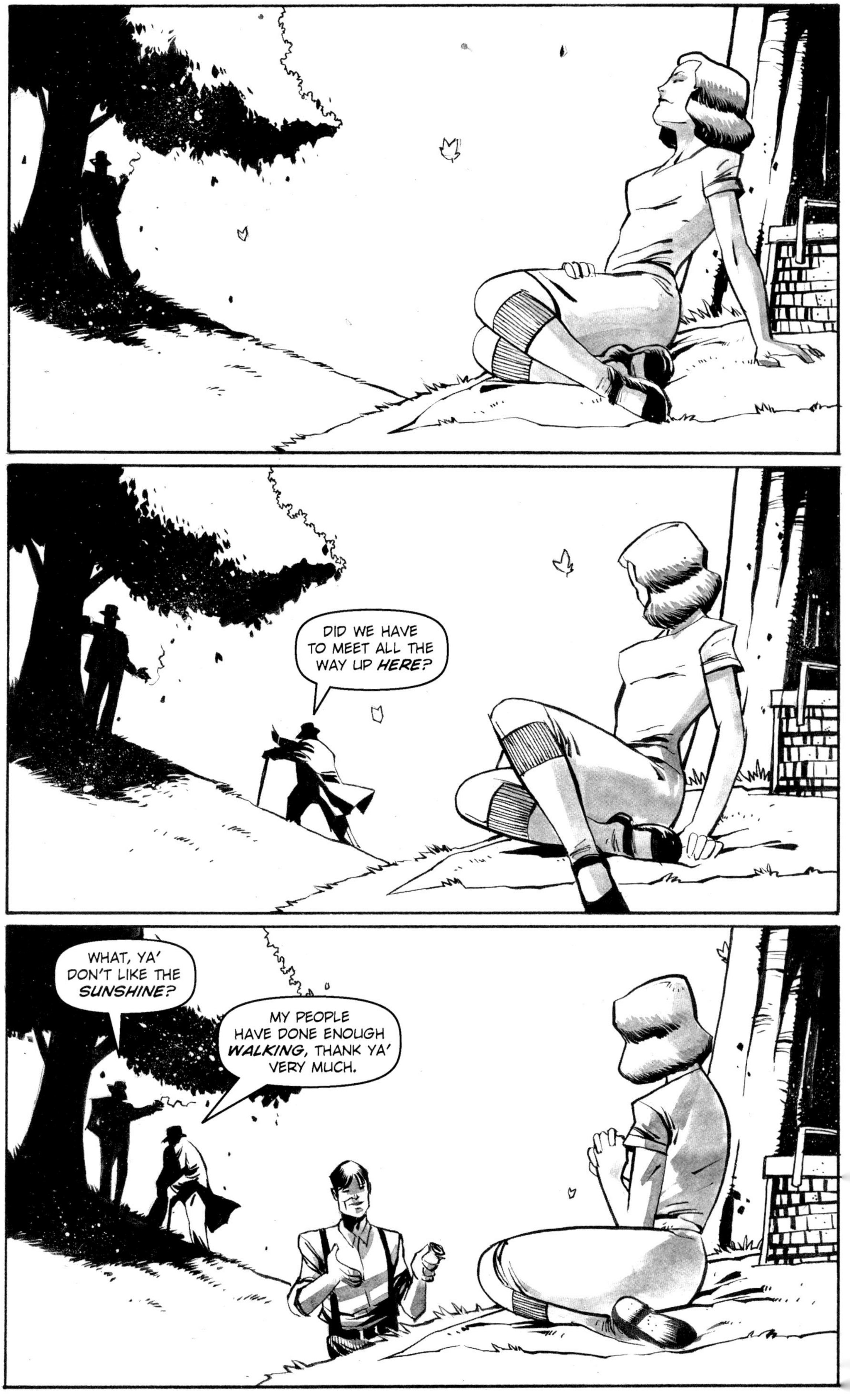
DID WE HAVE TO MEET ALL THE WAY UP HERE?
WHAT, YA' DON'T LIKE THE SUNSHINE?
MY PEOPLE HAVE DONE ENOUGH WALKING, THANK YA' VERY MUCH.

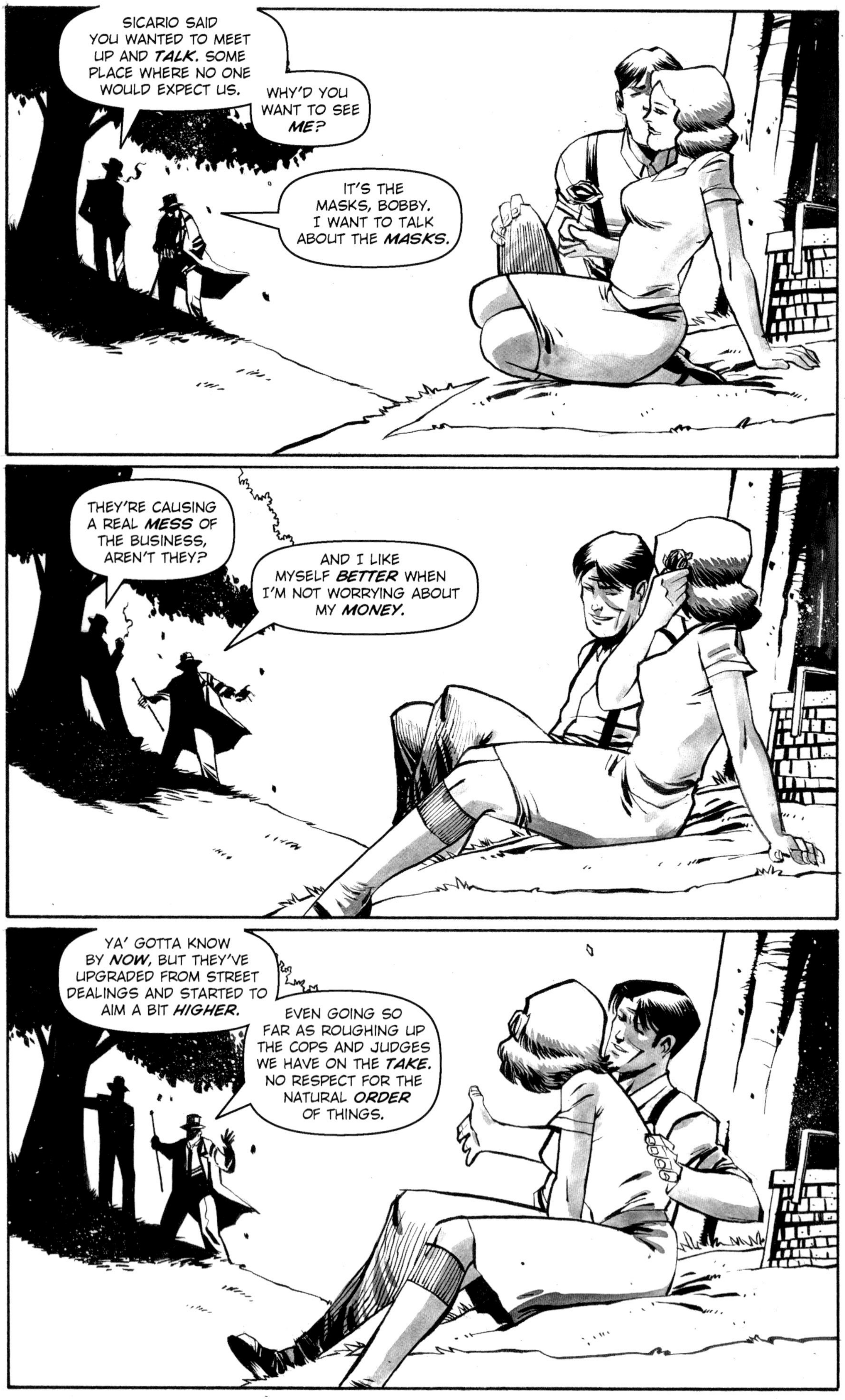
SICARIO SAID YOU WANTED TO MEET UP AND TALK. SOME PLACE WHERE NO ONE WOULD EXPECT US.
WHY'D YOU WANT TO SEE ME?
IT'S THE MASKS, BOBBY. I WANT TO TALK ABOUT THE MASKS.
THEY'RE CAUSING A REAL MESS OF THE BUSINESS, AREN'T THEY?
AND I LIKE MYSELF BETTER WHEN I'M NOT WORRYING ABOUT MY MONEY.
YA' GOTTA KNOW BY NOW, BUT THEY'VE UPGRADED FROM STREET DEALINGS AND STARTED TO AIM A BIT HIGHER.
EVEN GOING SO FAR AS ROUGHING UP THE COPS AND JUDGES WE HAVE ON THE TAKE. NO RESPECT FOR THE NATURAL ORDER OF THINGS.

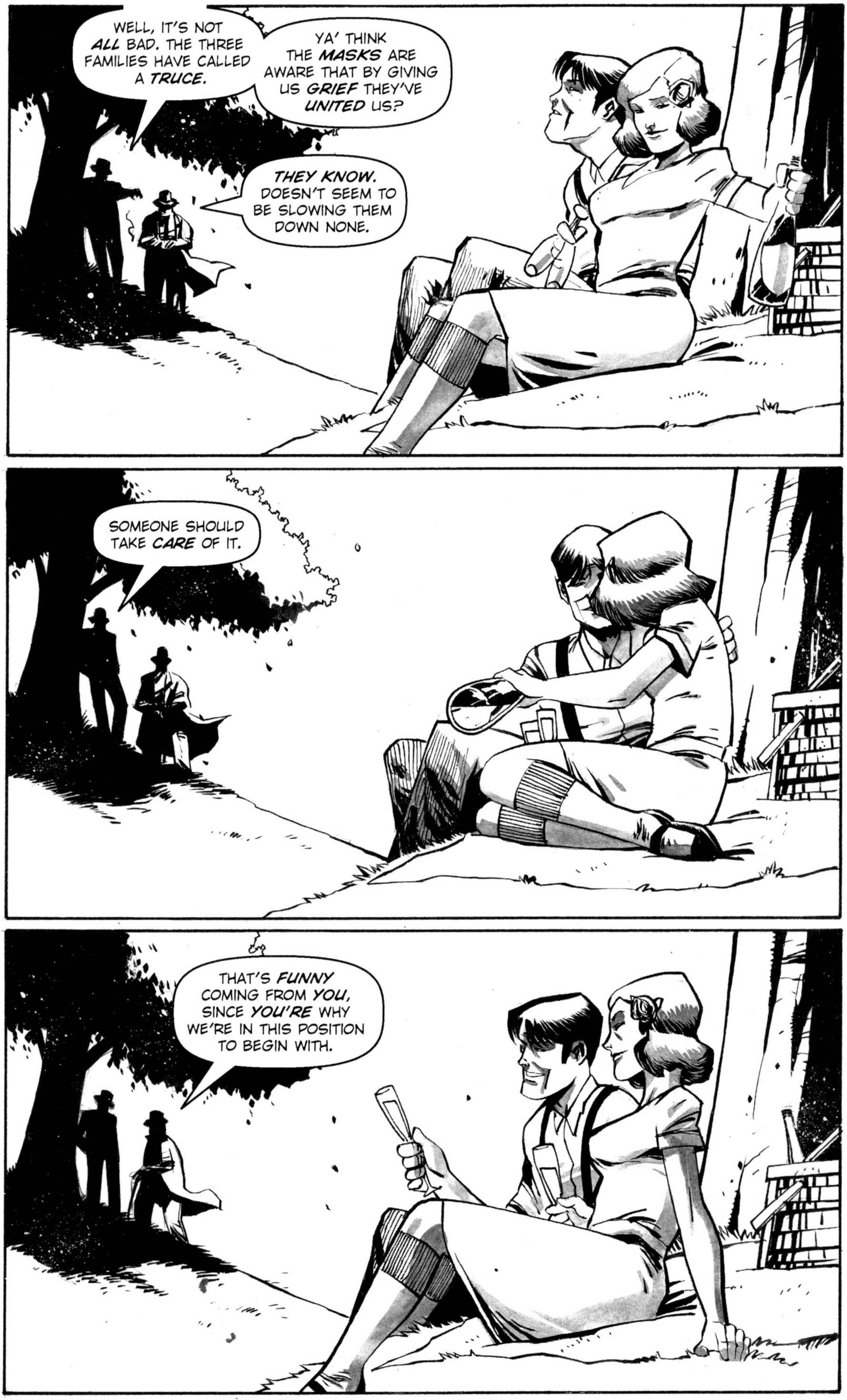

WELL, IT'S NOT ALL BAD. THE THREE FAMILIES HAVE CALLED A TRUCE.
YA' THINK THE MASKS ARE AWARE THAT BY GIVING US GRIEF THEY'VE UNITED US?
THEY KNOW. DOESN'T SEEM TO BE SLOWING THEM DOWN NONE.
SOMEONE SHOULD TAKE CARE OF IT.
THAT'S FUNNY COMING FROM YOU, SINCE YOU'RE WHY WE'RE IN THIS POSITION TO BEGIN WITH.

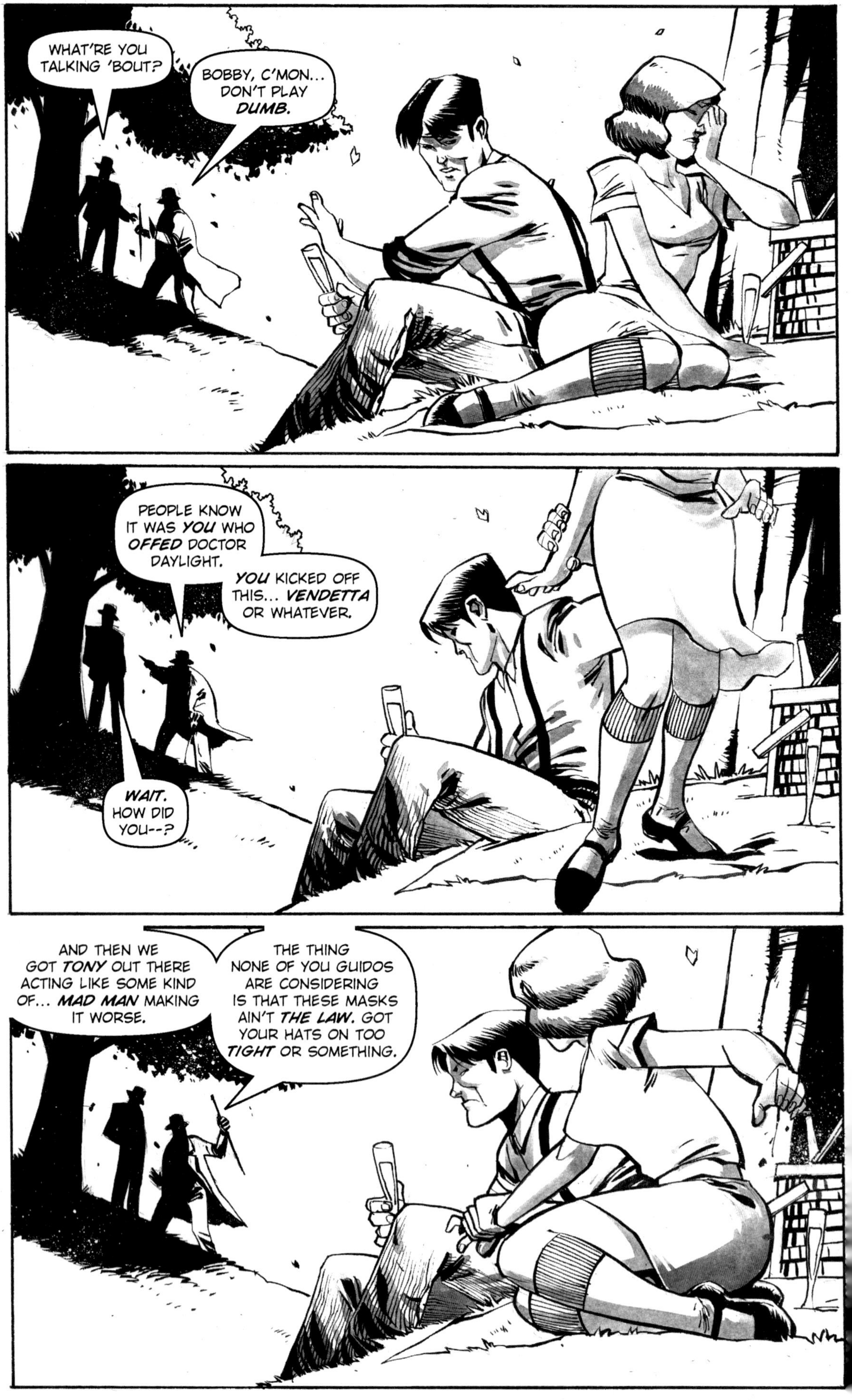
WHAT'RE YOU TALKING 'BOUT?
BOBBY, C'MON... DON'T PLAY DUMB.
PEOPLE KNOW IT WAS YOU WHO OFFED DOCTOR DAYLIGHT.
YOU KICKED OFF THIS... VENDETTA OR WHATEVER.
WAIT. HOW DID YOU--?
AND THEN WE GOT TONY OUT THERE ACTING LIKE SOME KIND OF... MAD MAN MAKING IT WORSE.
THE THING NONE OF YOU GUIDOS ARE CONSIDERING IS THAT THESE MASKS AIN'T THE LAW. GOT YOUR HATS ON TOO TIGHT OR SOMETHING.

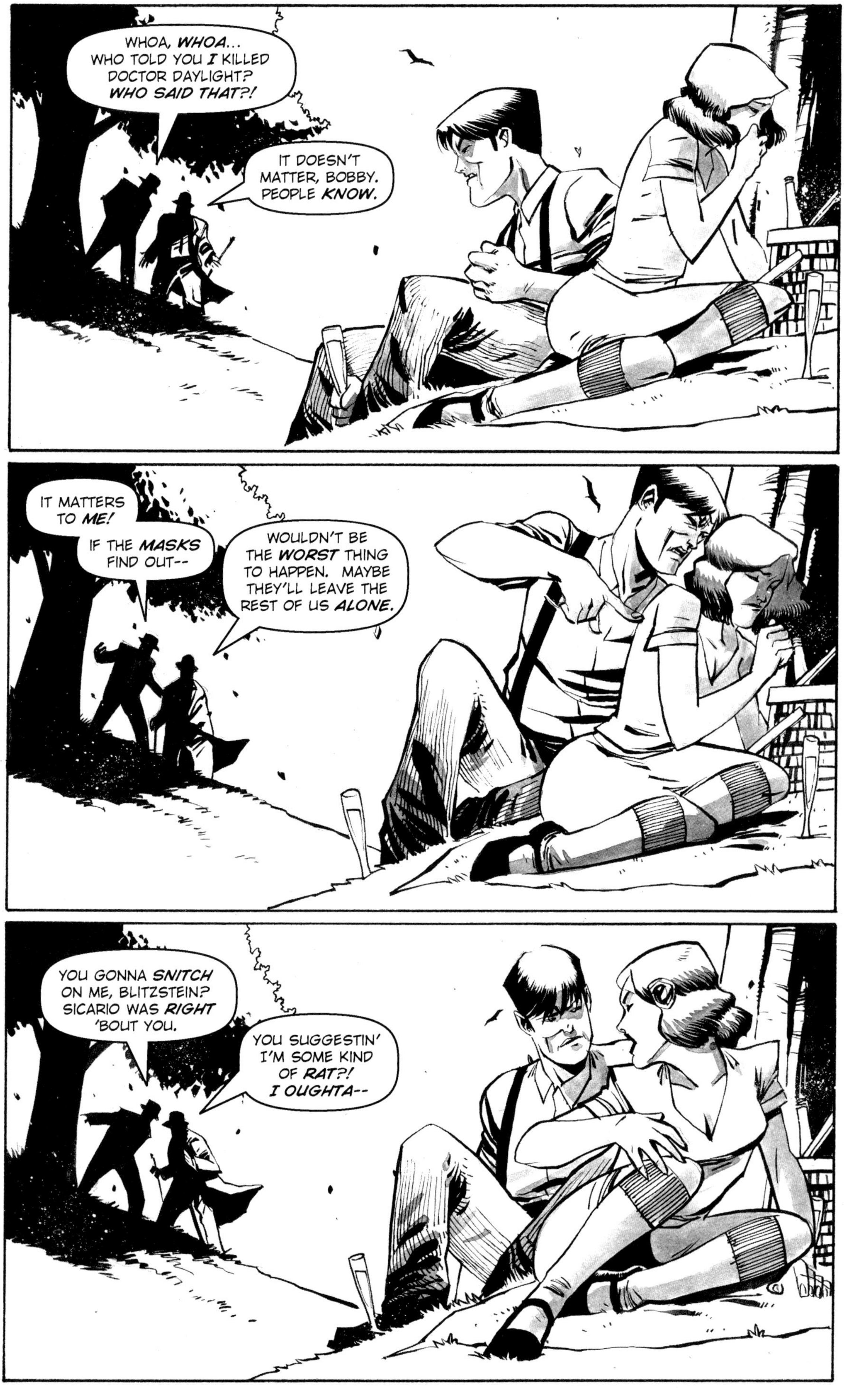
WHOA, WHOA... WHO TOLD YOU I KILLED DOCTOR DAYLIGHT? WHO SAID THAT?!
IT DOESN'T MATTER, BOBBY. PEOPLE KNOW.
IT MATTERS TO ME!
IF THE MASKS FIND OUT--
WOULDN'T BE THE WORST THING TO HAPPEN. MAYBE THEY'LL LEAVE THE REST OF US ALONE.
YOU GONNA SNITCH ON ME, BLITZSTEIN? SICARIO WAS RIGHT 'BOUT YOU.
YOU SUGGESTIN' I'M SOME KIND OF RAT?! I OUGHTA--

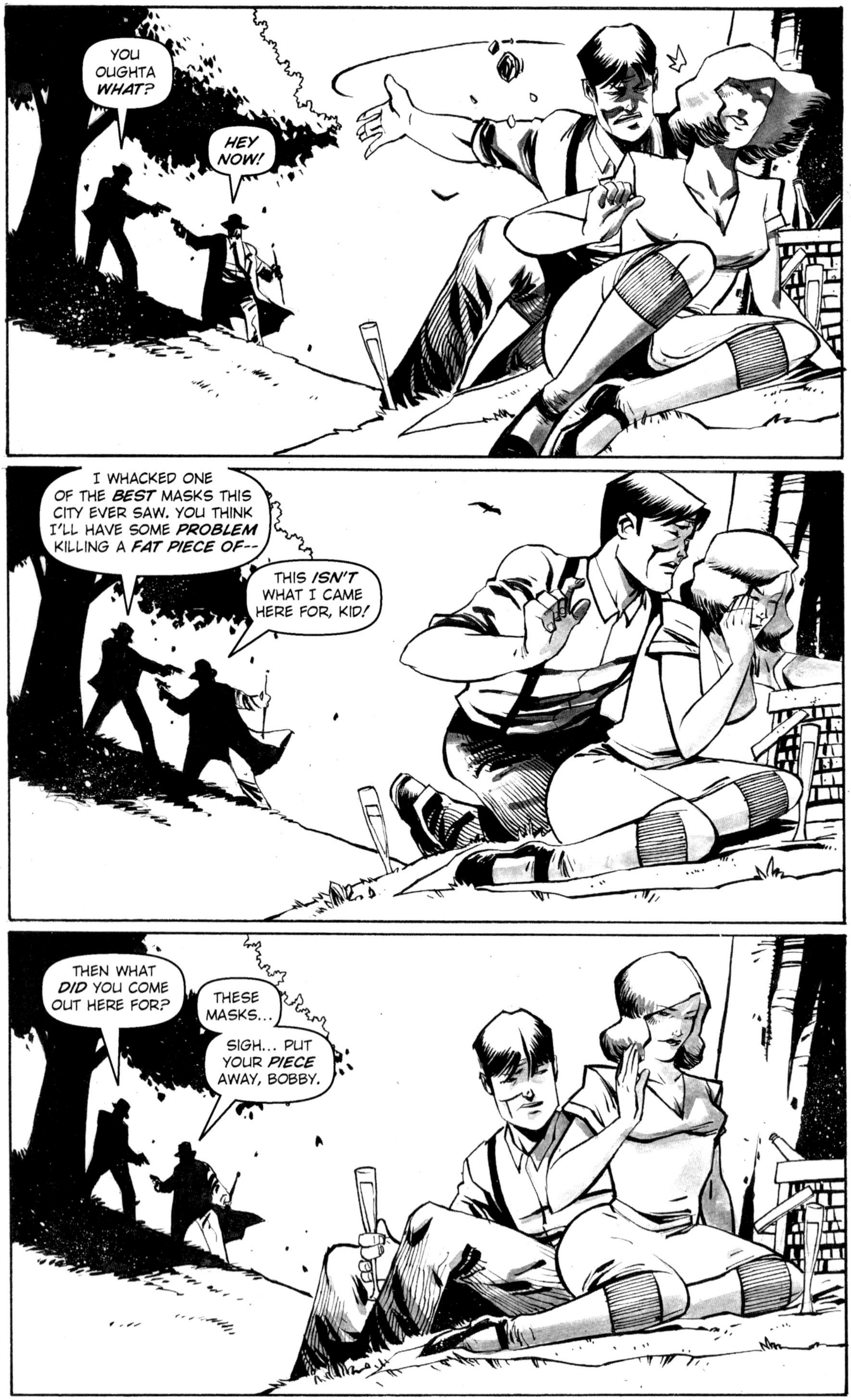
YOU OUGHTA WHAT?
HEY NOW!
I WHACKED ONE OF THE BEST MASKS THIS CITY EVER SAW. YOU THINK I'LL HAVE SOME PROBLEM KILLING A FAT PIECE OF--
THIS ISN'T WHAT I CAME HERE FOR, KID!
THEN WHAT DID YOU COME OUT HERE FOR?
THESE MASKS...
SIGH... PUT YOUR PIECE AWAY, BOBBY.

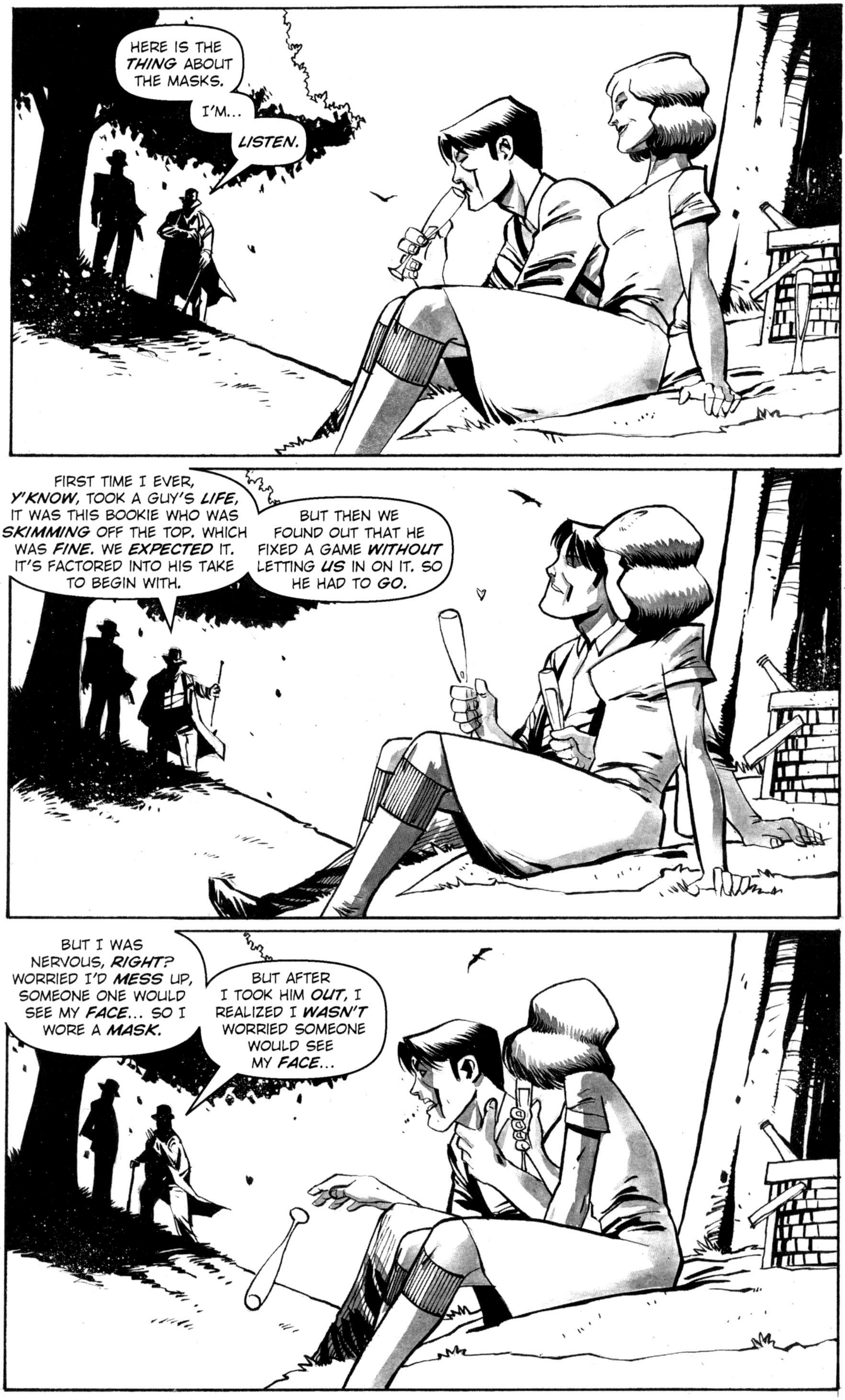
HERE IS THE THING ABOUT THE MASKS.
I'M...
LISTEN.
FIRST TIME I EVER, Y'KNOW, TOOK A GUY'S LIFE, IT WAS THIS BOOKIE WHO WAS SKIMMING OFF THE TOP. WHICH WAS FINE. WE EXPECTED IT. IT'S FACTORED INTO HIS TAKE TO BEGIN WITH.
BUT THEN WE FOUND OUT THAT HE FIXED A GAME WITHOUT LETTING US IN ON IT. SO HE HAD TO GO.
BUT I WAS NERVOUS, RIGHT? WORRIED I'D MESS UP, SOMEONE ONE WOULD SEE MY FACE... SO I WORE A MASK.
BUT AFTER I TOOK HIM OUT, I REALIZED I WASN'T WORRIED SOMEONE WOULD SEE MY FACE...

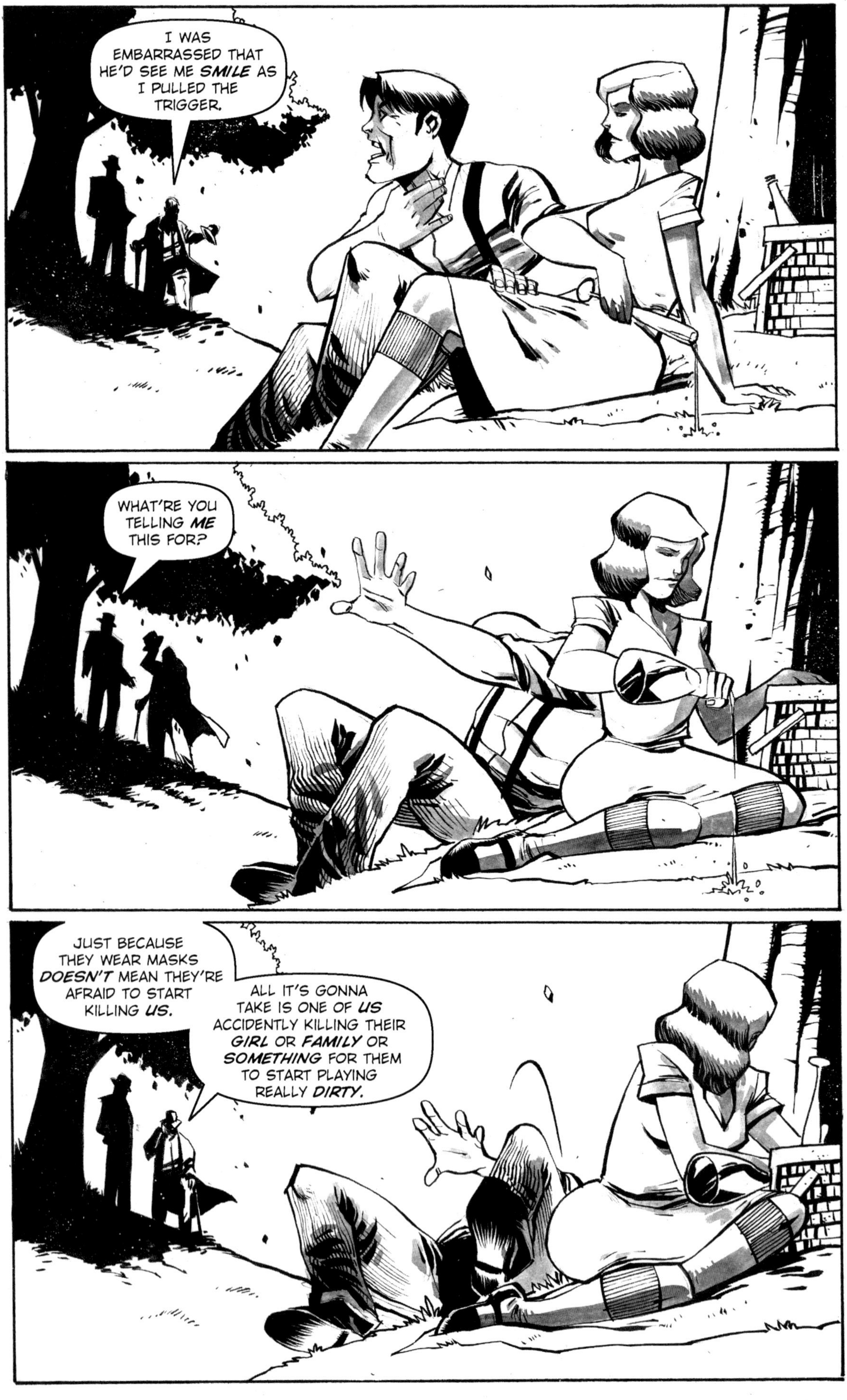
I WAS EMBARRASSED THAT HE'D SEE ME ***SMILE*** AS I PULLED THE TRIGGER.
WHAT'RE YOU TELLING ***ME*** THIS FOR?
JUST BECAUSE THEY WEAR MASKS ***DOESN'T*** MEAN THEY'RE AFRAID TO START KILLING ***US.***
ALL IT'S GONNA TAKE IS ONE OF ***US*** ACCIDENTLY KILLING THEIR ***GIRL*** OR ***FAMILY*** OR ***SOMETHING*** FOR THEM TO START PLAYING REALLY ***DIRTY.***

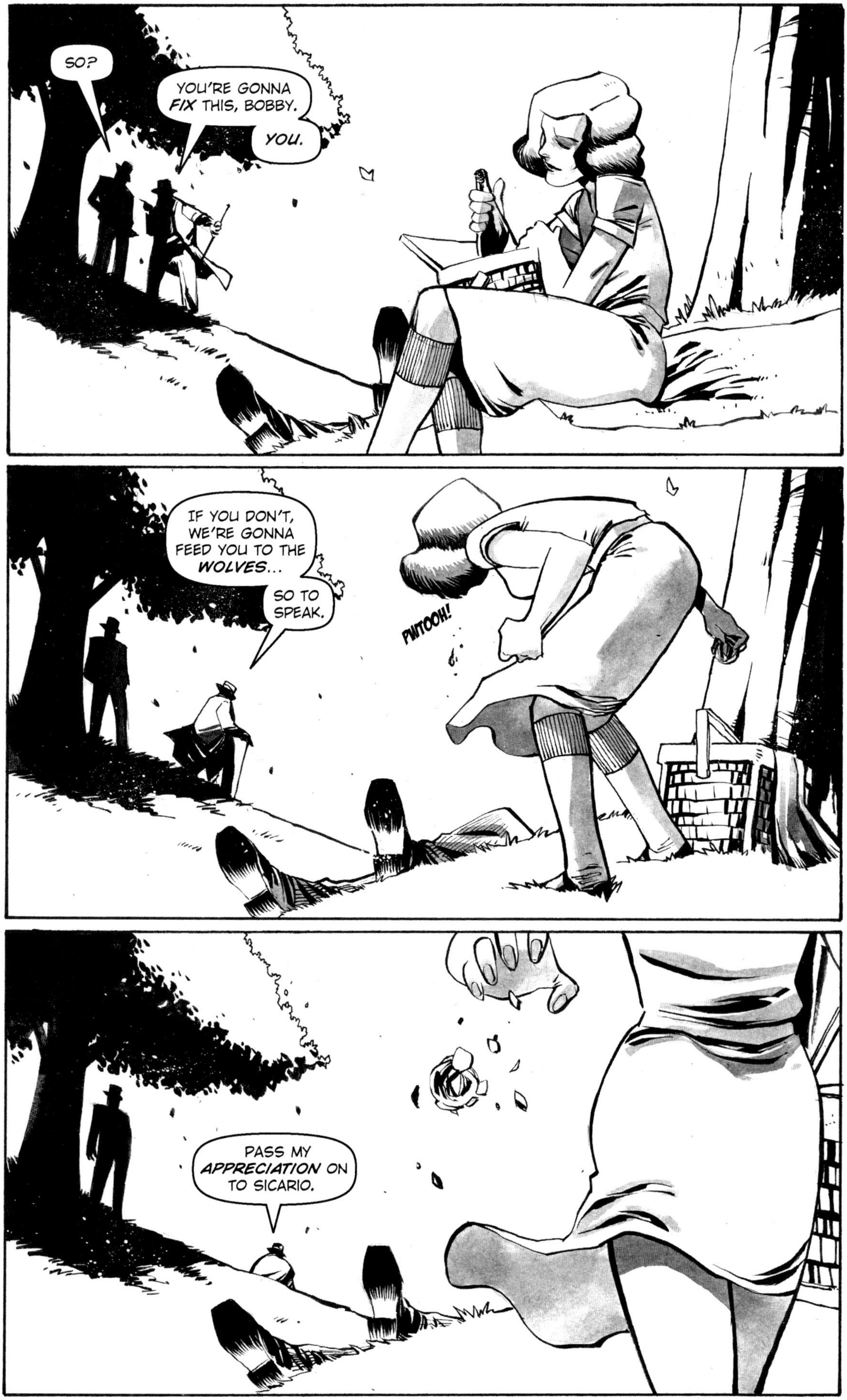
SO?
YOU'RE GONNA FIX THIS, BOBBY.
YOU.
IF YOU DON'T, WE'RE GONNA FEED YOU TO THE WOLVES...
SO TO SPEAK.
PWTOOH!
PASS MY APPRECIATION ON TO SICARIO.

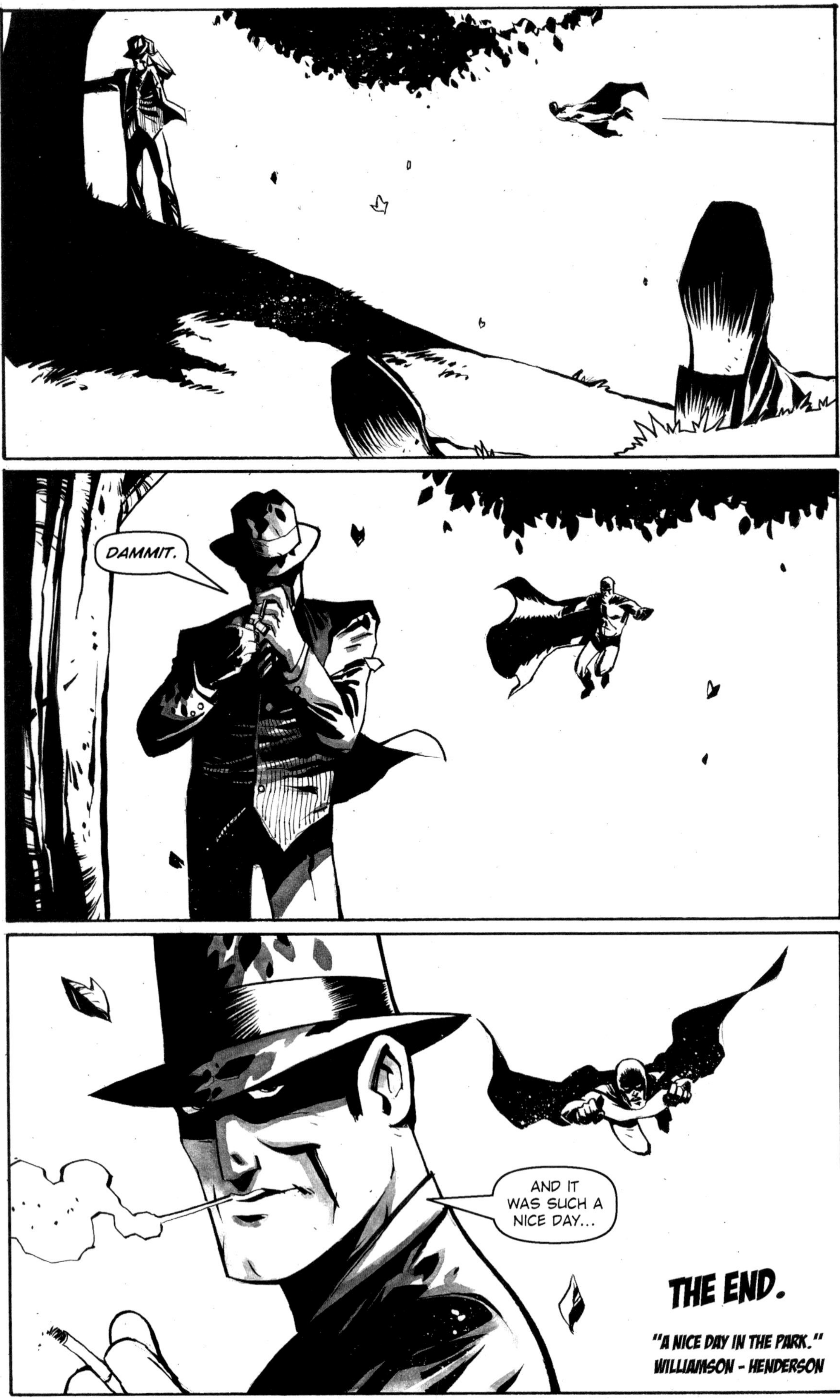
DAMMIT.
AND IT WAS SUCH A NICE DAY...
THE END.
"A NICE DAY IN THE PARK."
WILLIAMSON - HENDERSON

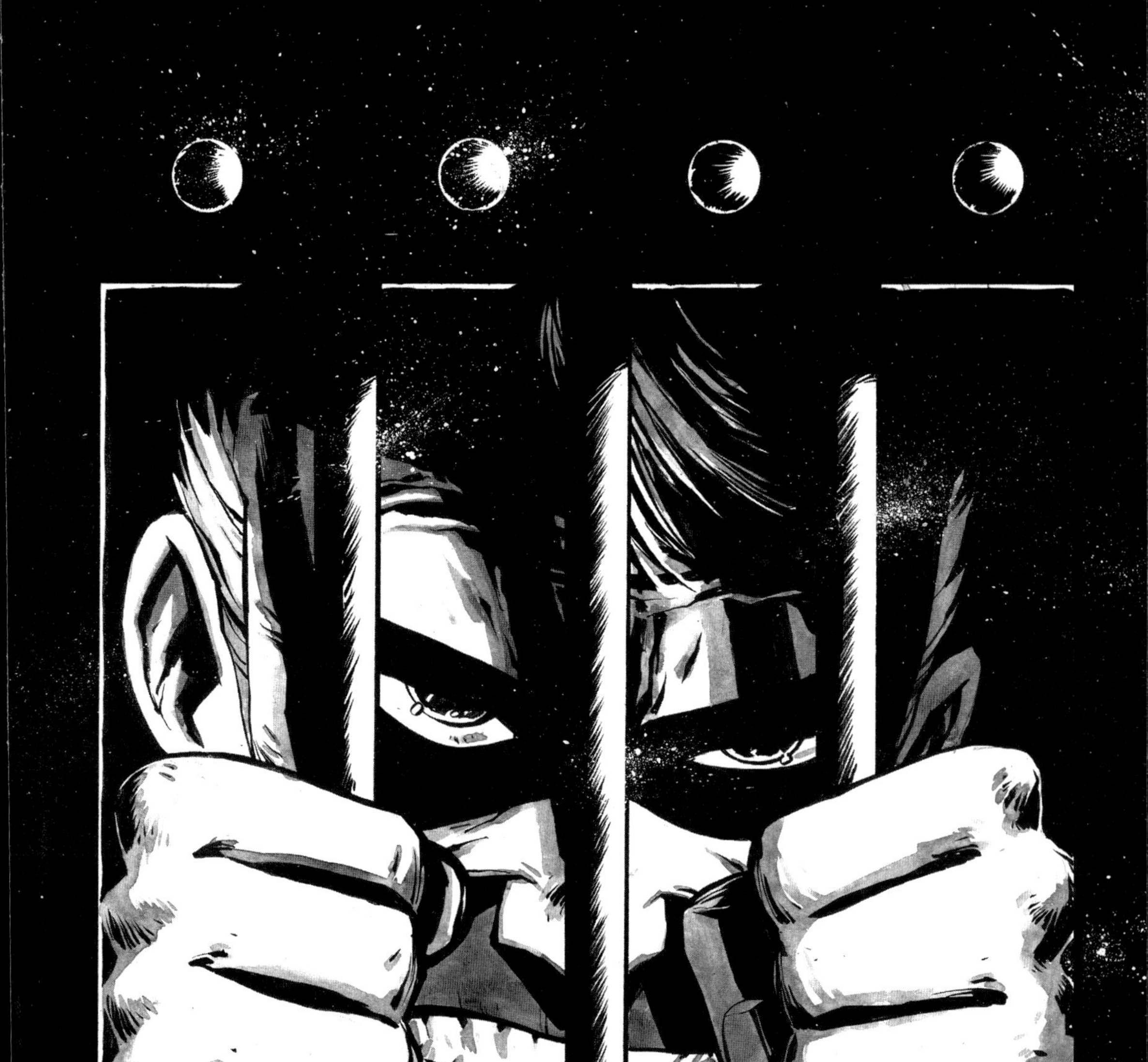

CHAPTER EIGHT

Ryan Cody's character designs. (top)
Mike's cover roughs for Chapter Eight. (below)

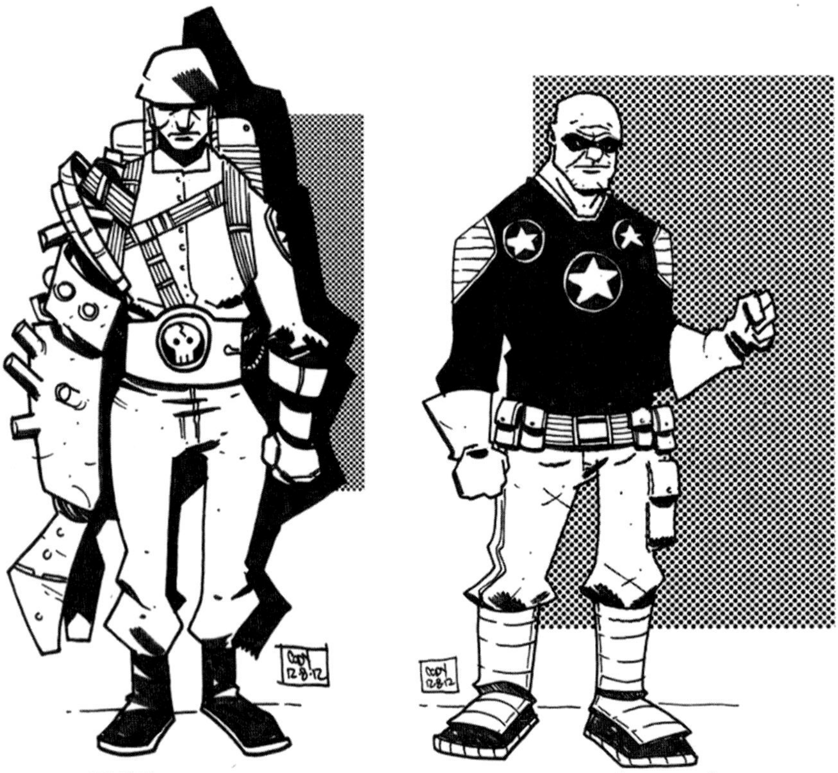

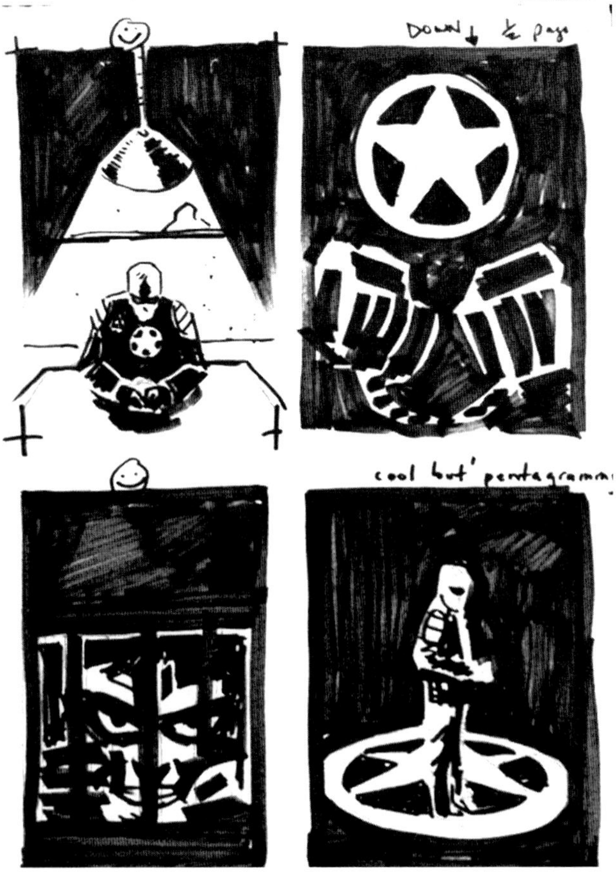
DOWN ↓ ½ page
cool but pentagram

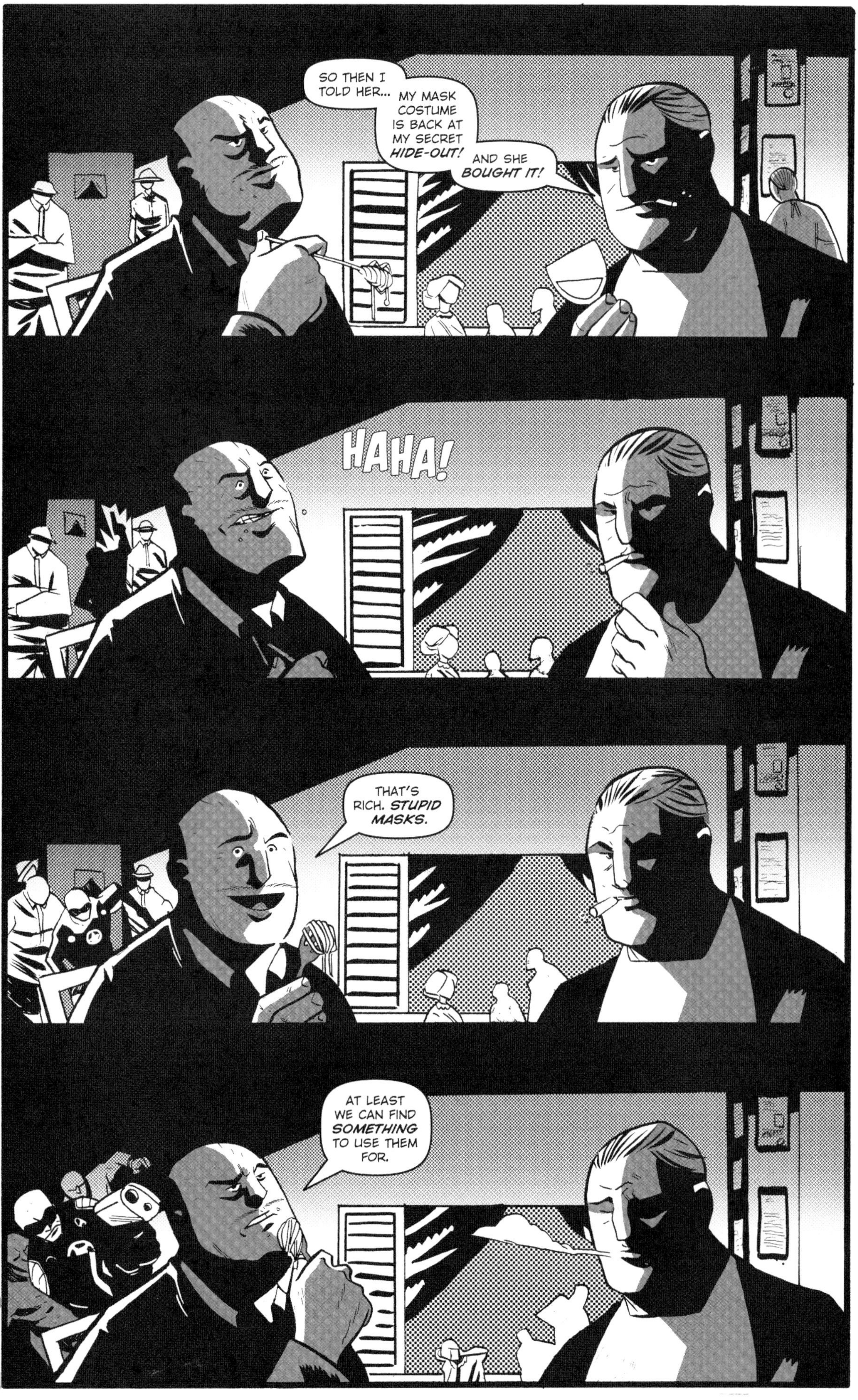
SO THEN I TOLD HER...
MY MASK COSTUME IS BACK AT MY SECRET HIDE-OUT!
AND SHE BOUGHT IT!
HAHA!
THAT'S RICH. STUPID MASKS.
AT LEAST WE CAN FIND SOMETHING TO USE THEM FOR.

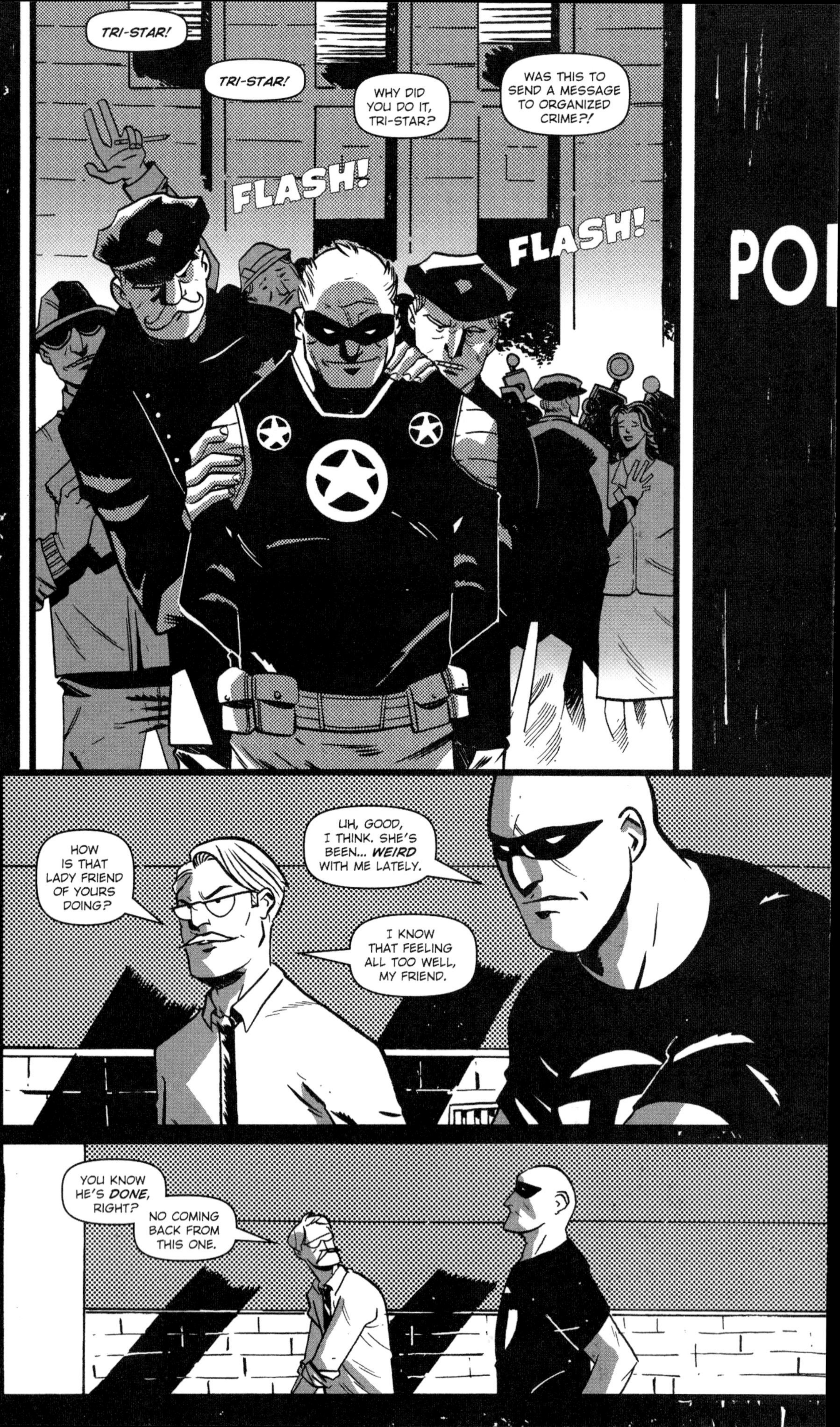
TRI-STAR!
TRI-STAR!
WHY DID YOU DO IT, TRI-STAR?
WAS THIS TO SEND A MESSAGE TO ORGANIZED CRIME?!
FLASH!
FLASH!
POI
HOW IS THAT LADY FRIEND OF YOURS DOING?
UH, GOOD, I THINK. SHE'S BEEN... WEIRD WITH ME LATELY.
I KNOW THAT FEELING ALL TOO WELL, MY FRIEND.
YOU KNOW HE'S DONE, RIGHT?
NO COMING BACK FROM THIS ONE.

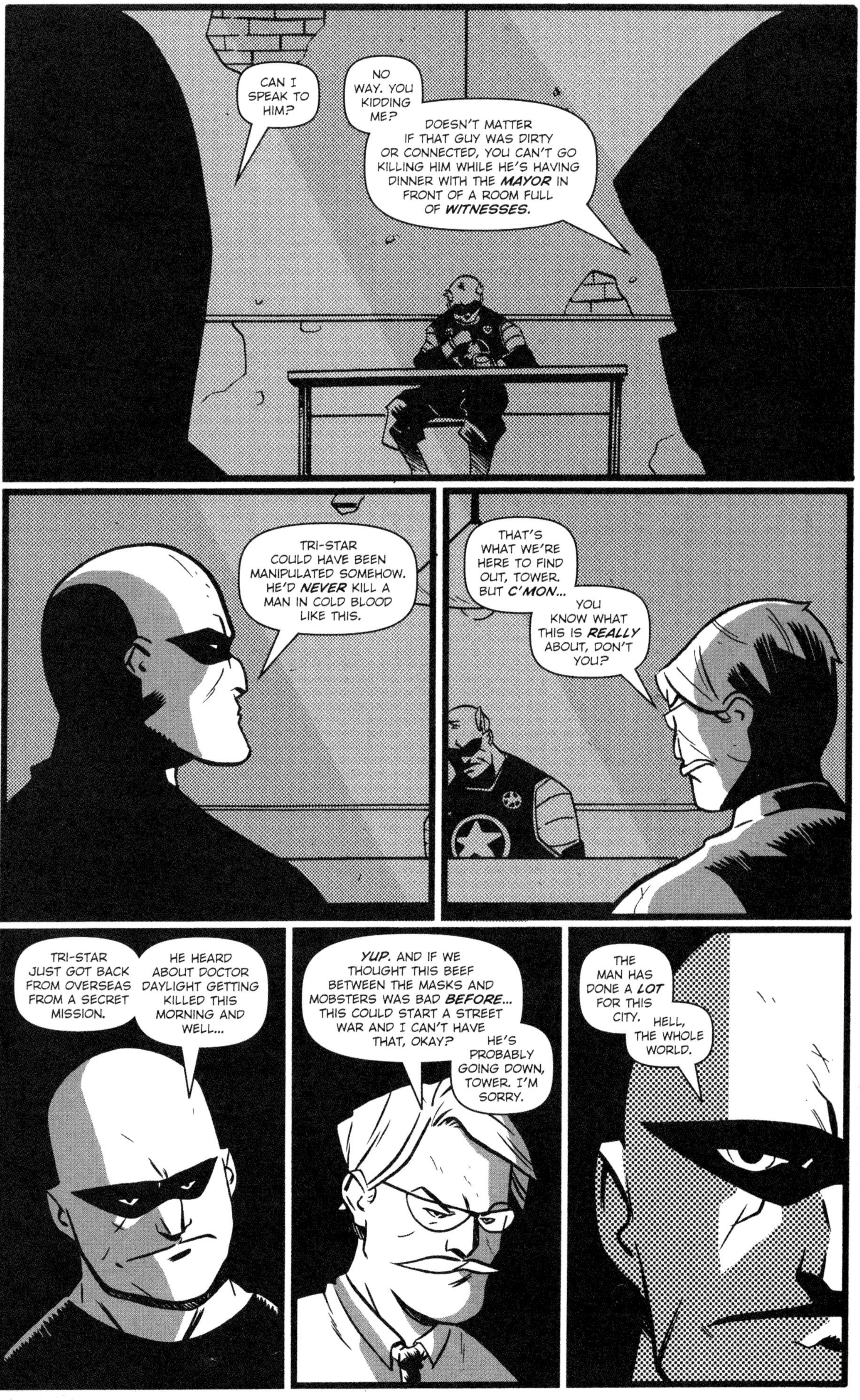
CAN I SPEAK TO HIM?
NO WAY. YOU KIDDING ME?
DOESN'T MATTER IF THAT GUY WAS DIRTY OR CONNECTED, YOU CAN'T GO KILLING HIM WHILE HE'S HAVING DINNER WITH THE MAYOR IN FRONT OF A ROOM FULL OF WITNESSES.
TRI-STAR COULD HAVE BEEN MANIPULATED SOMEHOW. HE'D NEVER KILL A MAN IN COLD BLOOD LIKE THIS.
THAT'S WHAT WE'RE HERE TO FIND OUT, TOWER. BUT C'MON...
YOU KNOW WHAT THIS IS REALLY ABOUT, DON'T YOU?
TRI-STAR JUST GOT BACK FROM OVERSEAS FROM A SECRET MISSION.
HE HEARD ABOUT DOCTOR DAYLIGHT GETTING KILLED THIS MORNING AND WELL...
YUP. AND IF WE THOUGHT THIS BEEF BETWEEN THE MASKS AND MOBSTERS WAS BAD BEFORE... THIS COULD START A STREET WAR AND I CAN'T HAVE THAT, OKAY?
HE'S PROBABLY GOING DOWN, TOWER. I'M SORRY.
THE MAN HAS DONE A LOT FOR THIS CITY.
HELL, THE WHOLE WORLD.

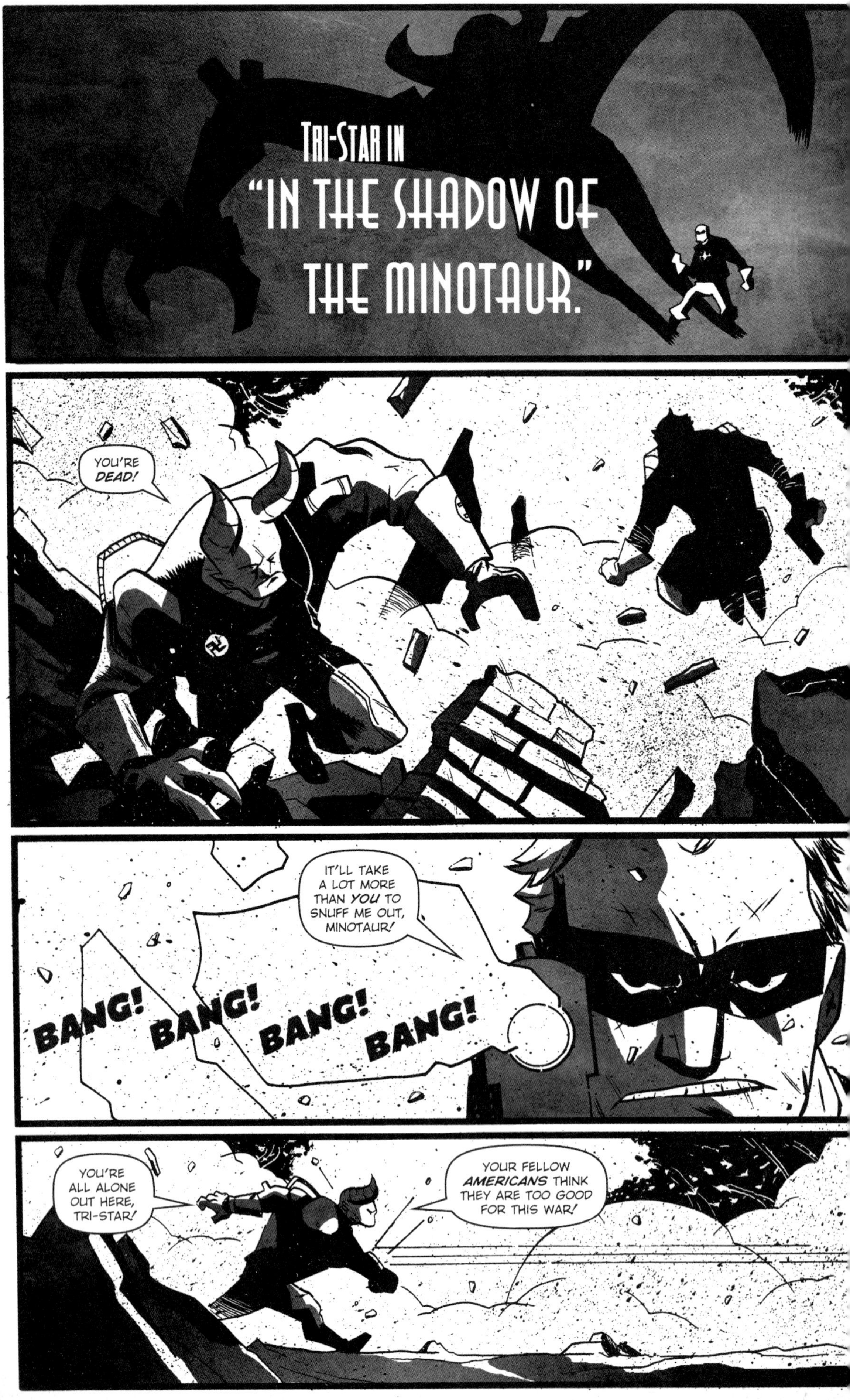

TRI-STAR IN
"IN THE SHADOW OF THE MINOTAUR."
YOU'RE DEAD!
IT'LL TAKE A LOT MORE THAN YOU TO SNUFF ME OUT, MINOTAUR!
BANG! BANG! BANG! BANG!
YOU'RE ALL ALONE OUT HERE, TRI-STAR!
YOUR FELLOW AMERICANS THINK THEY ARE TOO GOOD FOR THIS WAR!

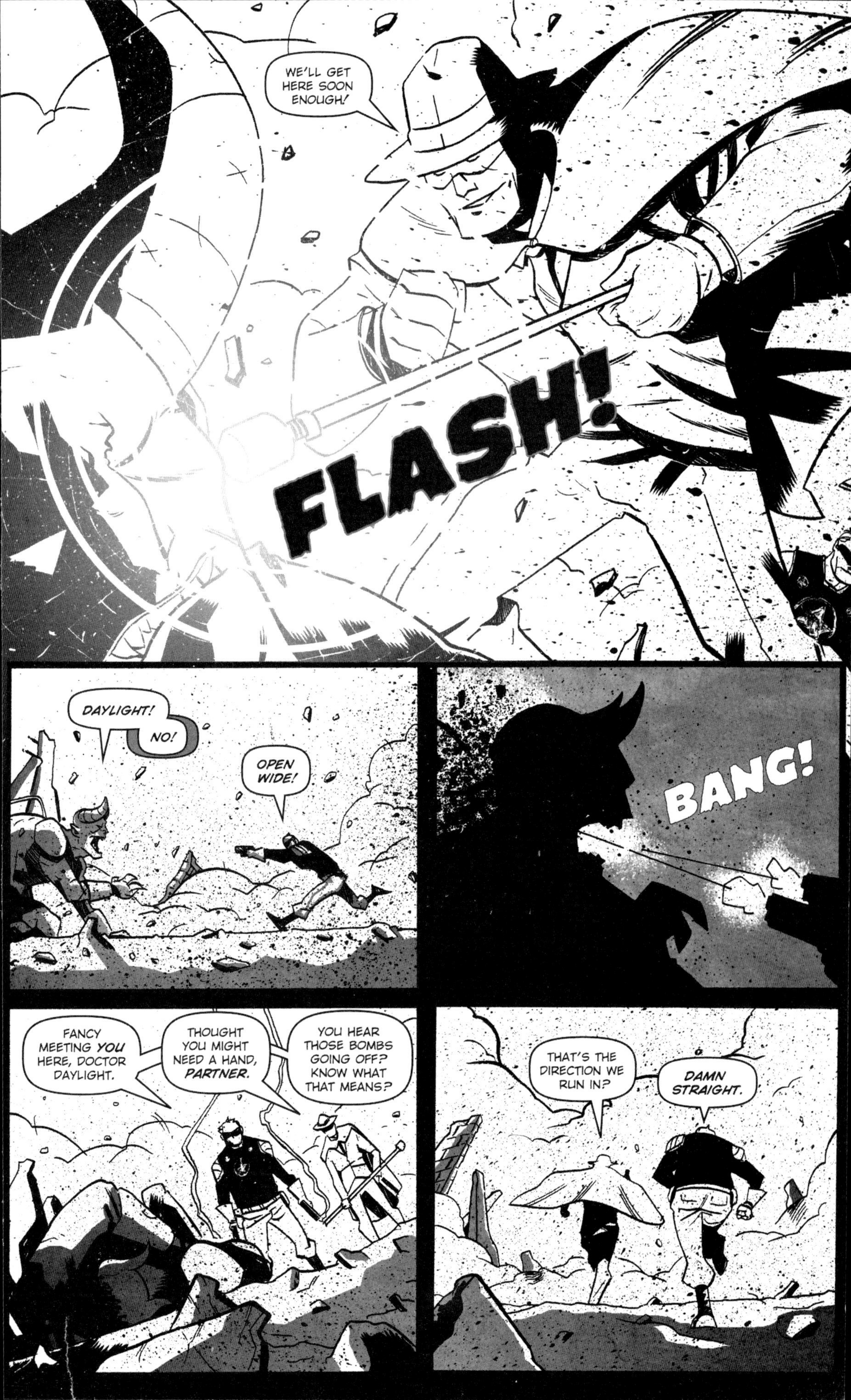
WE'LL GET HERE SOON ENOUGH!
FLASH!
DAYLIGHT!
NO!
OPEN WIDE!
BANG!
FANCY MEETING YOU HERE, DOCTOR DAYLIGHT.
THOUGHT YOU MIGHT NEED A HAND, PARTNER.
YOU HEAR THOSE BOMBS GOING OFF? KNOW WHAT THAT MEANS?
THAT'S THE DIRECTION WE RUN IN?
DAMN STRAIGHT.

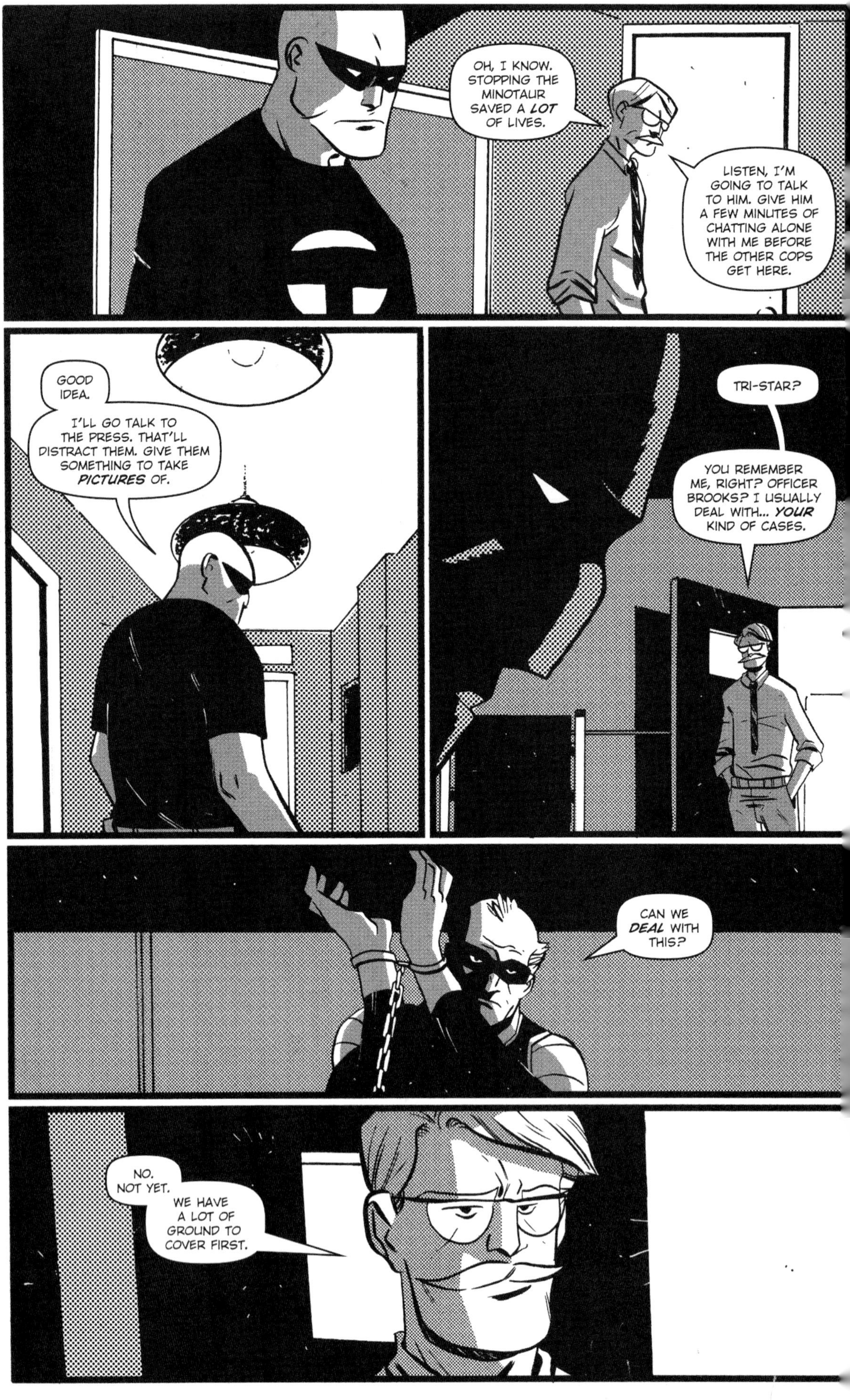
OH, I KNOW. STOPPING THE MINOTAUR SAVED A LOT OF LIVES.
LISTEN, I'M GOING TO TALK TO HIM. GIVE HIM A FEW MINUTES OF CHATTING ALONE WITH ME BEFORE THE OTHER COPS GET HERE.
GOOD IDEA.
I'LL GO TALK TO THE PRESS. THAT'LL DISTRACT THEM. GIVE THEM SOMETHING TO TAKE PICTURES OF.
TRI-STAR?
YOU REMEMBER ME, RIGHT? OFFICER BROOKS? I USUALLY DEAL WITH... YOUR KIND OF CASES.
CAN WE DEAL WITH THIS?
NO. NOT YET.
WE HAVE A LOT OF GROUND TO COVER FIRST.

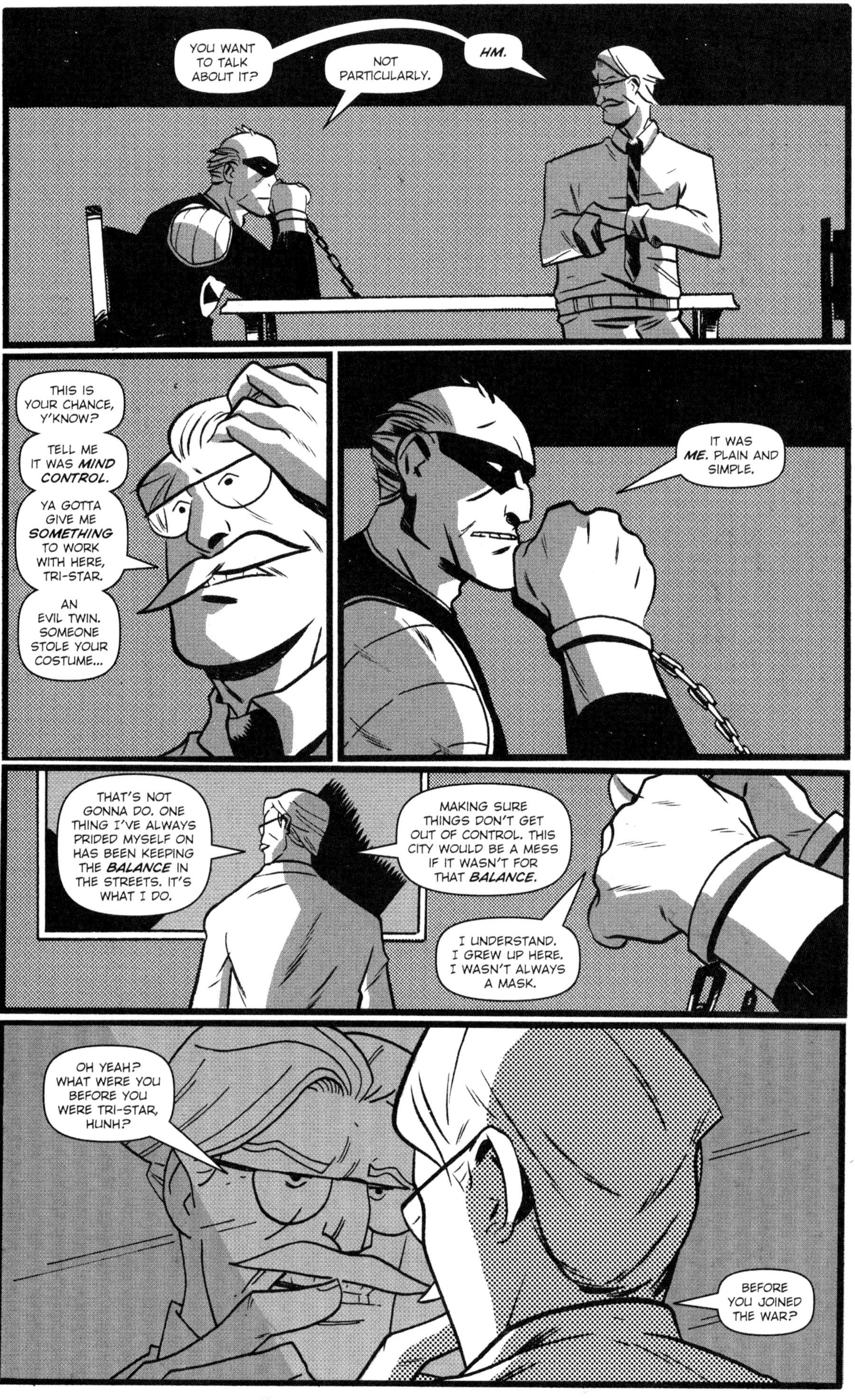
YOU WANT TO TALK ABOUT IT?
NOT PARTICULARLY.
HM.
THIS IS YOUR CHANCE, Y'KNOW?
TELL ME IT WAS MIND CONTROL.
YA GOTTA GIVE ME SOMETHING TO WORK WITH HERE, TRI-STAR.
AN EVIL TWIN. SOMEONE STOLE YOUR COSTUME...
IT WAS ME. PLAIN AND SIMPLE.
THAT'S NOT GONNA DO. ONE THING I'VE ALWAYS PRIDED MYSELF ON HAS BEEN KEEPING THE BALANCE IN THE STREETS. IT'S WHAT I DO.
MAKING SURE THINGS DON'T GET OUT OF CONTROL. THIS CITY WOULD BE A MESS IF IT WASN'T FOR THAT BALANCE.
I UNDERSTAND. I GREW UP HERE. I WASN'T ALWAYS A MASK.
OH YEAH? WHAT WERE YOU BEFORE YOU WERE TRI-STAR, HUNH?
BEFORE YOU JOINED THE WAR?

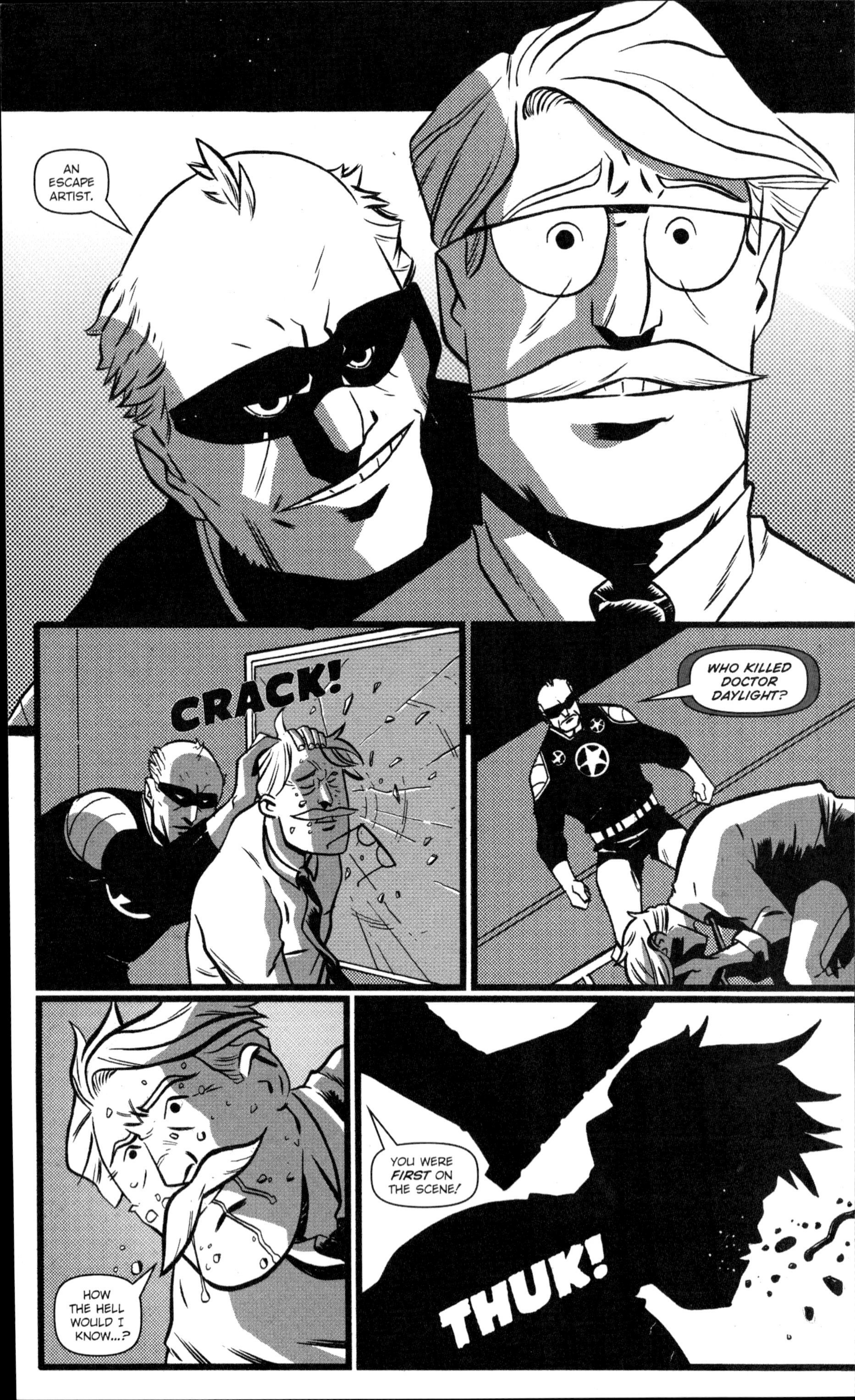
AN ESCAPE ARTIST.
CRACK!
WHO KILLED DOCTOR DAYLIGHT?
HOW THE HELL WOULD I KNOW...?
YOU WERE *FIRST* ON THE SCENE!
THUK!

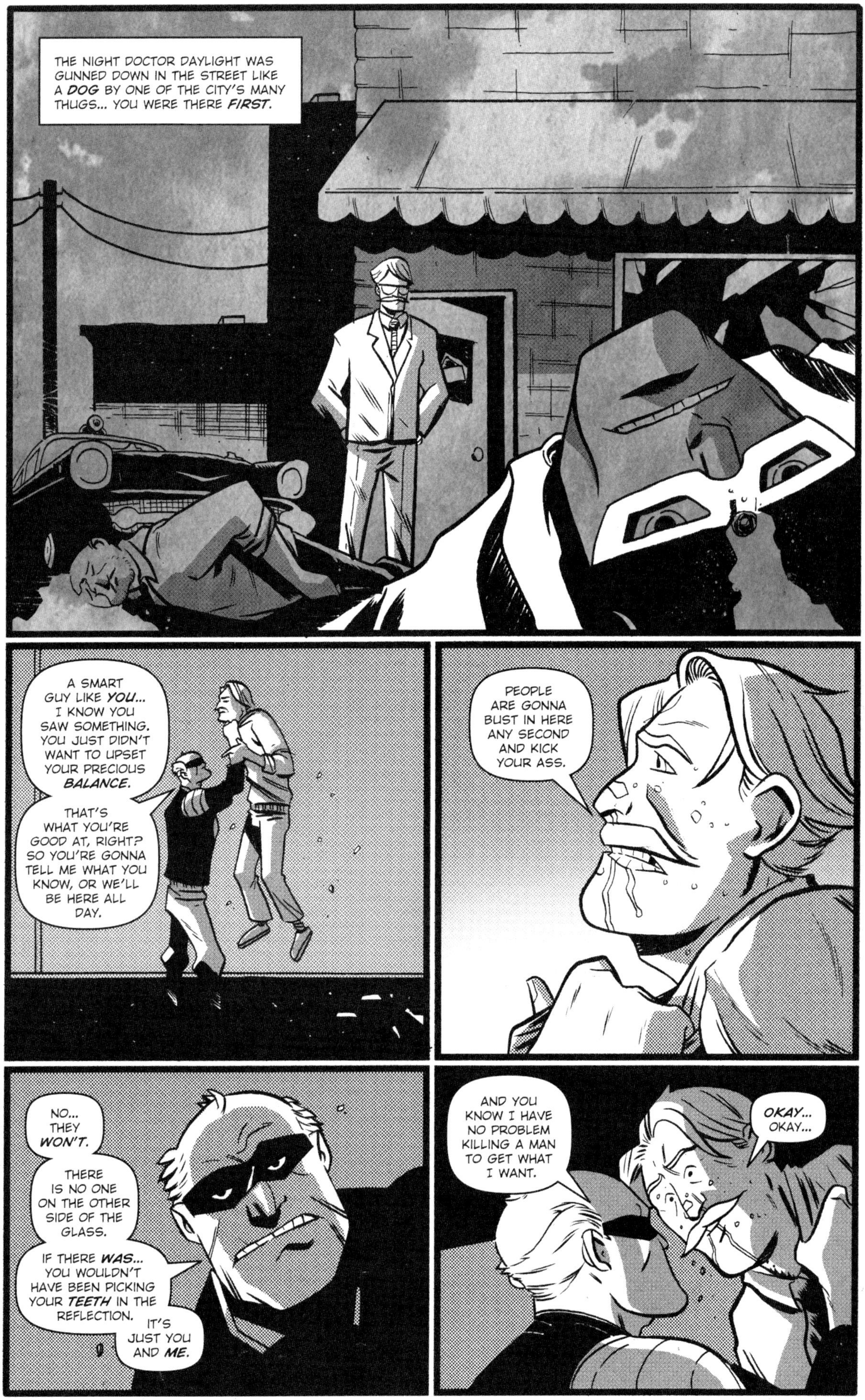
THE NIGHT DOCTOR DAYLIGHT WAS GUNNED DOWN IN THE STREET LIKE A *DOG* BY ONE OF THE CITY'S MANY THUGS... YOU WERE THERE *FIRST*.
A SMART GUY LIKE *YOU*... I KNOW YOU SAW SOMETHING. YOU JUST DIDN'T WANT TO UPSET YOUR PRECIOUS *BALANCE*.
THAT'S WHAT YOU'RE GOOD AT, RIGHT? SO YOU'RE GONNA TELL ME WHAT YOU KNOW, OR WE'LL BE HERE ALL DAY.
PEOPLE ARE GONNA BUST IN HERE ANY SECOND AND KICK YOUR ASS.
NO... THEY *WON'T*.
THERE IS NO ONE ON THE OTHER SIDE OF THE GLASS.
IF THERE *WAS*... YOU WOULDN'T HAVE BEEN PICKING YOUR *TEETH* IN THE REFLECTION.
IT'S JUST YOU AND *ME*.
AND YOU KNOW I HAVE NO PROBLEM KILLING A MAN TO GET WHAT I WANT.
OKAY... OKAY...

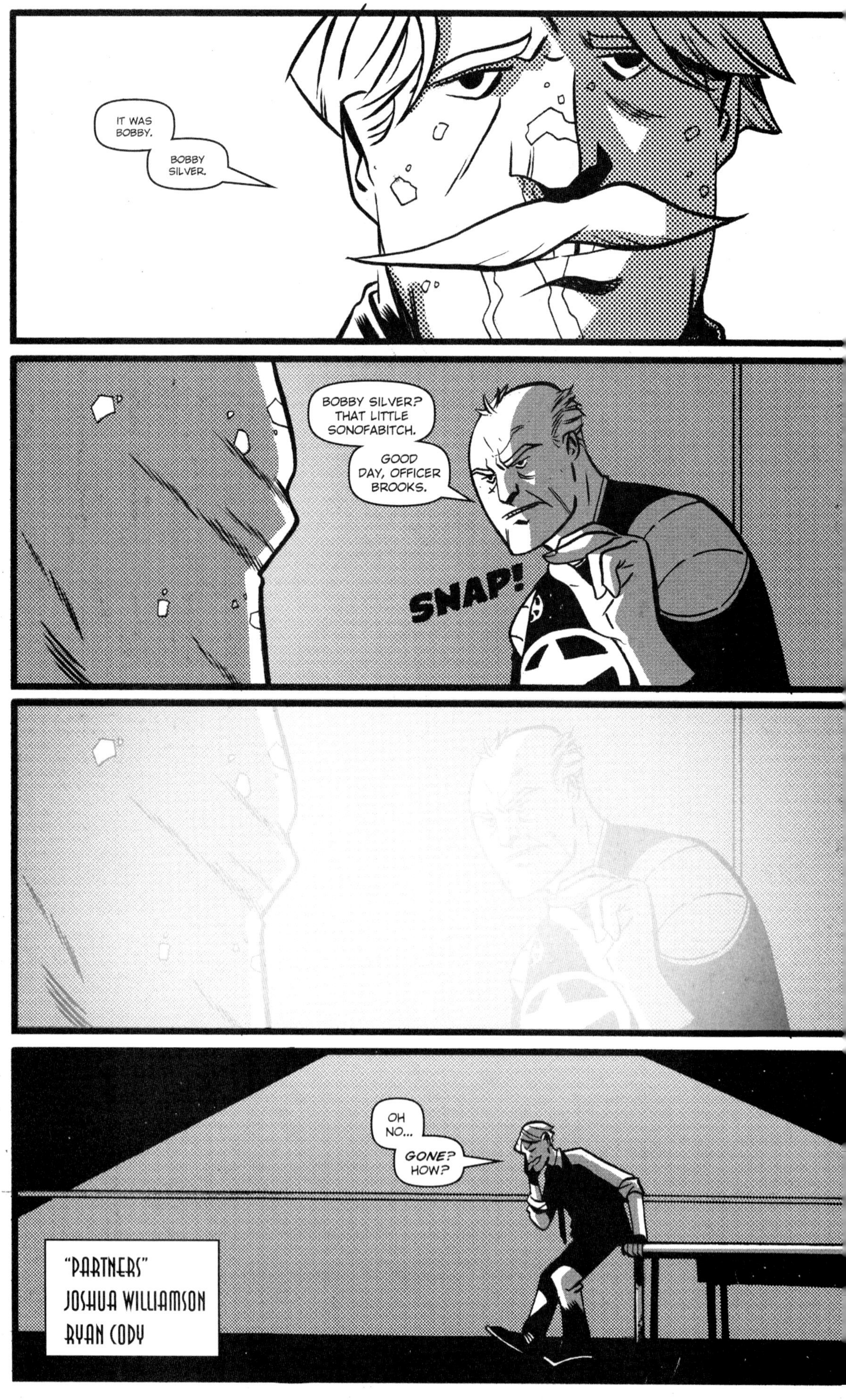
IT WAS BOBBY.
BOBBY SILVER.
BOBBY SILVER? THAT LITTLE SONOFABITCH.
GOOD DAY, OFFICER BROOKS.
SNAP!
OH NO...
GONE? HOW?
"PARTNERS"
JOSHUA WILLIAMSON
RYAN CODY

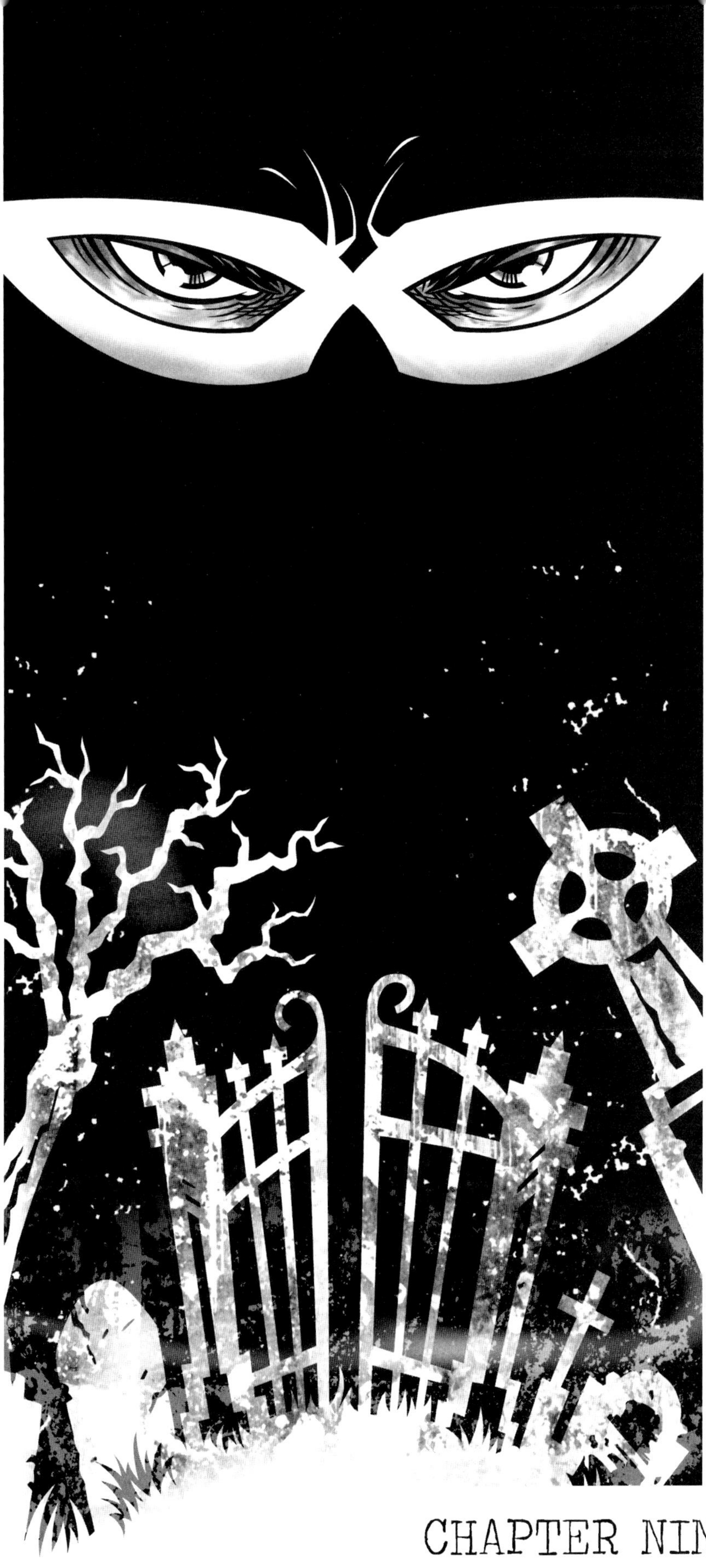

CHAPTER NINE

More of Scott Godlewski's designs

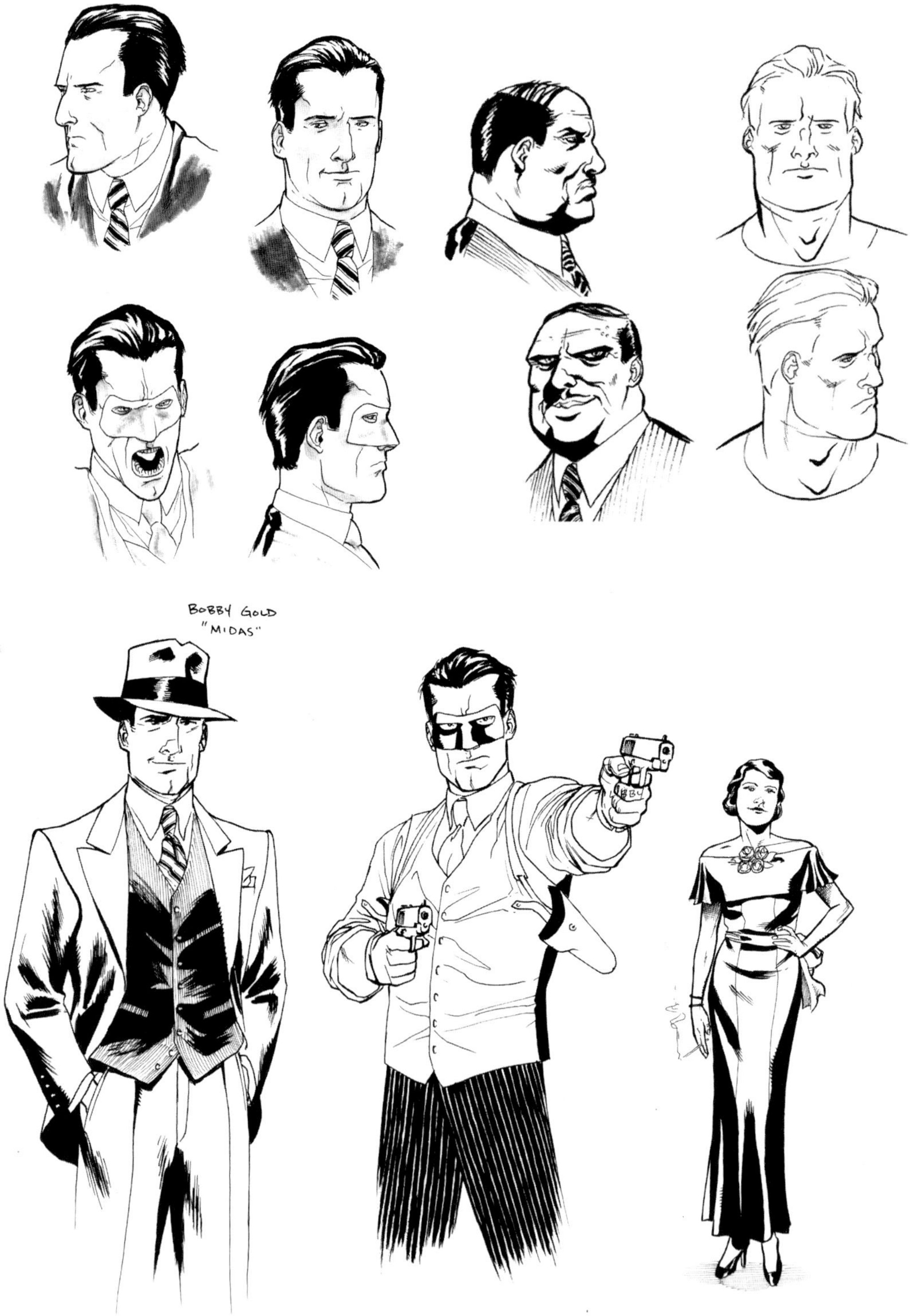
BOBBY GOLD
"MIDAS"

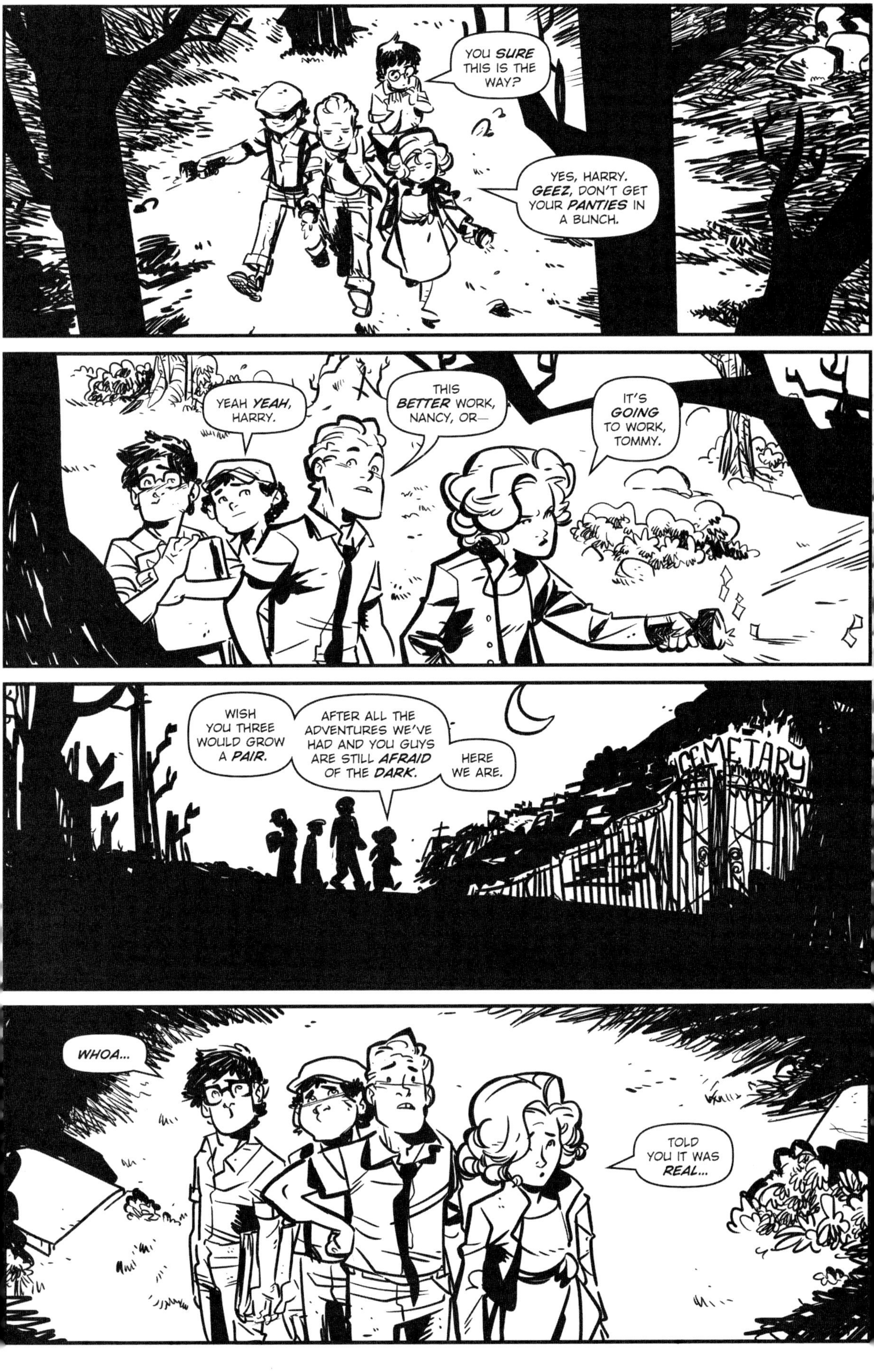
YOU SURE THIS IS THE WAY?
YES, HARRY. GEEZ, DON'T GET YOUR PANTIES IN A BUNCH.
YEAH YEAH, HARRY.
THIS BETTER WORK, NANCY, OR—
IT'S GOING TO WORK, TOMMY.
WISH YOU THREE WOULD GROW A PAIR.
AFTER ALL THE ADVENTURES WE'VE HAD AND YOU GUYS ARE STILL AFRAID OF THE DARK.
HERE WE ARE.
CEMETARY
WHOA...
TOLD YOU IT WAS REAL...

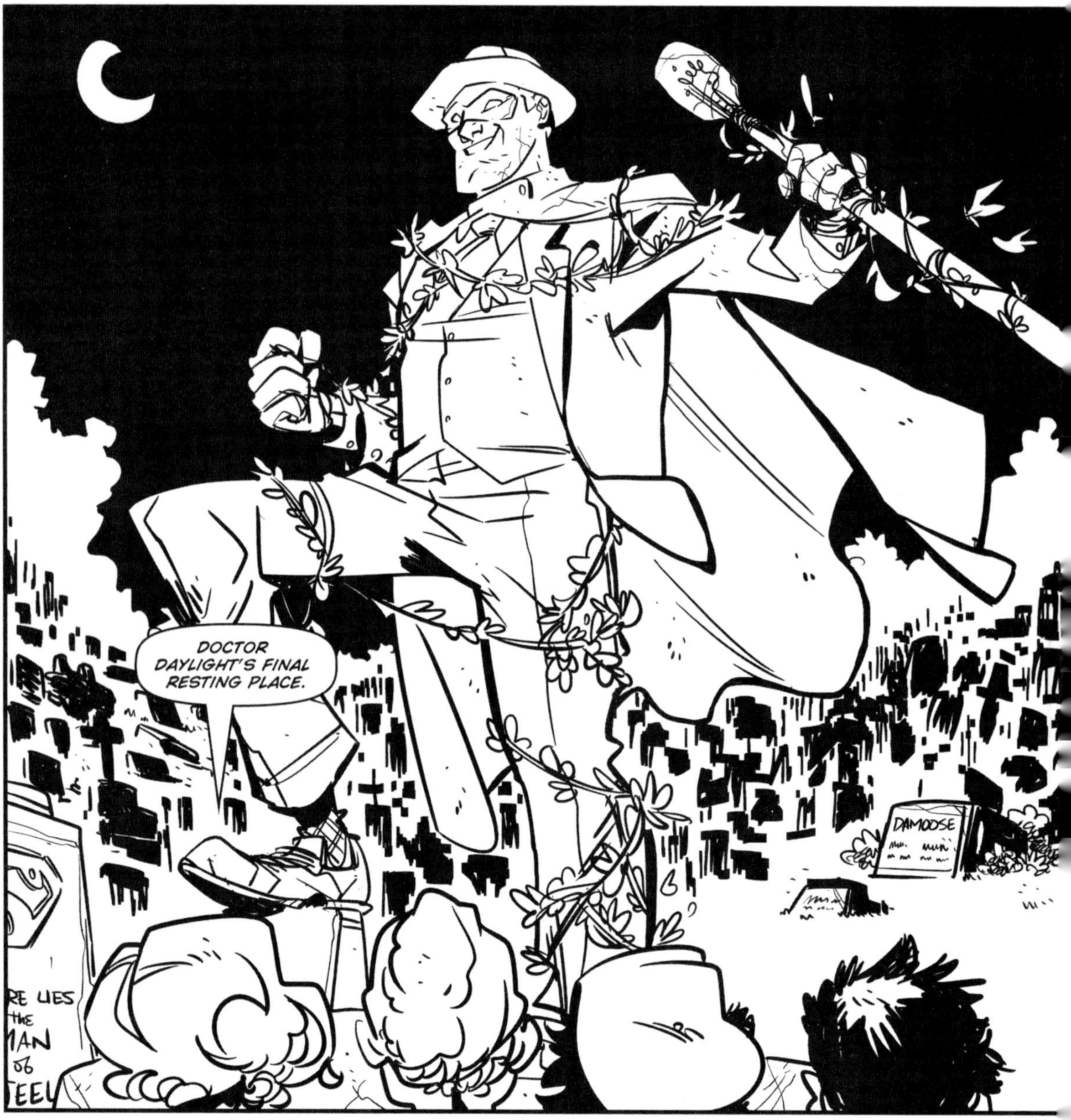
DAMOOSE
RE LIES THE MAN OF STEEL
DOCTOR DAYLIGHT'S FINAL RESTING PLACE.

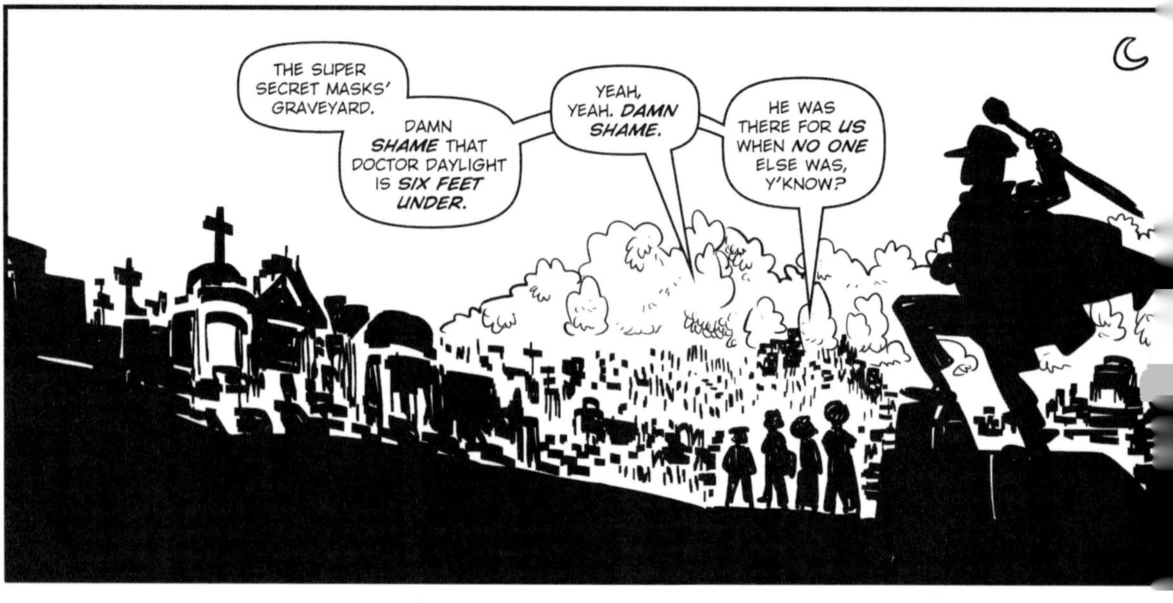
THE SUPER SECRET MASKS' GRAVEYARD.
DAMN SHAME THAT DOCTOR DAYLIGHT IS SIX FEET UNDER.
YEAH, YEAH. DAMN SHAME.
HE WAS THERE FOR US WHEN NO ONE ELSE WAS, Y'KNOW?

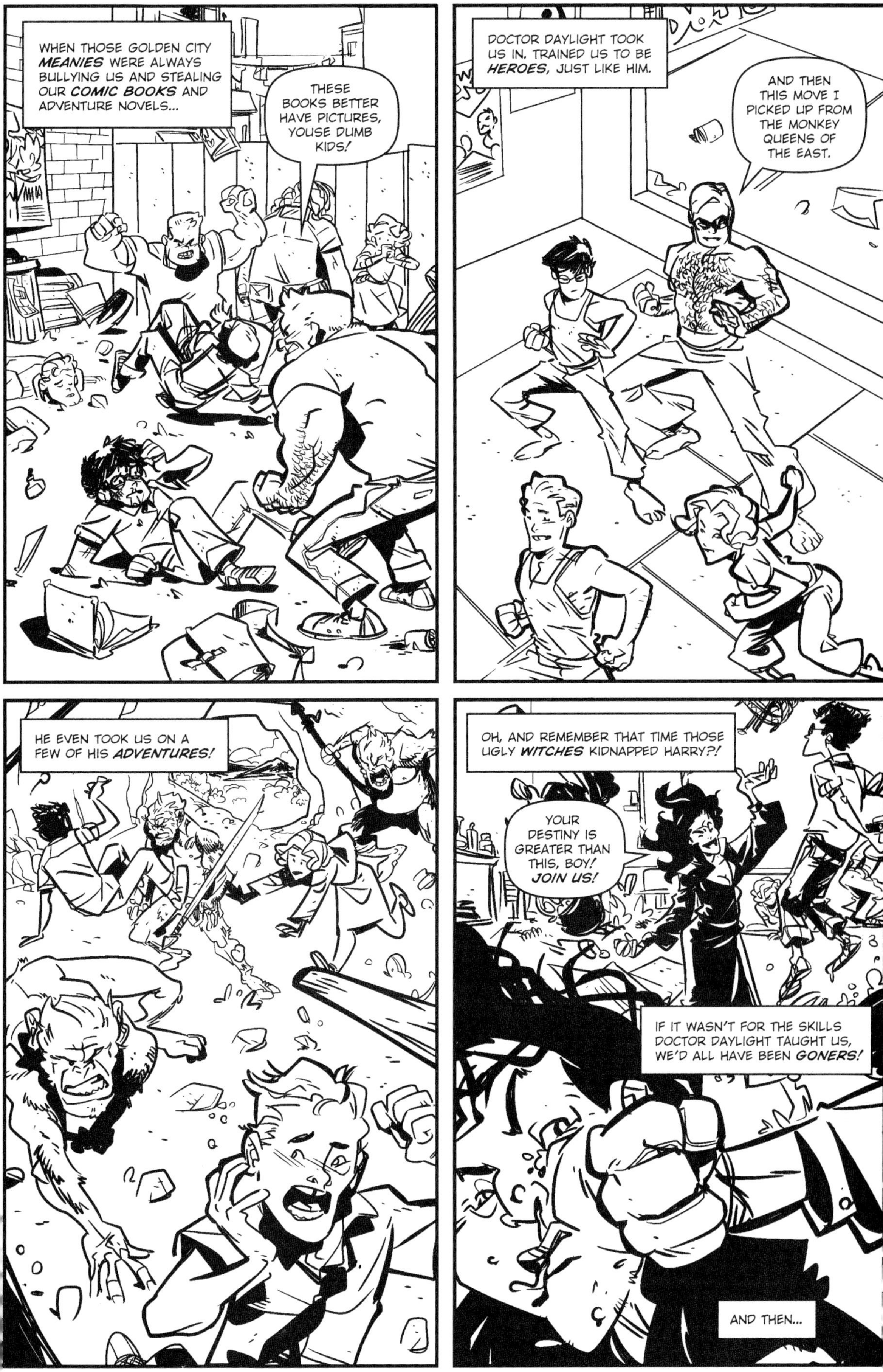
WHEN THOSE GOLDEN CITY MEANIES WERE ALWAYS BULLYING US AND STEALING OUR COMIC BOOKS AND ADVENTURE NOVELS...
THESE BOOKS BETTER HAVE PICTURES, YOUSE DUMB KIDS!
DOCTOR DAYLIGHT TOOK US IN. TRAINED US TO BE HEROES, JUST LIKE HIM.
AND THEN THIS MOVE I PICKED UP FROM THE MONKEY QUEENS OF THE EAST.
HE EVEN TOOK US ON A FEW OF HIS ADVENTURES!
OH, AND REMEMBER THAT TIME THOSE UGLY WITCHES KIDNAPPED HARRY?!
YOUR DESTINY IS GREATER THAN THIS, BOY! JOIN US!
IF IT WASN'T FOR THE SKILLS DOCTOR DAYLIGHT TAUGHT US, WE'D ALL HAVE BEEN GONERS!
AND THEN...

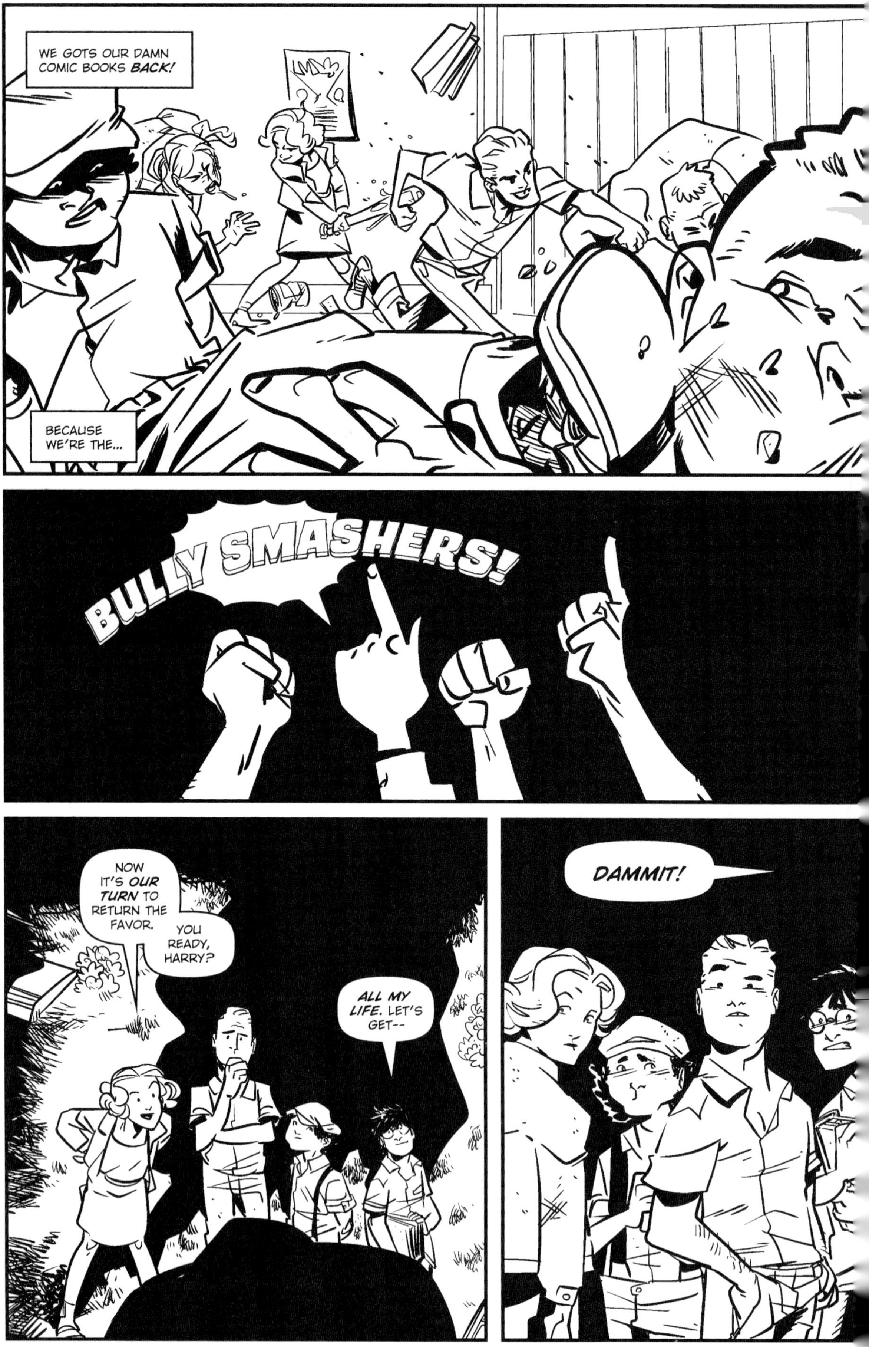
WE GOTS OUR DAMN COMIC BOOKS BACK!
BECAUSE WE'RE THE...
BULLY SMASHERS!
NOW IT'S OUR TURN TO RETURN THE FAVOR.
YOU READY, HARRY?
ALL MY LIFE. LET'S GET--
DAMMIT!

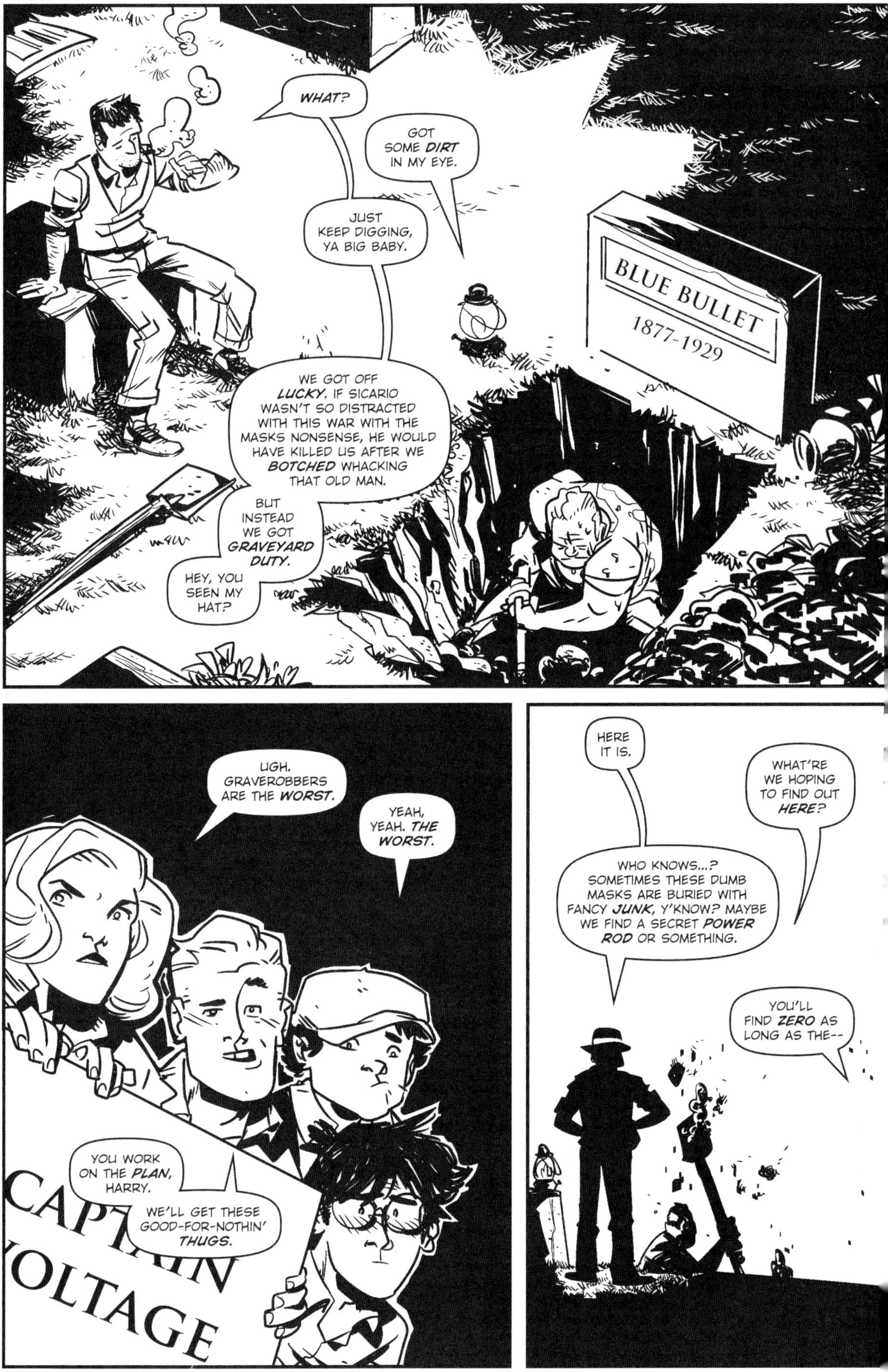
WHAT?
GOT SOME DIRT IN MY EYE.
JUST KEEP DIGGING, YA BIG BABY.
BLUE BULLET
1877-1929
WE GOT OFF LUCKY. IF SICARIO WASN'T SO DISTRACTED WITH THIS WAR WITH THE MASKS NONSENSE, HE WOULD HAVE KILLED US AFTER WE BOTCHED WHACKING THAT OLD MAN.
BUT INSTEAD WE GOT GRAVEYARD DUTY.
HEY, YOU SEEN MY HAT?
UGH. GRAVEROBBERS ARE THE WORST.
YEAH, YEAH. THE WORST.
YOU WORK ON THE PLAN, HARRY.
WE'LL GET THESE GOOD-FOR-NOTHIN' THUGS.
CAPTAIN
VOLTAGE
HERE IT IS.
WHAT'RE WE HOPING TO FIND OUT HERE?
WHO KNOWS...? SOMETIMES THESE DUMB MASKS ARE BURIED WITH FANCY JUNK, Y'KNOW? MAYBE WE FIND A SECRET POWER ROD OR SOMETHING.
YOU'LL FIND ZERO AS LONG AS THE--

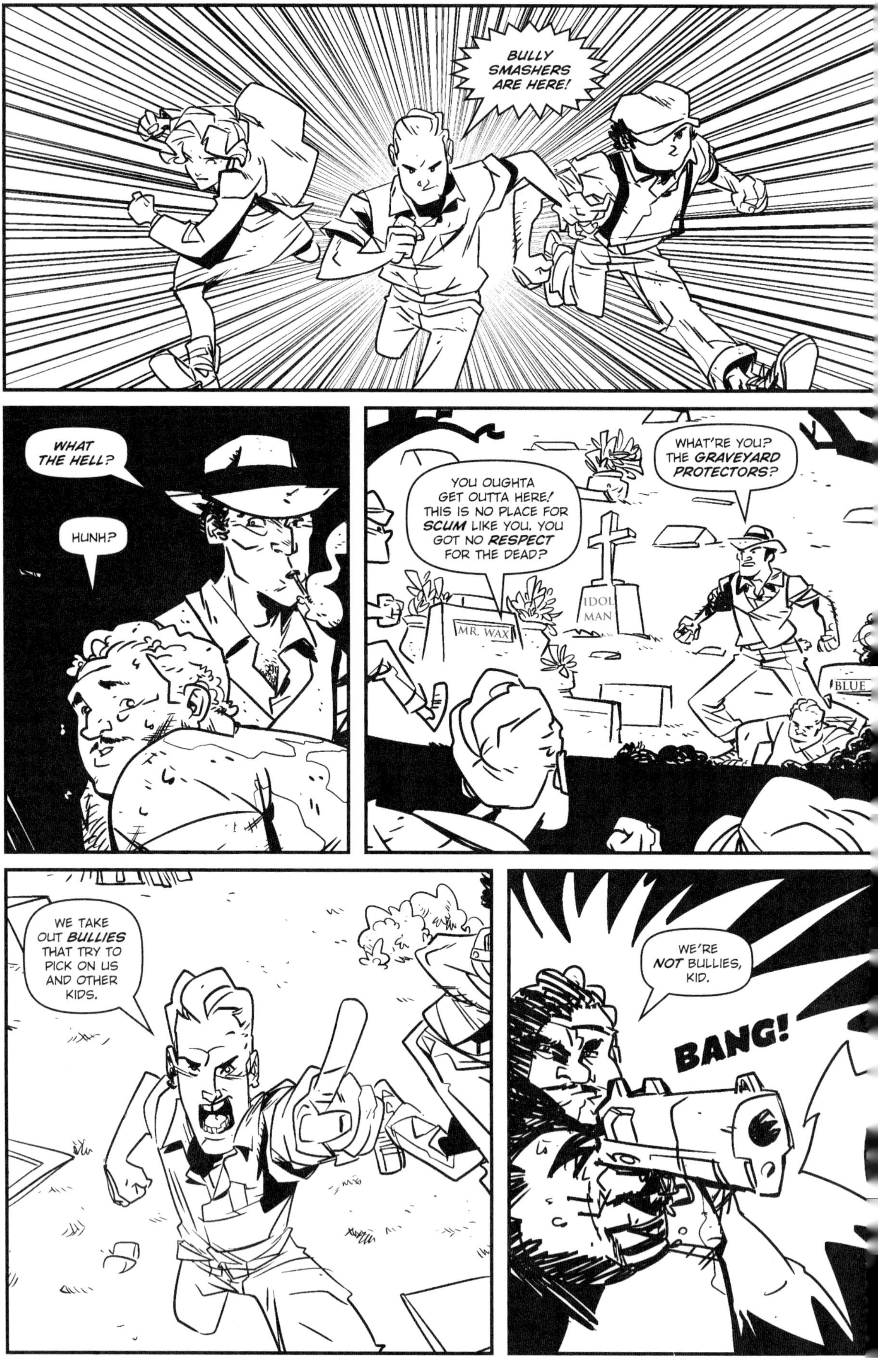
BULLY SMASHERS ARE HERE!
WHAT THE HELL?
HUNH?
YOU OUGHTA GET OUTTA HERE! THIS IS NO PLACE FOR SCUM LIKE YOU. YOU GOT NO RESPECT FOR THE DEAD?
WHAT'RE YOU? THE GRAVEYARD PROTECTORS?
MR. WAX
IDOL MAN
BLUE
WE TAKE OUT BULLIES THAT TRY TO PICK ON US AND OTHER KIDS.
WE'RE NOT BULLIES, KID.
BANG!

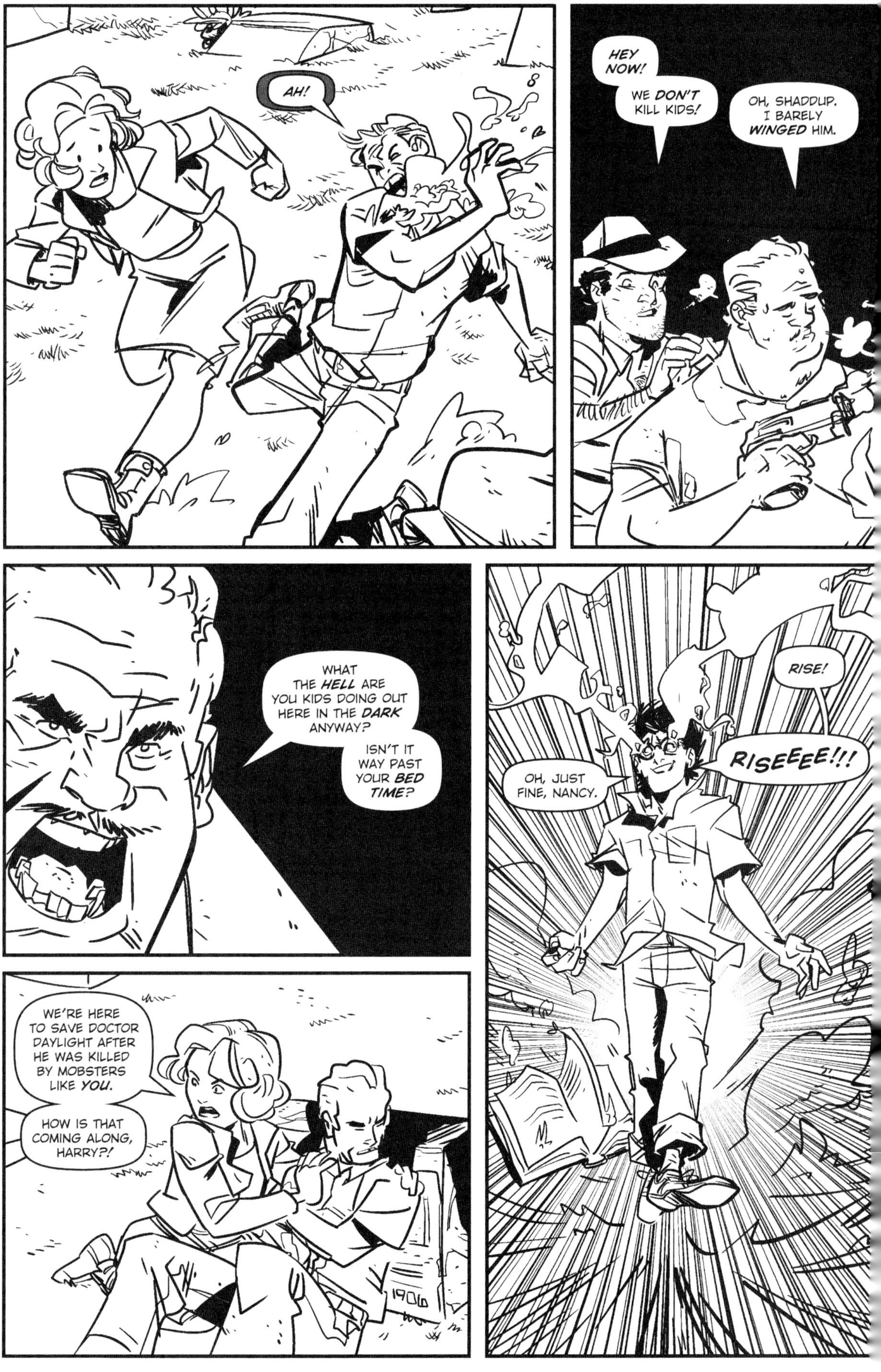
AH!
HEY NOW!
WE DON'T KILL KIDS!
OH, SHADDUP. I BARELY WINGED HIM.
WHAT THE HELL ARE YOU KIDS DOING OUT HERE IN THE DARK ANYWAY?
ISN'T IT WAY PAST YOUR BED TIME?
WE'RE HERE TO SAVE DOCTOR DAYLIGHT AFTER HE WAS KILLED BY MOBSTERS LIKE YOU.
HOW IS THAT COMING ALONG, HARRY?!
RISE!
RISEEEE!!!
OH, JUST FINE, NANCY.
1906

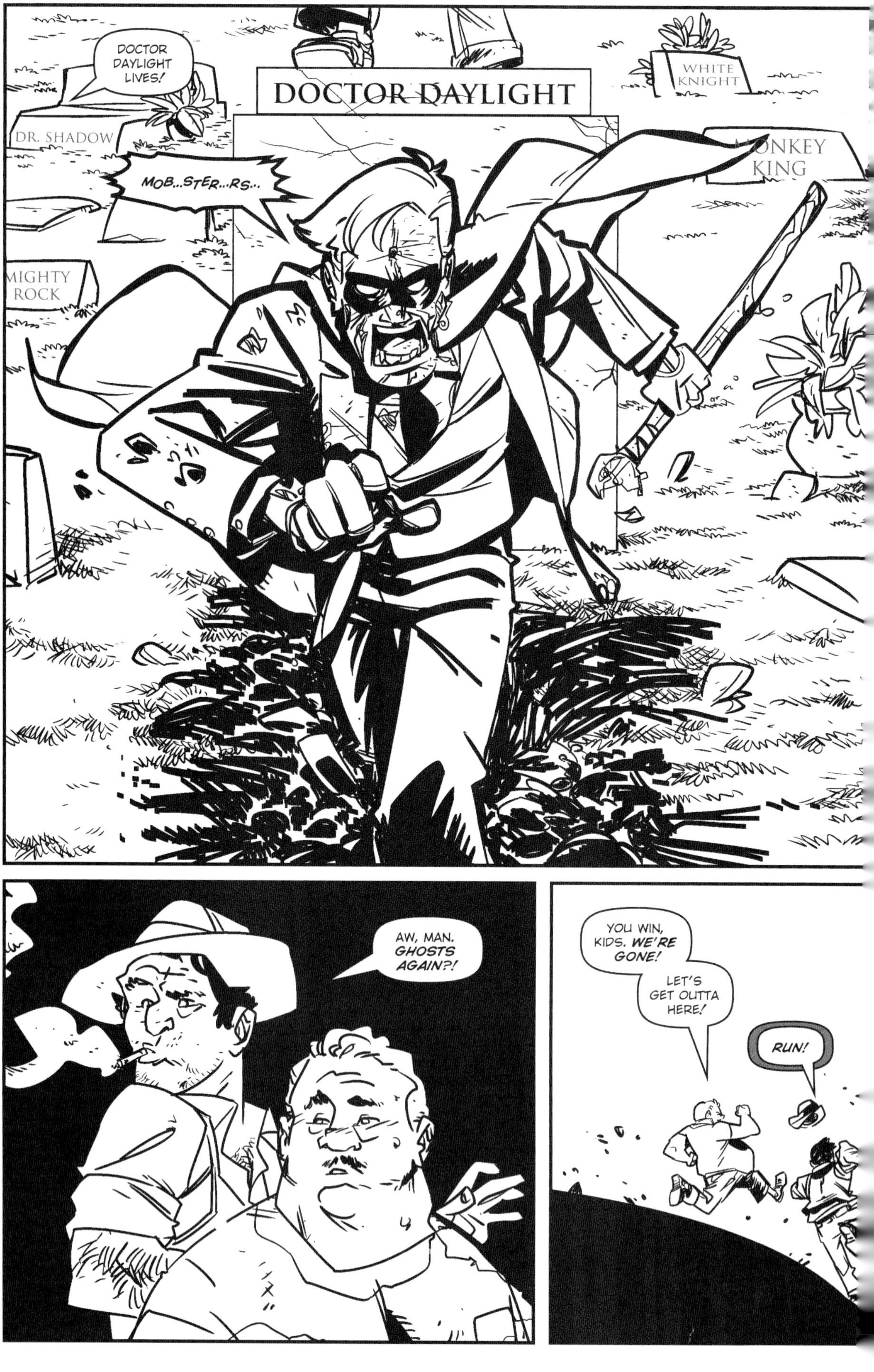
DOCTOR DAYLIGHT
WHITE KNIGHT
DR. SHADOW
MIGHTY ROCK
DOCTOR DAYLIGHT LIVES!
MOB...STER...RS...
AW, MAN. GHOSTS AGAIN?!
YOU WIN, KIDS. WE'RE GONE!
LET'S GET OUTTA HERE!
RUN!

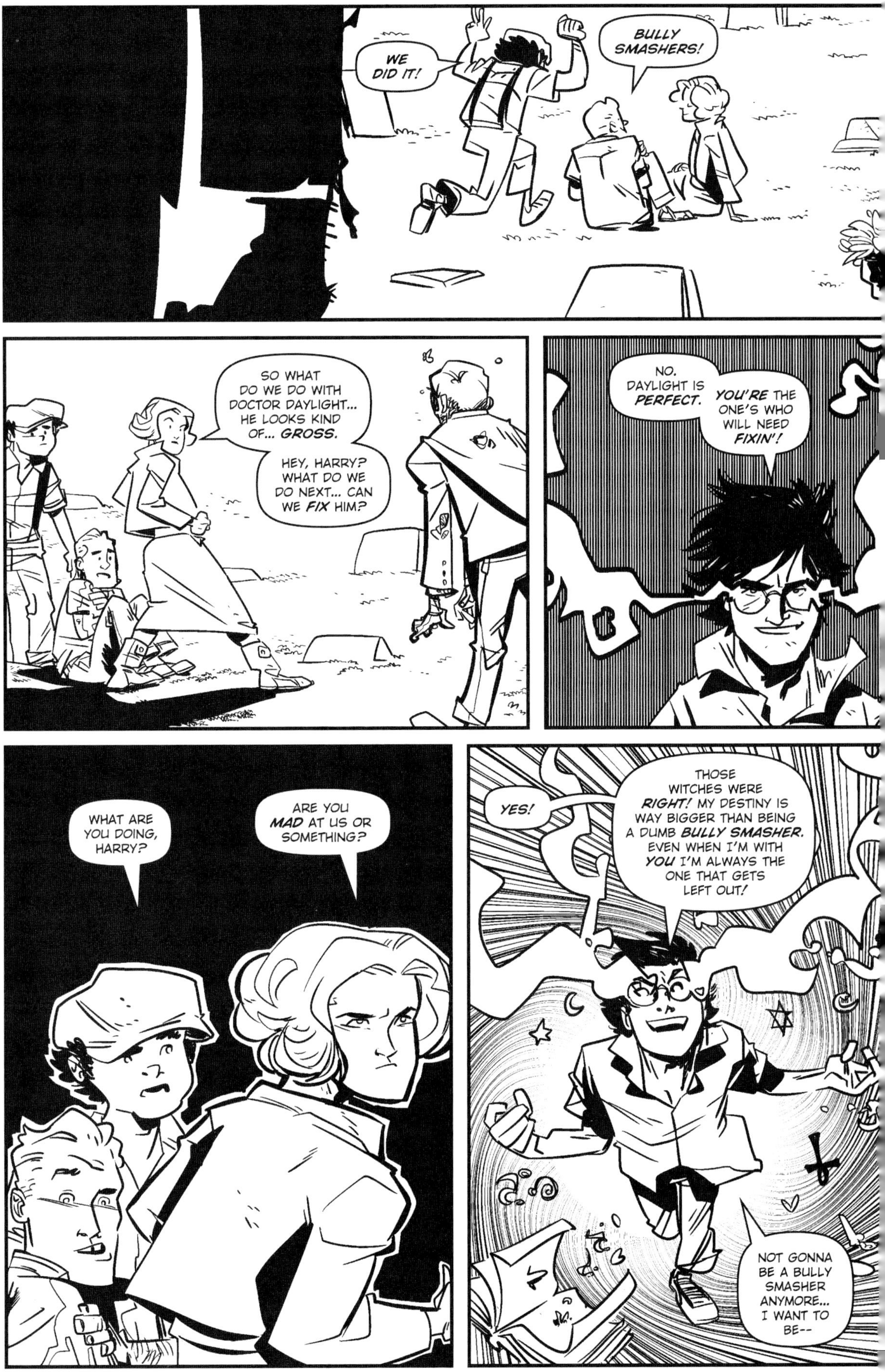
WE DID IT!
BULLY SMASHERS!
SO WHAT DO WE DO WITH DOCTOR DAYLIGHT... HE LOOKS KIND OF... GROSS.
HEY, HARRY? WHAT DO WE DO NEXT... CAN WE FIX HIM?
NO. DAYLIGHT IS PERFECT.
YOU'RE THE ONE'S WHO WILL NEED FIXIN'!
WHAT ARE YOU DOING, HARRY?
ARE YOU MAD AT US OR SOMETHING?
YES!
THOSE WITCHES WERE RIGHT! MY DESTINY IS WAY BIGGER THAN BEING A DUMB BULLY SMASHER. EVEN WHEN I'M WITH YOU I'M ALWAYS THE ONE THAT GETS LEFT OUT!
NOT GONNA BE A BULLY SMASHER ANYMORE... I WANT TO BE--

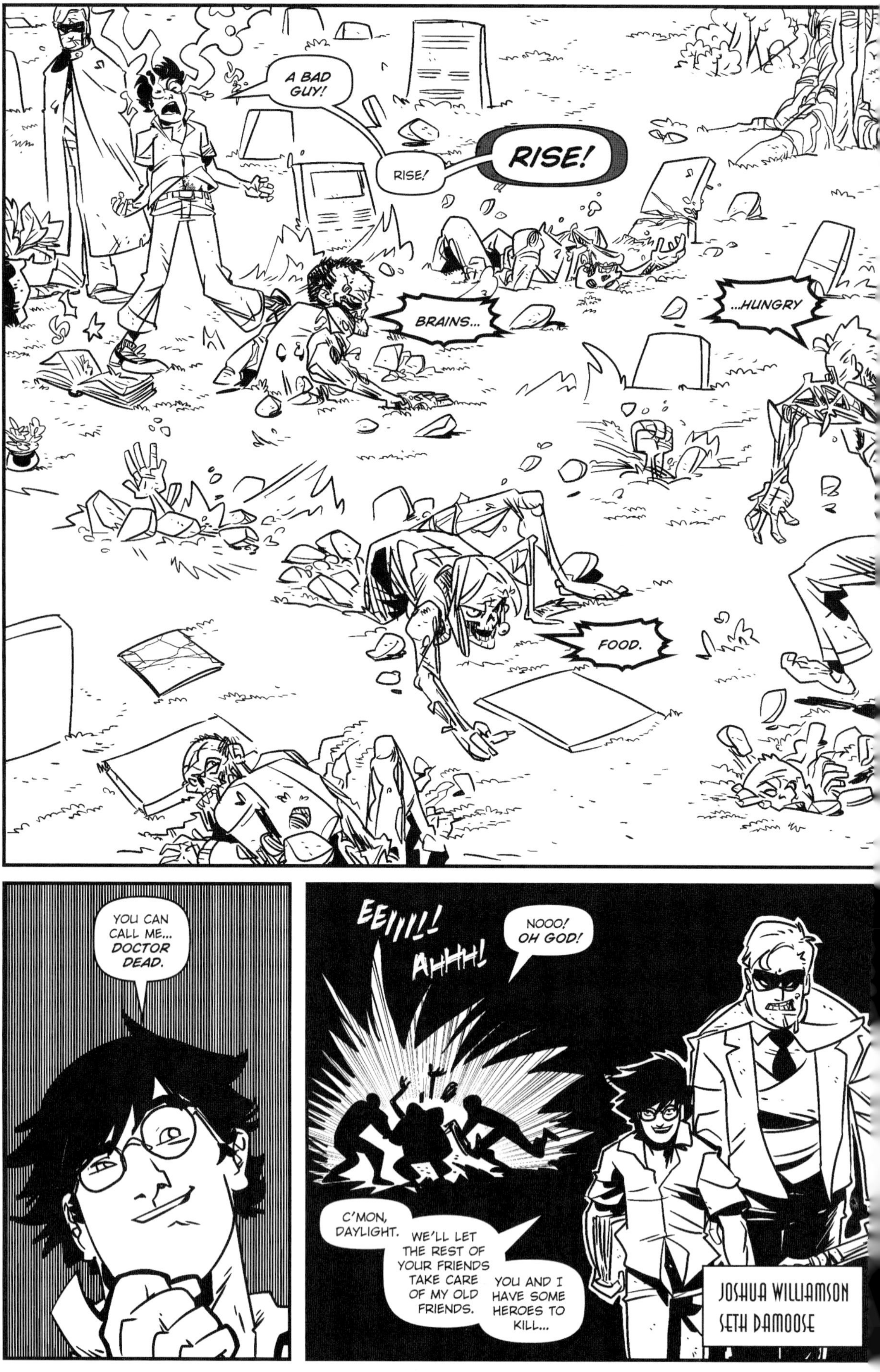
A BAD GUY!
RISE!
RISE!
BRAINS...
...HUNGRY
FOOD.
YOU CAN CALL ME... DOCTOR DEAD.
EEIII!!
AHHH!
NOOO! OH GOD!
C'MON, DAYLIGHT.
WE'LL LET THE REST OF YOUR FRIENDS TAKE CARE OF MY OLD FRIENDS.
YOU AND I HAVE SOME HEROES TO KILL...
JOSHUA WILLIAMSON
SETH DAMOOSE

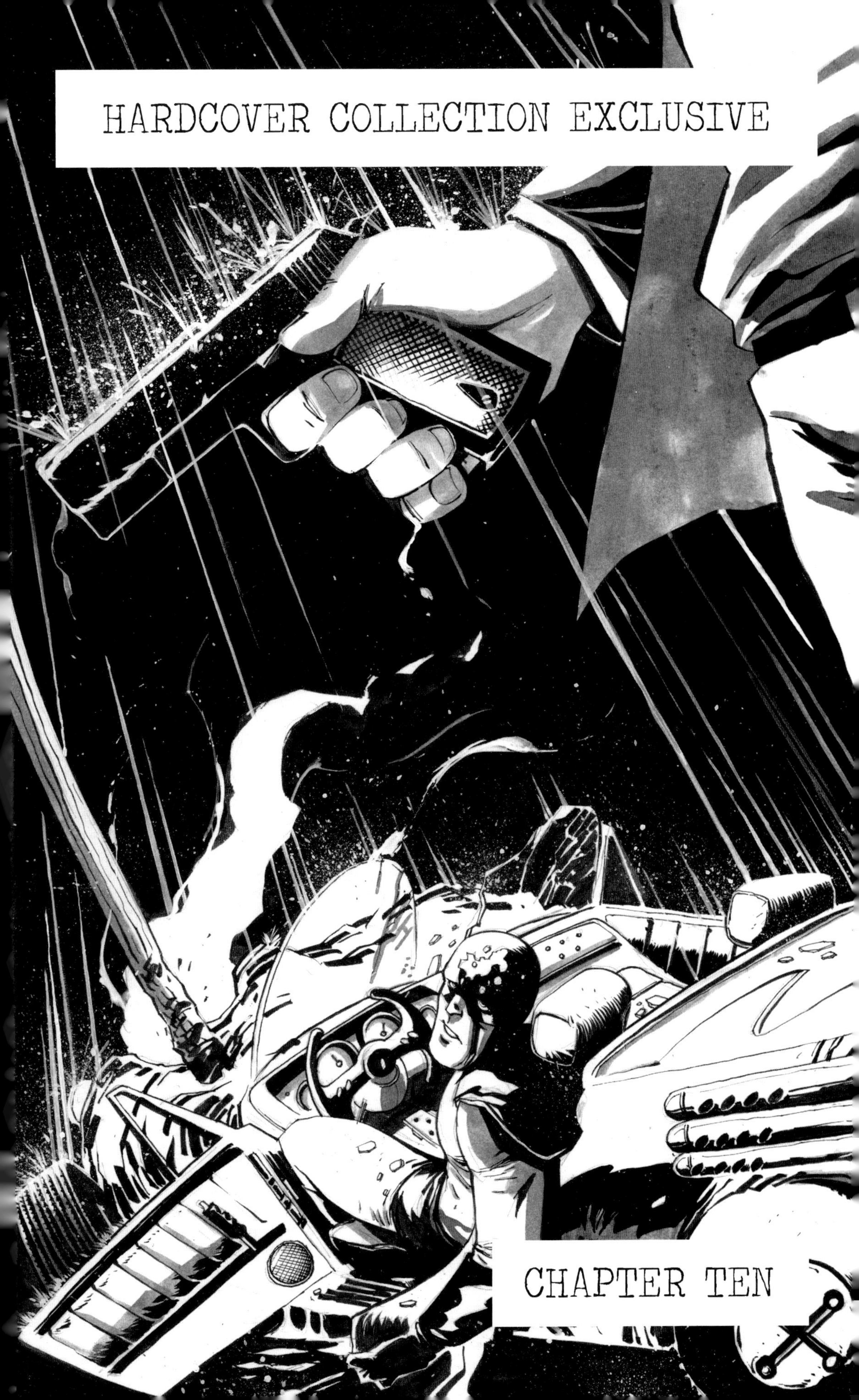
HARDCOVER COLLECTION EXCLUSIVE
CHAPTER TEN

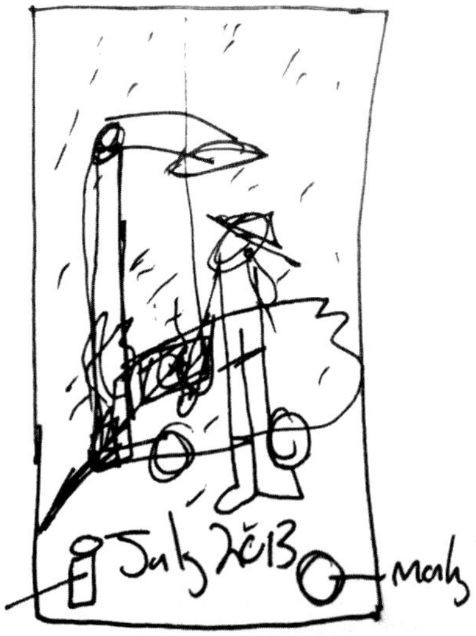
July 2013

Josh's crude original sketch for the cover of Chapter Ten (left).

And Mike's far more accomplished sketches for the same cover (below).

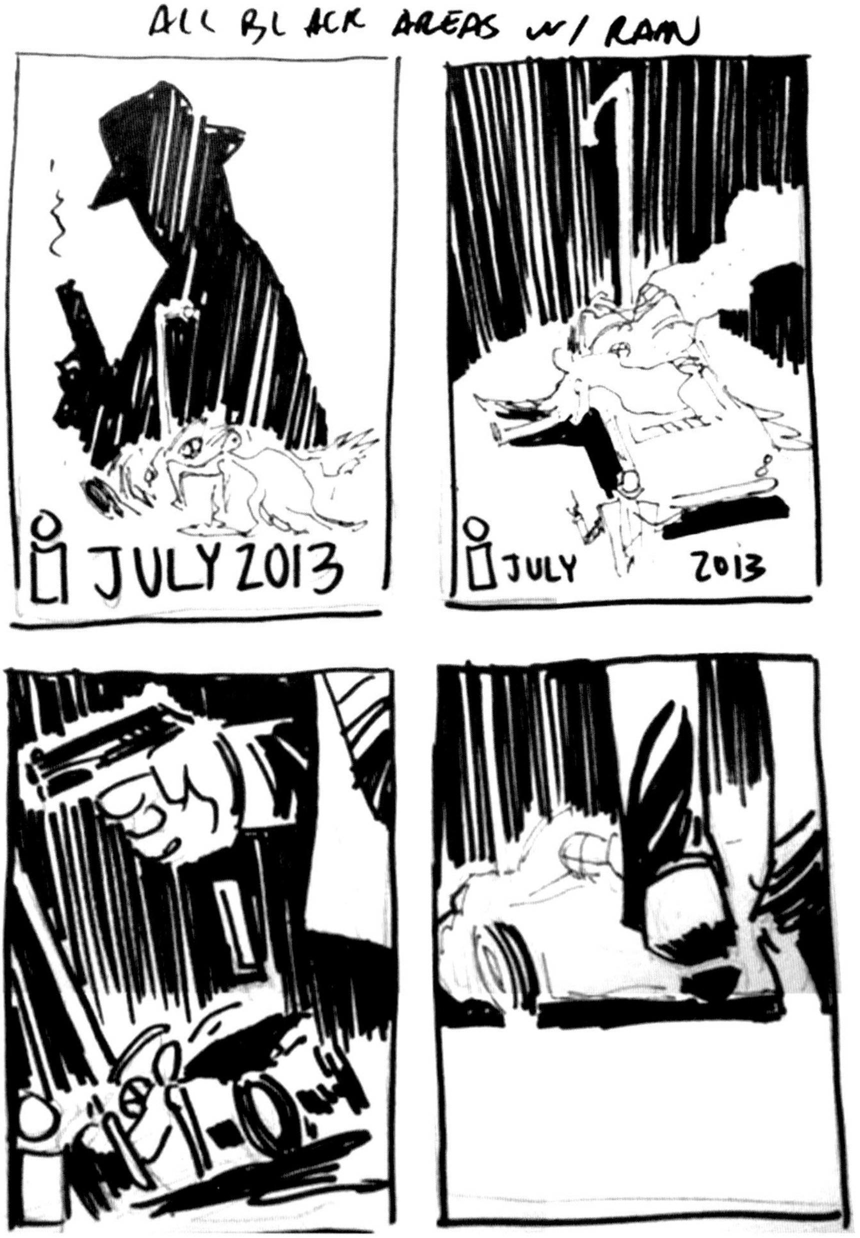
ALL BLACK AREAS W/ RAIN
JULY 2013
JULY 2013

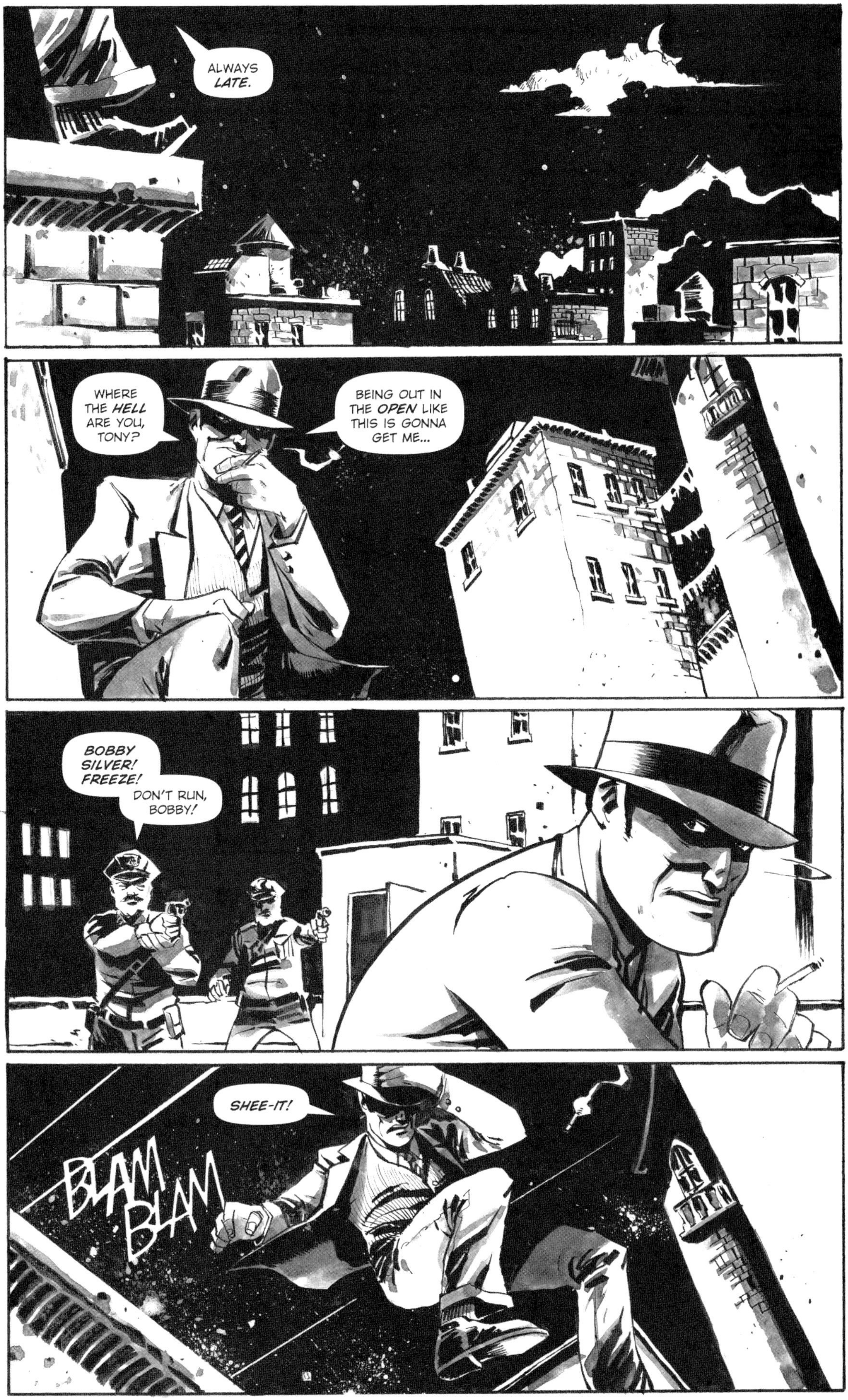
ALWAYS LATE.
WHERE THE HELL ARE YOU, TONY?
BEING OUT IN THE OPEN LIKE THIS IS GONNA GET ME...
BOBBY SILVER! FREEZE!
DON'T RUN, BOBBY!
SHEE-IT!
BLAM BLAM

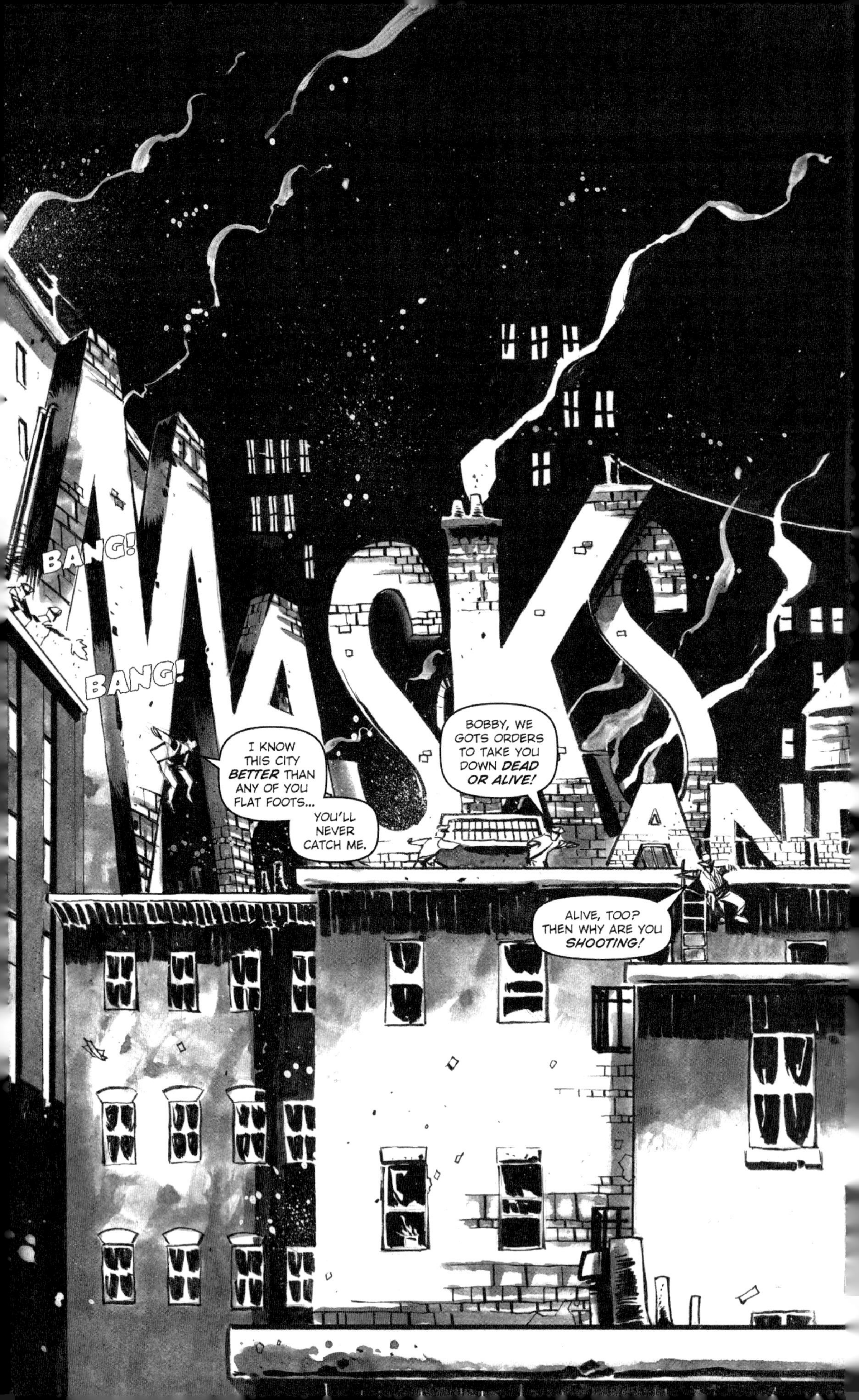
BANG!
BANG!
I KNOW THIS CITY BETTER THAN ANY OF YOU FLAT FOOTS...
YOU'LL NEVER CATCH ME.
BOBBY, WE GOTS ORDERS TO TAKE YOU DOWN DEAD OR ALIVE!
ALIVE, TOO? THEN WHY ARE YOU SHOOTING!

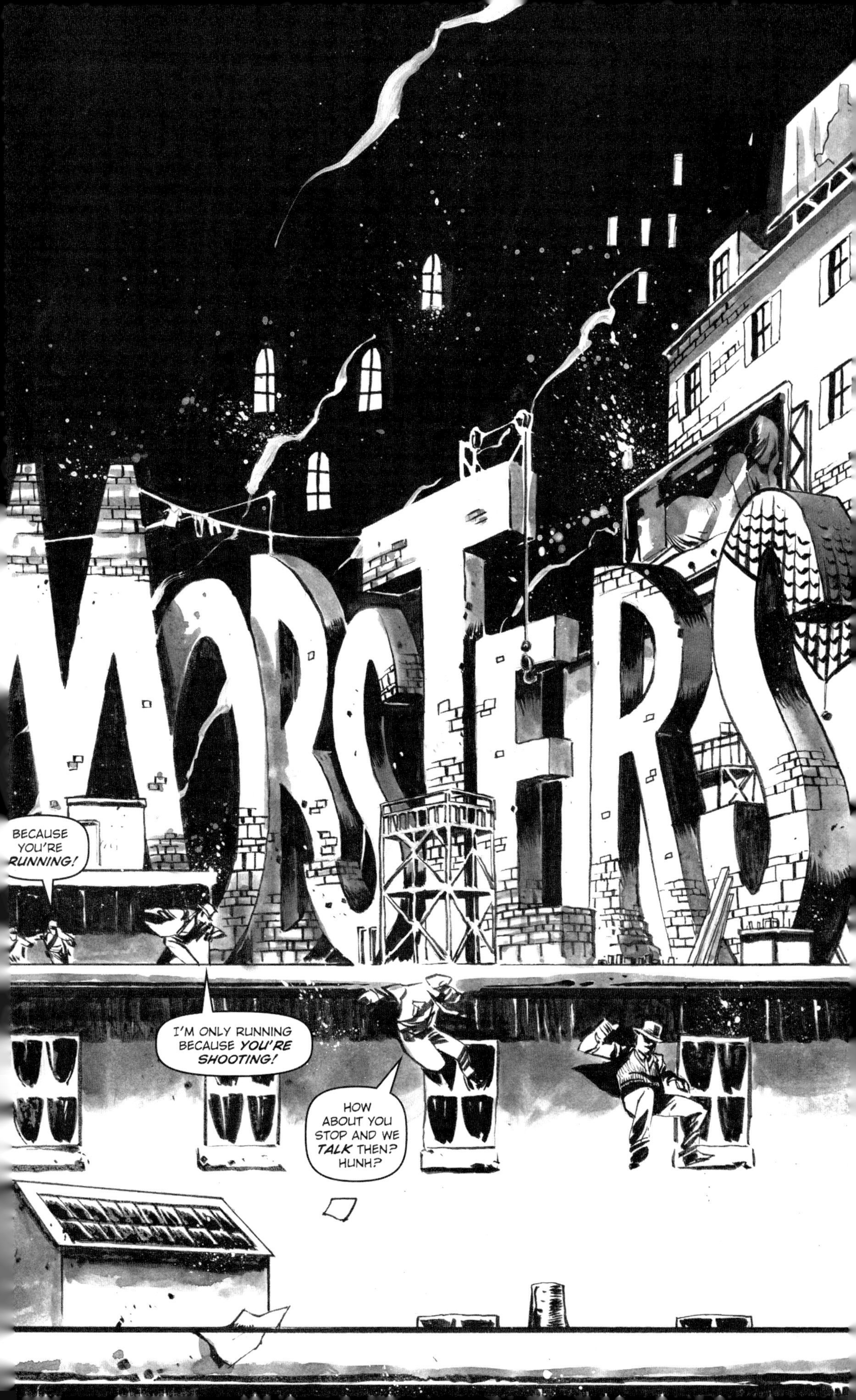
MONSTERS
BECAUSE YOU'RE RUNNING!
I'M ONLY RUNNING BECAUSE YOU'RE SHOOTING!
HOW ABOUT YOU STOP AND WE TALK THEN? HUNH?

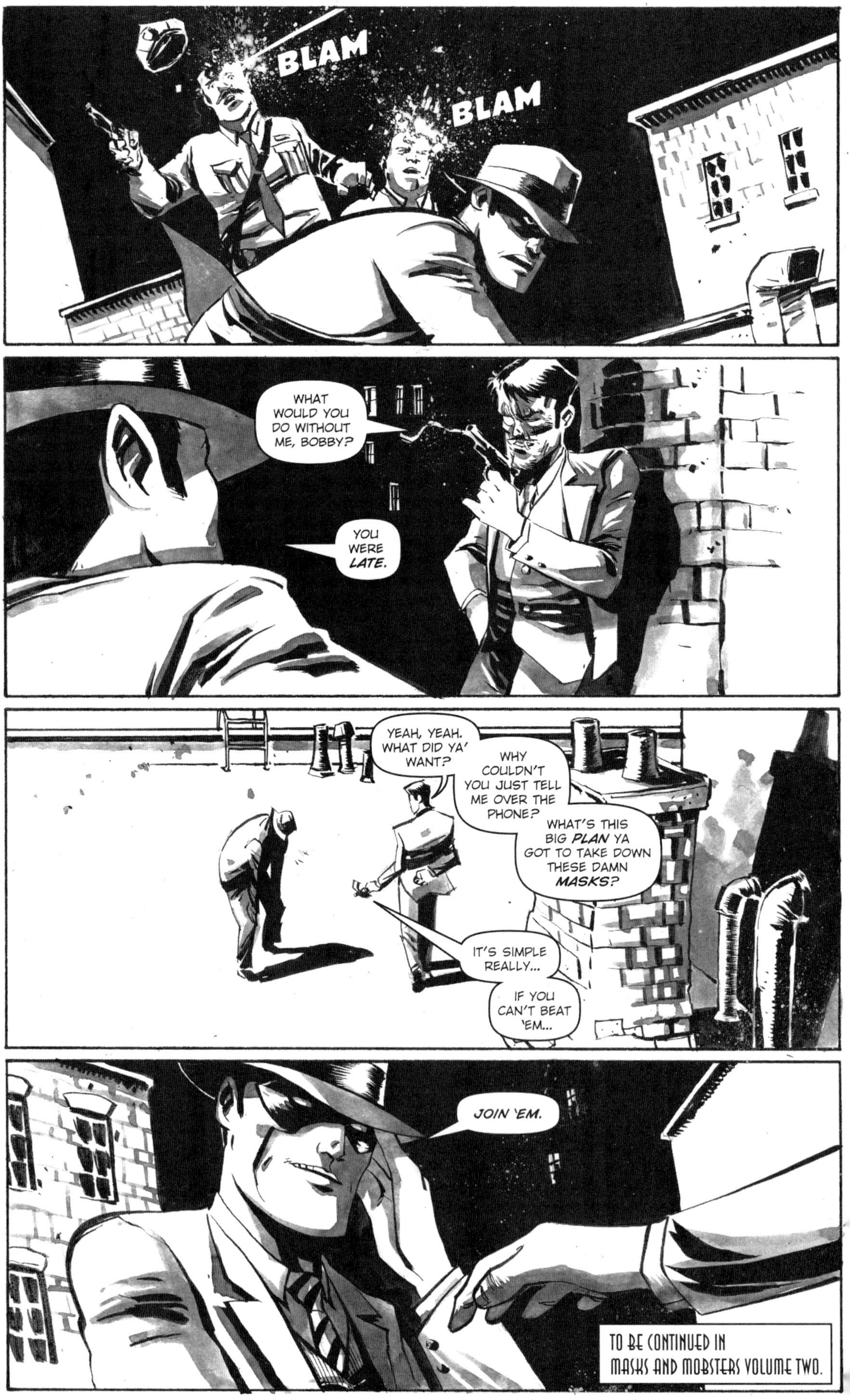

BLAM
BLAM
WHAT WOULD YOU DO WITHOUT ME, BOBBY?
YOU WERE *LATE*.
YEAH, YEAH. WHAT DID YA' WANT?
WHY COULDN'T YOU JUST TELL ME OVER THE PHONE?
WHAT'S THIS BIG *PLAN* YA GOT TO TAKE DOWN THESE DAMN *MASKS*?
IT'S SIMPLE REALLY...
IF YOU CAN'T BEAT 'EM...
JOIN 'EM.
TO BE CONTINUED IN MASKS AND MOBSTERS VOLUME TWO.

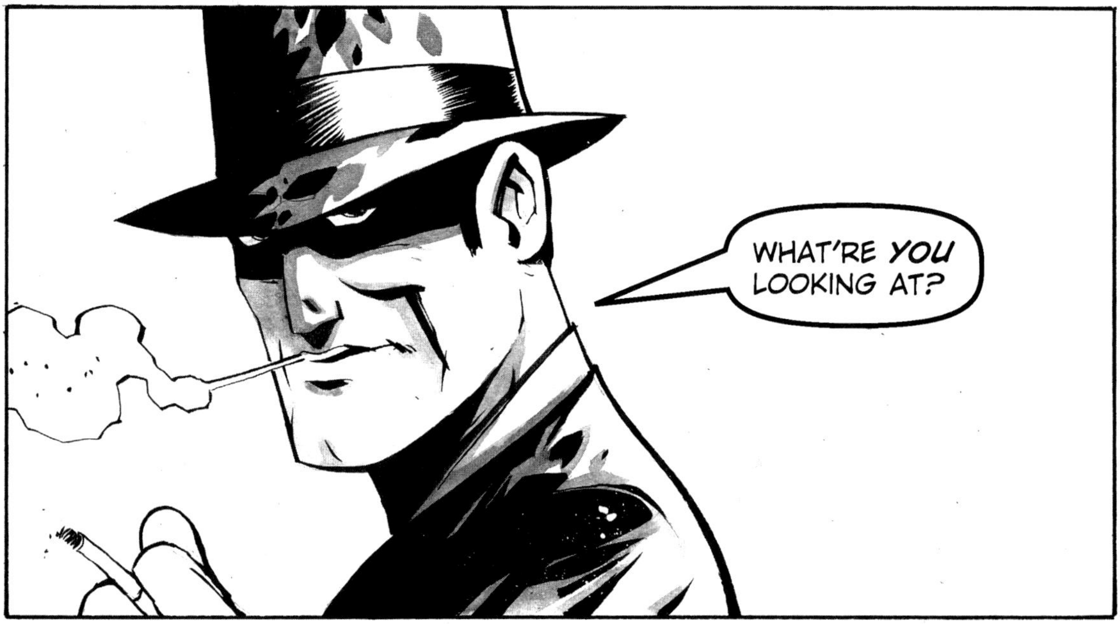
WHAT'RE YOU LOOKING AT?

JOSHUA WILLIAMSON writes comics, kids books and resides in Portland OR, home of big trees, rain and great beer. Williamson has written for a wide variety of publishers and titles including DC Comic's Superman/Batman and Uncharted, Marvel's Incredible Hulks, Image Comics with Dear Dracula, Sketch Monsters for ONI Press and Captain Midnight with Dark Horse Comics. His next creator owned title is GHOSTED with Image/Skybound Comics in July 2013.
Joshua writes comics because he can't sing or dance. Follow him on twitter @Williamson_Josh

MIKE S. HENDERSON, former student of the Joe Kubert School of Art, is a freelance artist for Marvel Comics, IDW Publishing, DC Comics and Nike. A native New Englander, gym rat and Scotch enthusiast, he resides on the East Coast for now. Follow him on twitter @MikeSHenderson."

JASON COPLAND is a freelance artist that resides in Vancouver, Canada. His work has been published by Image, Dark Horse and Villard/Random House, as well as in many small press publications. Jason has contributed work to two Eisner nominated anthologies, Trickster: Native American Tales and Postcards: True Stories That Never Happened. He is currently working on Kill All Monsters, a co-creator owned title. Follow Jason on twitter @jasoncopland or visit his blog at www.jasoncopland.com.

JUSTIN GREENWOOD is a Bay Area freelance comic illustrator, a fancy way of saying he likes to draw. After graduating from the Academy of Art in San Francisco, he worked on RESURRECTION and WASTELAND for Oni Press and is currently working on his first OGN STRINGERS. When not drawing, you can often spot him with his family, scouring the Farmer's Markets in search of the world's finest apple. Justin lives and works in San Leandro, California with his wife Melissa and their beautiful baby girl. Follow Justin on twitter @JKGreenwood_Art

RYAN CODY draws comics. He lives in Northern Arizona with his family. He has done work for Image, Red 5 & Viper Comics. Follow Ryan on twitter @@ryancody

SETH DAMOOSE spends his days with his beautiful wife and daughter while trying to find time to make funny books. Follow Seth on twitter @DamooseSeth

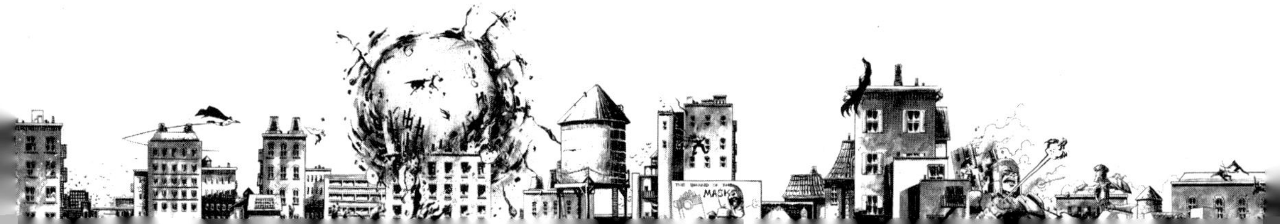

WE MAKE COMICS FOR FUN

ACTION CATS AESOP'S ARK AMELIA COLE ARTFUL DAGGERS BANDETTE DENALI EDISON REX FROST HIGH CRIMES KINSKI KNUCKLEHEADS MASK OF THE RED PANDA MASKS & MOBSTERS THE OCTOBER GIRL PHABULA RED LIGHT PROPERTIES SKYBREAKER SPIRIT OF THE LAW THE STARS BELOW SUBATOMIC PARTY GIRLS THEREMIN THOUGHTS ON A WINTER MORNING UNFAIR WANDER & MORE ON THE WAY.

monkeybrain COMICS

monkeybraincomics.com

More books by Joshua Williamson you're bound to enjoy...

With Vinny Navarrete

DEAR DRACULA
ISBN: 978-1-58240-970-2
$7.99 Hardcover

A heart warming story about a young boy, Sam, who writes a letter to his hero, Count Dracula and gets the surprise of his life when the King of Vampires comes to visit on Halloween night!

Now a charming animated feature from KICKSTART.
For children 6 years old and up!

With Seth Damoose

XENOHOLICS
ISBN: 978-1-60706-557-9
$14.99

A support group for victims of alien abductions find themselves in the middle of a larger conspiracy!
It's the X-Files and Fire In the Sky with tongue planted firmly in cheek for the not-so-serious conspiracy theorists among us!

FOR MORE INFORMATION ABOUT ALL *Shadowline* BOOKS AND WEB-COMICS, PLEASE VISIT US AT:
www.ShadowlineOnline.com
Follow SHADOWLINECOMICS on FACEBOOK and TWITTER

A Book For Every Reader...

ROBINSON

BRISSON/WALSH

LIEBERMAN/ROSSMO

WIEBE/ROSSMO

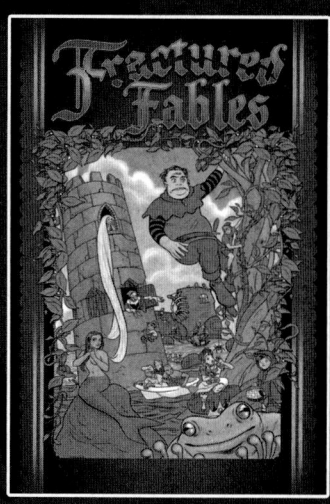
VARIOUS ARTISTS

WIEBE/ROSSMO

LIEBERMAN/LORIMER

BECHKO/HARDMAN

TED McKEEVER

FOR MORE INFORMATION ABOUT ALL *Shadowline*™ BOOKS AND WEB-COMICS, PLEASE VISIT US AT:
www.ShadowlineOnline.com

...A Book For Every Taste.

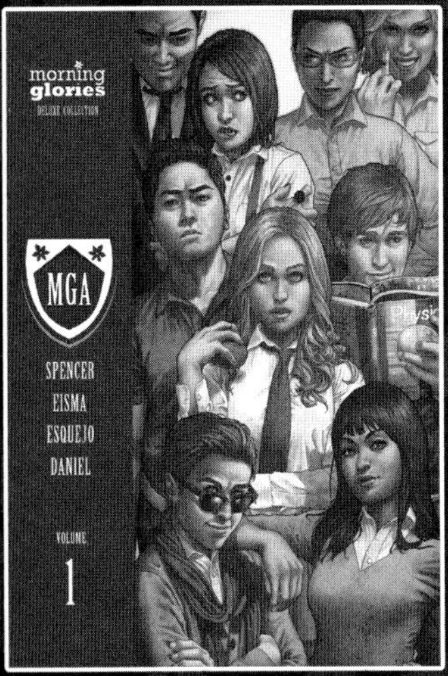
morning glories
DELUXE COLLECTION
MGA
SPENCER
EISMA
ESQUEJO
DANIEL
VOLUME
1

SPENCER/EISMA/ESQUEJO

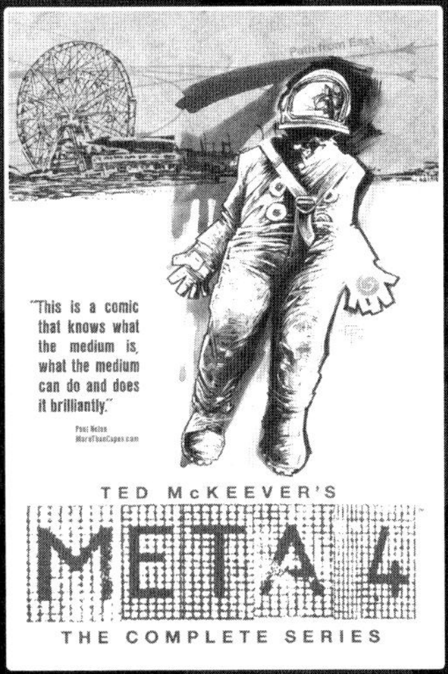
"This is a comic that knows what the medium is, what the medium can do and does it brilliantly."
TED McKEEVER'S
META 4
THE COMPLETE SERIES

TED McKEEVER

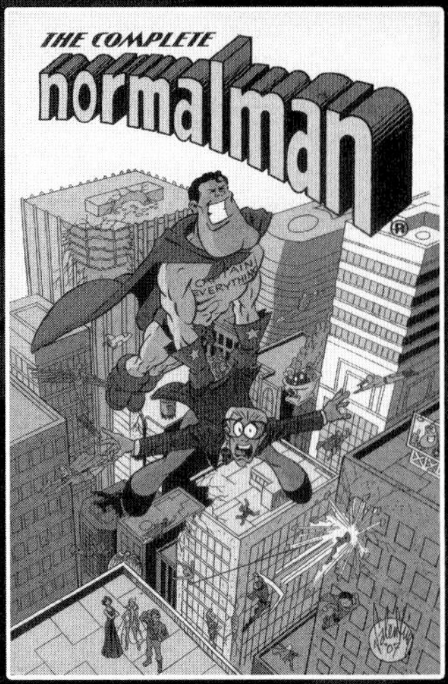
THE COMPLETE
normalman

JIM VALENTINO

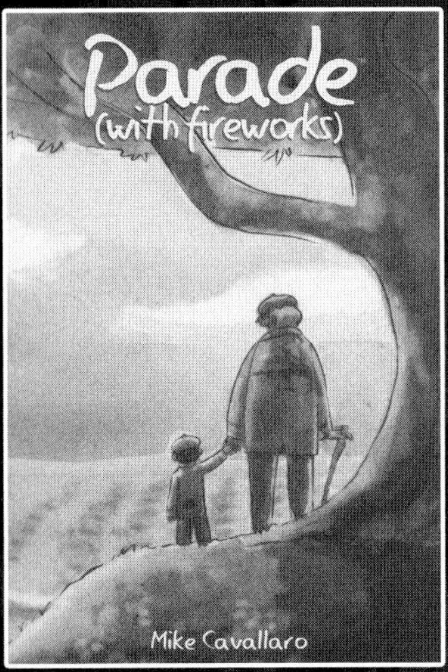
Parade
(with fireworks)
Mike Cavallaro

MIKE CAVALLARO

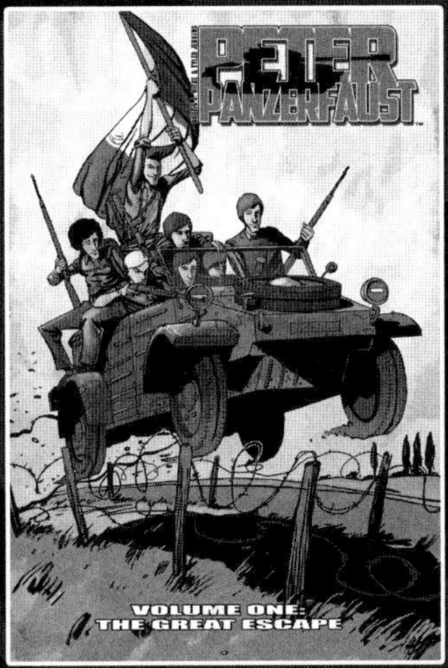
PETER PANZERFAUST
VOLUME ONE:
THE GREAT ESCAPE

WIEBE/JENKINS

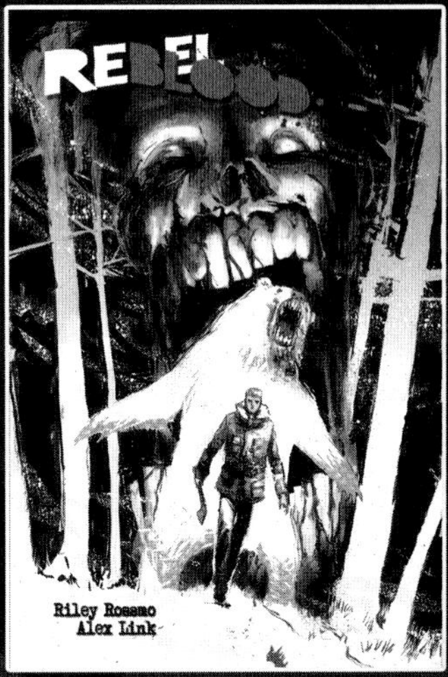
Riley Rossmo
Alex Link

ROSSMO/LINK

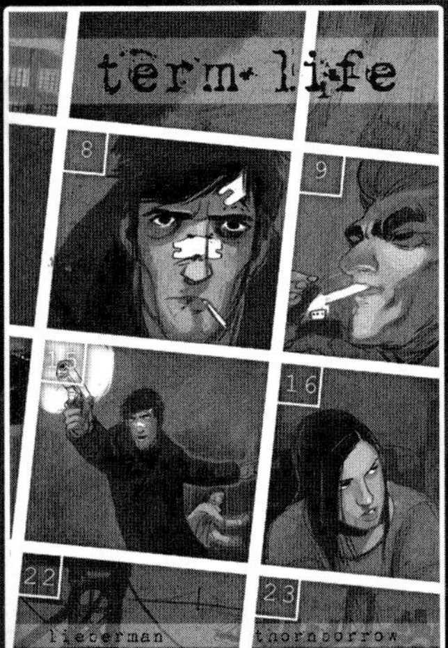
term life
lieberman
thornborrow

LIEBERMAN/THORNBORROW

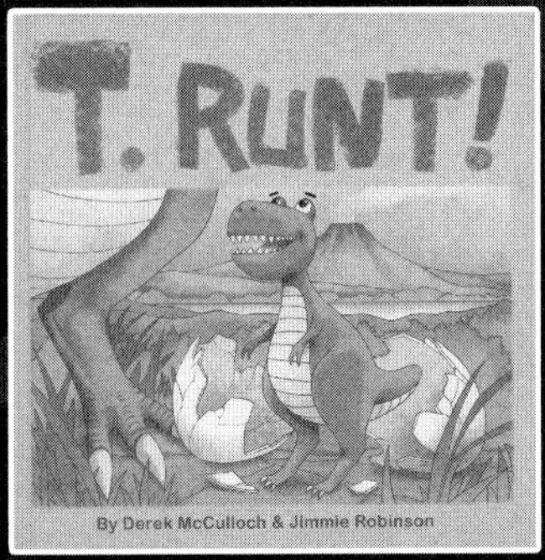
T. RUNT!
By Derek McCulloch & Jimmie Robinson

McCULLOCH/ROBINSON

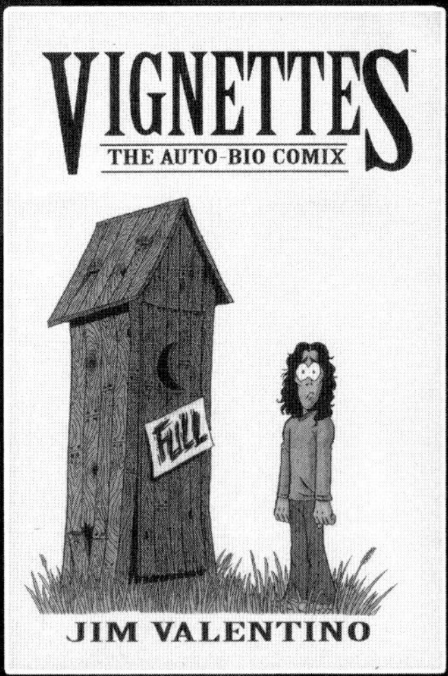
VIGNETTES
THE AUTO-BIO COMIX
FULL
JIM VALENTINO

JIM VALENTINO

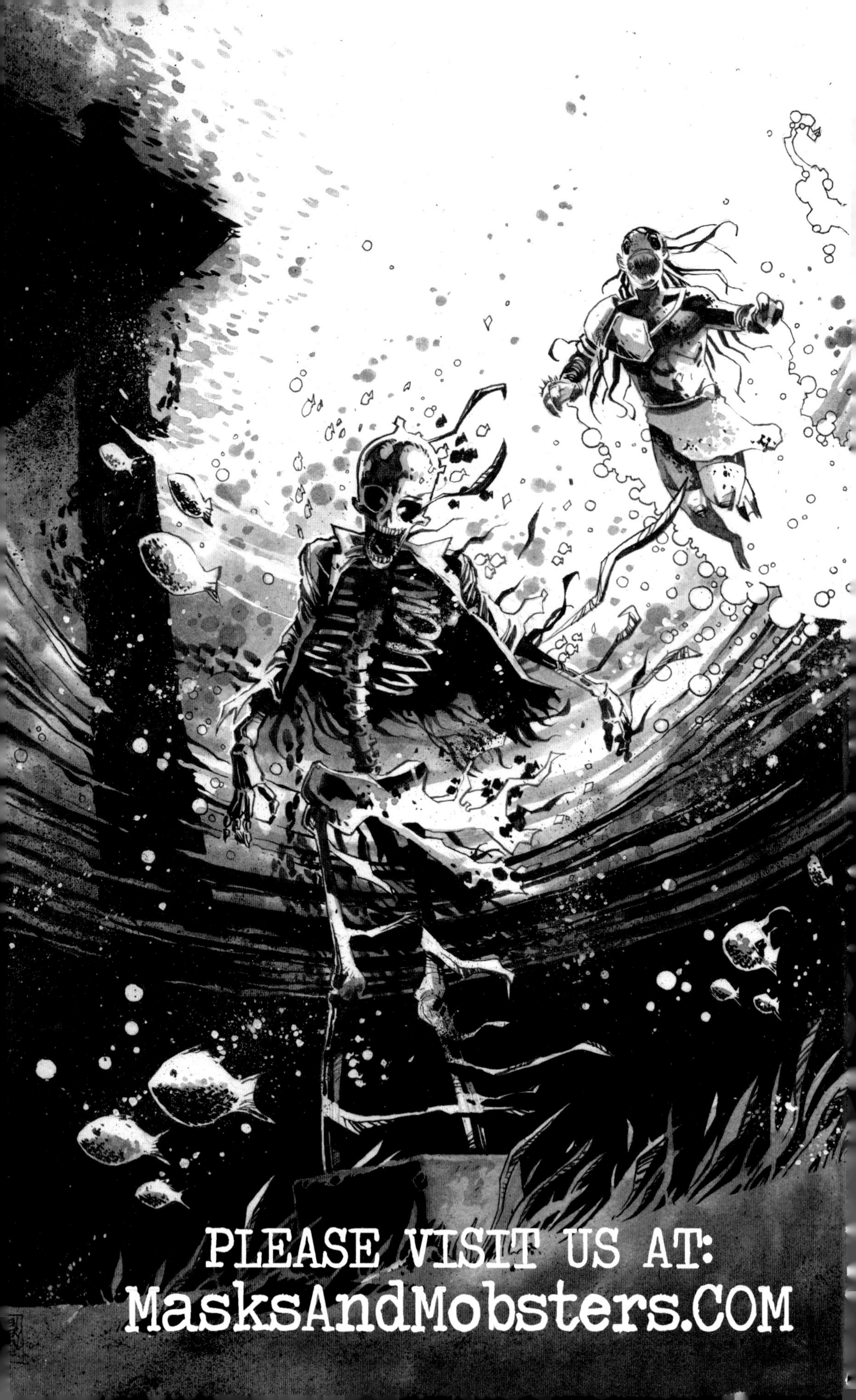
PLEASE VISIT US AT:
MasksAndMobsters.COM

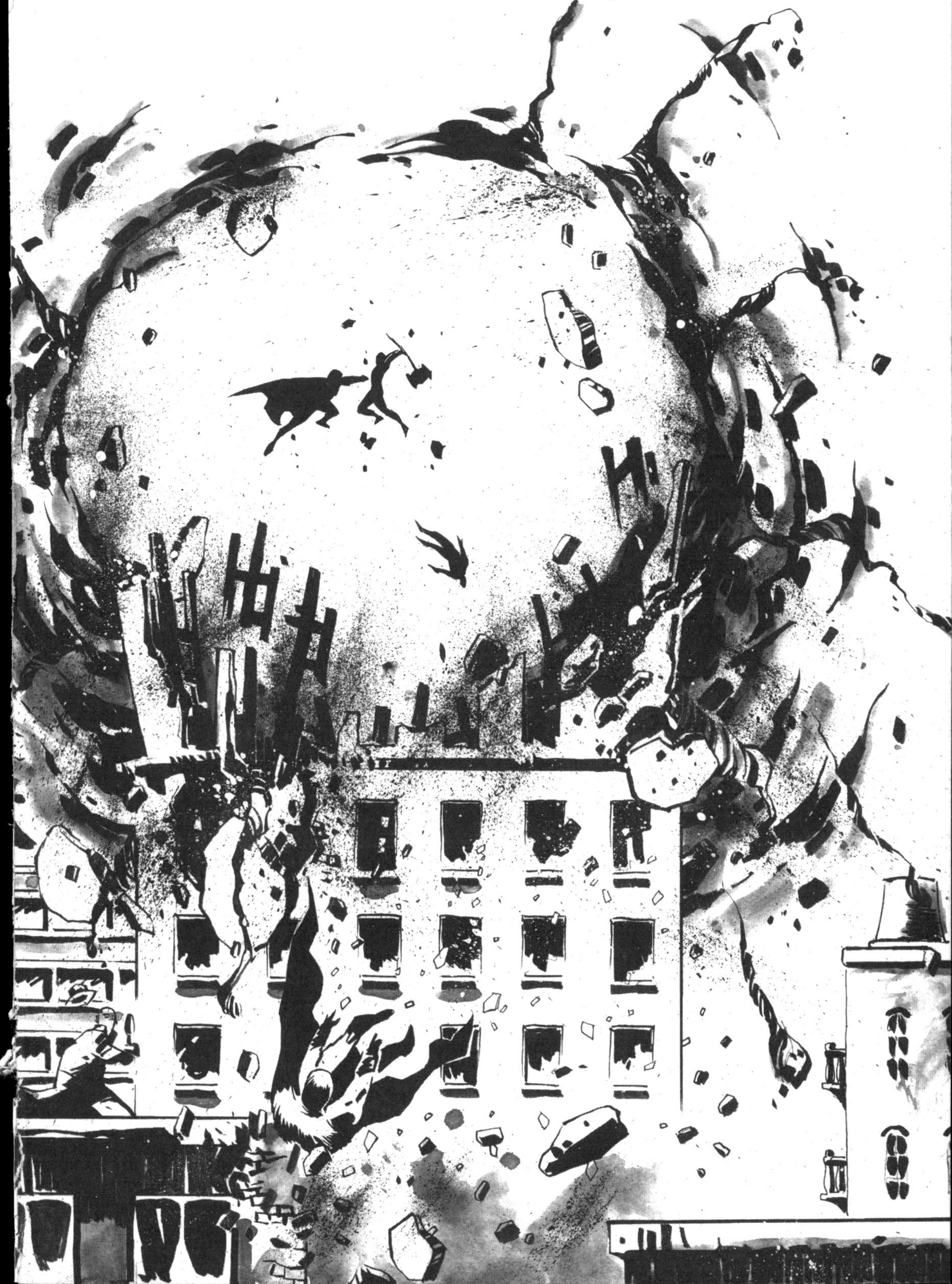

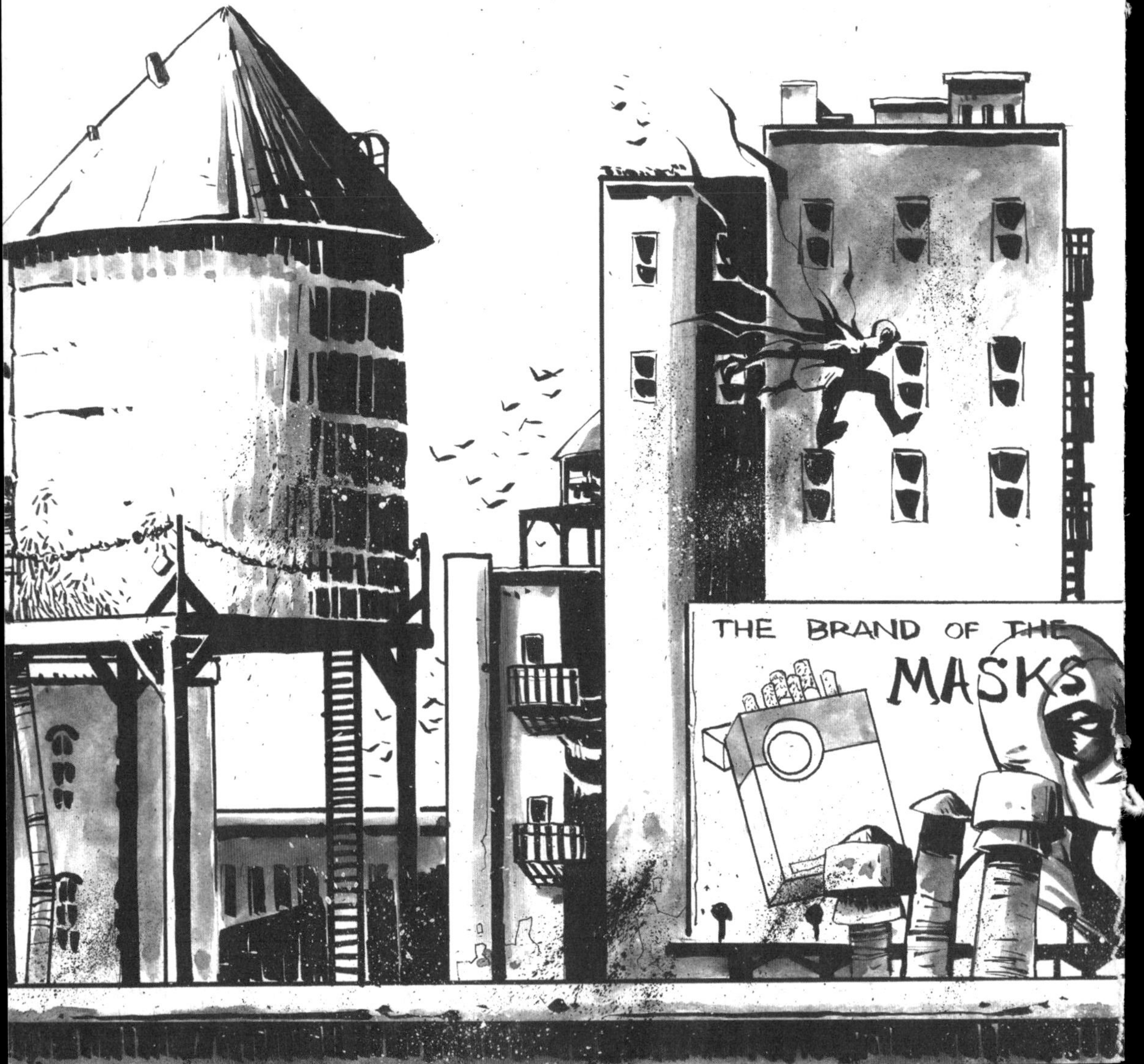
THE BRAND OF THE
MASKS